Erotica Omnibus Three

Erotica Omnibus Three

Pleasure Bound
Susan Swann

Playing the Game
Selina Seymour

Midnight Starr
Dorothy Starr

LIBRIS

An *X Libris* Book

This omnibus edition first published by X Libris in 1998
Reprinted 2001

Copyright © Susan Swann, Selina Seymour,
Dorothy Starr 1998

Pleasure Bound copyright © Susan Swann 1997
'Domia' first appeared in *Decadence* magazine,
copyright © Susan Swann 1994
Playing the Game copyright © Selina Seymour 1995
Midnight Starr collection copyright © Dorothy Starr 1996

The moral right of the authors has been asserted.

A CIP catalogue record for this book
is available from the British Library.

ISBN 0 7515 2580 4

Photoset in North Wales by
Derek Doyle & Associates, Mold, Flintshire
Printed and bound in Great Britain by
Clays Ltd, St Ives plc

X Libris
A Division of
Little, Brown and Company (UK)
Brettenham House
Lancaster Place
London WC2E 7EN

www.xratedbooks.co.uk

Pleasure Bound

Susan Swann

Contents

The Seven-Year Itch

STACEY PLUMPED UP the pillows and leaned against the headboard. She could hear Ross moving around downstairs and guessed that he was preparing a special breakfast tray.

She sighed. He tried, poor darling. But whatever he did she knew it would make no difference. They were in a rut. She still loved him, but the spark had gone. They were ... *comfortable* together. Cosy. Still, what could you expect after seven years of marriage?

When the door opened and Ross came in, she pasted a smile on her face. After all, you were supposed to be happy on your birthday. He had placed a single scarlet rose next to the freshly squeezed orange juice. There was a fresh peach, yoghurt with honey and toasted nuts, her favourite morning paper. The smell of freshly brewed coffee filled the room.

Ross tossed a bundle of envelopes onto the bed. 'Postman's just been. How's the gorgeous birthday girl?' he said. 'You don't look a day over twenty-five.'

'I *am* twenty-five, you fool.' She grinned. He could always make her laugh. And he had gone to some trouble to put all of her favourite things on the tray. She felt a rush of affection for him. I'm a selfish sod, she thought. I want it all – the fairy-tale, the lot.

Ross sat on the bed as she sipped her orange juice and opened her birthday cards. He looked handsome, having had his hair cut in a new, shorter style a few days ago. The spikiness suited his broad features and strong jaw. He was wearing a black denim shirt and jeans. Not the sort of clothes he usually favoured. Why the change? she wondered idly. He smiled, looking expectant.

'What?' she said.

'Did you think I'd forgotten your present? Look under the newspaper.'

Stacey looked at the slim black box, tied up with red ribbon. It would be chocolates, or a nightie, she thought, trying not to show her disappointment. But when she parted the layers of black tissue paper, she blinked in surprise. The pink rubber object was obviously some kind of sex toy. Slim straps were attached to the sturdy phallus and there was a strange appendage sticking out at a right-angle from the base of the shaft. She touched the oddly shaped wand. It was flat along one side and flexible.

'It's very . . . unusual,' she said, the corners of her mouth twitching. 'Whatever do you do with it?'

'Here. Let me show you,' Ross said, taking the tray and setting it on the floor.

Thinking that he was about to initiate some kind of sex, Stacey reached for him. Now you're talking, she thought, that's the kind of birthday present I want. But Ross had a strange look on his face. A new, steely glint in his eyes. She quickened with interest.

'Sit still. I'll put it on you,' he said. Stacey opened her mouth to protest, a giggle rising in her throat. 'Just – sit – still. Do as you're told for once. I mean it.' There was a hard edge to his voice.

Startled into obeying him, Stacey did as he asked. Ross folded back the bed-clothes and lifted the hem of her over-sized T-shirt. Stacey held up the garment as he instructed and looked down between her spread legs as Ross fitted on the contraption. She drew in her breath sharply as he lubricated the phallus and slipped it straight into her vagina. The thick stem felt intrusive, stretching open her entrance. She felt the urge to close her legs, but Ross's expression stopped her. He was totally absorbed in placing the flattened, flexible wand up the length of her sex, where it protruded slightly, the top of it veiled by her pubic hair. Ross gently arranged her labia so that they pouted around the wand.

'Ross,' she began, 'I really don't think—'

'Shut up,' he said, without rancour. There was still that unfamiliar hardness to his voice.

Stacey felt a flicker of sexual arousal. Ross was behaving so strangely. She didn't know him in this mood. Now he was securing the straps around her waist, reaching to settle the other fastening between her legs. Finally he took from his pocket a tube of lubricating gel, squeezed a blob onto his fingertip and reached under the shaped wand that bisected her labia. The gel was cool against the tiny hood covering her clitoris.

'Stand up,' he said. 'Walk around. How does it feel?'

Stacey did as he ordered. It was quite a shock to feel the thick phallus buried within her. Her sex was held open by the girth of the rubber penis. As she moved, the referred, slippery pressure of the flattened wand made her clitoris erect. The tiny hood of flesh retracted and the little nub was forced against the shaped and lubricated strip. The friction was ticklish and quite maddeningly erotic.

'Well? How do you feel?' Ross said.

'Strange. Sort of sexy. A bit wicked and. . .'

'And? Go on. Tell me exactly.'

'Well. A bit . . . ashamed that it's turning me on, actually.' She searched for the right words. 'It's like a forbidden pleasure, because you can't tell

4

that I've got a big, thick cock right up inside my pussy.'

Ross's mouth lifted in a crooked grin. She could tell that he was excited by her directness. 'That's the idea. This is a training harness. It's designed to keep you aroused for hours. When you wear it to work today, only you and I will know what's going on inside your hot little knickers.'

Stacey's eyes opened wide in horror. 'You can't mean it! I'm not wearing this thing outside the house. No. Ross. Sorry. It's impossible.'

She moved to untie the straps, but realised that she was oddly reluctant to take the harness off. She couldn't wear it all day. Could she? The idea was preposterous, but oh-so intriguing.

Ross stayed her hand, saying sternly, 'Oh, but you will wear it, darling. In fact, you'll do exactly as I say. I want your word on this, Stacey. You won't remove it until I tell you to. And I insist that you don't relieve yourself. No nipping off to the cloakroom for a bit of sly masturbation!'

The very idea! How could he even suggest that she'd do such a thing? She found herself nodding mutely. 'All right,' she said at last in a low voice. To be truthful, she was more aroused than she had been in a very long time. She liked the new, masterful Ross. When he kissed her she responded eagerly, melding her tongue with his in a long explorative caress. When he drew back she was a little breathless, her face flushed.

'I haven't finished yet,' Ross said. 'There's

another part to your present.' He produced a tiny box which held two small silver rings. 'Take off your T-shirt.'

While Stacey stood with her hands by her sides, Ross pinched her nipples until they stood out firmly. Wetting them with spittle, he teased each of them in turn through the tightly fitting rings. The nipples, like hard shiny beads, pouted outwards into little tubes of collared flesh. Stacey winced at the intense, pinching pleasure. Her nipples seemed sensitised like never before.

Reaching into her lingerie drawer Ross extracted a pair of plain white cotton briefs and a matching bra. 'Put these on,' he said. 'Nice and functional. A perfect foil for what's underneath.'

Stacey did so. The training harness was almost invisible. Just the tiniest little bulge showed at the front of her panties where the flexible rod emerged from her sex-lips. She had a sudden thought. 'Oh, I haven't washed this morning. I'll have to take this all off.'

'No you won't. I want you to smell natural. You wash too often anyway. I'm always telling you how much I love the smell of your lovely pussy, but you ignore me.'

It was true. She could never believe he relished her rich, female muskiness. Usually she used the bidet twice a day, slipping into bed at night pristine and smelling of soap. Now she was forced to accept that Ross had told the truth when he complained that she tasted like a cosmetic factory. The thought of him waiting for her to come home so that he could enjoy her natural sexual odour was oddly exciting. Oh well, she thought, if it was good enough for Napoleon and Josephine. By the end of a busy day in the office she would be as spicy and earthy as Ross could wish for.

'By tonight you'll be begging for it, my darling,' Ross said. 'I'll think of you, aroused all day, but duty-bound to do nothing about it. Oh, if you need to pee, you'll find that you can bend the rod out of the way. Better hurry now. You'll be late. Wear something plain. A white, high-necked blouse and a black, knee-length skirt.'

Ten minutes later Stacey stood in the lift beside Ross as they descended to the car park below the block of flats. She sat gingerly on the car seat, but found that the training harness did not hamper her movements in any way. It was just that she was constantly aware of it. Just before they left Ross had put another smear of lubrication under the strip of rubber. She hardly needed it. Her natural lubrication was flowing freely. Inside the virginal cotton knickers, the shaped wand slipped and rubbed against her firmly erect clitoris, teasing her with a remorseless pressure.

'Bye, darling,' Ross said, drawing the car to a halt outside the Georgian-fronted building where Stacey worked for a firm of solicitors. 'Pick you up at the usual time. We'll go out for a meal straight after work. Okay? Have a good day.'

She waved and watched Ross drive away. It was something she rarely did. Today she waited until the car disappeared into the traffic before she went inside the building. She imagined Ross as he sat at his drawing board, working. The thought of her in the training harness would give him a prodigious erection. Somehow she knew that he was also pledged not to masturbate to relieve himself. As she went to the cloakroom and exchanged greetings with her colleagues, she could not stop thinking about Ross. And about the heightened state she would be in by the end of the day.

The working day seemed endless. It took all Stacey's efforts to concentrate on her work. Even the lunch party with close friends to celebrate her birthday was only a brief distraction. Her attention seemed centred in her groin and between her legs, where the stout rubber cock kept her swollen labia and vaginal entrance held open. She was acutely aware that she was made ready, available for sex, by the presence of the hideously arousing thing which was strapped to her body. The dichotomy of herself as coolly efficient legal secretary and wanton sex-object was a powerfully arousing concept. How the hell had Ross discovered that this was just what she needed?

By the afternoon, as she walked from her desk, returning tapes and legal documents to her boss's office, shivers of frustration were tickling down her thighs. The gusset of her panties was damp with her juices and there was a sense of heaviness, a delightful, engorged pressure, to her spread-open labia. Her clitoris felt as firm as a tiny cock under the oiled caress of the shaped wand. Her breasts were hard and swollen, the pulled-out tubes of her nipples rubbing deliciously against the cotton of her bra with every slight movement of her body. It was all she could do to sit still. Her fingers itched to plunge between her thighs. Just a few subtle movements and she would climax.

'Thank you, Stacey,' her boss said as she handed him a list of documents pertaining to a difficult client. 'That's a load off my mind.'

She smiled warmly. Mr Johnson was a senior partner in the firm. He was pushing fifty with a kind face and immaculate iron-grey hair. She knew that he found her attractive, although he would never step over the divide between them. If only he knew what was going on beneath her rather severe skirt and blouse!

Somehow Stacey kept her mind on her work, managing to complete the day with a minimum of mistakes. When she used the toilet she found that she could bend the wand away from her body. The phallus inside her exerted an inner pressure against her bladder, so that she had to urinate in a slow, steady stream. The accompanying tingle and sweet pulsing of her clitoris made even peeing a sensual act. She dabbed at herself with toilet tissue, cleaning herself carefully, hardly daring to brush against her ultra-eroticised pudenda. If she was to make herself come, even inadvertently, she would have to confess the fact to Ross.

It seemed that by wearing the harness she was made acutely aware of her whole body. The nipple rings inside her bra made her breasts almost unbearably sensitive. She stood well away from the other people in the lift on the way down, imagining that she might well reach orgasm if someone were to brush against the front of her blouse. But that did not happen and she was left wanting, teetering on the precipice of orgasm. By the time she was hurrying down the steps to the street towards Ross and the waiting car, she felt wrung out with tension and sheer physical longing. The whole of her sex felt hot and swampy.

'Had a good day, darling?' Ross said, his eyes gleaming wickedly.

She leaned over to kiss his cheek, wishing that he would turn his head and claim her mouth. 'What do you think?' she murmured.

As he edged the car into the flow of traffic, Ross gave a low chuckle. The sound of it seemed to hit her in the pit of the stomach.

'Let's not go out to eat,' Stacey said on impulse. 'Can't we go straight home?' Hitching up her skirt, she crossed her thighs suggestively.

He smiled and glanced across at her, then shook his head. ' 'Fraid not. The table's booked. The magic belt worked, I see. Well you'll just have to hold on a while longer.'

Tears of frustration gathered in Stacey's eyes. She had been kept at fever pitch for hours. Her nerves felt like brittle threads. 'You bastard,' she hissed. 'I'm dying for you. Don't you know that? But of course you do. That's the object of this exercise. I haven't been able to think of anything all day but what you'll do to me when we get back. Christ, I'm as horny as hell. My knickers are soaked.'

Ross kept his eyes on the road as he drove smoothly through the traffic. She could feel the sexual tension in every line of his body. God, had she really thought that he was unexciting? With his short, spiked hair and dark glasses, he looked unfamiliar, a little mysterious. She wanted him madly in a purely physical, utterly obscene way.

At the restaurant she drank a glass of wine and ate her artichoke vinaigrette in silence. Ross tapped her on the back of the hand and leaned close to hiss, 'Go and take off those prim white knickers. Raise your skirt when you come back so that your bare buttocks are resting against the wooden chair.'

Without a word she rose and did as he asked. Her pulses were racing. She always wore stockings, so when she returned and sat down she indeed felt the coolness of wood against her bottom. The hardness of the chair-seat pressed the phallus more deeply inside her. Somehow she ate the rest of her meal, hardly tasting the pasta with saffron and cream sauce. Now and then Ross reached under the table to caress her naked thigh.

Once he reached between her legs to check the position of the instrument. She almost came when he ran a finger very lightly up the outside of the shaped wand and then gave her pouting labia an affectionate squeeze.

'You're really dying for it, aren't you? Tell me what you want,' Ross hissed in her ear. 'Tell me exactly what you want. I want to hear you talk dirty.'

While he sat back and ate his pasta, Stacey forced herself to give voice to her most private, wanton fantasies. Her cheeks burning, she said, 'I want your cock inside me. Hot and hard. No foreplay. Bloody hell, I've had a whole day of that. I want you to fuck my pussy while you suck my nipples and bite at the little rings . . .'

'And?' Ross said, his face impassive as he forked up the spicy tomato sauce.

'And . . . and . . . I want you to push a finger into my anus, while you suck my clitoris and lick up my juices. I want to make you come inside me.'

Stacey squirmed on the cool seat, pressing her pouting, thickened sex-lips against the now warm wood. Her juices had seeped down to pool on the chair. She could hardly believe she was saying these things. They usually didn't speak during sex. But that was then. Somehow this was now – a new time. A time of endless possibilities. Lord, what a birthday this was turning out to be!

Ross paid the bill while Stacey went to the cloakroom. She freshened her make-up and fluffed her short blonde hair, then studied her reflection. In the mirror she looked exactly as she always did. No one would guess that she was in such a state. On the way back to the flat, they did not speak. Ross ordered her to lift her skirt and open her legs wide, so that he could see the wand rudely bisecting her vulva.

'Stroke your pubes away from it. I want to see your pussy-lips,' he said.

Her face burning, Stacey used her fingers to part the damp hair. The inner surfaces of her labia were very red. They looked moist and fruity. She could smell herself – a rich, complex scent of aroused womanhood. All the way back she sat with her legs open, exposed to Ross's view, exposed in her own need.

As soon as they entered the flat, he took her in his arms and kissed her deeply. She responded with a desperate affection, hungry for his touch, his approval. Oh God, she loved him to distraction.

'Go upstairs,' he said. 'Raise your skirt and kneel at the end of the bed.'

Meekly she did so. It was a few minutes before he followed her. The bastard, he's making me wait, she thought as she pressed her thighs to the overhang of the duvet. She heard him come into the room, but did not look round. As he instructed, she made no move to help him when he untied the straps at her waist. When he drew the phallus from her body, she gave a little cry of distress. It slipped wetly from between her puffy labia, a hot rush of body-warmed rubber.

Stacey surged against the bed, her hips pumping beyond her control. She felt faint with relief. After being held so open, made so aware that – in a purely sexual sense – she was simply an object in need of being filled, she experienced a curious sense of emptiness. But it lasted only seconds. Ross knelt behind her, his erect penis pressing urgently against her hungry sex.

Stacey chewed at her bottom lip as he pushed straight into her. He gripped her waist, drawing her back onto the full length of his rigid cock. Then he drove back and forth, pushing deeply, thrusting without gentleness. His hard stomach slapped against her buttocks. She felt his balls brushing against her as, with each inner stroke, the head of his cock stroked her sensitised cervix.

It was what she had craved all day. The muscular walls of her vagina spasmed around his shaft. Stacey thought she would faint. She screamed as she climaxed. The pleasure was mind-blowing, the contractions so intense that she sobbed and writhed, calling his name again and again.

'Oh, Ross. Christ, I love you. Ross. Oh, Ross.'

Ross withdrew. He flipped her over onto her back, tearing at her blouse buttons and dragging her bra away from her breasts. Holding a breast in each hand, he held them up like offerings. As he mouthed her tormented nipples, his tongue flickering across the little rings, Stacey gasped and moaned. She was still hungry. Her thighs scissored around his slim hips as the pleasure prickled through her chest and down her belly. All she could think of was being penetrated again. But Ross drew away, slid down her body.

'This is what I've been anticipating,' he murmured.

He made little sounds of enjoyment as he feasted at her sex. His muscular tongue scooped up her juices, pushed into her vagina, lolled against her tingling clitoris. Gently he spread open her labia and licked the inner surfaces. Stacey climaxed again, turned on by Ross's own delight in her. When he moved back up to kiss her, she tasted her musk on his mouth.

As they locked together in an intensely erotic kiss, she lifted her thighs to welcome his cock back inside her. Now it was Ross who lost control. He bucked and surged against her, his slippery penis ramming into her again and again. Her ringed nipples were mashed against his muscular chest, the metal sliding on the thin film of sweat.

'Dear God. I can't . . .' she moaned. 'Oh yes, I can. I'm coming again.'

Incredibly Stacey felt herself building towards another peak. They climaxed together, laughing and crying at the same time. Ross held her tightly, like something unbearably precious.

It was some time before they could catch their breath. For a while they lay entwined, stroking each other in wonder and delight.

'How did you know?' Stacey whispered against Ross's mouth.

He grinned. 'Did you think you were the only one who was bored? Before we both succumbed to the seven-year itch I thought I'd find you a new man. Me. What's the verdict? Will I suit?'

'Oh, yes,' Stacey said happily. 'You'll do very well indeed. And I think you'll find you've got yourself a new woman!'

Julia's Burning

'THIS WAY, THE fire's through here. Oh, do hurry.' Julia clutched her long satin robe close, conscious that she wore only a few scraps of silk and lace beneath it.

'Stand back, madam,' the burly fireman said, putting out his arm to prevent her going back into the bedroom. 'I'll soon deal with this.'

She stood on the threshold, watching him as he crossed the room. In an instant he had quenched the fire. He turned and looked at her, a grin creasing his boyish face. Julia's pulses quickened. What a combination. That clean-cut face coupled with a big, obviously well-toned body was devastating.

'All done. Not much damage at all. Good thing you contacted us so quickly. Looks like an electrical fault. I'd advise you to have all the wiring checked.'

'Yes. Thanks. I will,' Julia said. 'I'm so grateful that you arrived promptly.'

'We were on our way back to the station. It's the end of my night shift.' He glanced at his wrist-watch. 'Actually I'm into free time now. My shift ended ten minutes ago.'

'Oh, I see,' Julia said, feeling guilty. 'Sorry for holding you up. I just panicked when that old electric heater started spurting flames. I suppose I could have tackled it myself . . .'

'No, you did right, madam. Best leave it to the experts.'

He smiled again and she felt a stab of heat in her belly. God, he was gorgeous. Those blue eyes and that firm, strong-looking mouth. The jacket of his uniform was open at the neck, showing an area of damp, honey-coloured skin. He seemed in no hurry to leave, despite being late already. In fact, the look in his eyes made her catch her breath.

'Would . . . would you like a drink?' she said. 'It's the least I can do to thank you for putting in overtime on my behalf.'

'Thought you'd never ask. Yeh, that'd be great. I'll just go down to the lads and tell them to go back to the station without me.'

When he left the room Julia hurried over to a pine dresser and looked in the mirror. She used her fingers to muss her hair and sprayed herself with perfume. Her eyes and cheeks glowed. She knew that she looked good. She wasn't pretty,

18

exactly, but the combination of her red-brown hair and pale skin gave her a definite allure. Besides, what she lost in fashionable features, she made up for in lush curves. She was quite proud of her unfashionable, hour-glass figure. She might not be model-girl material, but men found her a big turn-on.

Before she left the bedroom, she adjusted the neck of the satin robe so that it showed off her creamy chest and the deep valley of her breasts. As she descended the stairs, the fireman was closing the front door. There was another man with him. He turned and gave Julia a frankly appraising look. Her heart almost skipped a beat. Two of them – identical twins.

'Hope you don't mind if my brother joins us,' the first fireman grinned. 'We do everything together. By the way, I'm Tony and this is Max. If you object we'll leave. No problem.'

They seemed to fill the hall with their presence. The big uniformed bodies ought to have been intimidating, but Julia felt wildly aroused. She sensed no menace from them, only a sort of contained tension.

'Double trouble, eh?' she said. 'I think I can handle that.' This couldn't be happening. It was like a scene from a film. 'Come into the kitchen. I'll make tea.'

She almost laughed at herself. How English to offer tea! So much for her efforts to act cool.

'Tea's fine for me,' said Tony, gazing admiringly

at her cleavage and nipped-in waist. Max said, 'Me too. Have you got something to spike it with?'

While the men sat at the kitchen table, Julia filled the kettle, set out cups and took a bottle of whisky from a cupboard. They made small talk and Julia responded, but all the time she was aware of the potent male presence of the uniformed figures. The fire-proof jackets and trousers, the buckled webbing belts with attached instruments and the stiff gauntlets lying on the table seemed dangerous and incongruous in her neat, bright kitchen.

She poured tea with trembling hands, adding a generous tot of whisky to each cup. Even with her back turned she was conscious of their hot eyes on her as she moved. The satin clung to the rich curve of her bottom, the indentation of her waist. Her breasts seemed swollen, the erect nipples scraping deliciously against the lace of her bra. She felt herself getting wet between her legs.

'Thanks,' Tony said, accepting a cup of tea. Max grinned up at her as she leaned over to set a cup down beside him. He was not identical to his twin after all. His face was more angular, his jaw squarer. But his eyes were just as blue. There was a wicked, knowing gleam in them. A frank and unashamed sexuality. This man was a bit of a rogue.

It seemed that something clutched at Julia's womb. The rush of heat to her loins shocked her.

She was standing next to Max, her satin-clad thigh almost touching his protective trousers. As she went to turn away, he reached out a hand and grasped the belt at her waist. Julia did not pull away as he drew one hand down her satin-covered flank.

'Seems to me that there's another fire here for us to deal with, bro,' Max said. He winked at Tony. 'The lady's sorely in need of our expert attentions.'

Julia closed her eyes as the belt slithered to the floor and Max's hands closed on her waist. She hardly dared believe that this was happening. Her fantasy was going to come true. Max stroked her soft belly, reached up to feel her breasts, and then slid a hand down to cup her lace-covered pubis. One fingertip scratched lightly at the fabric triangle, scoring the slight indentation between her labia.

Julia felt her knees grow weak as he handled her. His touch was gentle, but proprietorial. Tony watched, a crooked grin on his mouth as his twin teased and aroused her. She swayed towards him, wishing that he would reach for her too. Max slid two fingers inside her panties, meshed them in the luxuriant bush of her pubic hair. Julia squirmed as he twirled the hair, stroking it away from her heated centre, but holding back from touching her slippery folds. God, how she wished he would touch her clitoris. It was throbbing and ticking with a life of its own.

21

'You know, Max,' Tony said, 'seems to me that we've been brought here under false pretences. There ought to be a penalty for wasting our valuable time.'

'Yeh,' Max said. 'You're so right, bro. What shall we do with you, Julia? You're guilty of wrongful use of council services. That's a serious matter. I'm afraid a cup of tea spiked with whisky just doesn't cut it.'

'I'm . . . I'm sorry,' Julia said lamely, trembling as his hands moved upwards now to grasp the cups of her bra.

'Oh, you will be,' Max said with a wolfish grin. With a swift movement he dragged her breasts free so that the full globes and dark nipples were exposed. Lifted by the cups and resting on the rim of boned fabric beneath them, her generous breasts were thrust into lewd prominence.

Julia made a tiny sound of distress deep in her throat as a blissful rush of shame swept her whole body. Tony now reached out his hand and slipped it into the top of her lace panties. He dipped between her legs, parted her labia, and slid one finger into her. 'Mmm. She's nice and wet. And look at those firm teats. Seems like she's expecting something.'

'Then we ought not to disappoint the lady,' Max said.

Julia couldn't speak for the desire which was like a burning presence in the whole area below her waist. When Tony withdrew his hand and stood up, she made no sound. Her legs seemed to have turned to water. When Max also rose, gripped her hips and pushed her belly down onto the kitchen table she gave a muffled protest. Her bare breasts were pressed against the cool wood. The sensation on her erect nipples was startlingly erotic.

'Now then, Julia. Time to take your punishment,' Tony said, raising the hem of the satin robe and tucking it into the band of her suspender belt in the small of her back.

Julia's cheeks flamed as Max dragged down her panties and left them cuffed beneath the underswell of her buttocks. He exerted a gentle pressure so that she was pushed further onto the table. Her stockinged feet slipped on the tiled floor and her legs splayed lewdly outwards. She imagined how she must look, her hair spilling over her face, her breasts exposed, and her big bare bottom sticking in the air. Her sex was clearly visible between her parted thighs, the wet red lips peeping through the luxurious red-brown hair. Oh Lord, it was so arousing to have both men desiring her.

'Nice arse,' Tony said. 'A bit too pale though. Have to remedy that.'

Julia bit her lip as the first open-handed slap landed squarely on her right buttock. She had gathered herself to meet the pain, but she was so worked up it felt more like a rough caress. So this was to be her punishment. But could it really be

23

called that if she enjoyed it? And she was loving every minute of it. While Tony spanked her right buttock, now and then stopping to circle the blushing flesh with a soothing palm, Max gave his full attention to the left.

She moaned and writhed with the stinging pleasure, feeling the wetness pool between her legs. How awful if she oozed onto the table. They would both see what a hussy she was. When her bottom was glowing, the spanking stopped. Julia was almost disappointed. She had liked the feel of both men handling her.

Tony reached underneath her and grasped her breasts. Kneading them, he circled the turgid nipples with his thumb. Julia held her breath. Her nipples were dark and prominent. She loved having them pinched. Another trickle of warm juice dripped from inside her. If Tony kept on doing that, she was going to climax.

Then something hard and cold was placed between her thighs. Julia jerked with shock and turned her head to see that Max had taken his fireman's axe from his belt. It was the stout rubber handle she could feel. It pressed against her soaking vulva, the domed tip brushing firmly against her clitoris.

Of their own volition her hips began to weave. She arched her back, pushing out her simmering bottom, spreading her legs wider, straining them apart, as the axe handle moved towards her hungry vagina. It circled the orifice, the tip edging

24

inside her, but not going in very far. Julia almost wept with frustration as Max and Tony teased her. She was sure that her syrupy juices must be trickling down the handle. The prickling throbbing of her nipples was maddening, echoing the thrumming of her stiff little clit.

'Hot little piece, isn't she?' Max said huskily. 'I think she's ready to be quenched. You first?'

'After you, bro,' Tony said gallantly.

The way they spoke about her, almost dismissively but with obvious admiration, drove Julia wild. They seemed used to sharing women and the thought made her eager for whatever they offered. When Max opened the buttons on his flame-proof trousers, she leaned towards him, eager to watch his cock spring free. The bulge tenting his underwear held great promise. She just knew that his member would be thick and veiny. Just the sort of cock she liked.

Max didn't take down his trousers, he just reached a hand in and drew out his penis. Julia licked her lips. It was just as she'd imagined. A flushed, robust stem, rising from a thatch of light-brown pubes. Not over-long, but thick and with a big shiny glans. Somehow seeing it sticking out of his uniform, collared by the open fly of his white boxers, was more exciting than seeing him naked.

Max put a hand on the back of her head, but she needed no urging to take him into her mouth. He was hot and tasted gamey. She smelled sweat and rubber, and something vaguely chemical from his uniform. Running her tongue down his length, she worked her mouth back and forth, sucking and spreading spittle along his length. Max grunted and stroked her face, meshing his fingers in her silky hair.

Julia became aware that Tony had moved between her thighs. His fingers were on her sex, spreading her swollen labia, fluttering over her inner folds. She imagined him looking down at her exposed sex and bucked as his hands brushed against her mildly sore buttocks, eager for the penetration that was to come. Tony pushed two fingers inside her while his thumb spread her juices upwards then gently circled her anus.

With his other hand Tony spread her buttocks apart until the tight, puckered orifice was lewdly stretched open. She steeled herself for the insertion of his thumb. As he pushed it into her, she cried out at the unfamiliar invasion. The base of his thumb was wedged up hard against the inner surface. With both Tony's fingers and thumb buried deeply inside her pulsing flesh, she began sobbing and working her hips in a shameless display of lust.

It was almost unbearably erotic to be manhandled in this way. Filled in three places at once, Julia felt the pressure of a climax building.

Max thrust into her willing mouth, his firm scrotum brushing against her chin. A drop of salty liquid slid on her tongue. He was near to orgasm. She rammed down onto him, relaxing her throat so that she could embrace the full length of him. With a gasp Max went rigid. His cock spasmed as his come jetted into her throat. At the same time Tony's clever fingers drew down the pleasure from her body. The subtle internal stroking behind her pubic bone, coupled with the meeting of his thumb through the thin membrane, tipped her over.

As she swallowed Max's come, the first ripples of her orgasm broke over her. Her vagina tightened around Tony's fingers, dry-milking him as she moaned with pleasure. She moved against his hand, grinding herself against his knuckles, wanting something, anything, everything. When the fingers and thumb were withdrawn she cried out with disappointment.

Tony chuckled as he opened his fly and fitted on a ridged condom. 'This fire takes some putting out! Good thing we're well equipped.'

Max moved away, tucking his softening cock back into his boxers. He bent and kissed Julia on the forehead. 'Don't worry,' he grinned. 'My bro's up to coping with any blaze.'

Then Julia felt herself filled by the full length of Tony's erect, covered penis. She was so wet and swollen inside that the slightest movement sent exquisite sensations raging through her pelvis. As he pounded into her, her upper body was pressed against the table. Her breasts lolled to the sides, the sensitive nipples chafing against the smooth, cool wood. As another climax built inside her, she lifted her bottom, loving the soft scrape of Tony's pubic hair against her sensitised buttocks.

'Christ!' Tony grunted. 'Oh, yeh. Oh, man.'

His pelvis rammed up tight against her as he emptied himself into the condom. Breathing hard, he bent over her, taking his weight on his hands, while the contractions of her vagina bled him of every last drop of pleasure. It was a moment before either of them could move. Julia was vaguely conscious of Max moving around the kitchen as, slowly, Tony withdrew. He bent and dropped a kiss on each scarlet buttock.

'Stay as you are,' he said. 'Max will see to the clean-up job.'

Julia relaxed as Max wiped her from front to back with a piece of kitchen roll. Then she rose unsteadily, pulled up her panties, and adjusted her bra. Her cheeks were as red as her buttocks. She could hardly bear to meet their eyes.

Tony and Max took their places at the table as if nothing had happened. Max picked up his cup, took a sip and screwed up his face. 'Ugh, tea's gone cold. It's not bad though, with the whisky.'

Julia smiled openly then. 'I'll make some fresh. And how about the usual? Scrambled eggs, bacon, mushrooms, beans, toast suit you? Can't have my two favourite firemen falling down on the job through lack of energy!'

Tony and Max laughed. 'If this was more than a once-a-month arrangement, we might need an energy transplant!' Tony said.

Julia gathered together the ingredients to make breakfast. 'Just you relax, boys. Your room's ready upstairs. After you've eaten you can sleep for a while. Then I think you'll find I've another fire for you to deal with – before your next shift!'

Looking-Glass

'WHERE'D YOU WANT it, love?'

Looking at the mirror again Josie wondered what had possessed her to buy it. Still, it had been a bargain for fifty quid. With that ornate gilt frame, all garlands, swags and cherubs, it had to be at least a hundred years old. It was so imposing, so ugly, that no one else had wanted it.

Josie had found herself bidding when the price dropped. Somehow she had known that it was meant for her.

'Well?' the delivery man said, losing patience. 'I haven't got all day. Which room? Up or down?'

For a moment Josie was nonplussed. She had not thought that far ahead. What was wrong with her? She was not given to making impulsive purchases. In fact, she was not impulsive at all – usually. It seemed to her then that she heard Sam's voice – his tone of bored annoyance, one she remembered only too well.

'Where the hell did you get that monstrosity? Are you mad?'

That decided it. She felt a surge of mild rebellion. I'll do as I damn well like, she thought.

'It can go in the bedroom,' she told the delivery man, who was still struggling to negotiate the front door. 'Upstairs on the right. Lean it against the end wall, in the alcove.'

The room was all hers now, since Sam had walked out on her. For the promise of an extra tenner, the delivery man was persuaded to help her hang the mirror. An hour later it looked down on her bed, adding light and space to the alcove. It would look better after she had cleaned it. She took a step back, rubbing at a spot on the glass with the cuff of her cotton sweatshirt. Her reflection stared back at her.

Not bad-looking. Dark blonde hair, longish face. Not exactly pretty, but striking, and she had good bones. Curious how light played tricks on glass. She could have sworn she saw a movement in the green-tinged depths.

Yes. There it was. A pale area – roughly oval. It came more clearly into focus the more she stared at it. A chill ran down her back. The shape looked like a face. She rubbed her eyes, looking again. Nothing. The misty, oval shape had gone. Josie's heart skipped back to its normal rhythm.

Sam would have said that she had been reading too many of her 'weird' books, as he called them.

That was another thing they had disagreed on. She had told him that 'occult' only meant hidden knowledge – the unknown – but he had not approved of her choice of reading material.

'Why can't you read romantic novels or sex-and-shopping, like normal women?' he had said contemptuously. 'Instead of all that bloody rubbish about ghosts and ghouls.'

She smiled wanly now, not surprised that she was seeing things. She knew that she was over-tired, tense. The doctor told her she was suffering from stress – the twentieth-century disease. Hardly surprising. It was only two months since the divorce had become final.

Roy, her best friend and owner of the antique shop where she worked, had suggested a simple solution.

'Go out and get yourself laid, love. Take two weeks off. It's our quiet time. Get away somewhere where there's sun and sand. You need a new man. Take it from me. It's a tried and tested cure.'

'Maybe for you, you old queen,' Josie said in a teasing voice.

Roy struck a pose. 'Dearie me! What's sauce for the goose, you know!'

She had taken the time off, but not the holiday. It was too soon. Sam had done a really good job on her. In his eyes she rated about as highly as an insect, when compared with his new love – a luscious brunette with money to back up her

32

over-active libido. Trouble was, Sam's opinion seemed to have rubbed off on her. In a few months maybe she would be ready for 'walking on the beaches, looking at the peaches', as Roy would sing.

Right now she felt like getting blind drunk. Thinking of Sam had that effect on her.

Josie took the bottle of brandy to bed with her. For a while she watched TV. The brandy and the re-run of one of her favourite films, 'Someone to Watch Over Me', relaxed her. When the film ended, she switched off the TV. Stretching out, still fully dressed, she leafed through a raunchy magazine – another of Roy's smart ideas. 'You can weigh up the talent,' he said with a laugh. 'You have to admit you're out of touch, love. What with having been married to a dinosaur for so long!'

The centrefold was a blond, beach-bum type, with a come-hither expression and a body to die for. Josie ran the pad of her thumb over his taut stomach and up over the prominent pectorals. Dipping down to the groin, she dragged her nails over the cock and balls. Shame he was not erect. It seemed stupid that all naked men in women's magazines were obliged to sport flaccid cocks. It wasn't exactly the greatest turn-on.

Still, something worked. Perhaps it was the beach boy's expression – macho but sort of 'I've got a soft centre'. Whatever, Josie felt a stir of interest. Roy was right. She did need a man in her life. Someone who fancied her madly, who would spread her out on the bed, kiss her all over, and tell her that she was the most fuckable woman in the world.

Trouble was, she was not ready for all the stuff that went with it. And for Josie, sex without a close relationship just didn't work. She was too hooked on commitment. Oh well, I suppose I'm going to have to face up to being lonely for a while, she thought resignedly, taking another swallow of brandy. She felt pleasantly woozy. There was an unfamiliar heaviness in her pussy, a slickness when she moved her legs. It had been a long time since she felt the urge to masturbate. Well, why the hell not. She deserved some pleasure, solitary or otherwise.

She fetched the vibrator she had bought at an Anne Summers party and settled back on the bed. The vibrator had been another impulse buy, she realised, a joke. She had never yet used it. It was made of some transparent pink material and had a plastic bubble, filled with little round beads, set partway down the shaft.

Reaching down, Josie unzipped her jeans and eased them down her legs. Sliding her thumbs into the waistband of her cotton lace pants, she took those off too. The sight of her reflection in the new mirror aroused her further. She looked wanton and sexy, naked from the waist down and with her hair all mussed. Her eyes glowed with a brandy-lent flame.

She still could not work out why she had bought the mirror, but it seemed like a better idea with each passing moment. She had never watched herself masturbate before. This would be a first. 'The start of a new Josie,' she slurred happily. 'Are you watching me, mirror?'

As she moved her hand down over her stomach, a feeling of warm tension spread around her pussy. She raised her legs and let her knees fall open, watching as the outer lips spread and the pink inner surfaces of her labia were revealed. Already they were glistening with juices. The opening to her vagina was a dark and mysterious shadow. It looked like velvet. Something about the mirror enhanced the look of her. Was her skin really that texture – like thick cream? And did her hair always have that sheen?

'Eat your heart out, Sam. You bastard. This is your loss!' she said aloud on a laugh.

Who needed him anyway? Josie shuddered with pleasure as she took in her enhanced mirror-image. God, she looked really sexy. She watched as her fingers spread her inner lips open more widely and began playing up and down the moist slit. Little ripples of sensation spread down to her thighs. She decided to put off using the vibrator for a while; save it as a treat, play with herself while savouring the thought of it.

She gave a little purr of pleasure. This was somehow more intimate than fucking. You could be making love with someone and not quite lose yourself. The other person claims so much of you, she thought, yet *you* feel guilty if they don't make you come. Self-love was entirely voluptuous. The selfishness of it was what appealed. Funny that she had never allowed Sam to watch her do this to herself. She was glad of that now. This act was hers alone. Let him pork that fat, brown-haired bimbo he had run off with! She didn't care any more.

There seemed to be a secret complicity between herself and the greenish glass reflection. Her hand worked faster, three wet fingers lightly circling her clit, varying the pressure. Slowly, teasing herself with the image and the reality, she inserted the tip of one finger into her vagina. Her mirror image did the same. How shiny her finger looked, how reluctant the slick pink flesh was to release it.

As Josie lifted her hips, flexing her knees and thrusting her belly upwards, the image in the mirror wavered. A flicker of light passed across the glass surface. Josie was too engrossed to notice for a moment. She strained her legs wide, opening her buttocks to reveal the tight rose-shape of her anus. It was moist, ringed with a few dark blond curls.

She tickled the little mouth with the tips of two fingers. It seemed a naughty, forbidden act. Never had she felt so wanton, so down-to-earth sexual. Her clitoris burned and throbbed as she stroked it. She smeared the juice seeping from her vagina all over her deliciously swollen pussy. Wetting her forefinger, she slipped it a little way inside her anus. There was some resistance at the entrance, then a feeling of acceptance as she pressed gently but remorselessly inwards. It felt like hot silk in there.

Oooooh, how naughty. Another first. Josie, you bad girl.

She pushed the finger all the way into her bottom, gasping at the mixed sensations that flooded her belly. In the mirror she looked wild. Her eyes glowed with a peculiar lambency as her body twisted and bucked. She could not look away from the delightful lewdness of the image. Her legs spread in wild abandonment, her pussy wet and glistening. Her fingers thrust inside her body, working and working to bring her to a sweet release.

Oh, it was magic or Heaven or both.

Pausing for a moment to reach for the vibrator, she twisted the base to turn it on. The low deep humming caused her pussy to throb with anticipation. As she caressed her soaking flesh with the bright pink phallus she shivered all over with a singular pleasure. On the brink of coming, she plunged the vibrator into her vagina. The feel of the clear bubble containing all the little buzzing, rotating beads drove her wild. Her hips wove madly as her orgasm rolled over her. She screamed and bit her lips, exulting in the sound she made, letting out all the grunts and groans of pleasure which she had kept caged from Sam. Her internal pulsings were deep and satisfying and seemed to go on and on.

When they faded, finally, she slumped back in exhaustion, replete as never before. In a while, she wiped herself with a tissue, cleaned the vibrator and put it away. Pouring herself another generous measure of brandy, she held up the glass to the mirror. 'Here's to plenty more shared good times,' she said with a wide grin. 'Mirror, mirror on the wall. You're a beauty – the best partner of all!'

She knocked the brandy back, then looked at the mirror in puzzlement. Pushing herself upright, she peered closely at the surface. There seemed to be a large smear on the glass. Head swimming with the after-glow of the brandy and the orgasm, she reached behind her for something to rub the mirror with. Her fingers closed over the damp tissue.

She rubbed at the patch and the glass came clean. It was only dust after all. Realising what she had used to wipe the mirror, she giggled. 'Oops, sorry, mirror. I've just smeared you with pussy juice! Hope you don't mind!'

The room spun around her. Josie fell back onto the bed, still laughing softly. She felt happy, carefree for the first time in many weeks. Groggily, she pulled off the rest of her clothes and dropped them onto the bedroom carpet. Flopping onto the pillows, she closed her eyes. Warm, relaxed, and sated, she fell asleep.

An hour later Josie awoke. Feeling cold, she sat up to pull the duvet over herself. Moonlight flooded the room through the slats in the Venetian blinds. The surface of the mirror looked silvery, as if it had absorbed every ray of light that penetrated the room.

She could see the clean spot where she had wiped the layer of dust with the tissue. Her eyelids drooped, then snapped open. The clean patch on the mirror was . . . glowing. Impossible. It could not be. But it was.

Josie watched with a mixture of fascination and horror. The clean spot was definitely getting bigger. Before her eyes the edges of the smudge pushed outwards. As it grew, the light followed it. Josie did not dare to move. Perhaps it was a brandy-induced dream. No. She was awake – muzzy-headed, but fully conscious. The glow was still growing. Finally it spread all over the surface of the mirror. There was a new depth inside the sumptuous frame. Josie could see right *inside* the mirror.

At first there was only a blank sheet of light, then the image condensed, sharpened. Josie swallowed audibly, finding herself gazing into a room. It seemed to be a boudoir. Red flocked paper covered the walls. There was a mahogany dressing-table with a mirror, a lacquered screen in one corner. Fringed velvet curtains masked the windows. The soft glow of an oil lamp illuminated the room. To one side there was a chaise longue.

Then the door opened and a woman stepped into the mirror-room.

She had thick red hair, a striking, longish face. Her hair was pinned up, leaving her slender neck bare. A froth of red curls framed her forehead. She wore a robe that had a deep collar of lace threaded with silk ribbons. Around her neck was a velvet choker with a cameo.

Josie was transfixed. More unexpected than anything that had happened so far was the fact that the woman had her face.

'My God. It's me. It's really me,' Josie breathed. 'I'm in the mirror. But it's a different me.'

She looked down, felt her limbs, pinched herself. Solid enough, real. Then it must be an image of herself she was looking at. She had read about doppelgängers. Was it possible? The fact that she felt no menace whatsoever stopped her from flinging herself off the bed and fleeing the room. Nothing but benevolence came from the mirror and its image.

Sitting sideways on to Josie, the mirror-woman patted her abundant red hair, tweaking the frothy curls at the front into shape. She bit her lips to make them full and red, then picked up a cut-glass scent bottle. Removing the stopper, she used it to apply perfume to her pulse points – behind her ears, in the crook of her elbow, on the insides of her wrists. Josie smelled the lavender and heliotrope notes of 'Jicky', her own favourite classic French perfume. With a mischievous smile the mirror-woman shrugged off the robe and applied a dab of perfume between her breasts.

Josie's pulses quickened. Her fear was fast fading and an unwilling fascination was taking over. The sheer natural sensuality of her other self exerted a powerful pull on her senses. The red-haired woman was obviously expecting a lover. And the glimpse of those full breasts jutting over the top of a tightly-laced corset sent a dart straight to Josie's stomach.

How pretty the clothes were, all those frills and flounces. She would like to wear things like that. It was Sam who had preferred her to wear tight jeans and clinging T-shirts. She wondered now why she had gone on wearing them. They were not even comfortable. She watched her alter-ego in the mirror, held by the spell of her. The woman looked innocent, but knowing at the same time. Do I look like that? Josie wondered.

The woman smoothed her black stockings up over shapely ankles, securing them behind her knees with frilled garters. Loose-legged, frilled drawers reached to her knees, only partly concealing the swell of her hips. The drawers were made of some thin stuff. Josie could see the faint shadow of hair on the woman's pubic mound. She turned now and bent to pick up the discarded robe and her drawers stretched tautly across her rounded bottom. Josie saw the indentation that marked the parting between the woman's full cheeks.

She could not help but admire the lushness of the figure before her. Sam had insisted that Josie dieted. Fool that she was, she had complied. Her body was angular now, her breasts almost flat, and her hips bordering on the boyish. She had the body that Sam wanted. Yet he had run off with the buxom brunette.

The woman in the mirror is me as I ought to be, she realised.

A new excitement gripped her as she saw that the scene in the mirror was changing. A door opened and a man walked into the boudoir. No words passed between the two figures, yet Josie was certain that the man and woman were on intimate terms.

The man was tall, broad-shouldered, blond. In fact, he looked rather like the pin-up in the magazine, which lay discarded amongst the rumpled bedclothes. The woman stood up and faced the man. Smiling slightly, she raised one leg and rested it on the stool, then began to fiddle with the toe of her stocking. The man said nothing, his eyes drawn to the drawers she wore. Because of her lifted leg he could see they were open at the crotch. The opening gaped, giving him a view of rounded thighs and the plump sex nestling between them.

One of the woman's hands strayed to her exposed thigh, stroking it gently, describing small circles on the creamy skin. Glancing up from lowered lashes, she gave the man a look of arch invitation. 'Shall I?' she seemed to be asking him.

'Yes. Oh, yes,' Josie breathed, lost in the sensuality of the scene as her alter-ego's finger toyed with her pubic curls before slipping into her parted slit. She's playing with him, teasing him, Josie thought. She had never had the confidence or the desire to do that to Sam.

The mirror-woman parted her legs and opened the lips of her sex with two fingers, exerting an upwards pressure so that her clitoris stood proud of the surrounding folds. At the expression on the man's face, Josie felt a tingle go right through her. The reddish hair on the woman's vulva glistened in the lamp-light. Her held-open labia looked swollen as if pouting and the man had a clear view of the moist inner flesh. Around the woman's vagina the flesh was a deeper red.

Josie licked her lips nervously. She would never dare to act that way. But her other self was totally at ease with her femininity. She really likes herself, Josie realised, while I never have.

The mirror-woman opened her thighs wide, letting the bent leg fall to one side. The man wore an avid expression. He looked as if he longed to press his mouth to that tender crevice, to suckle the flesh-hood and draw the nub of the clitoris into the curl of his tongue. He looked as if he wanted to drink her juices, smell the rich musk, to hear the woman sigh and moan under him.

Josie needed a man to want *her* like that. A good-looking man, strong yet sensitive. A man just like the one in the mirror. She found herself moving down the bed, nearing the frame that surrounded the intimate tableau. In a daze of arousal and need, Josie moved closer until she was looking directly into the mirror. The glass seemed to have melted. It had ceased to be a barrier. Surely it was a doorway.

Too late now for doubt or wonderment. Somehow Josie knew that if she refused to accept it was impossible, then it became reality. Reaching out her hand, she stretched her whole body towards the man. Without any apparent change of perception, she found herself looking directly up at him. She was conscious that she had one foot resting on a stool. From the corner of her eye she saw the lacquered screen and the lamp.

'I've been waiting for you a long time,' the man said, his intense blue eyes glittering.

Josie's heart turned over. The man's wide, sensual mouth curved in a smile of welcome. In that smile there was kindness, humour, and recognition. For a moment she was dizzy. But his hand in hers was strong, solid. Real. The chemise and drawers, the corset, felt strange and yet so familiar, so right.

Unable to resist, she turned and looked in the large ornate mirror which hung on the wall behind her. Do I still exist in the real world? she thought. With relief she saw the bedroom with its slatted blinds. In it she saw a thin, fair-haired woman sitting on a rumpled bed, a crumpled magazine beside her. She looked so unhappy that Josie felt sorry for her.

The man, her perfect lover, embraced the mirror-Josie. He ran his hands over her waist, stroked the rich swell of her hips. He smoothed the cambric drawers against her skin, hooking his fingers into the deep valley that bisected her generous rump. What was his name? It did not matter. It was what he represented that was important. Absorbing the truth of this, Josie gave a husky laugh and unlaced the front of her chemise, slipping the lacy neckline off her shoulders.

Her lover groaned as she freed her breasts and allowed them to fall forward. His mouth quested into the perfumed cleavage. He pressed kisses to the firm flesh, seeking a hold on a nipple. Josie sighed when he drew her nipple into his mouth and began lashing it with his tongue. After a moment he drew back and gazed admiringly at the full globes, the large, pale-pink buds.

Josie felt the urge to laugh with sheer happiness. 'You're perfect. The perfect lover.'

Her lover stroked her forehead, smoothing back the curls. 'I am for you, my darling,' he said softly.

An ache built within Josie. Her sex seemed actually to throb with lustful heat. Oh God, she needed desperately for him to bury himself in her liquid warmth. Her eyes met his. He seemed to know what she wanted. In a moment he had turned her around, bent her forwards over the broad stool. The drawers gaped open around her bottom. She smelled the sweet pungent musk of her own arousal. Then she was sinking back onto him, guiding the head of his cock into the tight purse of her sex. His flesh filled her, the stout head forging into her molten core.

She felt him shudder as he moved inside her, slowly at first, rimming her opening with the fat glans. Josie slammed her buttocks against the base of his hard belly, knowing that he felt the strong squeeze of her flesh-walls. Her lover cried out as he buried his shaft deep inside her, moving in time with her breathy moans.

'Do it to me, my darling girl,' he murmured. 'Milk me of my jism. Make me pant. Make me spend.'

The old-fashioned terms spurred Josie on. The cock leapt and twitched inside her. Never before had she felt such an all-consuming lust. His pubic hair ground against her bottom as Josie sighed and writhed on him. Moving her hand to the gap in her drawers, she rubbed herself as he pounded into her.

She could see their reflection in the large wall mirror – for mirror it had become again. The open drawers gave her a full view of her juicy quim, stretched wide around her lover's thick stem. She was wet and slick as a seal. Josie drank in the sight of her strong back; the perfect heart-shape of her generous, spread buttocks; the crumpled anus, pushed out slightly by the pressure of the rampant cock inside her; her sturdy thighs which took her lover's weight easily.

She loved herself like this, with rounded limbs and fat on her bones. How secure she felt, within the cushioning expanse of flesh.

'Oh, I'm spending. Oh Lord,' her lover cried.

Josie came too, the ripples of her contracting quim drawing the sperm from him. As her lover spasmed and emptied himself, her entire body tingled with the ecstasy of total release. She forgot Sam, the erosion of her self-confidence, the messy divorce, the long lonely nights. She forgot about Roy's advice and the fact that things like this could not happen. She believed. Let cynics like Sam hold on to their views if they wanted to.

Her lover kissed her gently before he left. 'I'm always here for you,' he whispered against her mouth.

Josie cupped his face in her hands and murmured, 'Thank you, for more than you realise.'

When he had gone, she looked into the mirror and saw again the image of the thin blonde woman on the bed. Moonlight crept in through the slatted blind. The other Josie was sleeping now, a smile on her untroubled face. The mirror-Josie knew that she must go back and enter the body of the woman on the bed, but that her alter-ego would always exist within the mirror. Her lover waited there too.

As she moved towards the mirror, the image of the boudoir behind her wavered and grew dark. She found herself looking down on her sleeping self and smelled the familiar odour of clean bed-linen and new paint. Then her cheek was resting against the cool pillowcase and all was peaceful.

In the mirror, the red-haired woman smiled tenderly. The lamp flickered and went out.

In the modern bedroom, the moonlight glimmered on a solid sheet of greenish glass.

Succubus

ROSE GAVE EMMA a lingering kiss, then fitted the key into the ornate front door.

'See you in the morning then?' she said, hoping that Emma would change her mind and stay in the house with her.

Emma shuddered and pulled up the collar of her black leather jacket. She looked up at the pointed-arch windows that seemed to stare down at the two women.

'It's a bloody mausoleum. I've always hated this house.' Her voice softened, became wheedling. She reached up to stroke Rose's cheek. 'You don't have to do this, you know. Come back to the flat with me.'

Rose grinned, enlivening her elfin face. 'I never go back on a dare. You should know that by now.'

'I won't hold you to it. We were both drunk. What is it with you and this house, anyway?'

49

Rose shrugged, the mass of striking red dreadlocks dancing around her shoulders. She opened the front door. 'You keeping me company or what?'

Emma's straight brows dipped in a frown. 'Sod you then, if you won't listen to sense. I'm off.'

She turned with a flick of her short black skirt, Doc Marten boots scuffing through the wet leaves that clotted the brick path. Rose watched her go, thinking that even now Emma might change her mind. She was not usually so stubborn. But Emma did not turn around. As her lover banged the wrought-iron gate shut behind her, Rose stepped through the front door.

Late afternoon sun streamed through the stained-glass door panel, casting coloured diamonds onto the floor tiles. The house smelled musty, sweetish, with the faintest trace of old lavender polish. Rose smiled, recalling childhood memories of visiting her grandmother. Gran's house had smelt just like this. It was a shame that Emma was still spooked by unpleasant memories of her dotty aunt. Anyone could see that the house was a gem. It belonged to the living. How could Emma even consider selling it?

She climbed the stairs, trailing her fingers along the carved bannisters, feeling the coldness of the wood under her palms. On her back was a holdall containing candles, food, incense sticks, a flask of coffee. Got to do this right.

Dust sheets covered the furniture. The rooms

seemed filled with white, lumpy shapes, iced rocks in the gloom. Nothing had been touched since the old lady's death. Somehow the house had escaped the notice of vandals and squatters. Odd, in this area, to see the red brick walls free from graffiti. Did everyone believe the ghost stories?

Rose made herself comfortable in one of the bedrooms. Maroon velvet curtains hung at either side of the window. More of the same fabric, this time swagged and threaded with gold cord, hung over the bed tester. A four-poster. Somehow she'd known Emma's aunt would have slept in one.

By the time she had eaten, and finished the coffee, the light outside was fading. She found four cut-glass candle sticks and put them to use. Then she set more candles around the room and lit some joss sticks. Tendrils of blue-grey, perfumed smoke snaked towards the plaster ceiling.

As she undressed, pulling off her studded boots, leather trousers and black T-shirt, she looked at her reflection in the large overmantel mirror. Her eyes looked huge in her narrow face. Candlelight flickered on her pale skin, the garish Medusa mass of her hair.She stood naked except for a fishnet body, admiring the slender curves of her waist, the flow of her hips. Behind her the bedroom had an odd look, somehow vibrant, larger than life. It was she who looked two-

51

dimensional, like a cardboard cut-out against the Victorian clutter.

It seemed that the house looked at her. Rose let it look. Stroking her hands over her breasts, she moved them downwards over the slight pout of her belly. She caressed the rose tattoo on her left hip, dipped her fingers between her thighs and stroked the dark hair that poked through the fishnet.

This house was a real turn-on. She had fantasised about it for months, ever since Emma showed her the place where the reclusive old girl had lived. She couldn't believe that the house would be Emma's one day. That night she had dreamed about living there. The obsession to spend one night alone in the house had begun soon after. The dare was just an excuse, a vehicle for her to have her own way. One night. That was all it would take.

'I'll make you mine,' she said to the shadows. 'Mine and Emma's.'

In the morning she'd bring Emma up to this room, persuade her with lips and tongue and deft slippery fingers that they should move in. They would lie on this bed together and make love in the dusty gloom. She would show her lover that there was nothing to fear. But first . . .

Slowly now. She breathed in the vanilla scent of incense. Light sparked on the jewel in her nose as she lifted her arms and untied the rags from her hair so that it spilled over her shoulders in a tangle of vibrant red. Shivering slightly with anticipation, she climbed onto the bed.

The dusty velvet coverlet was prickly against her skin. She closed her eyes. The house seemed to settle around her, the shadows moving in closer. A knot of excitement gathered in her stomach. Again she imagined lying on the bed with Emma. Her hands moved over her body in a slow dance. She spent a long time stroking her breasts, cupping the underswell, lifting and squeezing the firm flesh. She loved touching her breasts. The nipples were darkly defined and incredibly sensitive. When she was fully aroused they stuck out in wanton little tubes. Sometimes she came when Emma did nothing but suckle them.

Her breath came faster as she unfastened the fishnet body at the crotch, drew it up to her waist and tucked it tightly beneath her. The constriction around her waist, the nakedness of her hips and legs, excited her further. The fishnet made little indentations in the flesh of her breasts, quilting her. Her nippes were hard little nubs, bisected by thin black threads. The tactile feel of the cords made her shiver with lust.

Slowly, so slowly, she made circles on her bare lower stomach, working down to the patch of damp, scented hair between her thighs. Raising her knees, she let them fall apart and felt the caress of the dusty air on her parted sex. She sighed, the sound rustling into the room to be absorbed by the draperies. With the fingers of one hand, she pressed open her labia, exerting a slight pressure upwards so that her clitoris stood proud of the surrounding flesh.

Rose screwed her eyes shut, concentrating on the overall feeling of sensuality, of the cloying presence of the house all around her, and on the tension building, building between her thighs. She slid her hand downwards, dipped into the wet folds and touched the slippery moisture to the erect bud of her clit.

The whisper in her ear was subtle. The voice, soft and so husky with desire. Rose was startled, but somehow not afraid.

Her eyes snapped open. She searched the darkness, but could see nothing – no one. There was a new air of tension within the room. A faint smell of musk and lilies. Rose became aware of a presence. It was enticing. Amorphous. Something within her leapt to meet it.

The darkness was grainy, empty – gilded in small pools by candlelight and the thin shafts of moonlight that penetrated the stained-glass windows. Rose smiled, feeling disappointed. Wishful thinking. Too many vampire novels. Anne Rice and Freda Warrington had a lot to answer for.

Then the shadows moved.

The breath caught in Rose's throat. Her mouth went dry with anticipation even while a heady pulse ticked between her legs.

'Come then,' she said softly.

And the darkness changed. A faint glow appeared at its centre, thickened and took on form. A woman stood at the side of the bed. She was naked, dark-haired, pale and beautiful. Moonlight threw speckled shadows over her translucent flesh. Jewel colours against the white. The whisper came *inside* Rose's head. It was sibilant, insistent.

'Please. Let me. I beg you.'

Rose felt incapable of movement. Crazy images flooded her mind. This had to be a dream. An hysterical laugh bubbled up from deep inside her. But I'm awake. This is real. Her hands had fallen to her sides, the palms cupped as if in submission or supplication. Between her open legs, her exposed sex was beating like a second heart.

Then the woman bent over and kissed her. Her touch was cool, gentle at first. She climbed onto the bed and lay beside Rose; so light – she seemed weightless. Rose's thighs trembled as long white fingers played over her skin. Scented breath brushed her cheek, a wet tongue entered her ear. The arms encircling her were slender, pale, but very strong. Rose felt herself drawn into the woman's cold embrace. Full breasts pressed softly against her own. The woman moaned softly, beginning to move from side to side so that the tips of her big, firm nipples brushed backwards and forwards across Rose's own.

Rose felt slivers of pleasure flood her belly. She arched to meet the woman, making little sounds of urgency deep in her throat. The woman's skin grew warmer. It felt silky soft where it met Rose's naked flesh. The bunched-up fishnet was a barrier between them, but that fact excited Rose almost unbearably. The combination of skin to skin, the scratchy tightness around her waist and breasts, the dusty air on her lower limbs were all mesmerising.

Rose bent her head and closed her lips around a nipple. It was firm, rubbery. Drawing it deeply into her mouth, she lashed it with her tongue. She squeezed the breast hard, so that it was offered up to her, and released the nipple for a moment. Curving her tongue, she lapped at the taut bud, which was shiny, polished with her saliva. Then Rose felt herself pressed gently backwards, her arms held above her head.

Rose turned her face into the flesh of her own upper arm as long insistent white fingers began stroking her thighs. Pointed finger-nails played over her pubis and scratched gently up and down the sides of her swollen labia. Rose groaned aloud, biting into her own arm. She wanted the torment to end – she wanted it to go on . . .

Long black hair brushed her thighs and lay like a silk scarf across her stomach. Rose parted her legs, pushing upwards with her hips and arching her back. Long spiked fingers opened her sex, then Rose felt the first delicious sweep of a tongue on her wet inner lips. Her stomach grew taut, her hips worked back and forth as the hot tongue flicked upwards, feathering against the little flesh-hood covering her clitoris. The sweet, pulsing ache gathered momentum.

When Rose thought her pleasure would surely spill over, the contact was broken abruptly.

Before she could protest she found herself flipped over onto her stomach, her face pressed to the dusty velvet bedcover. Long claws dragged her buttocks apart and the hot lapping resumed. This time it started at the pouch of her sex, progressed up her cleft and over the tight pink ring of her anus. Rose cried out, her thighs rigid with tension, her wide-spread buttocks jerking and trembling as a firm tongue-tip entered her.

Somehow she held back as the knowing fingers dug into her flesh, holding her open and exposed. The velvet coverlet pricked her belly. Vanilla smoke tickled her nostrils. Now and then she felt long finger-nails scratching gently at her anus, probing into her soaking sex. When two fingers entered her, lifting gently, pulling in a backwards motion then slipping in and out, the first shudders broke over her.

In the very midst of her orgasm, she felt the bite of pain as sharp teeth scored her buttocks, long nails raked her back. Rose's cries echoed round the room, seemed to reflect back at her from the stained-glass window. The pleasure was so singular, so acute, that for a few moments darkness descended.

When she opened her eyes, she was lying with

her head hanging over the side of the bed. Her whole body seemed possessed by a tingling ache, as if it were reliving the experience at a new and deeper level. Rose lifted her head. The pale figure of the woman was standing a distance away, looking down at her. On her lovely face was an expression of pleading. It seemed to Rose that the figure was fainter. The line around her shoulders was smudged, half-absorbed into the darkness.

The whisper came again, hot inside Rose's head, but more hesitant this time.

'Only stay. And I'll come often to pleasure you. I exist only for you. I am what you make me. Please give me a reason to remain . . .'

The hand that reached out to Rose was almost transparent. The darkness crowded in, beginning to engulf the fading glow of the woman's body. Rose smiled joyfully. No wonder Emma's dotty old aunt had never left the house. What delights she had found within the sturdy walls.

She knew exactly what she must do.

Reaching out, she took hold of the fading swell of the woman's hips and pulled her close. As she wrapped her arms around the pale thighs, she felt them filling out and growing solid under her fingers. She pressed her face to the soft belly, her cheek against the curling hair that grew in a perfect triangle shape. As she breathed in the pungent scent of musk and lilies, she felt an instant reawakening of desire.

Bending her head, she parted the sex-lips with

her tongue, took her first taste of the rich salty flesh. The cold skin warmed again under her fingers. The hands that gripped her shoulders as she quested deeper were once again strong, the nails sharp, beautifully cruel. As Rose pulled the woman back onto the bed and pressed her thighs apart, she thought briefly of Emma who would be calling for her in a few hours. Emma who needed persuading.

A sense of certainty settled over Rose. The house was hers already. One night was all Emma would need.

Therapy

'SO, WHAT DO you do to combat executive stress? I love to go shopping myself. Nothing like a new outfit to give me a lift.'

The nasal voice of Linda the fashion editor floated into Anna's office as she sat staring at the screen of her Apple Mac battling with a feature which would not come right. She pushed back her chair in frustration and began paying attention to the conversation outside.

'I play squash. Sometimes treat myself to a facial or a leg wax.'

That was Corrina, deputy fashion editor. Both women in the corridor had recently joined the editing team of 'Pzazz' magazine, gaining the coveted jobs by calling in favours from high-ups in the trade.

Squash? A leg wax? Shopping? God help us! Anna thought. Is that the best they can come up with to fill their spare time? She had an impulse, quickly squashed, to go and tell them what she had planned for relaxation later in the day. How their perfectly made-up faces would go blank with disbelief.

Cheered by the thought, Anna opened her desk drawer and took out an envelope. Inside was the letter she had received that morning, along with three black and white photographs. Picking up the phone, she pressed the button for an outside line and dialled.

'Oh, hello. Anna Siegal here. Number two seems eminently suitable for my purposes. No problem with availability? Good. Look forward to our meeting.'

She replaced the receiver, a secret smile playing around her lips. Glancing at her wrist-watch she saw that she had two hours to go before she had to leave the office for the afternoon appointment. She poured herself a cup of black coffee, then turned her attention back to her Mac. Moving the mouse, she clicked on 'edit'. She'd have this feature finished before she left if it killed her.

Later, on her way to the lift, she passed Corrina, her arms full of an assortment of garishly coloured silk scarves.

'Accessories for the piece on Hermès,' Corrina explained. 'Off to the therapy centre for your regular session, are you? You never did say why you go there. What is it, some sort of Weight Watchers?'

'Not exactly,' Anna said breezily. 'It's more a whole body experience. Does wonders for one's well-being. Crouching over a desk all day is so draining.'

'Doesn't help the cellulite either, darling,' said Corrina, glancing meaningfully at Anna's bulging black leggings.

Skinny-arsed cow, Anna fumed, watching Corrina's stick-thin body diminish down the corridor. But despite her silent protestations, the pointed remark had hit home. As Anna drove across London to the treatment centre, she pondered on all the years she'd spent working on her insecurities. Today she prided herself on her ability to love her big, curvaceous frame. It was galling that, with a few words, Corrina had managed to transport her back to the days of her lumpy, spotty and painful adolescence.

Boy, did she need today's session! The therapy was an amazing confidence booster, leaving her feeling secure in the knowledge that it was downright sexy to be a generous size eighteen. On reaching Hampstead, she parked her car in a side street, then entered the door of the discreet clinic. The building was a restored Georgian town house. There was nothing in the black, wrought-iron railings or the window-boxes bursting with red geraniums and blue lobelia to suggest the nature of the therapies on offer.

Anna paused at Reception. The pleasant-faced woman behind the stained ash desk smiled at her.

'Ah, Ms Siegal. Nice to see you again. You are expected. Do go on up to treatment room three. Your therapist will be with you shortly.'

Anna thanked the woman and went up the stairs. The interior of the clinic was all marble columns, black tiles and white paintwork. On the second floor, she opened the door marked number three and went inside. The room was sparsely furnished. There were white Venetian blinds, a screen, a chair, a metal table with a lamp, and a leather-covered treatment table.

Anna slipped behind the screen and began to undress. There was a white cotton gown hanging up ready for her use. When she was naked, she put it on. It had ties at the front, unlike those hospital gowns that allowed your bottom to protrude rudely. As she emerged from behind the screen the door opened and a young man came in carrying a deep, covered tray. He was even more good-looking than in the photo. His shiny, dark hair was shoulder-length. It looked striking against his plain white regulation T-shirt and track pants.

'Good afternoon, madam,' he said. 'My name's James. I'm your chosen therapist for today.'

Anna smiled approvingly. His demeanour was perfect – friendly but courteous. Clients at the clinic were never addressed by name. Anna liked the anonymity, coupled with the knowledge that her express instructions would be carried out to the letter.

'Hello, James,' she said. 'I feel rather tense today. I'm very much in need of your specialist services.'

He smiled, showing even, white teeth. He was really sexy with his straight nose, olive-toned skin, and liquid brown eyes. Under the tight-fitting T-shirt, she could see the outline of toned pectorals and a flat, hard stomach. At the thought of his hands on her, her throat dried.

'I'm sorry to hear that you're stressed, madame. If you'd like to get up onto the treatment couch, I'll soon have you feeling better,' he said.

Anna made herself comfortable while James put the covered tray of instruments on the side table. He glanced swiftly at a computer print-out of her case notes, then said, 'No problem with your requirements. Ready to begin, madam?'

She nodded, feeling the usual mixture of anticipation. Each time she came to the centre her experience was slightly different. Her chosen therapist always found an individual way of meeting her particular demands.

'Let's just get you into the required position,' James said.

Anna trembled slightly as he untied the cotton robe and tucked the open flaps beneath her. Her pillowy breasts and big, round stomach were revealed. This moment always made her blush. It did not matter that she was totally in charge. Being naked before a handsome, desirable young man made her unbearably self-conscious. But she revelled in the flush of shame. That was part of the treatment. And there were worse indignities to come.

'May I say that madam has lovely breasts,' James said, looking her over appreciatively. 'They're big but firm. And your nipples are gorgeous. Prominent and such a pretty shade of pink. Your lovers must adore sucking them.'

He sounded sincere. She could almost believe that he had not been prompted by the explicit instructions on her record card. She sighed as he ran gentle fingers over her belly and soft, rounded thighs, before lifting each leg in turn and placing her feet in obstetric stirrups. She felt the cool air of the room between her thighs as they were drawn widely apart. Her face was bright red now. She did not meet his gaze as he slipped padded straps around the tops of her thighs, seating them high up under the swelling of her buttocks before securing them to posts at the side.

Anna began to feel excited. This handsome young man had an unobstructed view of her open sex. The urge to try and draw her legs together was almost overwhelming.

'Madam has a very generous figure,' James said, trailing his fingers over her skin. 'What a lovely soft belly. Such strong white thighs. And, if I may comment, a firm and well-made vulva. The labia are pink and nicely plump. It would be even better if you were depilated. I'll see to that for you at once.'

'Oh, do you think so?' Anna said, her pulses clamouring at the thought of him shaving her. 'Well, if you're sure . . .'

She loved this slow lead-up, the well-chosen comments, designed to make her feel like the most desirable woman in the world. James made certain that she was comfortable, positioning her so that her bottom was almost at the edge of the table. Then he adjusted the leather-covered rest behind her head and shoulders, so that from the waist up her body was slightly raised.

'I'm sure you'd like to see what I'm doing, madam,' he said. Lastly he placed her wrists above her head and secured them with bandages to the rail provided.

Deliciously helpless now, Anna watched James uncover the tray on the side table. She heard the snapping sound as he pulled on disposable rubber gloves. She shivered, awaiting the first touch, as he assembled the things he needed. Placing a chair between her legs he used an old-fashioned brush to apply a thick layer of shaving soap. The feathery bristles were a sweet torture as they flicked against her stretched labia and hardening clitoris.

Anna held her breath as he shaved her with long, expert strokes of a cut-throat razor. It was thrilling to feel the sharp metal skimming so close to her intimate membranes. All too soon it was over. James sluiced her pudenda with warm water and dried her.

'That's better,' he said. 'I can see your lovely stiff little clit more clearly now. It's standing proud of the surrounding labia as if greedy for attention. Naughty thing! It'll have to wait. Ready for the next stage?'

Anna did not trust herself to answer as he squeezed a large blob of transparent lubricant into the palm of one hand. She held her breath, anticipating the coolness of the gel on her hairless quim. But he did not go directly to stand between her spread thighs. Swooping down he pressed his mouth to hers.

The kiss was as prolonged as it was unexpected. A deep, sensual exploration. His tongue invaded her mouth, seeking, tasting. When he drew away she felt subtle tendrils of desire worming their way into her belly. She gave a muffled groan, no longer able to hold back the evidence of her pleasure.

'I think madam is ready now,' James said, satisfied that he had shattered her composure.

When he spread the lubricant on the folds of her sex, she gasped at the cold, oily feel of it. He stroked her gently, pulling at the labia until they swelled and stood out thickly. While he massaged her engorged sex-lips, he inserted two gloved fingers of his other hand and anointed her vagina with another generous blob of lubricant. She felt it dripping out of her, running warmly down the crease of her bottom.

It was difficult to stay still. She wanted to arch

her back, exert a pressure on the stirrups, flex her calf muscles and strain against the supporting straps which held her buttocks apart, but she controlled herself somehow. There was more to come, much more. She didn't want to peak too soon.

'How does that feel, madam?' James asked, rubbing her belly with one palm while continuing to stroke her exposed pudenda with a feather-light touch.

'Very good. So far,' Anna said with mock brusqueness. Lord, that was a gross under-statement! It felt bloody wonderful. It would be worth coming to the clinic for this alone.

James's forehead creased. 'Only . . . good? Then I've been sadly remiss. I'm sorry if madam is displeased. Let me hasten to put things right.'

Anna let out her breath on a sigh. James was playing the game for all he was worth. He bent over the tray and then took up his position between her thighs again. She felt his deft hands on her sex, two fingers gently holding her labia open while he inserted a small, slender phallus into her vagina. Anna chewed at her bottom lip as he moved the phallus back and forth.

'How's that? Does it suit madam?'

'No,' Anna said. 'It's too small. But keep it aside. You can use it up my bottom later.'

James withdrew the phallus. 'Very well. How about this one?' he said, inserting a slightly larger rubber cock.

Anna pretended to consider. It was hard to concentrate with James's hands on her lubricated sex and the dildo buried deeply inside her. 'It's . . . um, not right yet,' she said.

James looked crestfallen. Then his face brightened as he held up a large, bright-red rubber cock. Anna shook her head. 'That's far too big,' she said, her mouth curving with feigned distaste. The dildo was truly obscene. A shiny red monster with thick veins twisting down the shaft and a bulbous, flared glans. The thought of having it inside her both horrified and fascinated her.

James began to reassure her, as she knew he would. 'I'm sure you'll find it fits perfectly, madam. Do try it. I'll go very slowly and use lots of lubricant.'

'I said no!' Anna snapped with mock rage, beginning to struggle against the wrist-bonds as James brought the cock close to her vulva. 'No! Stop it! Do you hear me!' Oh, God, don't stop, she pleaded silently. Just the thought of the horrid thing squeezing into her tight channel almost made her come.

James was too well trained to be swayed by her outburst. His fingers reached for her labia again, pressing them open and exerting a slight pressure upwards. His gloved palm brushed against Anna's stiffly erect clitoris as he placed the cock's blunt glans at her entrance.

'James, I order you not to push that vile thing into me! Oh, you wretch. Take it out. It's stretching me horribly. Oh, it won't go in. I know it won't.' Her thighs trembled as the thick shaft slipped partway into her. Christ, it felt good.

James took hold of her oiled clitoris between his fingertips and pulled it gently back and forth. None of her other therapists had done this. He was using the nub of flesh like a tiny cock, masturbating it with measured efficiency.

'Oh, don't. You'll make me come too soon,' she moaned as the subtle drawing out of his fingers sent a spiked warmth flooding through her.

She felt herself loosening, opening up inside, accepting the impossibly big cock with ease. Lifting her head she peered between her thighs. The end of the cock was sticking rudely out of her. It dripped with lubricant and her own juices. The leather couch was awash beneath her buttocks.

She felt herself straining for release. Her orgasm was within reach. Then abruptly the stimulation was withdrawn. She almost wept with frustration. James chuckled. 'My, but you're wet, madam. I think we need the rubber sheet for the next stage.'

Anna let her head fall back against the leather rest as James lifted her bottom and smoothed the sheet beneath her. She ached to be penetrated again. It seemed that she was stretched from the intrusion of the thick red shaft. From the waist down she was a pulsing, throbbing mass of nerve-ends. James needed only to stroke her clitoris once or twice and she would climax.

He was approaching now, holding a rubber

douche-bag, a length of tubing, and a jug of warm water. Anna tensed, her ankles flexing in their supports. Oh, no. Not that. Even while she yearned for what was to happen, she dreaded the act itself. It was so shaming, so messy, and so . . . noisy.

'Please . . .' she said. 'I don't want . . .'

'Don't worry, madam,' James said soothingly. 'Almost finished now.' Swiftly he filled the douche-bag, attached the tubing, and hung the bag from one of the stirrups. There was a valve, operated by a cord which prevented the flow of liquid.

Carefully James inserted one end of the tubing into Anna's vagina. She made a sound of protest. But he smiled at the half-hearted gesture of defiance, knowing that pretending to be unwilling added immensely to her pleasure.

He held up the smallest of the dildos. 'Did you think I'd forgotten?' he said as he pushed it into her anus.

Anna closed her eyes as the slender stem filled her rectum. Filled front and back, she felt swamped by sensation. Penetrated by the tube of the douche-bag, her vagina was pulsing hungrily. Her anus convulsed around the slender dildo as if it would push it out. Then James did something else that none of her other therapists had done. He began to unzip his trousers. Taking out his cock he said, 'Look how hard you've made me, madam. I think you'd better do something about this.'

Oh, yes. Oh, God. Yes, she thought as he positioned himself beside her. His thick cock was near her face. The end of it was moist, the skin retracted to show the glistening purple glans. She smelt the salt-musk of his arousal and leaned across eagerly to take him into her mouth. As she began to suck, he groaned. A sound that seemed dredged up from somewhere deep inside him.

Anna shuddered, arching her back and straining against the constraints that made her subject to the delights of forced pleasure. As she pressed her buttocks to the table, the dildo was forced more deeply inside her anus. The tube of the douche-bag in her vagina was too small for her to gain purchase on. She bounced up and down, longing for the caress that would tip her over the edge.

'Oh, madam!' James said, his face screwed into an expression of bliss as she milked his rigid tool. Even as he started to come, he had the presence of mind to pull on the cord attached to the douche-bag.

As Anna felt his cock vibrate with the release of his sperm, a welcome surge of warm water entered her vagina. She swallowed James's salty come, a muffled scream rising to meet the flow as it slipped down her throat. As she climaxed the warm water poured out of her, spilling over the dildo in her stretched anus and splashing noisily onto the rubber sheet.

The sound of it, which seemed to Anna to be

the vocal expression of her forbidden pleasure, urged her on to experience a shattering, mind-blowing orgasm. The final paroxysms of pleasure were accompanied by the steady drip, drip, drip of water onto the floor.

James, having put his clothes to rights, went to stand between her thighs. He stroked and pinched her clitoris, making sure that she experienced two more climaxes before he deemed her satisfied. Anna's generous frame quivered and ripples ran over her fleshy belly as she orgasmed. The solid feel of her body as it gave itself to pleasure made Anna feel centred and at peace with herself. She felt that she'd truly died and gone to Heaven.

When the final pulsings had died away and she lay recovering, James said, 'Was the therapy to your liking on this occasion, madam?'

'Oh, yes. God, yes,' she breathed.

James beamed at her, his handsome face suffused with pride. 'It was a pleasure to service such a beautiful woman. Perhaps you'll choose me again?' And, even though there was no longer any need for him to humour his client, there was sincerity in his voice.

Anna basked in the warmth of James's regard. The glow of repletion lasted long after she left the centre and returned to her car. Later, when she returned to her office at 'Pzazz' she encountered Corrina in the cloakroom. 'Hi,' she said, giving the deputy fashion editor a dazzling smile. 'Busy afternoon?'

The Music Lesson

AS I MOUNT the stairs the feeling begins, low in the pit of my stomach, a mixture of dread and anticipation.

The porter carries my cello case into the room and places it by the window. I tell him to collect me in one hour. The room is empty – more than empty: bereft without you in it. I walk across it, my buttoned boots clicking on the bleached oak boards, and sit on the window seat, waiting.

The afternoon light streams in through billowing muslin curtains. Outside in the street a breeze rustles the leaves of the plane trees. I stare at the buildings opposite, their wrought-iron balconies crowded with tubs of flowers – lilies, mimosa, roses. The white stucco is dazzling in the summer light.

When the door to the studio opens, I do not look around immediately, wanting to suspend the moment until I see your face. When I turn, I see that you are not very remarkable. I know how you must seem to others, but you are large in my thoughts. Hair of mid-brown, a longish serious face, your fine eyes obscured by gold-rimmed spectacles.

But it is your mouth that drives me mad and haunts my dreams. It is wide, finely sculpted. A music teacher should not have such a mouth. It is the thing which betrays your nature. Can others see that too? I saw it at once.

You smile and greet me – casual meaningless words. I cross to the other window and open my cello case. Nothing unusual in that. No one watching would think anything is amiss. But I know better.

We are to play together today, a Puccini duet. Seated, I position myself. One hand poised on the strings, the bow in my other hand. You sit opposite, aware of my every breath, but holding back your eagerness to touch me. I understand that perfectly. Anticipation is its own reward.

Three times you tap with your bow. A staccato of wood on wood that echoes the racing of my pulse. We begin. The music swells, fills the room, concentrating my senses. How beautiful, how stark is the sound in this room. The vaulted ceiling provides perfect acoustics.

My breathing is shallow and I am aware of the tightness of my corset. I drew the laces more tightly than usual. You love my tiny waist. Are you thinking of it now? Aching to encircle it with those slim, artistic hands? Or are you transfixed by the tops of my breasts where they bulge above the frosted lace of my chemise?

We play and I feel wholly alive.

I close my eyes and let the music sink into my blood and bones. I am quite taken over by it; it is breath and life and sensuality. We pause, smile at each other – conspirators. And play again. This time it is Verdi. I am growing warmer. The effort to play perfectly makes me tense. But that is not the only reason for my tension.

Then I am playing alone and it begins.

I dare not look at you as you lay your bow aside, lean your cello against the chair. This is too fragile to speak of, even to acknowledge. The music carries you to me and now you stand behind me. Before you touch me, I feel you. A slight difference in the air, perhaps your breath, tobacco-scented, on my neck.

Then a touch, a finger brushes my nape, just below the upsweep of my hair. I do not falter in my playing or give any sign that I have noticed your proximity. And you touch me again, twining one chestnut curl around your finger.

'You are playing well,' you say softly. I nod to acknowledge your approval – such a subtle gesture for something which means so much.

Another touch. This time your lips trace a path down my neck and pause at the slight bump of my spine, which is prominent when I bend my head to play. I shudder when I feel your tongue moving on that place – hot, tactile.

Your hair smells of hay and is silky when it brushes my bare shoulder. I wore this dress today because of its wide neckline and I'm glad that I did. There's the tiniest sound when your lips kiss my shoulder, almost lost in the music, little more than a sigh. But I hear it. Oh, I hear it.

Fingers on my buttons, undoing each peach-flushed pearl, one by one. I hold my breath when you part the fabric of my tight bodice and draw it back over my shoulders. I am wearing russet velvet today over a skirt of ashes-of-roses figured silk. I know these colours please you. They make the paleness of my skin seem opalescent and deepen my hazel eyes to lion-gold.

Your whisper is loud in my ears. Oh, you break the rules! Except for the music instruction we have always been silent, but I forgive you. I knew today would be special.

I play on, even though your fingers move over the tops of my breasts. I am trembling now. The bow screeches. It needs resin, but my need is greater.

Outside in the carriage my father waits for me. I am his pride, his possession. His head is cocked to listen to the music. If I were to falter he would clump slowly up the stairs, demand to know why we are wasting his money talking.

Today I am bold and turn my face towards you. I see that you are surprised. You think me innocent, unknowing, but I learn fast – a model pupil. Perhaps you disapprove, but you do not disappoint me. Our lips meet. How tender is your mouth – the mouth you should not own. You taste of brandy and cigars, and something else . . . indefinable. A young man's taste. You are like a symphony. Is that too trite? Certainly it's not original. I do not care.

Your fingers slip below my neckline, into the top of my chemise and close at once over my breast. Ah, this is punishment for my wantonness. You intend to shock me. I gasp, my hand falters and the cello complains, but she forgives me at once.

My lips open beneath yours and I revel in the texture of your tongue. So tender, I want to bite it, suck it, but I repress the urge as your other arm slips around my waist. I lean back against you, feeling your strength. Arching my back I move my hips a little and your fingers become busy at my breast, stroking, pinching. Sweet pleasures trickle over my skin like notes of music.

You whisper to me, 'I'll make you come this time.'

I am dizzy with shock. You have never been so bold, nor I so unrestrained. The hand at my waist moves down and you withdraw your other hand from my breast. I am lonely without it, but not for long. When you have lifted the layers of my skirts and found my thigh through the split in my cambric drawers you return.

Now I feel you on my naked flesh in two places at once. My breast seems to swell as it welcomes your return. The other hand is caressing my inner thigh, moving up slowly, trailing like silk on my skin and, even now, you find the moist red heat of me. I tense, afraid for a moment. I should not allow this, but it was inevitable. And was so from that first time in the lesson when you stopped playing and I carried on without question or pause.

'Oh,' I breathe, when your fingers begin to stroke me . . . there.

Such a little sound, but it echoes inside me and melds with the music. Would I love you if you could not play the cello? Probably not. 'Oh,' again as your fingers describe circles, pressing and smoothing, dipping between the widely spread folds to caress the small bump which is burning, throbbing.

Now I am lost in your kiss and I play by rote, my arm moving the bow with the expertise of long practice, of many painful lessons when my fingertips bled. My knuckles remember the punishment of a wooden ruler. My first teacher. Not you. A new rhythm is building, building inside me and I follow the cadence of your voice. Another symphony.

'Reach for it, my little Clara,' you say with your soft, European accent. I love the way you say my name.

How can I let go – make myself vulnerable to you? That is to give you too much power. Where can this lead? But I cannot stop. As I continue to play, you stroke me, your slender, beautiful musician's fingers playing out their matchless tune on my most intimate flesh.

It seems as if all of me is poised, waiting. Always waiting. I am lost in the magic of the moment. The sun streams in and makes bars of gold on the pale oak floor. I smell lavender polish and resin, the warm leather lining from my cello case by the window. Your breath, a fragrant benison.

I can hardly stop myself calling out. How exquisite it feels to have you touching me. And now entering me in two places with tongue and fingers. Though my flesh sheathes you I cannot move my lower body very much: the cello, my position, prevents it. So I must endure and trust you to lead me. And you do. Like the impresario you are, you lay the notes one on top of the other.

The piece is almost finished. I must reach a peak before I draw the bow across the strings for a final time. Can I do as you wish? You have been training me expertly and I do not want to fail. Oh, my cheeks are burning with shame and exertion and I feel you licking the slight sheen of sweat from my top lip. Your tongue so hot, questing. I almost beg you to stop.

Lord, I am strung as tight as my bow. But it is beginning now.

'Ah, yes, Clara, my angel. Let it go,' you whisper softly against my ear.

It is the final movement and I feel myself gather, break, convulse. How like music it is, sinews and membranes resonating to a top note which spreads and flows over me, enervating, enriching. You capture my groans in your mouth, taking the sounds deep into the warm cavern of your throat.

And I give them to you, my music master. A most singular duet, don't you think?

Your fingers are deft as they pull up my bodice and fasten the pearl buttons. When you take your seat you smile, just for an instant. Behind your spectacles your fine dark eyes are filled with pride. What an obedient pupil I am. Picking up your bow, you tap out the notes. Wood on wood, staccato, echoing the rhythm of my racing pulse. You join me in a duet. Faultless, never a note wrong.

And the last moments meld together, until – silence.

In the carriage outside, Father is nodding his head with satisfaction. His money has not been wasted, neither have I wasted a precious moment by stopping to talk. My playing is improving immensely. Soon I'll be ready for another teacher, he says.

But for now I shall continue to come here once a week. I stand, shake out my crumpled skirts, and put my beloved cello inside its case. The porter is at the door now, waiting. He picks up my cello and I follow him to the top of the staircase.

'Well done, Clara,' says my teacher, softly. 'You are almost ready.'

I do not look back. Downstairs father is waiting impatiently.

The Huntress

AS THE SMALL chartered plane began losing altitude, curving around in a graceful arc, Ruth Shepard leaned forward in her executive-class seat. Through breaks in the clouds she could see the ocean far below, a vast gleaming expanse of aquamarine.

Ruth smoothed the skirt of her designer suit then glanced at the woman who sat next to her, an eye-mask covering the upper part of her face. Nancy Brogan, a high-up in a prestigious American design company, was snoring softly. She had been asleep since their conversation at the start of the journey. Ruth wished she was calm enough to doze, but her mind kept dwelling on what Nancy had said. When Ruth asked her if she had received a letter, Nancy had replied, 'Sure. Mine came in the mail at my company office. I expect this is going to be another of those hare-brained schemes to hone my management skills. You would not believe the seminars and courses I've attended.' She rolled her eyes and shrugged. 'I just do as I'm told. He-who-must-be-obeyed holds the corporate purse-strings!' She opened a Gucci handbag and unfolded a single sheet of paper. 'This is the letter. I guess every woman on this plane has one similar.'

Ruth had glanced at the letter. It was exactly the same as the one she had received. Nancy had been told to pack and go to the airport. All travel arrangements were taken care of. She could expect to be away for a minimum of five days. There was no question of choice. The letter was a demand.

'If you're here, then I guess someone pulls your strings too, huh?' Nancy said, when Ruth handed the letter back.

Ruth nodded. 'Behind every successful woman . . .'

'There's another successful woman or man, waiting to push you aside and claw their way to your desk!' Nancy chuckled.

'Exactly.' Ruth laughed with her. 'That's why I've accepted this challenge. No questions asked. I'll do whatever I need to to give me an edge over the competition.'

'Smart lady.' Nancy grinned. 'These high-powered aptitude tests are the fashion right now. Who knows what'll be flavour of the month next?'

Ruth thought it was more likely that they were

all being head-hunted by a multi-national company. If that was the case, then she was part of a most exclusive short-list. Everyone on the plane was an expert in their chosen profession.

'We're about to land,' Ruth said now, peering intently at the thickly forested hills.

Nancy sat up, took off the eye-mask, and stretched. 'Where the hell are we? Oh, God is that the runway? It looks like a goat track! Better hold on tight, ladies!'

As Ruth stepped out of the plane, the heat pressed against her face like a hot, wet blanket. Within seconds she was dripping, her expensive haircut drooping and clinging to her skull. She felt a surge of irritation. The last thing she wanted was to arrive looking sticky and dishevelled. She hoped there would be time to freshen up before the welcome meeting. Ruth always travelled with a barrage of cosmetics and toiletries.

It was a relief to step into the relative coolness of one of the waiting vehicles. Twenty minutes later the four-by-four drew up in front of an Hawaiian-style village of bamboo walled apartments, complete with palm-thatched roofs and a pool-side bar. Bowling-green-quality lawns surrounded the bungalows. Brightly coloured tropical flowers were everywhere. Men dressed in spotless white uniforms came to welcome the women and show them to their rooms.

'Please to come this way, ma'am,' a young man said to Ruth.

'See ya later, alligator,' Nancy called.

Ruth's room was small, but charming. A basket of fruit stood on a bamboo table. Next to it was a welcoming card. She was instructed politely to change into suitable clothes, then to meet for further instructions in the building she could see from her window. She unpacked shorts, a white cotton shirt and a pair of sandals before taking a shower. After dressing and finger-drying her thick brown hair, she applied fresh make-up. It was cool in her room, due to the air-conditioning. She did not relish stepping out into the fierce tropical heat again.

Ruth was a city girl, born and bred. She liked order and neatness in her life. The sprawling lushness of the vegetation, just feet away from her bungalow, made her feel uneasy. Well, there was no help for it. She needed to know what was going on. Hastily plaiting her damp hair, she left it hanging over one shoulder. As she left her bungalow, she saw another of the women leaving her apartment. She recognised Sarah Reynolds. Sarah worked for a firm of London bankers. The two women fell into step.

'Have you any idea what to expect?' Sarah said. She was slightly built and had curly dark hair caught up high on her head with a towelling band. She looked enviably cool in a white halter top and tailored shorts. Her slender legs were shown to advantage by strappy high heels.

'None at all,' Ruth said, wishing that she'd

worn prettier sandals instead of settling for comfort over style. 'But I've a feeling all is about to be revealed.'

Ruth and Sarah entered the meeting place together. The other women, except for Nancy, were already there. They sat on woven grass mats which covered the beaten earth floor. How incongruous we all look squatting here in our designer shorts, our perfect make-up already starting to melt, Ruth thought.

'Hiya, gals,' Nancy said, breezing in through the door. 'Oh, am I last? Story of my life!' There was a polite ripple of laughter. Nancy looked stunning in an emerald green bathing suit, with a Hermès scarf tied sarong-style around her waist.

'Welcome, ladies,' said a deep male voice. 'May I have your attention?'

A tall man dressed in a white linen suit stepped from behind a bamboo screen which had been in half shadow at the back of the single room. Ruth's heart gave a lurch when she saw that sculpted, perfect facial structure framed by sun-streaked hair. She recognised this man. He was the owner of an airline company, amongst other things, and was known for his ruthless business dealings. He was also extremely eligible, wealthy, arrogant, and too attractive for his own good.

'I'm here to give you instructions,' Joel Matheson said. 'Make certain you listen closely. I cannot stress this enough. After you leave this room, you're on your own.' Matheson grinned narrowly. 'You'll be engaging in a contest – an ancient rite. This challenge is like nothing you've ever experienced. The islanders who used to live here had a name for the ceremony. The rite was enacted every mid-summer. The most beautiful women would be chosen to take part. Just like you've been chosen. Roughly translated the native word means 'Animal woman takes power from the Sun'. There'll be one winner. The woman who triumphs over the rest will receive my personal cheque.' The amount of money he spoke of was obscene.

Ruth tried not to let her surprise show on her face. The other women were staring at Matheson openly, one or two of them making it quite clear from their expressions that they would do *anything* to become the victor in this bizarre contest.

'So we have to compete against each other?' Nancy said, flicking back a lock of her blond hair. 'You've brought us all this way to tackle a native obstacle course?'

Matheson smiled slowly, his teeth very white in his tanned face. 'Oh, nothing so pedestrian. Give me credit for presenting you with a much more compelling challenge. You'll all need to get in touch with your base natures. In short, throw off the veneer of civilisation completely, return to a simpler, more savage time.'

When he finished speaking there was a stunned silence. Ruth was the first to speak. 'To what purpose? I mean – what's the goal?'

Matheson turned his dark blue gaze on her. For the first time she felt the full force of his persona. His charm was almost hypnotic. He grinned slowly. 'In the old times a male was chosen and the women would run him to ground and overpower him – sexually. Are you capable of abandoning yourselves entirely to your essential female natures, or are you constrained by what the world expects of you?'

Before their astonished gazes he undressed. Wearing only a brief leather garment around his waist, he stood up and faced them. Ruth felt the urge to giggle. Matheson was the quarry. Me Tarzan. You Jane. What an arrogant bastard. The prospect of running him to ground was ridiculous, but she could see that Matheson was utterly serious. And the amount of money he had dangled before them as a prize made this whole venture far more than the crack-pot game of a bored playboy.

'Everything you'll need is in the knapsacks behind the screen,' he went on. 'This island's covered in jungle. There's no wild animal large enough to harm you – if you're careful. There's plenty of water and food to be found. And you can't get lost. In two hours you can walk from shore to shore in any direction. My people here will keep tabs on you, but they won't make themselves known unless you need medical help. Are there any questions?'

'When do we start?' Sarah Reynolds said, her

face flushed and her dark eyes glittering with excitement. Drops of perspiration sparkled on her curly hair.

'The contest's already begun. Whatever you're wearing, that's it. There's no returning to the village. Anyone who wants to drop out can do so. But the plane won't return for three days.'

'And no doubt there'll be a less than complimentary letter to our company bosses if we refuse to take part,' Ruth said dryly.

'Very astute,' Matheson said, raking her with a measuring gaze.

Ruth was grateful now that she'd instinctively worn practical clothes. Sarah glanced down at her high-heeled fashion shoes in dismay. Matheson grinned nastily and Ruth felt a surge of dislike. He had deliberately refrained from forewarning any of them about what was to come in the hope that they'd put themselves at every disadvantage. But then, that too was part of the challenge.

She felt a heat in the base of her belly and knew that, despite herself, she was stimulated by the prospect of what was to come. Lifting her chin she looked straight at Matheson, trying to ignore the fact that he had the most perfect body of any man she had ever seen. Anyone else would have looked ridiculous with the scrap of leather around his waist, but he managed to look virile and poised.

It would have given him the greatest satisfaction to know that she was wondering what his skin felt like to the touch. The thought of besting him was exhilarating. That sculpted mouth was made for kissing . . .

'And when one of us catches you,' she said levelly. 'What happens then?'

Matheson's eyes sparked wickedly. '*If* any of you do. Use your imagination. The islanders had a saying: "When woman is queen, man must bow before her and offer himself for her pleasure." Conquer me and you become the victor. You'll know what to do. Take what you want from me. That is your right.'

And with that he disappeared out of the door. After Matheson had gone, there was consternation. Ruth did not bother to join in with the questioning. To her mind any more discussion was futile. She reached behind the screen and extricated a haversack. As she sat on the floor and began looking through the contents she found herself joined by Nancy and Sarah.

'Jeeze, I wish I'd put on shorts and a blouse,' Nancy said, plucking at her emerald swimming costume.

Ruth took out tubes of insect repellent and sun block and began to apply both. 'I doubt if we'll need to worry about clothes. It's hot enough to fry by day and I'll bet it's not much cooler by night.' At the door she glanced back. 'Good luck, everybody. See you in the jungle.'

Just a few yards from the village the jungle

pressed in, surrounding Ruth on all sides with a verdant ripe softness. There was a smell of heat, mildew, and something rich, like fruit cake. The humidity was incredible. Her shirt and shorts stuck to her wet skin. Rivulets of sweat trickled from under her hat band.

She used the knife she found in her pack to chop away at the vegetation on either side. But that was tiring, so she simply went slower, pushing aside the tough shiny leaves in her path. Her hair snagged on low branches and whippy stalks scratched her bare legs. When she backhanded her forehead, smears of greasy make-up came away. Oh, what the hell, she thought, who's going to care what I look like in this heat? Resolutely she ignored the inner voice which told her that this whole situation was ridiculous, that she had no more chance of tracking down Matheson than of flying to the moon.

In her private and working life, Ruth refused to contemplate defeat. But the habit of self-control had become an obsession. In her career any sign of weakness was scented out by the bloodhound wannabes in the offices on the floor below hers. She'd had to be strong and ruthless to get ahead. But she denied, even to herself, that she had sacrificed something inherently female in doing so. Matheson had hit a nerve when he challenged her to abandon herself to her essential feminine energies. When did you last feel sexy? the secret inner voice said. When did you last allow yourself to want a man just for his body and not for what he could get for you in the company?

Her sandals were silent on the thick leaf mould underfoot. Insects whined and buzzed. She swore when she tore a nail on a rock, but somehow it did not seem very important. Back in London, a broken nail would have had her hurrying to a specialist salon to get it expertly wrapped. The heat pushed oily fingers under her skin. Runnels of perspiration trickled down inside her bra. The waistbands of her shorts and pants were soaked. Yet the discomforts seemed minor, compared to the beauty all around her.

Before long she found that she was walking with a loose open-hip sway, quite unlike her usual clipped stride. She could smell her body sweat and musk and gloried in the natural odours untainted by the false notes of manufactured perfume. Inside she felt as if she was melting, oozing out to meet the throbbing tropical heat.

A few yards on she came to a stream. It burbled and frothed over moss-covered rocks. With a cry of delight, she untied her sandals and slung them around her neck. Then she entered the water. The coolness around her ankles and calves was delicious. As she started downstream, making for the faint thunder of a waterfall, she felt herself uncoiling slowly, her body unravelling like a spring that was finally relieved of tension.

Apart from the cries of brightly coloured birds

and the shrieks of tiny gold monkeys, it was quiet in the dappled shade of tree ferns. Now and then she thought she glimpsed one of the other women, but no one answered when she called out. Then she caught herself, laughing. Fool, to call out to them! We're all in competition. All of us want the cheque that Matheson has promised.

The sunlight flashed on jade, emerald, scarlet, as tiny flies skittered around banana palms. Some of the bananas were ripe. Ruth cut some from the central stack. They were tiny and tasted creamy, not at all like supermarket fruit. She drank some water from the stream, then filled a canteen and slung the strap over one shoulder. Already it was growing dark. She hadn't thought about the time when she left the village. Now she realised that she must spend the night alone in the jungle.

She felt a dart of fear, then remembered that Matheson had assured them all that no wild animal on the island was big enough to harm them. Still, for precaution's sake, she looked for a safe place to sleep. She found a tree with huge twisted roots, beneath which was a small chamber. Crawling inside, she found it dry and clean. Curling up on the dry moss, Ruth blinked through the cage of roots.

One moment it was growing dark, then it was night. There was no twilight, just sudden moonlight when every leaf was silvered and the jungle sounds changed. The rhythm of the night sang in Ruth's blood. She felt a strange contentment. She knew that she must look a wreck, but she could not have cared less. Tree frogs croaked, plum-purple shadows gathered around her. Ruth stretched out her legs, pillowed her head on her arm, and slept.

It seemed that only a moment passed before a movement woke her. Something soft and hot was pressed to her stomach. A silken pressure moved up the inside of her thigh. Half asleep, Ruth stretched and allowed her head to fall to one side on the mossy pillow. This dream was so real. It was too delightful to break by opening her eyes, so she lay still, allowing the sensations to continue. The buttons of her blouse were being undone and her bra eased gently aside. Then she felt the sweetly pulling pleasure as her nipple was suckled. The hand on her thigh dipped under the hem of her shorts. Fingers moved over her underwear, stroking her pubis through the damp cotton. She was getting wet between her legs, her labia thickening, swelling. When a finger slid into her moist channel, she opened her legs and pressed down, wanting that subtle touch on her clitoris.

Suddenly Ruth was jerked awake. This was no dream! She sat up, her legs scrabbling on the moss, clawing backwards. In the darkness two eyes gleamed at her. She saw moonlight silvering a sculpted face, making hollows at cheeks and eye sockets. A man laughed huskily.

'Matheson! You bastard!' she hissed, ashamed

at her body's ready reaction to his caresses. 'What the hell are you playing at?'

He grinned, his teeth very white in the moonlight. 'I've been tracking you. It was almost too easy. Now I've come to claim my prize.'

'But I'm supposed to find you! You made no mention of taking some kind of forfeit if you should find one of us first.'

'Didn't I? I must have forgotten to mention it. But you didn't seem exactly unwilling just now.'

Ruth prickled with mortification. Despite his arrogance she could not deny that she wanted him. She could feel the wetness on her inner thighs. An insistent throbbing was spreading from her clitoris up into her lower belly. How was it possible to desire a man so much when you disliked him intensely?

'Oh, I get it now,' she said. 'This whole set-up is just for you. You get to seduce all of us in turn. We're the quarry! The rite you mentioned is a load of rubbish!'

'Oh, the rite existed as I explained and I intend to honour my promise – *if* one of you runs me to ground. But you see, I just don't think any of you are capable of doing so. The primal female energy no longer exists in the modern woman.'

'Don't be too sure of that,' Ruth said, drawing back as he bent over her.

His mouth came down to claim hers, his tongue pushing strongly into her mouth, tasting and possessing her. She meant to bring up her hands and push him away, but somehow she found herself clasping his shoulders. The voice of the jungle was loud in her head, the night heat acting like a spur to her senses. The hardness and warmth of Matheson's bare chest seemed to burn through her half-opened cotton blouse. Suddenly he was tearing at her clothes and she was helping him.

She had hardly time to wonder at herself, to marvel at the hunger raging through her, before she was wriggling out of her shorts. He used his thumbs to push down her pants, then he leaned into her. The column of his cock pressed against her inner thigh as she spread herself under him. As her body opened to his, she saw a mental image of an exotic flower with petals peeling back to reveal a moist centre, drenched with sweet nectar.

She made little moans of eagerness as the cock quested bluntly towards her, nudging past her parted labia and slipping deeply into her. He was hot and hard. Her flesh seemed to suck at him, drawing him in deeper, until the swollen head of the cock nudged against her womb.

'Oh, God . . .' Ruth lifted her legs and wrapped them around Matheson's lean hips. Raising her lower body she rubbed herself against him as he pounded into her, tipping up her hips so that he drove downwards into her red heat.

She had never felt anything like this. There was no finesse, no tenderness, nothing but a joint and urgent need. Their sweat-slick skin chafed and slid. She could not pretend, even to herself, that she did not crave the thrusting hardness, the sensation of being totally filled. Clawing at his taut buttocks, she surged back and forth, gasping with pleasure, her head thrown back in total abandonment. Something seemed to give way in her head. There was a sound in her ears, like throbbing drums. The jungle beckoned. Her clitoris mashed against his pubis and her climax built rapidly, rising to a crescendo that left her uttering guttural little cries as her body convulsed around Matheson's invading maleness.

A moment later he drew out of her and spilt himself onto her belly. Hardly pausing to catch his breath, he sat back on his haunches and reached for the scrap of leather.

'So you're something of a gentleman, despite evidence to the contrary,' Ruth said dryly, wiping her stomach with her shirt. Now that they had pulled apart, she found that she could not look him in the eye. Her cheeks burned. God, what had possessed her to act like a sex-starved cat on heat? She had not even thought of protection, until now. At least Matheson had had the grace to come outside her.

Matheson grinned wolfishly. 'I singled you out from the others. You're different, special. I'd like you, at least, to have a good opinion of me. Despite what you think, I do have a code of honour.' He began moving backwards out of her temporary shelter. 'Sleep well,' he said, before disappearing into the darkness.

Ruth slumped back on the carpet of dried leaves. If it had not been for the tingling and pulsing of her sex, the faint smell of semen and male sweat, she would have believed that she had just imagined the whole thing. *What is happening to me?* She did not recognise herself. Never had she given herself to anyone like that. And further more, she was still aroused. Tentatively she put her hand between her legs.

Her sex was hot and swollen, the labia puffed-up and her vagina awash with juices. She pushed a finger into herself, amazed at the muscular, fecund feel of her inner flesh. Almost without thought she slid another finger into her body and began rhythmically to push them both in and out. She began moving, weaving her hips back and forth, opening her legs wide. This was incredible. Why did she not feel guilty for touching herself? She always had before. That was why she rarely masturbated. Lowering her other hand, she tapped gently on her clitoris, feeling the way it swelled under her touch. Parting her fingers, she rubbed gently either side of the swollen bud. It felt so good. She panted audibly as she teased herself.

Rich, buttery juices coated her fingers. She drew them out to smear the slickness over her clitoris. A tension built inside her as she stroked and rubbed and stabbed at herself in an access of selfish pleasure. Her climax when it came was deep and satisfying, the sounds of her completion echoed in the moist tropical night, joining with the chorus of insects' chirrups. With her sweat cooling on her body, she snuggled naked into the dried leaves and slept.

The next morning Ruth crawled out from under the tree roots and looked around her. The jungle glittered in the sunlight. She breathed deeply of its loamy smell. The air was scented with vanilla and felt soft against her skin. Inside herself, she felt a further loosening as if some essential element had slid away during the night. Something was happening to her: the jungle had laid claim to her.

Deciding not to dress, she stuffed her clothes into her knapsack, then reached for the tube of sunscreen. Her hand halted in midair. Moved by an impulse beyond her control, she brushed aside the thick covering of leaves underfoot and scooped up handfuls of fragrant wet soil. Haltingly at first, she smeared the mud onto her skin, then began applying it with relish until her body was covered. The mud felt delicious. As it dried, some of it fell off in flakes, but most of it remained, affording protection from the sun's rays and providing her with natural camouflage.

Ruth's mouth curved in a smile as she thought of what had happened in the night. A new resolve had been born within her. She knew that she must find Matheson and prove him wrong. But how?

Setting off, she noticed a broken strand of a fern. In the soft earth there was the imprint of a bare foot. As she concentrated, she saw other, more subtle signs of Matheson's passing. With growing confidence she set out after him. As she walked, she came upon bushes bearing fruit and knew instinctively which to eat and which to leave alone. Picking a handful of berries she crammed them into her mouth. They were tart and chewy. The red juice streamed over her chin and dripped onto her breasts. Pausing only to rub the back of her hand over her mouth, she plunged more deeply into the undergrowth.

The sun was low, casting long shadows from the moss-covered rocks she passed. A purple-throated hummingbird whirred close, its tongue extended to probe the depths of a cream orchid. Ruth heard a faint sound and paused, scenting the air like a cat. Dipping low, she slid silently through the tangle of vines and ferns, emerging at the edge of a clearing. A pool sparkled in the near distance. On a flat, sun-warmed rock, a yard or so away, there were two figures.

Ruth sank into the dappled shade of a tree fern, obscuring herself from view. The two naked women had not heard her approach. They were engrossed in each other, oblivious to anything other than their own pleasure. Ruth's eyes widened as she took in the sight of Nancy Brogan and Sarah Reynolds kissing with animal passion. *Has the jungle changed them too*? She found herself transfixed by their languid movements, the way they strained against each other, pressing breast against breast.

When Nancy slid her hand between Sarah's thighs, Sarah moaned loudly and ground herself against her lover's fingers. Nancy whispered endearments, mouthing Sarah's shuddering skin as she stroked the curling hair on her mons. Ruth was so enthralled by the sight of the two women that it was a moment before she saw the figure in the bushes off to one side. Matheson. It had to be. And she knew that he had not detected her presence.

She felt a fierce excitement, knowing that this was the best chance she would have of surprising him. Stealthily she moved backwards and began circling around the clearing. As she grew near to where he was hiding, she lay on her stomach and began using her knees and elbows to propel herself forwards. Faintly she could hear Sarah's moans and Nancy's answering cries. Through the screen of vegetation she saw that Nancy was kneeling between Sarah's thighs, her head moving slowly back and forth as she tongued the other woman's vulva. Against the backdrop of the jungle, with the tropical sun beating down, the sight was somehow primeval, beautiful.

She smiled. Matheson was intent on spying on the lovers, waiting for them to finish before he revealed himself and claimed a forfeit. What a surprise *he* was going to get.

She could see him now. Only feet away, he was a shadowy form against the backdrop of an oleander. Silently, slowly, she edged forward and around the back of the bush. The two women's cries increased in tempo. She was close enough to hear Matheson's breathing and to know that he was aroused. She could actually smell his excitement, sense the pounding rhythm of his blood. Without pausing to contemplate just how she had become so super-sensitive, she slid through the long grass beside him and with a smooth, sinuous movement reared up before him.

Matheson's face went white. His mouth gaped. For a moment she thought he was going to have some kind of a seizure. A word escaped him. She had never heard it before, but she knew that it was the name of an ancient deity.

She nodded and held out her hand. 'I claim my right over you.'

Moving slowly, like a sleep-walker, Matheson fell to his knees. His face was filled with awe and longing. 'What . . . what do you require of me?' he stammered.

Ruth gestured, exulting in her power. Her breasts swelled and her nipples hardened, pushing against their coating of mud. She had forgotten how she must look, with her naked body caked with greyish powder, her thick brown hair matted and tangled with leaves. But Matheson's expression reminded her. His handsome face was stricken by wonder. He had not believed the old stories, she realised, but he did now.

'On your back,' she ordered. 'Lie over that rock.'

Matheson did as he was bid. With his back curved over the rock, his head and arms hung back helplessly. Muscular parted thighs balanced his body weight. His body was curved into a bow, his erect cock sticking out potently. His scrotum was exposed, held in tight to his body. Ruth straddled him. Looking down at his white face, she felt herself grow gravid with power. The power of the jungle.

Slowly she bent her legs, sinking down towards the twitching column of flesh. Matheson groaned, suffused by fear and longing. Under the pressure of his erection, his foreskin had slid back to uncover the purplish glans. A glistening drop of pre-emission oozed out of the slitted cock-mouth. With the tip of one finger, Ruth scooped up the clear fluid and leaned forward to smear it across Matheson's sculpted mouth. He moaned, tremors passing over his skin as he circled his lips with his tongue.

Grasping the cock, Ruth swooped down to impale herself. As she sank down, enclosing the rigid flesh inside her hot and hungry vagina, Matheson gave a strangled scream and bucked against her. His hands clutched at air and he tossed his head from side to side. Ruth rode him mercilessly, lifting herself almost clear of his cock then slamming all the way down until her pubic hair ground against his.

She did not allow Matheson anything, but took her pleasure entirely for herself. Sweat snaked down her skin, making runnels in the dried mud. With her strong internal muscles, she milked him, forcing him to eject his semen in great shattering bursts while his chest heaved and he gasped, almost weeping in his ecstasy. Even then, she had no mercy. And Matheson did not expect any. He remained stiffly erect as she worked herself up and down on him, crying out in the acuteness of her pleasure while forcing him to spurt inside her again and again.

The feel of his hot organ as it pulsed against her flesh-walls, giving up its life-force at her command, drove her on to orgasm after orgasm. She was almost delirious in her sexual hunger and her domination over him. He was simply a male, an object for her pleasure.

When Matheson was sobbing unrestrainedly, trembling all over while in the throes of a final, merciless paroxysm, Ruth looked up to find herself observed. Sarah and Nancy were standing a few feet away, their arms linked fondly, expressions of wonder on their faces.

'Dear God. Ruth?' Nancy said, a slow smile coming over her face. 'Well, who'd have thought it!'

Ruth felt as if a haze was lifting from her brain. The jungle seemed to realign itself around her. Suddenly she was once again aware of the noises of insects, birds, and the gurgling of a spring that emptied into the pool ahead. She straightened slowly and felt Matheson's shrinking cock slip out of her. Silver runnels of semen slid down her thighs, but she ignored them, smiling at the women. Matheson struggled up from the rock. Throwing himself at her feet he pulled up handfuls of soft moss and began wiping her clean.

'I adore you,' he murmured. 'Adore you. No one's ever bested me. I've been waiting for you all my life.'

Nancy lifted an eyebrow. 'I'd say the cheque's yours. But somehow I can't see you being too bothered about business from now on. Do you know what you've taken on, honey?'

'I've never been clearer about anything in my life,' Ruth said, looking down at the man who knelt before her.

He was just as striking and arrogant, with his perfect face and his sun-streaked hair now dark with sweat. Anyone who knew him would see no change. But Ruth knew that there was something different about him. The acknowledgement of female power had changed him forever. And that was why she was certain about her destiny.

She knew now that she need no longer suppress any part of herself to get ahead in her professional life. What she had found in the jungle would never leave her entirely. Without a backward glance she walked towards the pool. Sitting in the shallow water, she began washing the mud from her body. A long shadow fell across her body.

'May I join you?' Matheson said, his voice uncertain and tinged with respect.

She smiled up at him. 'You may. And I think I should call you Joel from now on. Since we're intimately acquainted and likely to remain so.'

Wet Nurse

JEHANNE SAT BY the side of the road, waiting for the stage coach. It was almost noon and the sun beat down on top of her straw bonnet.

She was tired already, but there was still far to go. Her head drooped with dejection. She could do nothing but wait. At least the farmer had promised to meet her with his cart when she alighted at the coaching inn.

Jehanne knew that she ought to think herself lucky. Positions for wet nurses were getting fewer these days. Untying her pack, she took out the hunk of bread and piece of cheese she had saved for the journey. It did not take her long to finish eating. She opened the stopper on a leather bottle, but there was no water left. Sighing, Jehanne chewed on a stalk of grass. The green taste of it made her feel less thirsty.

It was another half hour before she felt the faint

vibration of iron-shod wheels on the road. The plume of dust was visible before the coach itself came into view. Wearily Jehanne pushed herself to her feet and picked up her pack. Gathering her long skirts around her, she climbed aboard. Her full breasts pressed against her stays when she lifted her arms. She winced at the soreness.

The atmosphere inside the coach was stifling. It smelled of leather and tobacco and old sweat. As the horses moved off with a jangling of harnesses, Jehanne tried to open a window and let in some air, but both of them were jammed. She closed her eyes and sagged back against the seat. The handkerchief clutched in her hand was already sodden with her own sweat.

The only other occupant of the carriage, a strong country lad, had fallen into a half doze. Jehanne opened her eyes and studied him. He was sturdily built, with great shoulders and thick muscular thighs. He had a coarse, honest face under a shock of untidy fair hair. The colour of ripe wheat, she thought, and so it should be, for a farmer.

Jehanne drew in a sudden breath against the pain in her breasts. It had been a whole day since she had given milk and they were hard and engorged. A trickle of sweat ran down her cleavage. She mopped at it ineffectually, flapping the wet handkerchief in the vain hope of creating a cool breeze.

Outside the coach, the countryside sped past.

Acre upon acre of forest, which gave way to the bright patchwork of fields. Now and then she saw an expanse of acid-green where hop fields stretched away into the distance. Farmhouses nestled in folds of land, their walls washed with pastel pinks, blues and yellows. Looking at them, Jehanne felt a surge of longing.

It would be early morning before they reached the village where she was to take up her new position. If only it was not so hot and airless in the coach. She might have slept, but for her discomfort which was growing with each passing moment. The heaviness in her breasts had become a throbbing bruising ache. Her situation was desperate. Somehow she must relieve the pressure.

She glanced again at the sleeping farmer. His head had fallen back and his mouth was open. He snored softly.

Deciding all at once, she fumbled with the fastening of her bodice. Her low-necked chemise was wet around her nipples where the milk had leaked. The tops of her stays dug into the under-swell of her swollen breasts, chafing and reddening the taut flesh. With savage eagerness, Jehanne pulled her bodice open, unable to bear the sore heaviness a moment longer.

'Ah, thank God,' she murmured as she unhooked the top of her stays and her breasts sprang free.

She dabbed at her exposed skin, rubbing her

fingertips in soothing circles over the warm, sticky flesh. Sweat beaded her top lip and she could feel the heat prickling all over her body, but the pain in her breasts had eased somewhat. She sighed deeply and lifted her head, palming the leaking nipples.

And found herself looking straight into the open eyes of the young farmer.

In confusion she looked away, plucking at her bodice as if she would draw the open garment to cover herself. But it was too late. He had seen. She chanced a look at him and saw that he was watching her steadily with something like understanding on his big-featured, plain face.

'Can I help?' he asked quietly after a moment.

Shocked, she did not know how to reply. Did he understand what was wrong with her?

'My sister has a new babe. I know how it pains a woman when her breasts are full and the babe won't feed.'

His voice was soft, his expression kindly. A sharp pain shot through one of her nipples. Jehanne barely suppressed a wince. She looked at him again. There was nothing of guile in his expression. Making a decision, she nodded, her eyes downcast, while a flush rose to stain her cheeks. Let him make the move. She was unable to give voice to the words, to ask him for what she needed.

The young man moved towards her and dropped to his knees. With trembling fingers

Jehanne cupped one of her breasts and held it up towards him. The white skin was fretted with blue veins, the nipple prominent, pushed out by the pressure of her milk, and as brown as bark.

The young man bent his head, hesitating for a moment more.

'So beautiful,' he murmured, then he opened his mouth. Jehanne placed the nipple on his tongue and he closed his lips.

He sucked gently, his mouth warm and careful of her. The pressure did not ease. After a few moments Jehanne shifted uncomfortably against his lips. He freed the breast and looked up at her.

'What is it? Am I doing it wrong?' He looked so eager to please.

Jehanne smiled, charmed by his gauche demeanour. She no longer felt self-conscious and seemed to have found her tongue.

'Well now. I expect that you're long out of practice. It's some time since you were a babe in arms. Let me help you.'

The practical side of her nature rose to the fore. Having given herself over to the situation, it felt natural for her to take charge.

'What is your name?' she asked.

'Hamish. Hamish Sawyer.'

She told him her name. 'Then let us be comfortable, Hamish. And I'll show you what to do.'

Hamish took off his rough tweed jacket. Under it he wore a striped workman's shirt. It was well laundered, but faded and frayed around the collar band. The scent of his strong young body reminded her of elderflowers. Jehanne settled down on the floor of the coach, bunching up her parcel of spare clothes to form a backrest for herself.

'Now then. Lie at my side. Settle in the crook of my arm. That's the way. And take the whole of the nipple into your mouth, not just the tip. Use your tongue to press it against the roof of your mouth. Now, suck hard. You need not be too gentle.'

Hamish did as she told him and gave a practice suck. 'Like this?'

Jehanne felt the tingling which meant that her milk was ready to flow. 'Ah, yes. Just like that. That's perfect.'

Jehanne closed her eyes as the sweet drawing down of her milk began. Having mastered the technique, Hamish sucked lustily, swallowing great warm mouthfuls with audible enjoyment. The full breast was pressed tight to his mouth. Jehanne's other breast wept with sympathetic pleasure, the pearly drops rolling down her white skin. She was embarrassed and made a move to reach for a cloth to staunch the flow.

But Hamish made a sound deep in his throat and reached out a hand. He stroked the leaking nipple gently, letting the milk roll over his fingers. He seemed completely at ease. Jehanne relaxed. As Hamish's mouth clamped more firmly against her, she let out a long breath of satisfaction. It was quiet inside the coach, but for the subtle wet sounds of Hamish's mouth.

After a while he paused in his ministrations, looked up at Jehanne and smiled. A thin trickle of her bluish milk threaded from the corner of his mouth. Just like a baby, thought Jehanne, as she wiped his mouth clean with the heel of her hand.

'Is it good?' she asked him mischievously.

'So warm and sweet. I did not expect it.'

In a short time Hamish emptied one breast. They changed position so that he could begin on the other. Partly due to the heat in the coach and partly because of her feeling of well-being, Jehanne began to feel drowsy. Her head slipped backwards and she fell into a slight doze as Hamish's warm mouth worked away at her. While he sucked on her full breast, he reached up to gently knead the other one, now slack and pear-shaped.

The coach rumbled along the stony road, its interior filled with the warm milky smell of her and with the spice of their joint body heat. All at once a new sensation brought Jehanne rushing back to full wakefulness. There was a ticklish pleasant feeling in one of her breasts. Satiated and full, Hamish had drawn away a little and was licking and nibbling at her drawn-out nipple.

Jehanne smiled, completely at ease. Indeed, Hamish was like a child – though he might be a hulking great young man – a child who has fed well and is inclined to playfulness. Well then, let him nuzzle and suck at her a little. She did not mind. At first she lay back indulgently, feeling quite detached from the situation as Hamish tongued the now soft teat.

He has a nice mouth, she thought, though his face is unremarkable and verging on the coarse side. Then, as he kept up his attentions, nipping gently at her with relaxed lips and using his hands to cup her softened breasts and roll them together for his pleasure, she began to feel something. A coil of heat gathered in her belly.

Now Hamish sucked again, drawing strongly on the slack flesh. Filling his mouth, he parted his lips and allowed a mouthful of milk to trickle between her breasts. It ran down onto the upper part of her ribcage, exposed by the open front of her stays. He bent his head as if to lick up the spillage and made a little sound of disappointment.

'Oh, I cannot reach to clean you,' he said innocently. 'Will you unfasten your stays a little?'

Jehanne's breath came faster as she did as he asked. Why not? He had helped her and she was grateful. Besides, the feel of that naughty warm mouth on her skin was doing something wonderful to her. The bones of her stiffened basque creaked as she loosened the laces.

'There, you can reach now,' she said.

For a few moments Hamish licked at the skin exposed by her open stays. There were red marks where the whalebone had pinched. Hamish ran the tip of his tongue over the imprinted flesh. Jehanne shuddered at the unexpected delicacy of his touch. It was both soothing and arousing. She could not remember when she had so relished the touch of a man.

'You could take off your skirts,' Hamish said shyly. 'It would be cooler that way.'

Jehanne did not hesitate. 'Help me then. My skirts are heavy.'

Hamish fumbled with the fastening of her waistband. She let him open her skirts, then untie the cord that held up her petticoats. As he pushed the thick bunched fabric down over her hips she lifted a little to help him. She wore no drawers and was naked under her skirts.

She would have liked to be more beautiful for this eager young man. There was a slackness at her belly and pale, silver scars across her hips, but Hamish seemed not to notice.

'God. Oh, God,' he murmured, running trembling fingers over her soft white thighs, then trailing them lightly across the frosting of hair at her groin. 'You are so lovely, Jehanne.'

The wonder in his voice touched her. He was such a mixture of gentleness and brute young strength. Could it be that he was sexually innocent?

'Have you never had a woman, Hamish?' she said gently.

He hung his head and would not look at her for

116

a moment. When he spoke his voice was low and filled with longing.

'Never. But I want you badly. Will you show me what to do?'

Jehanne felt flooded by emotion. It was a curious mixture of power and humility and affection. It seemed right that they should lie together. She wanted him too – her whole body was crying out for fulfilment. And it would be a payment of sorts – she had no money, after all. An honest transaction, she thought, smiling.

Drawing him close, she cupped his face, feeling the stubble on his coarse skin. She fingered his strong, square jaw, looking into his eyes. They were hazel, with flecks of copper-brown around the irises. Pressing her lips to his she kissed him deeply. His lips were firm and he tasted faintly of tobacco. Hamish moaned against her mouth. Her blood seemed to catch fire at the simple, raw sound of his passion.

Reaching down to the flap of his moleskin breeches, she unbuttoned him and took his strong young cock in her hand. He was breathing quickly and it would soon be over if she did not manage him carefully.

'Lie down, Hamish. Be patient now. It will be good for us both this way. I promise.'

When he was quieter and lulled by her kisses and slow caresses, she opened her thighs to him and told him to lie between them. He did so, content for her to take the lead. The smell of her rich female musk and the spice of heat rose between them.

'Is this the scent of all women?' he asked in wonder.

She nodded. 'Does it frighten or repel you? Not all men savour it.'

'Nay. It is wonderful. Like the earth or new bread. I have never seen a woman's quim up close. May I . . .? Will you permit me to . . .?'

'Yes,' said Jehanne. 'Look your fill. Do what you will.'

Hamish spread her sex, his movements gentle as he gazed at her. Jehanne steeled herself to lie still, but it was difficult not to arch her back as he tentatively stroked her. He obviously did not realise that he was giving her pleasure as he explored her moist folds with the roughened tips of his thick fingers. His innocence, coupled with unselfconscious enthusiasm, was a potent lure to her senses.

As he bent and took a first delicate taste, Jehanne marvelled that such an intimate act should seem natural to him. Many of her lovers had not dreamt of such a thing and others thought it demeaned them. She found herself beginning to breathe faster and had to bite back a groan as he used his mouth and tongue as he had done when suckling her earlier.

Wrapping her fingers in his thick flaxen hair, she urged him on to keep licking as her pleasure grew. Her flesh grew slick and swollen under his

118

touch. By accident, it seemed, he pressed gently against the firm bud of her pleasure, lolling his tongue back and forth against the tiny hood of flesh. Her climax built swiftly, taking her by surprise. As she crested, then broke, she rubbed herself urgently against his mouth, gasping and crying out as the waves consumed her. The aftershocks of her orgasm ebbed finally and her body quelled.

Hamish moved up her body and kissed her, so that she tasted herself on his mouth. She felt the blunt head of his cock at the entrance to her sex. Placing her hands on his buttocks she exerted a gentle pressure, but he needed no urging. She was wet and ready for him and raised herself to receive him. He pushed into her, giving a loud groan as he buried himself to the hilt.

Jehanne raised her legs, giving him deeper access. He bucked against her, his potent young flesh sliding deliciously against her vaginal walls, making her feel tight and new again. Incredibly she felt a second climax building. She cried out and all at once she was sobbing with the deep pleasure of it, her cleated flesh pulsing around the thick stem buried within her.

Hamish's face screwed up into an expression of surprised delight. His mouth opened wide. With a hot gush, he emptied himself inside her. Jehanne held him while he thrashed and spasmed and finally grew quiet. In a while he raised his face and smiled down at her.

'You did not have to show me everything after all.'

She smiled tenderly. 'There is nothing anyone can show you about being a man.'

'I did well?'

'Oh, yes,' she breathed. 'More than you know.'

He kissed her again, with affection and pride, his rough hands stroking her hair and cupping her chin.

As the coach sped on, swaying and rumbling across the countryside, day gave way to night. Moonlight silvered the tops of trees and hay-ricks. A vixen's harsh ghostly call echoed in the night. Inside the coach, Jehanne and Hamish slept in each other's arms. Near morning, when the dawn glow lit up the thatched roofs of a village, the coach drew under the stone archway of the inn's courtyard.

Fully dressed now and composed, Hamish helped Jehanne down from the steps and handed her the parcel of clothes. Jehanne shivered as a cool breeze played about her bare ankles. Hamish leaned out of the open coach door as she stood on the cobble-stones of the forecourt. Jehanne looked up at him, lost for words. Now that they were to part, she was suddenly shy. What was there to say, except goodbye? But it did not seem enough. She tucked a lock of hair inside her straw bonnet and tied the ribbons firmly under her chin.

In the near distance, in the road, she could see

the farmer – her new employer – sitting atop his cart, waiting for her. His figure was a shadowy bulk, topped by a shapeless hat.

'I'm to be married. Next month,' Hamish blurted suddenly, as if by disclosing this secret he had given her a treasure. 'My wife-to-be has a farm and a babe newborn. Her husband was killed a year since.'

Jehanne smiled, a trifle sadly. Then she recovered herself. 'I wish you every happiness. Your wife is a lucky woman.'

'I live in the next village. It's but a day away by cart,' he said. 'We'll be neighbours. Perhaps . . .'

The coachman cracked his whip and the team of horses began to move off, their breath steaming in the chill morning air.

Jehanne stood and waved. 'When you need a wet nurse, you'll find me here,' she called.

Hamish smiled and waved jauntily. But she did not know whether he had heard her over the clattering of the horses' hooves.

War Story

'THE BAND DOWN at the Palais is supposed to be ever so good,' Monica said, shouting over the noise of the munitions factory. 'You should come out with me tonight instead of sitting at home brooding night after night. Your Ken shouldn't expect that of you.'

Hazel Price smiled and tucked a few stray fair hairs back into her headscarf. 'He doesn't. He's not dull really, not when you get to know him. It's just that it wouldn't be right. We only got engaged on his last leave.'

'Where's the harm in a few dances, a few drinks? Most of the girls have sweethearts in the forces, but they go out. Oh, say you'll come, do.'

Hazel glanced across at Monica, whose big bosoms pushed against the buttoned front of her overalls. There was a smear of grease on her good-natured face. Monica was considered to be brassy by some of the other girls, but Hazel found her lively and amusing. Before she knew it she had agreed to go out dancing.

'I'll call for you at seven,' Monica said. 'It'll be a lark, you'll see.'

Now hurrying down the road towards the bus stop, Hazel felt a mixture of excitement and reluctance. She drew level with a florist's shop, the window criss-crossed with sticky tape to prevent glass flying out if a bomb should land nearby. Despite her lateness Hazel glanced in, admiring the floral buttonholes on display. The bunches of snowdrops and anemones were pretty, but one in particular caught her eye. A beautiful white camellia, just like the actresses in Hollywood films wore. One of those would liven up her shabby dance dress.

She loved to dress up and wear nice things, but Ken said that it was vain and foolish when so many people had to make do. Still, he was proud of her slim figure and shapely legs. He called her his Betty Grable. Everyone said that she and Ken were the perfect couple. And he was what she wanted, wasn't he? Well set-up, reliable, honest, even if he could be a bit pompous at times.

She tried to conjure the image of his face in her mind. It alarmed her that she could hardly remember a thing about him, not the feel of his hair nor the smell of his aftershave. Perhaps if there had been more . . . contact between them. But Ken said it was a sin to do that thing before

123

marriage. That was right and proper, of course. She felt guilty for wanting more.

One Christmas after too many sherries, he had pushed his hand up under her jumper and fondled her breast over her brassière. Shocked and ashamed by the warm melting feeling between her thighs, she had pushed him away. He had apologised and she had not dared to ask him to touch her again. But oh, how she had longed for him to stroke the inside of her thigh above the top of her much-darned stocking, to slip his hand inside the loose leg of her cami-knickers.

The heat rose into her face as she recalled how, later, in the quiet and dark of her own bed, she raised her nightie and touched herself between her legs. The fleshy folds there were wet and swollen. When she stroked and rubbed the bump inside the pouting little slit she had felt all tingly. Guiltily she had jerked her hand away. Nice girls shouldn't have those urges.

Hazel gave a guilty start, suddenly remembering where she was. She felt all hot and bothered and wondered if her thoughts showed on her face. The shop girl inside the florist's looked quizzically out at her. Hazel coloured, realising that she had been staring blankly in at the window for some time. Oh, crikey – the bus! Whipping around she almost collided with an American soldier as he walked into the flower shop.

'Sorry,' she mumbled, pushing past him with hardly a glance. She noticed only that he was a G.I. and tall with dark hair. She was breathing hard when she joined the queue at the bus stop. A few seconds later the bus drew to a halt. Hazel moved forward ready to board it.

'Pardon me, ma'am,' came a voice at her shoulder.

Hazel turned. The tall American G.I. held out a floral buttonhole. 'I wonder if you'd accept this,' he said. 'I saw you admiring it. I'm not trying to be fresh with you. It's . . . well. It's just that this is a great country. You English are such darn nice folks.'

Hazel's face registered her shock. It was the white camellia. How had he known which one to buy? 'I . . . No. I couldn't possibly . . .' she began, grasping the rail, ready to jump onto the bus.

A gentle hand on her arm restrained her. 'Please take it. I'd look pretty foolish with it pinned to my jacket.'

A woman standing on the bus platform looked back at Hazel and raised her eyebrows. The bus conductress looked from Hazel to the American. 'Well, miss? You coming aboard or staying here for the duration?' she said.

'I'm . . . I'm coming,' Hazel stammered, her instincts telling her to ignore the soldier. The blind cheek of him! All the Yanks were the same, flashing their money about, expecting a girl to fall right into their arms. Well, she wasn't the sort of girl to have her head turned by flattery.

She looked at the G.I. closely for the first time. He had a nice face, with regular features. His straight mouth was parted in a grin. There was an air of sincerity about him that was very attractive. Despite her reluctance she found herself smiling back. She reached for the buttonhole. 'Thank you. It's a kind gesture.'

He lifted his hat. 'A pleasure, ma'am,' he said, before turning on his heel.

The bus conductress gave a theatrical sigh and rang the bell. 'Yanks,' she said under her breath. 'Overpaid, overfed, oversexed, and over here!'

The downstairs passengers laughed at the popular cliché. As the bus pulled away, Hazel found her way to a seat. How extraordinary. She had no idea who the American was and was not likely ever to see him again. But his elegant gesture had brightened her day. She brought the camellia to her face and took a breath of the fresh sweet scent. These sort of things didn't happen in real life. They belonged in films. Just wait until she told Monica.

Later that night, when she and Monica stepped into the dance hall of the Palais, the band was playing a fair approximation of Glenn Miller's 'In the Mood'.

'Ooh, I love this tune. Don't you?' Monica said, wiggling her shoulders so that her full breasts jiggled provocatively.

Hazel agreed that she did – the sound of brass

instruments always caused a shiver to run down her spine. Her feet began tapping in time to the music. The floor bustled with dancing couples and the air was filled with the scent of warm bodies, perfume, and cigarette smoke. She smoothed her hands down the front of her dress, feeling self-conscious.

'What if no one asks us to dance?' she whispered to Monica.

Monica rolled her eyes. 'Don't be daft. With regiments stationed all around the county there's three blokes to every girl here! Give it a mo. We'll be fighting them off!'

Almost immediately two Polish soldiers appeared at their side. 'You like to dance?' they asked.

'Don't mind if we do,' Monica said, grinning archly. 'Come on, Hazel.'

Before she could answer Hazel found herself swept onto the dance-floor. After each dance finished there was someone else waiting to partner them. The dance hall, draped festively with flags and swathes of coloured fabric, buzzed with the sound of accented voices. They danced with British and Norwegian soldiers who bought them drinks and produced photographs of their families back home. When pressed to dance again, Hazel refused, smiling. 'I'll just sit and catch my breath first. You go on, Monica.'

'I'll stay a minute or two,' Monica said, winking at Hazel to indicate that she did not intend to spend the whole night with the first men who paid her attention. As the soldiers moved off to find other partners, she said, 'Glad you came now, aren't you? You're much too pretty to shut yourself away.'

Hazel nodded, sipping her drink. Monica was tipsy. Her laugh was a bit loud and raucous, but Hazel didn't mind. She felt happy and light-hearted. This was just what she needed. She was tired of the drudgery of war-time. Five years it had lasted, so far. Like many others, she couldn't remember the last time she had slept the night through without being woken by sirens.

Suddenly she spotted a tall figure making his way through the crowd towards her. At the sight of him, her fingers relaxed on her glass. She almost dropped her drink. 'Oh good heavens,' she hissed. 'Monica. It's him!'

'What? Who?' Monica said.

'The G.I. I told you about. The one who . . .'

At that moment the American reached her table. He grinned. 'Well, this is a surprise. Hello again. I see you're wearing the corsage. It's very becoming.'

'I er . . . Yes,' Hazel stammered. 'It's lovely.'

Monica nudged Hazel in the ribs and hissed out of the side of her mouth, 'You didn't tell me he was gorgeous! He could be Robert Taylor's brother! Ask him if he's got a friend.'

'Monica, shush!' Hazel felt her cheeks burning.

The American grinned. 'That's okay. Sure I've

got a friend. Hey Barney, come on over here and meet this pretty lady.'

Monica fluttered her eyelids at Barney as he took a seat next to her. He was fair, fresh-faced and cheerfully brash. 'Hi, sugar. What's cookin'?' he said, putting an arm around the back of her chair. Monica pursed her lipsticked mouth, edged close to the brawny G.I. and nudged him in the ribs. 'Well hello, Barney. What's your friend's name then or hasn't he got one?'

The tall American chuckled and leaned on the back of Monica's chair. Although he addressed her friend, his eyes sought Hazel's face. 'Say, we haven't been introduced. I'm Angelo. Angelo Gallone. And you are?'

'Monica. The shy pretty one's Hazel. She doesn't say much. She has hidden depths.'

Mortified by her friend's forwardness, Hazel stood up. She wished her skin was less fair. Her face must be like a beetroot. 'Would . . . would you like to dance?'

'Sure thing.' Angelo took Hazel's arm and led her onto the dance-floor.

Hazel found herself held firmly and led expertly around the floor. Close to, Angelo seemed even taller than on their first meeting. He was broad and strongly built. Next to him she felt light and fragile, a new sensation for her. Ken and she were almost the same height.

'So. Is it true? Do you have hidden depths?' Angelo said, lowering his voice. Hazel could not help laughing. She felt a little strange. Her fingers were tingling where Angelo held them. There was an unfamiliar tension in her body. He really was very good-looking. How had she not noticed that properly at the bus stop?

'Hidden depths? Like a mill-pond. Ever so deep,' she joked.

Angelo smiled down at her, suddenly perfectly serious. 'I'll just bet you do too.' His grey-green eyes were intense. A girl could drown in those eyes, she thought.

Hazel looked away, her throat suddenly dry. What was happening to her? She was aware of every inch of her body. The bits of her that were pressed against Angelo seemed to throb and burn. His breath smelt of peppermint and was hot against her cheek. She realised that she was damp where her knickers pressed against her privates. Even when Ken had kissed and fondled her, she had never felt so . . . trembly, so warm and syrupy between her legs.

To cover her confusion, she ventured a comment. 'That buttonhole . . . Are you always so impulsive?'

He grinned. 'Sure. Where's the sense in holding back? You never know how long you've got left. Got to live for today. Save something for too long – you lose it.'

That was true enough. Everyone said things like that these days, but somehow, when Angelo said it, it had a different reality. An image of Ken came to mind, his features blurred and indistinct like a faded photograph. You could live your whole life waiting for something to happen, she thought. Suddenly she knew that she didn't want that. She wanted to feel alive. To experience everything, however wicked or forbidden. She was fed up with trying so hard to do the right thing.

The night whirled around her in a glitter of bright lights. With only brief rests for refreshments they jitterbugged, waltzed, jived, and did the rumba and the tango. Hazel couldn't remember when she'd had more fun. She felt as if she was walking on air. Monica was still dancing with Angelo's friend, Barney. She waved as they passed by, but Monica, gazing raptly up at the enormous blond-haired soldier, didn't notice.

'Looks like your chum's fixed herself up, huh?' Angelo said.

Hazel nodded, not really listening. The smell of Angelo, his hair oil, the newly laundered uniform, the subtle underlying scent of his maleness, was making her feel quite dizzy with desire. Her blood seemed to fizz with bubbles. As the last dance drew to a close, she felt a mixture of disappointment and anticipation.

'Landed quite a catch there,' Monica said when they went to collect their coats. 'Looks like he knows how to treat a girl. Best make the most of him tonight.'

'What do you mean?' Hazel said. 'I'm not that

sort of girl!'

'Don't kid yourself, we're all that sort with the right man. But I didn't mean that. Angelo's moving out tomorrow with the rest of the boys. Barney told me they're just passing through here on their way south to the airfield.'

'Angelo didn't say,' Hazel said. 'Oh, well. Easy come, easy go.'

'That's the ticket. There'll be someone else like him tomorrow.'

Despite her carefree tone, Hazel's heart plummetted. Angelo made her feel desirable, reckless. It was something in his eyes, his smile, the way he held her. Well, too bad. As she left the cloakroom her steps felt leaden. Serve her right. It was a good thing temptation was going to be removed. The sooner Ken came back and made an honest woman of her the better.

Outside, Angelo looked even more imposing in his greatcoat and peaked hat. 'What's the matter, honey? You look so glum.'

She told him what Monica had said. 'It's true,' he said. 'We're pulling out tomorrow.' He drew her away from the entrance to the Palais, then turned her towards him and tipped up her chin. She could hardly meet his gaze. His grey-green eyes glinted with contained emotion. 'Look, maybe I'm crazy, but the minute I set eyes on you I knew you were special. Oh, I suppose all the guys tell you that, huh? You're so pretty. You must have any number of admirers . . .'

'No. No I haven't. You're the first person I've been attracted to in a long time.' There was a hot pressure in her stomach. It was true. She didn't care if Angelo was leading her on. She loved the way he made her feel. If only this night could go on and on.

'I gotta a coupla hours before I have to be back at the base . . .'

'We . . . we could go for a walk,' she said on impulse, tucking her hand into the crook of his arm.

'Swell! You're in charge. So – where are you taking me?'

Hazel laughed. She felt anything but 'in charge'. 'Would you like to walk down by the river?'

The moon shed a pale silver-grey light over the open fields. They did not speak, both aware of the tension between them. It was cold, with the smoky smell of frost in the air. When Hazel shivered, Angelo put his arm around her. It seemed natural to turn into his embrace and lift her chin for his kiss.

When his mouth covered hers, she felt such a jolt in her womb that she imagined he must have been aware of it. At first his lips were cold against hers, the skin of his cheek smooth and smelling faintly of cologne. He pressed open her lips and slipped his tongue inside, probing gently at first, then exploring her more insistently as she melted against him. He tasted of peppermint gum and

Lucky Strike cigarettes. She seemed to feel the effects of the kiss right down to her toes.

Angelo pulled her into the angle of a stone wall, where they were sheltered from the cold wind. She strained against him, returning his kisses with unfamiliar passion. Lord, but it had never been like this for her. Ken's closed-mouth pecks on her lips were nothing like these hot, demanding probings. The firm tongue plunged deeply into her mouth, making her think of another, more intimate penetration.

She did not protest when Angelo unbuttoned her coat and slipped his hands inside. Nor did she pull away when she felt his touch on her bare stomach. As his hand slid upwards, the curled fingers trailing over her ribs and then moving to cup her breast, she made a small sound of protest in her throat.

'I'll stop if you want me to,' Angelo said, drawing away.

'No. Don't stop,' Hazel gulped, clutching at him. She gathered her courage. It was now or never. The next words all came out in a rush. 'I've never felt like this. I want you to do . . . I want . . . everything. Show me, please?'

His hands began their slow, tantalising stroking again. 'You're sure?'

She nodded, biting her lip as he found a nipple and began squeezing it gently. The pleasure of it made her head swim. 'What's that you said? You have . . . to live for . . . now?'

He grinned crookedly at her. She knew he was amused by the breathless sound of her voice, her untutored passion. 'Yeh. Something like that. Do me a favour, honey? Stop talking. Just relax.'

She nodded, beyond words anyway. Looking down at her, he watched the play of emotions across her face as he explored her body. Hazel found it almost unbearably exciting to have his hands on her, doing things to her which Ken had never done. She tried to hide the evidence of her pleasure, but knew that her shining eyes, flushed cheeks and parted lips gave her away. He allowed her no modesty. When she pleaded with him not to look at her he shook his head, smiling in that crooked way he had. She was actually trembling with shame and need. She did not know which emotion was the stronger.

Angelo pushed her dress up to her waist and caressed her inner thighs. His fingertips were butterfly-light on the strip of flesh above her stocking tops. She felt her belly tighten as he stroked her skin. He reached for the waistband of her knickers and pulled them down. Leaving them lodged around the top of her thighs, he sought out her moist and throbbing centre.

Hazel bit back a moan and pressed her burning face against his shoulder as his fingers parted her swollen labia. Little shocks of sensation spread outwards and upwards, fanning over her stomach and thighs. She had never imagined that such pleasure could be had from simply being stroked just there. It was nothing like when she touched herself. Angelo's hand was almost unmoving against her flesh. He used just the pad of his thumb to press and roll against the stiffly erect little bump within her slippery folds. The feeling was exquisite. She found her hips working lewdly. Hoarse sounds escaped her lips.

What must he think? She felt like a hussy. Oh Lord, it felt so good. Her wetness seeped onto his fingers and the gentle, liquid pressure went on and on. Her thighs shook as she opened them wider. Now he had a finger inside her. His mouth was on hers again and the twin sensations were too much. She could not stop the pleasure building, building – then suddenly she gave a cry and shuddered against his hand, grinding herself against his wrist as great rolling waves of pleasure spilled over her.

When she grew calm, Angelo tipped up her chin. 'You okay? That was your first time, wasn't it?'

She nodded, scarlet to the roots of her hair. Her whole body seemed to glow. So that was why people were tempted to sleep together before marriage. She felt grateful to Angelo for showing her. Reaching up she put her arms around his neck and brought his face down to hers. When they kissed again she felt the need and tension in his long frame. He had been so kind and unselfish. Now she wanted to repay him.

'Show me how to do it to you,' she murmured against his mouth.

Angelo smiled. 'Yeh? You're quite a gal. You know that?' He unbuttoned his fly and placed Hazel's hand inside his trousers.

She touched him hesitantly, fascinated by the heat and hardness of the penis which pushed against his under-shorts. She liked it when Angelo groaned. It made her feel good to know that she could do this for him. When he unfastened his waist band she closed her hand around the silken stem, moving her fingers back and forth so that the skin slid along the shaft.

'You sure you haven't done this before?' Angelo said, his breath coming in short bursts.

Hazel grinned. 'I haven't, but my friend told me what to do. It seemed shocking then. But somehow now . . .' She remembered something else that Monica told her. It had sounded vile, an unbelievable thing to do. She hadn't believed that men liked you to suck them. But now she wanted to do it.

On impulse she sank to her knees. Angelo's penis looked very red. The tip was dark and moist. His pubic hair was dark and the thick organ thrusting up from it looked potent, a little dangerous. Before Hazel lost her nerve, she leaned forward. Opening her mouth she drew the glans in and sucked it gently.

Angelo's knees almost buckled. 'Oh, God,' he said. 'Oh, yeh.'

He tasted faintly of salt. She smelled soap and the faint tang of sweat. Growing bolder she took more of the shaft into her mouth. Using her tongue she explored him, lapping at the flared ridge around the glans. Angelo moved his hips, thrusting the cock in and out of her mouth. She sensed that he held himself back from plunging deeply into her throat. His leashed passion was very arousing.

'God. Oh, God,' he said again, through gritted teeth, his hands meshing in her hair as she moved her mouth over him. 'You're good at this. You'd better stop soon. I'm going to . . .'

Not on your life, Hazel thought. She wanted to do this properly. Covering her teeth with her lips she worked her mouth down the rigid shaft, once, twice, three times. Angelo gave a strangled moan. She slid her other hand beneath his balls, cupping them, feeling the tightness as his climax approached. On impulse she pressed her hand inwards, pushing one finger into the moist crease of his buttocks. Angelo's bottom tightened and he bucked against her. 'Here it comes.'

The warm flow spurted into her mouth. Hazel swallowed the chalky-tasting fluid. She felt proud of herself. And loved the way Angelo seemed so helpless at the moment of his climax. She stood up and laid her head against his chest, her hand still encircling his subsiding penis.

They arranged their clothing and cuddled for a while, exchanging kisses in which there was passion, but also a sense of friendship and peace. Both knew that their futures were divided. The interlude, while poignant, was just an episode in the story of so many in the war. After a while Angelo walked Hazel home. They embraced at the end of her road, oddly formal at the moment of parting.

'Goodbye, Hazel. Thanks for a great night,' he said. 'The memory will keep me warm on the way south.'

'Goodbye, Angelo. You take care,' she said. She watched him walk away, feeling sad that she would probably never see him again. As she walked the few yards to her garden gate, she saw an image of Ken in her mind.

Extraordinary how clearly she saw him now. She felt a rush of affection for him. It was only weeks until his next leave. When he came home she would make sure he had some rather special memories to take back with him. After all, you had to live for the moment. Some things were just too good to deny yourself.

Domia

THE CARD FABIENNE found in Howard's pocket bore one word.

Domia.

The print was gold and the embossed card of good quality. She turned it over. On the reverse side was the address – 14 rue St Honoré.

So Howard did have someone. She had expected as much. His excuses for being late for their dates had been growing more feeble. Fabienne's chin came up. The eyes which stared back at her from the mirror were cold with fury.

She knew that she looked good. Damned good. Her face was pale under the stylishly cut black hair. The subtle make-up suited her – understated eyes, full lips outlined with pinkish-brown pencil. No lines yet on her face, breasts still high and firm, legs long and slim. Men stared after her in the street all the time. Howard saw how they looked at her, their eyes avid but regretful. He liked men to look at her. She was not for them.

It was all for Howard. So why this?

He had phoned earlier that evening to cancel their dinner date. His voice on the answerphone, explaining that he had to work late, had been falsely bright.

'Sorry, darling. I'll call by the flat early tomorrow. Take you out to breakfast at our favourite restaurant. Okay?'

Fabienne scrunched the card into a ball and threw it across the bedroom. No it bloody well was not okay!

Howard would be with her now. Domia. It sounded Italian. Maybe she was a high-class whore. Someone young who would flatter him and do all the things he liked. Moan in the right places. Italian girls could be beautiful when young, but they soon grew fat, she thought bitchily. All that pasta and rich sauce.

Furiously she pulled a black silk sheath over the expensive lacy underwear that Howard liked. Steady now. She did not want to tear the dress. Howard wasn't worth it. She slipped her feet into zipped ankle boots. Sweeping her long black hair back from her face she clasped it at the nape and reapplied make-up.

A different look. Pale face, strong eyes with black liner, red lipstick – the shade of ripe cherries. Moments later she slammed the front door and ran down the steps, her black velvet cloak fanning out behind her.

As the taxi crawled through the warren of streets, Fabienne watched the traffic pass in shining streaks, headlights reflecting off wet roads. Shop windows gave onto a park and there were the spires and turrets of the cathedral. She loved the tall building with its Gothic arches and huge brooding buttresses.

The address on the card was in the old Latin quarter. As they approached the area, which although run-down had a tawdry charm, Fabienne's lip curled. Howard had always fancied himself as something of a bohemian.

'Stop here, please,' she ordered the driver.

'You wish me to wait? It is not safe for a lovely woman to be alone.'

'No. Thank you,' she said, tipping him well because he was young and handsome, yet thoughtful of her safety.

Trees lined the street. The gutters were awash with litter. Crumbled cigarette packets floated like boats down to the drains. The air smelled of rain and car exhausts. City smells. The houses had narrow fronts, closed shutters.

She turned into an alley, lit by a single cast-iron street lamp. Her heels clattered on stone cobbles, noisy in the silence all around. She glanced uneasily behind her, half regretting her decision to dismiss the cab driver. No need to be fearful. She was simply spooking herself. Slowly she walked forward. Halfway down the alley, in shadow, she saw a black-painted door with number 14 in red enamel letters. Above the door was a neon sign.

Domia.

Fabienne laughed aloud. Domia was a club – not a woman. Then why the secrecy? She hesitated for a moment only. What the hell, she had come here to find out. Pushing open the door she stepped inside.

It was very dark. Candles in sconces flickered on red velvet walls. Scented smoke filled the room. Suspended from the ceiling, a sequinned ball cast motes of light over the people who sat around. Mostly men sat at the tables which were clustered around a circular stage.

Two women sat on high stools near the bar. One in fishnet and leather, the other wearing a rubber dress, so tight that it showed every line and curve of her body. Both women were young and beautiful. They looked at her with doe-eyes, smiling slightly.

Tight-lipped, Fabienne returned their smiles. She glanced around. She could not see Howard. Perhaps he would be along later, when he finished work or whatever it was he was doing.

She liked the place, the air of expensive rather run-down seediness. There would be a show later, she thought, a striptease. Or maybe a live sex show. Two sad people humping and sweating under harsh lights – no more a turn-on than the display on a butcher's slab. Cheap thrills.

'You're showing your age, Howard,' she murmured under her breath. She couldn't wait to see his face when he saw her there. She ought to get plenty of mileage out of this. Oh, how she would make him grovel and beg before she forgave him this time.

A couple came into the club. Fabienne smelled expensive perfume, saw the glint of jewellery. Diamonds, emeralds. Her discerning eye told her that the gems were real. The women wore designer clothes, daring and beautifully cut. Leather with studded straps and black net that revealed more than it concealed. Gaultier, probably. Next came a number of men wearing dinner suits, as immaculate as penguins. One of the men was a high-up in publishing. She recognised him from a magazine.

Not wanting Howard to see her as soon as he came in, Fabienne headed for a dark corner. Someone seized her by the arm and spun her around. Amused, she turned to see a young man dressed all in black, buckles and straps across his chest. He had a beautiful face, an elegant, toned body. Gold rings glinted at his ears and in his nose. His hair was fashionably short in what the Americans called a buzz-cut.

'You're late. I'd given up on you,' he said, giving her no chance to speak. 'Come this way, quickly.'

Intrigued, she followed him through a curtained alcove. This was even better. She could watch from backstage as Howard incriminated himself. Explanations could come later. She was enjoying herself.

The beautiful young man led her down a narrow corridor which smelled of dust and grease paint. 'In here, quickly.' He opened the door, shouted inside, 'You've got barely ten minutes. Andy says to make it really good tonight. There are faces with big money out there.'

Fabienne hesitated for just a moment. Now was the time to speak up. The moment to leave. She kept silent. Stepping into the room, she saw that a woman with full blonde hair sat at a mirror. The woman turned as Fabienne entered. Her eyebrows arched in surprise as Fabienne took off her cloak and hung it up.

'Well, well. You're not what they usually send. A bit understated, aren't you? But I like the look. It's classy. Different. Are you new with the agency?'

Fabienne smiled, not yet understanding. 'Yes.'

Her heart was hammering with excitement. Why not? Howard wanted thrills. She would give them to him.

'I'm Nancy. You wanna fluff? I'm finished with the mirror.'

'Thanks. I'm Fabienne.' Fabienne sat down and began reapplying lipstick, powdering her nose.

She tried not to stare at Nancy, but it was difficult not to. Nancy was tall and strikingly beautiful. The studded collar encircling her neck threw her heart-shaped face into prominence. She wore a body harness that left her large breasts free and fitted tightly at the waist. A high-cut narrow strip covered her pubis. Her hips swelled out lusciously below the constriction of the belt.

As Nancy raised her arms to secure a black leather mask, her exposed breasts were lifted. The red-brown nipples were erect and gleaming with some kind of sparkling powder. They jutted out pertly, asking to be touched.

Fabienne felt a lurching jolt as Nancy's eyes met hers in the mirror. Nancy smiled knowingly as she pulled on long black boots and began to lace them up. Fabienne smiled back, her lips trembling slightly with a quite unexpected anticipation.

'Keep that look,' Nancy said. 'It suits you. Kind of innocent, but knowing. The punters'll like that. We're to provide a bit of fresh colour. Some new pussy. Gets them in the mood. After us it's the usual free-for-all for the regulars.'

She smoothed the fingers of her elbow-length gloves until they fitted sleekly.

'Ready?'

Fabienne stood up and turned around, her pulses hammering, suddenly aware that she had no idea what to do.

'I'll follow your lead,' she said, with a confidence she did not feel.

'Sure you will,' Nancy said. 'It'll be a pleasure to instruct you.' Leaning close, she brushed Fabienne's lips lightly with her own.

146

Fabienne swallowed hard. The point of Nancy's tongue had squirmed into her mouth. It had been hot, muscular. She wasn't sure how she felt about kissing a woman.

'A real pleasure,' Nancy said again, grinning confidently as she clipped the collar and leash around Fabienne's neck.

'I . . . Wait a minute.' Fabienne protested.

'Shut up. We're on.'

As they walked out onto the darkened stage, the music began. Nancy strutted along, head held high, breasts thrust forward. Her lovely face was set in a severe expression. She jerked on the leash, almost dragging Fabienne along behind her.

Fabienne was in a state of heightened tension that bordered on shock. This was not what she had expected. She felt afraid, but somehow aroused at the same time. It was a potent mixture. Two bullet beams of light flicked on, illuminating the centre of the stage. The rest of the club was in darkness. Fabienne could not see if Howard was in the audience, but she no longer cared very much. He had assumed less importance.

Nancy led her to centre stage where there was now a black leather chair with deep rounded arms and a wrought-iron rack with a selection of objects. Above it was a pulley with cuffs and restraints that could be raised or lowered at will.

'Stand on that chair,' Nancy ordered. When Fabienne was slow to obey she gave her two stinging slaps on the buttocks.

Fabienne gasped with shock and climbed onto the chair, the tight skirt of her silk dress making it difficult. Nancy ordered her to raise her arms and slip her wrists into the leather cuffs. Then she raised the pulley until Fabienne's arms were pulled up tight and she was balancing on the tips of her toes, her high heels making indentations in the leather.

Fabienne struggled to stand upright. The cuffs were padded and she was not uncomfortable at first, but soon the tension in her arms and legs became an ache.

'Please. Loosen it a bit,' she whispered.

'Now you don't really want that,' Nancy said, laughing softly. She slid her hands up the outsides of Fabienne's thighs, raising the tight skirt of the dress as she did so. Fabienne's shapely legs, in sheer black stockings, were revealed, then her lace garter belt, and finally the triangle of lace at her groin.

Fabienne bit back a cry of distress as the dress was bunched up tightly around her waist. Nancy turned her, so that she faced the back of the stage, presenting the audience with a view of her taut rounded backside, bisected by the strap of her black G-string.

Fabienne sensed the gathering tension in the club. The silence was thick. She heard someone strike a match. There was a moment of calm before she felt the slap, then her head snapped back with surprise.

Nancy placed another open-handed smack on Fabienne's buttocks. Then three more, swiftly, one after the other. Fabienne jerked as each slap connected. She bit her lips, working her hips back and forth in an effort to escape. A memory rose in her mind of being called in to the headmistress's study at her old girls' school. She had been spanked for some minor misdemeanour and recalled feigning tears to disguise the fact that she had enjoyed the punishment.

Forgotten feelings surfaced as Nancy administered a similar punishment and became her surrogate headmistress. Fabienne felt her buttocks tremble as Nancy struck them with her palm, concentrating on one at a time until they burned and throbbed. The warm pain radiated through her, sending shock waves of pleasure into her groin. When Nancy paused, Fabienne sagged, letting the pulley take her weight, her knees bouncing against the padded leather back of the chair.

Nancy bent down and took one of Fabienne's feet in her gloved hand. She lifted it high, so that Fabienne felt the strain in her knee and thigh, then she unzipped the ankle boot. She repeated the process with the other boot, placing them carefully side by side next to the chair.

Fabienne felt the leather of the chair against the soles of her feet, through the nylon of her stockings. It was warm and giving, like skin, and provided a sharp contrast to the seething heat of her bottom. The twin sensations sent a new spasm of pleasure through her.

Nancy drew the dress up higher, pulling it over Fabienne's head. Uncuffing her wrists briefly, she discarded it. Now she turned Fabienne to face the front of the stage and pushed the lace cups of the bra aside. Pulling her breasts free, she left the shaped band to cup the under-swell, forcing the exposed breasts to jut up and out.

Fabienne swallowed her protest, knowing that it would be ignored. Even if she begged, Nancy would not stop. With shiny, gloved fingers Nancy stroked her breasts, murmuring compliments and bending briefly to suck on the nipples. Fabienne felt the heat and wetness gathering between her thighs. She closed her eyes briefly, unable to contain a groan of pleasure.

Nancy's lips were warm. The sensation of sucking, the subtle pulling on her flesh, was hypnotic. The thought of all the watching eyes added to her pleasure. Then her eyes snapped open as Nancy pinched her nipples with gloved fingers. When the pressure was withdrawn, Fabienne let out a sigh. The feeling of throbbing discomfort could not be called pain. At its bitter heart there was the same poignant longing she experienced from being spanked.

Now Nancy began stroking Fabienne's breasts lightly with a flexible crop. The strokes went back and forth, teasing her sore nipples into hard peaks. Jagged flares of lust dipped down to

Fabienne's belly. She arched her back, thrusting her breasts towards the crop tip which Nancy continued to play gently across the flesh of her breasts. It was too much. She had not expected to feel this way – to feel so much. The bastion of her self-imposed repression threatened to crumble around her. She felt her eyes filling, her mouth twisting as she bit back grateful tears.

Nancy's lovely hard mouth curved with satisfaction at the evidence of Fabienne's confusion. Her eyes gleamed through the black mask. She reached down to the garter belt, slid a gloved finger into Fabienne's groin and pushed the lace triangle covering her sex aside.

Taking hold of Fabienne's pubis she tugged at the dark fleece, claiming the tight little plum with a force that bordered on cruelty. Fabienne whimpered and almost cried out. Ah, how she loved this game, this sexual sparring, this exchange of energies. It was something she had never before found with a woman. And with many men, the dominance was too crude, too pure.

When Fabienne tossed her head, Nancy crooned to her and stroked her face gently, commenting on her pretty flushed cheeks, her trembling mouth. Fabienne did not know that she wept, until Nancy caught a single tear on one gloved finger and carried it to her mouth. Their eyes met through the mask and something passed between them. Fabienne held her breath.

151

Then Nancy broke the thin sides of Fabienne's G-string and tore the lacy scrap free.

Now she adjusted the pulley, so that Fabienne could bend her knees and squat down, though her arms remained secured overhead.

'Rest back in the chair. Right back. Spread your knees and loop your legs over the arms of the chair. Come on, darling. Spread them wide. Show the punters that pretty pussy.'

Fabienne's face grew hot as she tried to do as Nancy ordered. It was impossible. She could not abase herself in public like this. Not even to get back at Howard.

But now her thighs were gripped and opened, her sex spread apart for all to see. She knew that she was wet, the inner flesh-lips puffy and swollen. Nancy stroked the dark pubic curls away from the rosy sex, exposing the inner labia and vaginal entrance to the audience. Using two fingers she began tapping the hood that covered Fabienne's clitoris.

Fabienne was swept by a riot of emotions as the subtle spanking proceeded. Never had she imagined this caress, which was both wicked and sublime. The muscles tensed in her inner thighs as she tried to drag them together, to shield herself from the eyes which watched from the darkened area beyond the stage. It seemed dreadful that her awakening must be observed, though she knew also that, but for Nancy and this accidental lesson in the majesty of dominance, she might have stayed asleep forever.

Waves of sweet submission lapped at her consciousness, making her bear down and push her sex towards Nancy's gloved hands. She thought briefly again of Howard, but now she no longer cared whether he watched or not.

Nancy raised her gloves to Fabienne's lips and pushed a finger into her mouth, so that Fabienne could taste her own smoky juices. Then she bent and began to kiss Fabienne on the soft insides of her thighs. In a moment Fabienne felt the subtle change in rhythm as Nancy bit her – not hard enough to break the skin, but enough to send ripples of new sensation deep into Fabienne's belly.

Fabienne began tossing her head from side to side, moaning loudly. She had found a new dimension within herself. All her senses, her screaming nerve ends, seemed centred on Nancy. Nancy who was so knowing, so wise, whose every considered touch, every spiked caress, sent new thrills of submission and pleasure through her.

Her arms ached with tension. The leather armchair was hot and sticky against her skin. The insides of her knees, the crease of her stretched and tender buttocks were damp with sweat. She slipped against the leather as she strained towards Nancy.

'Don't stop. God, don't stop,' she murmured, hardly knowing what it was that she was pleading for.

She felt the pleasure pooling, building. Someone had put a tape on. Sound crashed onto her.
The throbbing music filled her ears. Trent Reznor
singing 'Head like a Hole'. The light from the
bullet beams blinded her. Her senses were
running on overload. She smelled cigarette
smoke, the tang of leather, Nancy's perfume, her
own arousal – salt and musk. There was nothing,
no one in the world, except herself and Nancy.

'Oh, my God. Please. Nancy . . .' she sobbed as
the first wrenching wave of a climax threatened to
break.

As she hung on the edge, Nancy leaned over
and thrust two gloved fingers deep into her.
Fabienne spasmed, her hips working as she
sheathed herself on Nancy's fingers. Nancy
pressed her lips to Fabienne's mouth, kissing her
hard, lashing her muscular tongue around the
inside of her mouth. Fabienne gave a final groan
and felt the vibration of it in Nancy's throat.

Neither of them heard the applause. In a dream
Fabienne stood up. Her legs were shaky. She felt
completely drained.

Nancy unfastened the wrist cuffs, bending
swiftly to place a kiss on the inside of each wrist.
She picked up Fabienne's dress and threw the
crushed silk to Fabienne, who caught it and held
it close.

Nancy beckoned. 'I don't need to tether you, do
I? Good. Come with me.'

Swinging the collar and leash against her high

boots, Nancy strode from the stage. Fabienne followed obediently. Her thigh muscles ached and she could feel the places where Nancy had placed lovebites. She was acutely conscious of her still glowing buttocks, her sensitised breasts. Her entire body felt sore and yet more alive than ever before.

In the dressing room she looked into Nancy's eyes and smiled. Nancy smiled back, a look of complete understanding.

'You need a bath and some more attention, darling. My place or yours?' she said, taking Fabienne in her arms and kissing her with expert thoroughness.

'Mine,' Fabienne replied, returning Nancy's kiss with a newfound eagerness. 'I'm not expecting anyone. I had a date for breakfast. But I'll break it. It's not important. Not any more.'

With Kid Gloves

ON THE TRAM going home, Lily stared out of the window. A casual observer would have assumed that she was watching the scenery, but someone more astute might have noticed that her hands kept fluttering back and forth over the wrapped parcel in her lap, as though with pride or guilty pleasure.

Lily was not quite sure what had possessed her to buy the pair of exquisite black kid evening gloves. But buy them she had. They rested in the wrapped box on her lap, folded between layers of violet tissue paper. She was not a frivolous young woman, nor one given to acting on a whim. Indeed she prided herself on her common sense and level-headedness, two qualities which made her indispensable as upstairs maid to Lady Eleanor Soames.

Even now she was tempted to get off at the next

tram stop and retrace her steps to the Royal Emporium, there to hurry through the fashionable new store with its glass display cases and glittering lights, and ask to exchange the package for something more practical. What she had *meant* to buy was a pair of sensible winter gloves, hard-wearing and durable.

Oh, it was too ridiculous. She would never have occasion to wear the evening gloves – and yet she was aware of feeling happy, light-hearted. In the pit of her stomach was a warm feeling. It did not matter if the gloves had cost her a month's wages. Simply owning them made her feel special – like a lady of quality.

The tram drew to a halt and Lily alighted, the wrapped box now placed in the shopping bag along with the other purchases for her ladyship. A few minutes later she entered the imposing, red-brick townhouse by the back door. She was engrossed in her thoughts as she walked along the tiled hall to the coat- and hat-stand. Suddenly the tall figure of the butler stepped out of the shadows and loomed close, making her catch her breath with fright.

Unabashed, Samuel winked at her. 'Make you jump, did I? How's my lovely Lily today? Been out buying unmentionables for her Ladyship?' His hand slid over her skirt as he patted her bottom.

Lily's cheeks flamed, but she did not react. Two chambermaids were coming down the back stairs and she was unwilling to make a scene – as Samuel well knew. Really, butler he might be, but he had no right to take such liberties in public! The next time he tapped on the door on her attic room late at night she would be sure to tell him so in no uncertain terms. Just because she had allowed him certain intimacies, that gave him no right to act as if she were a common street girl.

When the chambermaids had passed by on their way to the scullery, she flashed Samuel a pert look of disapproval in which there was still enough warmth to fan his interest. 'I had a most satisfactory trip, thank you for asking, Mr Mackey,' she said, careful to keep her voice neutral.

He hovered behind her as she took off her hat and coat. She could smell the macassar oil on his smooth black hair and the peppermint on his breath. 'How about a kiss? No one's about. Aw, come over here, Lily. Don't take on so high and mighty. Who knows better than me that you're not as cold as you make out?'

Ignoring him, she marched smartly upstairs. She did not need to look over her shoulder to know that he stood at the bottom of the stairs looking up admiringly at her swaying derrière. Although she was mildy annoyed with him, she could not deny that she was flattered by Samuel's advances. Giving in to an impulse to tease him she lifted the hem of her skirt, giving him a brief flash of her lace-trimmed petticoat and neat ankles clad in buttoned leather.

Samuel gave an audible sigh. 'You're a cruel young woman, Lily Harrison,' he said in a penetrating whisper. 'What must I do to melt your heart?'

'Oh, I'll think of something,' Lily said airily, her lips curving in a secret smile.

He was a handsome rogue to be sure, with his fair Irish skin, wavy dark hair, and startling blue eyes. At one time or another each one of the prettier maids had fallen under his spell only to be discarded when he had tired of them. Lily had other plans. She wanted Samuel Mackey, but it would be on her own terms.

Before she took Lady Eleanor's purchases through to her, she slipped quickly up to her own small room and put the box with the gloves inside on top of her pine dresser. She patted the slim box, hearing the soft rustle of tissue paper inside. Somehow she resisted the urge to take out the gloves and try them on again. That would have to wait until much later, when she had completed her duties.

She was tucking stray tendrils of her red hair into her lace cap when, from the floor below, she heard Lady Eleanor's well-bred voice raised in annoyance.

'Where *has* that girl got to? I want her to dress my hair for dinner.'

'Coming. I'm coming,' Lily muttered under her breath as she hurried down the stairs and went in to Lady Eleanor's boudoir.

By the end of the day Lily was tired and looking forward to retiring for the night. She was subdued as she took her supper in the kitchen with the other servants. Although she was aware of Samuel's eyes on her throughout the meal she took pains to give no sign that she had noticed his gaze flickering over her pale skin and abundant red hair.

As she drank her tea, she began to relax. The conversation of the other servants went on around her. She made no attempt to join in. They in turn let her be. She knew that they thought her haughty, with ideas above her station, but she did not care. She had always wanted nice things and was determined to have them. The evening gloves were an emblem of her aspirations. Samuel caught her eye and gave her one of his blinding smiles. Lily lowered her eyes. No one at the table would guess that her heart had turned over and a heat crept into her lower belly.

When Samuel looked at her like that she felt reckless, tempted to give in to her desire for him. But she knew that would be foolish. It was her coolness, her reluctance to give away more than a kiss, a hurried and stolen caress, that kept him burning for her.

Lily poured more tea, pleased that her hand was steady although her breathing was rapid, her pulses quickening. Her breasts felt swollen and heavy inside her chemise, the nipples pushing against the fine embroidered cotton. Samuel had that look which meant that he would tap softly on her door when the rest of the household was asleep. The memory of what they had shared already made her feel hot. There was a melting sensation between her legs.

Perhaps if Samuel was extra charming to her she might permit him to lift her nightgown and look at her plump thighs. Just look, mind. Once, greatly daring, she had allowed him to loosen the drawstring at the neckline of her chemise and lift her breasts free. She was rather proud of how high and round they were, the nipples as well defined as two copper coins.

How Samuel had groaned as he stroked the firm flesh, begging to be allowed to kiss them. He had pinched her nipples gently until they stood out like hard little buds – as hard as they were at this moment. She permitted herself a secret smile as she remembered the avid look on his handsome face. But Samuel was not a man to be satisfied for long with being held off. He had to be encouraged, played like a fish on a line, otherwise he would look elsewhere for more rewarding prey.

As much as she desired Samuel, Lily was determined not to go the way of the last woman he took a fancy to. Poor Maudie had been packed off back to her parents with a week's wages and no reference. That was why Samuel had to be taught some respect. She wanted to be more than his flighty piece. Oh yes, she wanted far more from him than that.

Finishing her meal, she stood up and took her used china and cutlery into the scullery. Then she said good night to Cook and the maids, nodded to Samuel and went up to her room. Her preparations for bed did not take long. She hung up her gown and petticoats, then, after washing, brushed her long hair until it poured over her shoulders in a mass of soft curls. With a gathering sense of excitement she reached for the box on the pine dresser.

The black kid evening gloves nestled between the folds of violet tissue paper. They had a softness and a sheen like velvet. There was an opening on the inside of each wrist which fastened with a number of tiny covered buttons. The elbow-high tops of the gloves were trimmed with sparkling black beads and feathers. They were so – refined, so ladylike. As Lily stroked them she felt an echo of her earlier emotion.

An idea came to her. She smiled a secret smile. Now she knew why she had bought the gloves.

It was not long before the soft tap came on her door. Lily was ready. She sat on the single high-backed wooden chair, her hands clasped in her lap, a flounced cotton dressing gown buttoned up to her neck. The room was dark except for the flickering light of a single candle.

'Come in,' she said.

Samuel closed the door softly behind him. In the small room he looked enormous, his bulk magnified by the shadow climbing the wall behind him. For a moment Lily faltered. Was it possible that she could impose her will on this man? Then she thought of the evening gloves and what they represented and was once again aware of her power – the power of women, deep and dark at heart and as old as time.

Samuel looked at her in surprise, perhaps affected by some subtlety of her expression. Obviously he had expected to find her in bed or sitting nervously on the counterpane. Her composure seemed to disconcert him.

'Lily? Is something wrong? Are you unwell?'

Lily smiled, her hazel eyes dancing. 'Oh, no Samuel. I'm very well. In fact I think everything will be perfectly all right. I think . . . I mean . . . I want us to become lovers.'

A flush appeared on Samuel's pale face. He seemed speechless at her daring. Then his blue eyes darkened with excitement. 'You want me too? Lily, darling! You won't regret this. If you knew how much I've longed for you. Watching you every day has been a torture to me. There's been no one like you. You're so cool and poised, but I knew that you burned underneath your starched skirts. Oh, Lily. All the others meant nothing to me.'

She smiled again. He probably believed that he spoke the truth. How many others had he said that to?

Crossing the room in two strides, Samuel knelt before her. Reaching out he encircled her waist and pressed his cheek to her bosom. 'My dearest girl,' he whispered. Then he became aware that beneath the cotton robe she was wearing a black satin corset. With a hoarse little groan he reached for the buttons at her throat. In a moment he had unbuttoned the robe to her waist. Unable to contain himself he reached inside and grasped her breasts, holding them together to form a deep cleavage. Then he pressed kisses all over the swollen flesh, lapping at the shadowed rift with his eager tongue.

Lily shuddered with pleasure at his touch. It was difficult to remember that she must control herself. Samuel's hot mouth closed over one of her nipples. She felt the urge to arch her back at the delicious pulling sensation as he sucked and nibbled the taut little nub. She wanted to touch herself, to cup her breasts and offer them up to him. Somehow she managed to place her hands on Samuel's broad shoulders and push him away.

Samuel looked up at her, his eyes glazed by lust, his sculpted mouth shaped into a soft 'O' of surprise. A lock of his black hair had tumbled forward onto his forehead. He looked so much like a naughty schoolboy that she wanted to laugh. He was not the imposing butler now. That was when she knew that everything would go to plan.

'Samuel – Sammy,' she said. 'You do want to please me, don't you? You want me to let you come to my room again after tonight? And for us to do all sorts of forbidden things together?'

'Yes. Oh good Lord, yes,' Samuel said in a strangled voice.

'Then you must do as I say. Downstairs you have a certain position of power. And I respect that. But here, in *my* bedroom, I'm *your* mistress.'

Samuel gulped. 'I don't understand.'

Lily chuckled softly. 'Of course not. How could you? You've had things your own way for far too long. But that's the way it's to be, Samuel. If you don't like that fact, you can leave right now. But if you stay . . .' She let the sentence trail off, pinning Samuel with a look that held desire, promise, and forcefulness.

There were beads of sweat on Samuel's top lip. His pale face was flushed high on his cheekbones. She thought that he had never looked more handsome, more desirable. For a moment her heart fluttered. Had she gone too far? If Samuel was to get up now and leave, she would lose him.

'What . . . what must I do?' Samuel said haltingly.

'What must I do, mistress?' she corrected him, hardly able to contain her exultation. He repeated the phrase by rote, putting extra emphasis on the word 'mistress'.

'Good, Sammy – I shall call you that when we're alone together from now on. Now. Stand up.'

Samuel did so. Lily rose from the chair and unbuttoned the robe from the waist down. Shrugging it from her shoulders, she dropped it to the floor then stepped out of the crumpled folds. Samuel caught his breath as she stood before him clad only in the black corset, which left her breasts bare, and black woollen stockings held above her knees by frilled garters. When he would have reached for her again, she shook her head. 'Wait there.'

Turning her back, so that he was treated to a view of her generous naked buttocks, she took the black kid gloves from the pine dresser and began pulling them on. She faced Samuel now, as she fitted the supple black kid to her lower arms, sliding the fabric down each of her fingers in turn, then smoothing the rippled folds up to her elbows until each glove fitted snugly. Samuel watched avidly, unable to take his eyes from her. She held out her hands, palms up, for him to fasten the covered buttons.

With a hoarse moan Samuel grasped her slim wrists and brought them to his mouth. Pressing his lips to the slitted openings he kissed her white skin, touching his tongue-tip to each bluish vein, each bounding pulse. Lily shivered, feeling the wetness gathering at the folds between her legs. She had never been so aroused, never felt so strong and womanly.

'Fasten the buttons, Sammy,' she said after a few moments.

Samuel did as she told him. He seemed mesmerised by the black silkiness of the gloves which looked startling against her fine-grained skin. She sensed his reluctance to let go of them. Gently she pulled away. 'Now, Sammy. Strip to your drawers.'

Samuel blinked in astonishment. 'But I can't. Not like this. You . . . you're not going to watch me?' he said.

'Oh, yes I am,' she said softly, but with the slightest hint of menace. 'Surely you have no objection? Don't you know what happens to disobedient servants?'

Samuel swallowed audibly. 'They . . . they get beaten?'

'They do indeed,' Lily said, delighted to hear the note of hopefulness in his voice. 'It seems that I must give you your first lesson. For I expect to be obeyed at once, without question. Now – disrobe!'

Samuel flinched as her voice cracked like a whiplash. Hurriedly he slipped off his boots, unbuttoned his braces, shirt and trousers and laid them aside. His vest and socks followed. Soon he was clad only in his linen under-drawers. He stood slightly hunched over, his hands hovering at his groin trying to shield his huge erection.

Lily chuckled inwardly as she stepped forward, grasped his wrists and placed them firmly at his sides. Samuel's stiff cock tented the fabric of his drawers, nudging at the buttoned opening as if eager for escape. She had never seen him wearing anything less formal than his butler's uniform and had been unprepared to find his body so well-made. His shoulders were broad, his chest deep with a sprinkling of dark hair, and his stomach was ridged with muscle. Lord, but he was as fine a figure as the huge navvies who worked on the canals.

She touched his chest, moving her gloved hands over his biceps, then stroking down to where the dark hair grew in a point up to his navel. It was odd, exciting, to be touching him so intimately, but to feel nothing through the black gloves. Samuel breathed fast, his belly tautening as she trailed her gloved hand down to his waistband and slipped inside.

'Oh, Lord,' Samuel gasped, looking down at her shiny black fingers.

She ran a finger up his engorged cock, then circled the firm sac of his scrotum while he arched towards her, helplessly aroused, his cheeks flaming with shame and need. Slowly she unbuttoned the opening of his drawers and drew out his rampant cock. It was rigid, deeply flushed, the cock-skin drawn half back over the moist glans. The column of flesh, rearing up from the gap in his drawers, looked almost obscene and heavily potent. Cupping his scrotum she drew his balls through the gap too.

She had an almost overwhelming desire to bend her head and taste him, flick her tongue over the swollen glans, but in a moment she had mastered the urge. Punishment he had been promised and that was what he must have. For Samuel was a man who would feed on any woman's weakness, press home any advantage.

That did not daunt her. After tonight things would be different. Tonight she felt strong, beautiful, in control – the evening gloves adding more than a touch of glamour and wickedness to her new persona.

'Turn around,' she said sternly.

He looked blankly at her for a moment, then turned around so that his muscled thighs pressed against the mattress. Deftly she encircled his waist and unbuttoned his waistband. Samuel made a strangled sound in his throat as his drawers slipped to lodge halfway down his buttocks, revealing the firm flesh of his bottom. Giving in to a devilish impulse Lily grasped his drawers and dragged them down his thighs. They slipped further, falling in folds around his ankles. Pushing gently at the small of his back, she said, 'Lie forward on the bed, Sammy. On your belly for me.'

For a moment she thought he might balk. His back straightened and there was a stubborn set to his shoulders. Then he bent at the waist and stretched himself out as she ordered. She left him lying face down for a moment, while she picked up a hairbrush from her dresser. He did not turn his head to look at her as she moved around the room, nor did he look up when she tapped the back of the wooden brush against her gloved palm. The subtle sound of wood against leather was penetrating in the silent room.

A tremor passed over Samuel's back and his

buttocks twitched as if in anticipation or fear. 'Now, Sammy,' she purred. 'This is going to be your first lesson. I do not doubt that it will be the first of many. But you will remember this one because it is special. Think of it as . . . as,' – she searched for an appropriate word – 'as a baptism.'

Raising her hand she brought the back of the brush smartly down on Samuel's left buttock. Although he flinched with surprise he did not cry out or protest. Emboldened by his response she spanked him again. Then again. Soon the punished flesh glowed pink. She admired the contrast between the as yet untouched right buttock. Samuel's fingers were clenched on a fold of her counterpane, his head buried in the folds of white cotton.

When she began spanking him again, this time on his virgin cheek, he gave a whimpering cry of eagerness. She laid to with a will, plying him with the back of the brush until both buttocks glowed a deep peony red. Her knees felt quite weak with the flooding feeling of power and excitement. As she moved, the swollen folds of her quim rubbed slickly together. A pulsing beat seemed to penetrate deep inside her.

'How does that feel, Sammy?' she said huskily. 'Have you been punished enough?'

'Oh Lord, mistress,' he said. 'Oh, please. No more . . . Don't stop . . . I mean . . .'

Lily smiled confidently. He was almost hers. 'Just a little more, I think. And I order you not to lose control. Do you hear? If you spill your jism onto my counterpane I shall have to order you back for another session just like this one.'

Samuel moaned softly, pressing his belly more closely against the cool cotton. Deliberately Lily turned the hairbrush over and brought the bristled surface down onto Samuel's sensitised flesh. He gave a muffled howl and his hips began pumping as he mashed his member between his belly and the surface of the bed. Quite out of control now he humped and gasped as Lily spanked him on both cheeks at once. Sensing that he was near to breaking she brought the brush down in a rough stroke so that the bristles scraped across the burning flesh and penetrated his cleft, spiking deliciously at his clenched anus.

'Lily, darling! Mistress! Oh good Lord!' Samuel choked, convulsing with the pleasure-pain and the indignity.

Straining backwards, he arched his back so that his reddened bottom was tipped up towards the punishment. His hips wove and he thrust shamelessly into the counterpane as if he was pushing his cock into Lily's willing body. Lily brought the brush down between Samuel's legs and stroked the bristles gently across his taut and straining sac.

Suddenly Samuel tensed and lifted his head. The cords stood out in his neck and shoulders as he spent himself, threshing and grunting in ecstasy, his hands plucking bonelessly at the quilted counterpane.

Lily laid aside the hairbrush and stood by,

waiting for Samuel to recover. It took a long time for him to stop twitching with after-shocks of pleasure. Still breathing hard, he pushed himself backwards onto his knees.

'Oh dear, oh dear,' Lily said sternly, looking at the creamy wet patch on the counterpane. 'It seems as if you'll have to come back for some more training. But not until I give you the signal. From now on you'll wait until I tell you that you're welcome in my bedroom. Understand?'

Samuel nodded mutely.

'One more thing. You'll treat me with the respect due to a lady – your mistress – from now on. No more bottom-pinching and stolen kisses. And no cheeky talk when others are within earshot. Any lapses and I'll deny you all favours. Is *that* understood?'

Samuel nodded. 'As you wish, Lily darling . . . I mean mistress. Might I be allowed to ask one favour?'

Lily stroked her chin as if considering his request while inwardly she was exultant. Oh, what times they would have! 'You may,' she said at length. 'Just one, mind.'

'Please will you . . . will you wear those gloves next time? You're like a different person with them on. I hardly know you. Dear God, Lily. I'm your slave!'

And Lily threw back her head and laughed. A month's wages they had cost, but they were worth more – a whole lot more.

Peep-Show

I HAD HEARD of them, of course. Grace Jones had herself been portrayed as a peep-show entertainer for a publicity campaign to promote an album, some years back now. My lover and I had made love often to one track – 'Warm Leatherette'.

But I had never seen a real peep-show. In fact, I didn't know if they still existed or were some sort of throw-back to the Sixties, like Betty Page and *Tit Bits* magazine. I had to admit that I was shocked by my lover's suggestion.

'You mean actually go to one of those places?' I couldn't believe he was serious.

A friend had told me that he'd been to one of those peep-hole affairs while on holiday in Europe. He said laughingly that someone had actually been vacuuming the little cubicle while the girl on the turntable postured and pouted for the customers! But that was Europe. I didn't think we in Britain could ever be so dismissive about sex.

'Paying to watch women expose themselves. It's so . . . seedy,' I said, imagining the unsavoury darkened booths, the men in raincoats huddling in their seats, hands jiggling at themselves while their eyes were pinned to the anonymous woman on show.

Even as I protested, I felt a flicker of excitement. Seedy, yes, but also titillating.

'Isn't that the attraction?' he smiled, seeing that I was interested. 'I've heard of a place, newly opened. It's classy, the "in" place to go. There's more to this establishment than tired whores gyrating in shabby underwear for a pound a minute.'

I put my arms around him and lifted my mouth for his kiss.

'And how do *you* know what happens in these places?' I asked teasingly, feeling even more turned-on by the thought of my lover sitting in one of those dingy little booths. 'Have you been to one?'

'Of course,' he said lightly. 'I went with a group of friends from the office once, for a laugh. It was a long time ago. Before I met you.'

I didn't believe him, but it didn't matter. Whatever he did when he was not with me was none of my concern. The snatched hours, the occasional overnight stays in his stylish, riverside flat in Docklands, were crystalline moments in the ordinary landscape of my life.

His tongue slipped between my lips and I sank against him, loving the way he tasted, the way he explored my soft inner flesh with such expert thoroughness. I knew that I was going to agree to go with him. I always did what he wanted, because I wanted it too. And because he was young and beautiful. It was my pleasure to indulge him.

Soho by night has a sort of seaside town brilliance. It's as tawdry as an over made-up drag queen. I loved the spice of excitement, the smells wafting out as the doors of restaurants opened and closed, the razor cut of danger in the air. Neon signs in yellow, orange, electric blue lit up the streets and made them one long amusement arcade. Sex shops, selling plastic penises, rubber items, day-glo French ticklers and a riotous assortment of garish underwear, plied their trade like static whores.

I clung to my lover's arm as we walked, both of us enjoying the stares, the glances of startled appreciation. Maybe some of them recognised me. I could almost hear their thoughts. 'Isn't that . . . No, it can't be.' My lover was so obviously a lot younger than me, but I was still quite a catch. I have an ex-model's slender figure and good legs. The slim designer dress and high heels showed them off to advantage.

My lover pointed across Great Windmill Street. 'There,' he said. 'That's the place. Interesting, eh?'

I couldn't agree. The doorway was next to a shop which seemed to vibrate with garish neon signs. 'Striptease', 'Exotic Shows', 'Adult Videos', the signs proclaimed. And over the doorway next to the shop a similar sign glowed redly. 'Peep-show downstairs.' Was this a joke?

Despite my reluctance, my pulses quickened as I followed my lover into the darkness. Downstairs we entered a womb-like basement; red carpet, swirly red-flock wallpaper, red light. The colour bleached out the features of the haggard man sitting at the counter. My lover handed him a sheaf of notes. We passed by with a nod.

I felt the man's eyes on me and smiled at him and swung my hips. They couldn't get many women in a place like this, at least, not anyone other than 'working women'. Certainly not like me: mature, well-groomed, wearing black silk by Versace and matching, hand-made shoes.

We walked along a landing until we came to the booths. Six of them. The atmosphere was close and there was the smell of cigarettes and something else, almost antiseptic. A middle-aged man slanted me a look. His eyes slid quickly away when I smiled back without a trace of embarrassment. Some of the booths were occupied, their doors hanging open. I saw a youngish man in one. He wore a heavy overcoat and was hunched over, making small movements inside the shelter of his coat. It was what I had expected, after all.

For some reason I found it all sad and dreary.

But it was also as seedy as I'd imagined it would be and that rather excited me.

'In here,' my lover said, taking my arm and directing me into one of the booths.

It was very dark and cramped. My eyes took a moment to adjust. There was only a narrow bench to sit on. In one wall there was a window the size of a letterbox opening, covered by a metal plate. Beneath it was a coin slot.

My lover propped the door open deliberately. Now anyone walking past could look in and see us. I was unnerved by that, having always preferred to take my guilty pleasures in secret. But I did not protest. My lover never did things by accident and I wondered – what was his purpose?

For a moment nothing happened. I waited, expecting the metal covering over the narrow oblong window to be removed.

'Don't we have to put some money in the slot?' I whispered.

My lover shook his head. 'We've paid for a special show. Be patient, darling.' His fingers traced the contour of my cheek.

I leaned against him, wanting to feel his warmth against my skin. My dress was sleeveless and I shivered when he ran the tips of his fingers up my bare arm. His lips moved to my neck. They were firm, demanding. I knew what he wanted and parted my thighs.

Under the dress I wore only a black satin suspender belt and lace-topped, sheeny stockings.

I shuddered when he pushed up my dress and rested a hand on my thigh. Just then, a light went on in the room beyond and the metal covering the narrow window was removed.

Viewed through the oblong opening, there was a woman on a bed. She wore only an open-cup, lacy bra and a lace G-string. Covering her face was a frilly black mask. She was positioned on all fours. As she moved to and fro, arching her back and weaving her hips, her breasts swung lazily. The nipples poked rudely out of her scanty bra. She had a good body; firm generous breasts, slim waist, a taut curvy bottom.

A wash of pinky-red lit the room, giving a surreal quality to the woman's skin and turning the blackness in our booth to violet-toned twilight. As I watched, the woman moved to the edge of the bed. She was graceful, her movements fluid and sexy. Her curly dark hair spilled over her shoulders.

'Wouldn't you like to make love to her?' I whispered to my lover.

He didn't answer, which pleased me. In the grainy light he smiled and kissed my mouth. His fingers described tiny circles on my inner thigh and I felt the beginnings of that special ache in my sex. My nipples hardened, brushing against the cool black silk of my dress as I strained towards his hand.

When his fingers closed possessively over my pubis, I gasped, anticipating his touch on my moist vulva. I knew that I was swollen and receptive, the dew seeping out of me, but he denied me the intimacy of the caress I wanted so much. He contented himself with stroking my pubic hair, teasing the springy curls into strands. The tension coiled within me as he sat calmly watching the woman in the other room while caressing my mound with almost casual familiarity.

'Please . . .' I whispered. 'Touch me. Feel how wet I am.'

He shook his head. 'Not yet. When I'm ready.'

For a second I hated him. He was so self-assured, so certain of his attractiveness. But the feeling passed almost immediately. It was his refusal to compromise in any way which kept my interest.

Sitting on the edge of the bed, the woman raised her hands to the tips of her exposed breasts and took hold of her nipples. As she twisted them, pulling them out into little tube shapes, I felt an answering pull in the base of my belly. How deliciously painful that looked. Her nipples were large and of some dark colour, brownish-red or copper, I imagined. In this light, colours were deceptive.

With her other hand, she reached down and pushed the G-string aside. She had a lot of black pubic hair. As she began stroking herself, pushing aside the silky hair to probe her labia, I glimpsed the shadowed parting of her flesh. The red lips looked bleached by the artificial light. Her fingers were wet and she began moving her hips as she rubbed her clitoris. She seemed to be enjoying herself. If she was acting, she was good.

'Get up on the bench,' my lover whispered hoarsely. 'On your knees, bottom in the air.'

I did as he asked, feeling the narrow board under my knees, the wood hard against my stockinged shins. As the toes of my expensive shoes were bent against the hard surface, the muscles in my calves protested. Standing behind me, straddling the bench, he rolled my skirt up to my waist. The close, fusty air of the booth was soft on my bared buttocks and the tops of my thighs. Grasping the neckline of my dress, he yanked it down so that my breasts spilled out and hung down beneath me.

'Oh,' I breathed, feeling an exquisite sensation wash over me. My lover knew how I loved to take on the submissive role during our sex-play.

Now I must look like *she* had when the shutter was removed and the pink-washed room came into view. It was almost as if we had changed places.

My lover curved his body over mine and his erection sprang up between us, the length of it nudging against the parting of my buttocks. He was hot and hard. Adjusting his position he slid straight into me – so slick and smooth. His hands cupped my breasts, stroking, then pinching, and I writhed under him – loving it, loving him.

Turning my head, I watched the woman masturbating and imagined that she could look out of her narrow window to see me being fucked, my body moving in time to my lover's deeply penetrating thrusts. Would she enjoy watching us? I chewed my bottom lip as my pleasure mounted and hers seemed to follow a similar path.

Look into my eyes and see me, I groaned inwardly. My lover and I are your peep-show. But she seemed oblivious to the eyes watching her from the other booths, her entire concentration centred on bringing herself to orgasm.

'You're like hot silk inside,' my lover said, his voice distorted by passion. And I started to come.

I couldn't hold back and he knew it. He rode me hard now, the way I liked it. I spasmed and bucked against him, helpless as I dissolved and broke into splinters of pure sensation. He was so deep inside that I could feel his balls brushing my buttocks as he pounded into me. The twisting, pinching movements of his fingers on my nipples was sweet torture.

I cried out as the pleasure pulsed right through me and my inner muscles contracted around his buried shaft. 'God. Oh God . . .' I moaned.

In the other room, the woman had thrown back her head. Her face screwed into a rictus of ecstasy as she came, her fingers buried in her vagina, her thumb circling circling the glistening bud of her clitoris. I felt that she and I were kindred spirits, but I was so much more circumspect. I admired her for her total lack of inhibition.

How did it feel to know that you were the centre of attention? That every man watched you, wanted you? What a challenge it would be to find out.

My lover moaned and gave a long sigh. I felt his breath on my neck as he emptied himself into me, making the inarticulate little noises that I cherish. How special is the moment just after he has climaxed. He is so vulnerable then. I felt him growing soft inside me, but my body was reluctant to let him slip free. Turning my head I reached back over my shoulder and brushed my lips against his damp hair.

Then I froze.

For the first time I glimpsed the back of the booth, which had been partially screened from my sight by the open door. The door was closed now. I saw the second letterbox-sized slit, the darkness beyond. And in the darkness I saw the reflected points of light from the eyes – many eyes – watching me.

My lover laughed softly. 'How does it feel to have other men watching you, each one of them wanting you?' he asked. 'Each of them listening to your cries of pleasure?'

I smiled rather shakily, absorbing the fact that his words so nearly mirrored my thoughts. 'I don't know. You haven't given me time to absorb the fact that we *have* been watched. I'm too shocked to react.'

In fact I was very calm. There seemed a perfect symmetry to the situation. As he helped me sit up and straighten my dress, he said tenderly, 'It was a rotten trick to play. You're not angry with me?'

'No. Of course not. I always enjoy your games. But perhaps you should have told me about the other peep-hole. Then I would have known what to expect. It seems the fair thing to do.'

'Ah, but it was my secret pleasure to keep it from you. To enjoy you in your innocence, knowing that you belonged solely to me and they could do no more than gaze upon you. I loved knowing that only I can have you.'

Selfish boy, thinking of his own pleasure. I kissed him deeply, then bit his bottom lip to punish him just a little. The saltiness of his blood on my tongue was satisfying and his wince, the cool inrush of his breath, like a caress.

'The next time we come here I'll know that I'm being watched,' I said. 'And I'll put on an even better performance – for you as well as them.'

'You actually like it? You enjoy the thought of being watched?' he said, his voice, for the first time, unsure. Was that just a flicker of self-doubt in his fine dark eyes?

And I laughed, enjoying the shock on his beautiful arrogant face and the fact that I had robbed this wicked boy of his victory. At least – for the moment.

Charity Begins . . .

MISTRESS CHARITY PENN set down the pail of slops and wiped her forehead with the back of her hand. The sun beat down overhead and trickles of perspiration ran down her armpits and soaked into the top of her stays. Inside her woollen stockings her legs itched and prickled, but she dared not leave off the garments. Someone would be bound to notice her bare ankles.

Inside the stockade there was a rich stew of odours – wood smoke, roasting meat, horse dung, and the acrid stench from the tannery. In the stifling heat of the Virginia summer, the air was filled with the sound of toil as the settlers went about their daily work. In their black clothes, relieved only at collar and cuff by starched white lace, they looked like so many magpies.

Charity sighed, picked up the pail and continued on her way to the pig pen. Outside one of the square wooden houses, Jacob Hawkins was chopping wood, his shirt-sleeves rolled up to reveal brawny forearms. At the sight of his broad shoulders and narrow hips, his muscled thighs moving under his leather trousers, her knees went weak.

She knew that it was immodest to stare so, but she could not help it. Jacob was as near beautiful as any man got. His long fair hair was caught at the nape with a thong, but loose strands of it had escaped. Wisps of it whipped around his bronzed face as he worked and stray hairs clung to the damp skin of his shoulders. Chips of wood flew into the air as he brought the axe down squarely onto a log, splitting it so that one perfect half fell either side of the block.

The sappy smell of chopped wood seemed to her to be the most alluring scent in the world. Before she could think better of it, she found herself calling out a greeting.

'Good morrow, Jacob. Is it not a beautiful day?'

Oh Lord, she hoped no one else had heard her raise her voice. Calling out to a man like a common fishwife, that would be a black mark against her. Jacob did not seem to mind. He grinned and paused in his work. Leaning on his axe-handle, he watched her as she passed by.

'Good morrow to you too, mistress,' he said. 'Indeed it is beautiful, especially from where I'm standing.' He sounded amused by her presumption. His eyes, sweeping lazily over her, quickened with more than passing interest.

Charity slowed her steps. Perhaps she would risk a few words with Jacob. Surely the censure of the community would not fall upon her for exchanging innocent pleasantries with a young man in the good open air. She was shaping the words in her head when the sound of a harsh voice at her elbow made her start.

'Be about your business, Mistress Penn,' said Minister Barber. 'The Devil makes work for idle hands. And it would behove you to use less lace in your dress-making.'

Charity prickled with outrage, but bit back the retort that rose to her lips. The deep lace collar she wore was the work of a whole winter spent indoors when the mud was so thick inside the stockade that it was a misery even to run to the privy. She was proud of her lace-making skills and did not think God would begrudge her the chance of displaying the fruit of her labours. But the generous and loving God she spoke to in her heart seemed to be a different deity from the one Minister Barber spoke of, his harsh voice booming out from the pulpit of the church on the Lord's resting day.

'Well? Get on with you now,' the minister said. 'Go and draw your water from the well.' He made shooing motions with his hands. As if I were a mouse in the hay-rick, Charity thought, and not a young woman of marriageable age. And I'm not going to fetch water. If he had been at all interested in her, he would have seen that her pail was already full of pig food.

Although she glared her defiance, the minister did not stop to remonstrate with her but strode away, certain of being obeyed. From the tail of her eye she saw Jacob wink at her, the corners of his mouth pulling away in a wicked little smile. That made Charity feel better. She returned the smile, then without a backward glance hurried on to the pig pen.

The reddish Virginian dust rose up around her buckled shoes as she walked. As she drew nearer she heard the sound of raised male voices. In between the laughter and shouts of encouragement, there came a veritable cacophony of grunts and squeals. Puzzled, she rounded the building which screened the communal pen from view and stopped in amazement. A number of men, mostly the elders amongst the settlers, were grouped around the stout wooden fence.

Inside the pen, the sows were running back and forth in a frenzy of excitement, while the huge saddle-back boar sniffed at their haunches. One of the men leaned forward, waving his arms and shouting instructions. Through the space that opened up, Charity had a brief glimpse of the proceedings. The boar raised its head, its muddy wet snout questing the air, then it gave a throaty squeal and launched itself across the pen.

She had a brief impression of the boar's curling organ, erect and dripping, before the beast gave a lusty grunt and covered a willing sow. The reddened porcine eyes closed and the boar's teeth ground together with pleasure as it began thrusting vigorously. At the sight of the great ballocks, swollen with the fluid of generation and swaying between the boar's thrashing haunches, Charity's cheeks reddened. She knew that she ought not to look, but fascination drew her feet forward. Besides, the men were too preoccupied to notice her.

'That's it, my lusty. Give it to her!' one of the men shouted.

'Aye. Rut away! Make the sow squeal like a wench in childbed!' said another.

The ribald comments and coarse laughter made Charity prickle with embarrassment. Could these be the same men who berated any young woman for the slightest act of assumed immodesty? She felt uncomfortable being the only female in all-male company and was about to slip away when one of the men turned and saw her. For a moment he did not speak, but looked her up and down, his eyes sparking with animal lust.

Even in her innocence of men, she knew that he was aroused by the spectacle of the boar servicing the sows. His glance seemed to undress her where she stood. Inside, she cringed away from the hot, cruel eyes, but she would not lower her gaze and give the man the satisfaction of knowing that she was shamed by having been caught watching the mating. If it was considered fitting for men to watch, then why not women too? For surely in a farming community everyone knew how piglets got started.

The man nudged his neighbour. In a moment Charity found herself censured by all eyes. She felt an agony of self-consciousness and wished herself a hundred miles away, but she looked them all in the face. A silence fell. Then there were murmurs of consternation. Someone muttered, 'Disgraceful conduct!' A few of the men shuffled their feet, exchanged furtive glances. She heard someone say, 'She's but newly arrived at the settlement. Mayhap she does not know our ways.'

Before she could identify the speaker and flash him a smile of grateful thanks, another voice rang out.

'This is no place for you, mistress, nor for any modest woman.' Charity recognised the man as Josiah Wainwright, one of the pillars of the community. He was a thin man with reddish hair, hollow cheeks, and a jutting chin. 'Did you not know that all women were told to avoid the animal pens this day?'

Charity shook her head. 'I heard no such announcement.'

'Indeed? Then you should stay to listen to the minister's promulgations in church after the end of the service,' Josiah said severely. 'Instead of running off to the house of that disreputable, half-breed woman who serves the settlement as midwife!'

Charity coloured at the slur on her friend. Samaseta – better known by her anglicised name of Sarah – was the only person with whom she could be truly herself. Despite being looked down upon because of her Indian blood, Sarah did not judge or preach the judgement of hellfire, as did the pious wives and daughters of the settlement worthies. And she listened patiently, always answering Charity's questions with honesty.

'Berate me if you must, Master Wainwright, if you deem it necessary for the good of my soul,' Charity said coolly. 'But I would ask you not to pass comment on one who is not present to answer for herself!'

There was a shocked silence. Josiah's bony face paled. Charity lifted her chin defiantly, waiting for the explosion of righteous anger which would surely follow. Just then, the boar gave an ear-splitting grunt of pleasure. The sow he covered let out a warbling squeal and jerked forward. Sliding off the sow's back, the boar stood snorting and trembling, his still erect organ shiny and dripping. It looked shockingly red. Charity tried not to stare at it.

'He's ready for another,' one of the men said, his voice thick with admiration at the boar's prowess. 'See how his pizzle is still standing.'

'Aye, and the sows be glad of it! Look how they present themselves ready for him.'

'You'd best begone,' Josiah said in a voice that held ice. 'Lest you be corrupted by such bawdy talk. I'd advise you to pray for modesty, mistress. Aye, and you've yet to learn to afford the proper respect to your betters! I'll be speaking to the minister about you.'

'I don't doubt that you will, Master Wainwright,' Charity said pertly, dipping a shallow, almost insulting curtsy. There, let the nasty creature find fault with that! She had the satisfaction of knowing that Josiah was fuming inwardly, but he could not actually take her to task for any lack of manners. She was annoyed too that the minister had not seen fit to warn her about the mating when he spoke to her earlier.

Dumping the pail of swill at Josiah's feet, she said with laboured politeness, 'Perhaps you will see to it that my pig is fed after she has been serviced, Master Wainwright, since I am not permitted to attend her this day. No doubt she will relish her meal after her strenuous labours. I'll call back for the empty pail later when you have all gone home to your good wives.'

Smiling to herself she strode away, the sight of Josiah's furious impotent face imprinted on her mind. She walked with shoulders set and her back straight, her head held high. As the boar set up a lusty grunting, she heard the mocking laughter of the men floating after her. I hate them all, she thought. They are so secure in their superiority.

She felt in a bad temper after leaving the men and ill-inclined to go back home where a dozen or more tasks awaited her. Nothing was so pressing that it could not wait. On impulse she decided to go and visit Sarah, Josiah's words having put her in mind of her friend. Sarah's cottage was outside the stockade, beyond the fields of maize. As Charity skirted the fields of ripening corn and entered the canopy of trees, she took off her broad-brimmed hat and untied the straps of her lace cap. No one from the settlement could see her here and berate her for immodest behaviour.

The dappled sunlight on her bare head felt wonderful. She shook out her hair so that it tumbled over her shoulders in shining brown coils. The path to Sarah's cottage was well worn. At one time or another all the settlement women had need of her services. Sarah was far more than a midwife. She had knowledge of secret things – things to which men were not privy and which they would have been outraged to discover.

As Charity approached the cottage, she saw Sarah seated outside. She was shelling beans into a large basket of woven grass. Sarah always wore Indian dress. Her tunic of bleached doeskin was decorated with beads and feathers. Ebony plaits hung down to her waist. Catching sight of Charity, Sarah looked up and waved, her generous mouth curving in a smile of welcome.

'Good morrow, Charity,' she said in the perfect English she had learned at the mission school. ' 'Tis good to see you. Will you come inside and take a cup of sassafras tea?'

Charity followed Sarah into her cottage. The interior was cool and spotlessly clean. It smelled of dried herbs, jerked meat, and lamp oil. Sarah sat on a trunk which was covered by a brightly patterned Indian blanket. They spoke of inconsequential things whilst the tea was brewing. Sarah stirred honey into the tea and passed Charity an earthenware cup, then suggested that they take the steaming brew outside.

'And what's amiss with you, my friend?' Sarah said, when they were seated on the wooden bench.

Charity took a sip of her tea before she answered, looking up over the brim at Sarah's handsome face. With her shining black hair, honey-coloured skin and strong features, she was a striking woman. Charity was no longer surprised by Sarah's perception. There had been many similar incidents in the past.

'You always know when something is wrong,' she said.

'I have the sight,' Sarah said simply.

Charity found it easy to tell Sarah about what had happened at the pig pen. 'I hate those men,' she said. 'They are worse than animals. They are coarse beasts. I think that I shall never marry if I have to do that ... that ... filthy thing with a man!'

Sarah chuckled. 'You hate all men? Even young Jacob Hawkins?'

Charity smiled briefly. 'Well, perhaps not him.

He seems different. But for all I know he's no better than the rest of them in one respect. Oh, Sarah, the way they were all encouraging the boar. They were so excited by its stiff pizzle and the way it thrust itself into the sows, I saw them drooling with envy. But they tried to hide the fact when they saw me.'

'And you?' Sarah said evenly. 'Never mind the men. They're foolish and deny their own natures. Were you excited by what you saw?'

'Sarah!'

'Oh, you need not pretend to be shocked. This is me, remember?'

Charity lowered her eyes and remembered the swimming, light feeling in her stomach as she watched the boar serving the sow. 'Yes. I was excited,' she said haltingly. 'Why is that? It is wrong, is it not, for women to feel so? I know that there is no pleasure in the act of generation for us. That is why it is forbidden to speak of it. It is ugly and unpleasant. But we must suffer it because of the sin of Eve.'

Sarah sipped her tea, her hands cupped around the earthenware vessel to absorb the warmth of it despite the heat of the day. She was silent for a while as if considering her answer, then she said, 'Did the sow seem to be enjoying the boar's attentions?'

Charity nodded. 'As far as I could tell. I could not see very much.'

'Then do you not think that a woman can enjoy a man in the same way?'

194

'Indeed not! We are not animals to take our pleasures where we will!'

'Ah, but we are, my poor innocent. It is because there *is* pleasure to be had when man joins with woman that the act is surrounded with rules and secrecy.'

Charity was stunned. 'I cannot believe this! Sometimes, in the sewing circle, the married women make certain . . . comments. They speak of their duties with such distaste that I shudder to think of what they endure.'

Sarah threw back her head and laughed. 'Those silly geese! What a rod for themselves they make! The marriage-bed need not be such a barren country. Listen to me. I have never lied to you, have I?'

Charity shook her head. 'No. But we have never spoken with such a lack of modesty before.'

'Modesty! What's that but another of the ties that bind you? Forget all you have been taught for the present. There is the world you must live in, my friend. And there is the world inside you. In order to be true to yourself, you must discover that the two go hand in hand. We hold the secret of our own pleasure inside our bodies. Women of all times have had to open themselves to this truth in order to be happy.'

Charity was not sure she understood. Sometimes Sarah spoke in riddles. Her friend thought the settlers lived comical and unnecessarily complicated lives, but it was all very well for her to judge when she was able to go her own way. There were rumours that Sarah had a lover, an Indian brave, who visited her cottage from time to time, but who lived with his people for much of the year. Charity sighed, wishing that she understood more about men and women.

Sarah seemed to empathise with her. 'You need to see something for yourself, then you will understand what I speak of. When you leave here, do not go back across the cornfield, but make a wide circle and enter the settlement by the postern gate.'

'Why?'

Sarah smiled sagely. 'You'll find out. Only remember not to judge too harshly. Learn from what you will see. I am giving you knowledge. Use it as you will, but do not abuse that knowledge. You will understand what I mean later.'

When Charity took her leave of Sarah, a short time later, she was still puzzled. Whatever could she expect to learn by simply taking a walk through the forest? She shrugged, trusting in Sarah's integrity. As she walked she swung her bonnet and lace cap against her full skirts. The rhythm was soothing and dulled her into a mood of relaxation. Before long, she found herself enjoying the beauty of the forest.

Many of the leaves were tinged with the yellow and russet which presaged the approaching fall. Dappled light, like gold coins, coloured the forest floor and the scent of pine resin rose from cushions of slender green needles as she walked over them. The grey-brown bulk of the settlement was visible through the trees and she kept it always on her right, making certain that she did not venture too far into the wilderness where tribes of unfriendly natives dwelt.

Gradually she found herself thinking of her conversation with Sarah. Just recalling the subject made her feel hot and ill-at-ease. Whatever her friend said, she would never be convinced that there was anything of pleasure for a woman in the act of generation. Woman was born to suffer, so said the scriptures, and kick against the goad though she did, she felt at heart that this was the truth.

Her high spirits plummeted as she walked. The men would tell their wives what had taken place at the pig pen. She could imagine the sidelong looks, the expressions of righteous indignation. Well, she was certain of one thing. She would never marry, never engage in that painful disgusting act. It was only beasts and men who saw any merit in it at all.

A flash of colour and a movement between the trees arrested Charity's attention. The sound of laughter high and carefree floated to her on the breeze. She paused, surprised that there should be anyone else in the area at this time of the afternoon. Perhaps a group of children were out checking snares for conies. Then she heard the laughter again. Definitely a woman. Soon after, she heard a man's deep baritone and knew that she had stumbled on a lovers' tryst.

Slowly, taking care to move quietly and hold the folds of her gown against her legs, she advanced towards the source of the laughter.

Ahead of her, she could see that there was a glade, ringed all around with silver birches. Grassy hummocks dotted with wild flowers formed a natural couch for the two figures who reclined there. They spoke in low voices, in which there was a tension that was almost tangible. As Charity watched, the woman sat up, giving Charity a view of the man whose body she had obscured.

'My Lord! Josiah Wainwright,' Charity said under her breath.

And indeed it was he, with a look on his face she had never thought to see. His hollow-cheeked visage was flushed and animated, his flat blue eyes alight with honest lust. He smiled up at the woman, his lips curved with eagerness.

'Hurry and disrobe, Mary. I have longed for thee so and can hardly wait to tup thee,' he said thickly.

Charity's eyes opened wide with shock as she recognised Mary Barber, the minister's wife. She remembered Josiah's words to her and felt a surge of righteous anger. The hypocrite! She took a step forward, was on the point of marching into the glade and demanding to know just what was going on when something stopped her. This was no business of hers. Besides, it would be a crime to see the expression drain from Josiah's face. He looked almost handsome, and happier than she had ever seen him.

Mary too was giggling like a schoolgirl, and her a respectable married woman!

As Charity watched Josiah fumbling with the laces on Mary's woollen basque, she felt an odd fluttering sensation in her belly. It was just like the morning at the pig pen. She recognised the feeling now as anticipation. There was such an air of sexual tension and unbridled enjoyment in the glade that she wanted to see more. Just then Josiah pulled open Mary's basque and dipped both hands into the neck of her shift. With a groan deep in his throat, he drew Mary's breasts free and buried his face in her shadowed cleavage.

Mary gasped as he kissed the fat globes, pressing them together before sucking noisily at her nipples. Writhing against him, she threw back her head, her eyelids fluttering closed with enjoyment. Charity wondered how it must feel to have a man's hot mouth close over her nipple and suckle it like a babe.

When Josiah moved back for a moment Charity saw the thrusting teats which had gathered into hard, puckered buds. They were wet with Josiah's spittle and glowing like dark cherries. Josiah pinched Mary's nipples until her breath came fast and her capacious bosom heaved up and down.

'Oh, Josiah, my lusty. Help me with my skirts. I can hardly wait. I long for thee so!' Mary whimpered with eagerness as Josiah fondled her stockinged calves then slid his hand higher.

'Wait awhile, sweetheart,' Josiah said, moving his hand back and forth beneath Mary's petticoats. 'I'll make thee as slippery as an eel before I tup your sweet quim.'

'Oh, say more of that. When you talk that way, you make me so hot for you,' Mary gasped, sighing with pleasure and rubbing herself against his hand. She opened her legs wide. 'You're a wicked, sinful man with clever, lewd fingers. And I love what you do to me.'

Josiah chuckled huskily. 'Aye, and I do relish you too, my juicy dumpling. Your dimpled thighs, your white breasts, and your wonderful rosy quim are like manna from Heaven to a starving man.'

Charity could hardly believe her ears. This was not the hatchet-faced Josiah she knew. Juicy dumpling! It was laughable, but she felt anything but humour. The place between her thighs was pulsing sweetly. Her own breasts had swollen inside her dark gown and the nipples pushed firmly against her shift. When she made the slightest movement, they scraped maddeningly back and forth, sending little shivers of sensation down to her throbbing groin. She wished that a man would stroke her between the legs, like Josiah was doing to Mary. She too wanted to experience that dream-flush that made the minister's wife so pliant and languorous.

For the first time, she began to see what Sarah meant. There was one world of reality, where everyone must bow to the conventions of faith and law, then there was the inner world of personal experience. Sarah had implored her not to judge, but simply to learn. And she was doing that right enough. She had never imagined that anyone would do what Mary was doing now!

'Oh, Josiah. Enough or I shall spend. Lie back. Let me attend you now,' she said, pushing him back to lie on the ground.

Efficiently she dealt with the buttons on his leather breeches. Chuckling she ran her hand over the bulge at his groin, before sliding her hand inside the opening and pulling down his white linen drawers. With a sound like a low growl she drew out Josiah's erect member, stroking it as if it were a friendly dog. Then she bent her neck and placed a delicate kiss on the skin that covered the cock-tip.

Charity muffled a cry of surprise. Who would have thought that Josiah possessed such a fine crested cock? It had a thick shaft, all fretted with veins, and it reared up from a nest of curling reddish hair. It was all Charity could do to stay silent. She pressed her knuckles against her mouth, watching intently as Mary began licking Josiah's rampant member. After smoothing back the cock-skin with eager lips, Mary took the swollen tip in her mouth and sucked lustily.

Josiah closed his eyes, his face bound by an expression of bliss. 'Oh, Mary. You lovely wanton,' he breathed, his hips working beyond his control and his hands stroking her bulging cheeks. 'You've the lips and tongue of a Jezebel. Ah, you'd best stop soon, or I'll spend in your mouth and be of no manly use to you.'

Mary sat up. Her lace cap was askew and her dark hair stuck out all around her pretty face. Her cheeks were pink and her mouth swollen with kisses. Charity was doubly amazed. In church every Sunday, Mary Barber sat next to her minister husband, her small mouth clenched sourly and a severe expression on her face. Charity had never seen her wearing anything other than high-necked black gowns, trimmed sparsely with white, and her hair stuffed completely under a plain linen coif.

Now Mary looked like a wood nymph. If Charity had been in any more doubt about women receiving pleasure from 'the act', one look at Mary's glowing face would have convinced her otherwise. Mary lay back on a grassy hummock. With both hands she began raising her skirts. She looked gloriously wanton with her naked breasts spilling richly out of her opened basque, her stockinged legs sprawled apart. Josiah knelt between her thighs and helped roll up her skirts until they lay around Mary's waist.

Glancing down between her spread thighs, he

gave a groan. 'Did ever God create a more fragrantly wicked morsel? I would taste you, my lovely, but I fear I cannot wait any longer.'

'Nor I. Do me now, Josiah.'

Placing a hand on the grass on either side of her, Josiah gave a thrust of his narrow hips and plunged his stout member into Mary's willing body.

Charity felt a potent surge of lust and a warm liquid seeped out of her. She could feel the slippery stuff on the insides of her thighs and wondered if it was normal to seep like that. She soon had evidence that it was. She was unable to take her eyes off Josiah's pumping hips and the dark mouth of Mary's wet quim. When Josiah rose up with each thrust, she could see his balls and the base of his cock and the juicy stem as it slid in and out of the hairy red aperture.

Mary groaned loudly and clutched at Josiah's buttocks. 'Ride me, my lusty,' she moaned. 'Ah, yes. That's the way. Do me. Take me. Cleave me in two. Plough me. Plunder me.'

Urged on by Mary's coarse speech, Josiah's hips wove from side to side as he strove to drive her towards her ultimate pleasure. Mary's plump shapely legs waved in the air. She brought her heels down and dug them into Josiah's buttocks, drubbing at him as if she had been wearing spurs.

'Dear Lord, woman. You hot piece. You're insatiable. You'll be the death of me!' Josiah panted.

'Aye! But what a wonderful way to go!' Mary said. 'More. Give me more. Tup me, my lusty. I am almost at my peak.'

Josiah toiled valiantly, his cock so swollen it looked like a knobbly staff. Bending his head he bit gently at Mary's nipples, then nuzzled her white neck.

'Oh. Oh. I'm spending,' Mary moaned, her face twisting into an expression of the purest pleasure. She lifted her hips, her legs spasming and her heels drumming madly on Josiah's bottom.

'So am I. You have undone me,' Josiah said, his breath expelling in a series of loud grunts. 'Ah God, woman. You've milked me dry.'

Charity pressed her hands into her lap, trying to still the ache and throbbing in her sex, but she knew that nothing would make this new longing go away. Nothing would assuage the hunger inside her, but the touch of a man. Now she truly knew what it was to perform the act of generation. And she understood why the act was bound around with secrecy and rules and prohibitions. For if everyone was to follow his or her own natures, then everyone would be doing 'the act' all the time.

And that would never do, because the sacred and beautiful would become boring and mundane. God's greatest gifts were meant to be treasured.

While Mary and Josiah were lying side by side, stroking each other tenderly in the aftermath of their passion, Charity stole silently away. She felt grateful to Sarah for granting her enlightenment and she felt less angry at the men for making her feel uncomfortable earlier. Now she understood that they were guarding their maleness from the greed of women.

With a secret smile she realised that she now had power over Josiah Wainwright. She did not intend to abuse that power, but surely she ought to be able to dissuade him from running to the minister with tales of her misdeeds.

But her thoughts, as she made her way back to the settlement, did not settle on any of these things. The image which crowded her mind was that of Jacob Hawkins in his shirt-sleeves, the muscles of his forearms flexing as he chopped wood, and the way his taut buttocks rolled maddeningly inside his tight leather breeches.

Playing the Game

Selina Seymour

Chapter One

'*KATE . . . ?*'

'I know.'

Steven flinched. Know? How could she know? They never knew until he told them. That was his way. He felt, for a moment, that he was losing control. He swung on his heel and looked at his reflection in the mirror. The sight pleased him and he frowned slightly: not because he saw any flaws, but because frowning, he knew, suited him.

Kate, on the other side of the room, also frowned – but at the flaws that were now etched in her memory for ever. Then, with strong, confident strides, she walked round the bed and stopped, beside Steven, in front of the full-length mirror.

They stood there, looking yet not looking at each other. Steven, accustomed to summoning his feelings when he wanted, began to experience the rare and unwelcome sensation of embarrassment. Kate's face bore no hint of the emotion she felt. Her eyes were blank, refusing to acknowledge that treachery was staring at her. 'I know,' she said, 'because I saw you.'

'Ah.' So he had lost, for the first time, the element of surprise. He shivered imperceptibly. 'So you know that it's over?'

'Yes.'

Steven wanted to look elsewhere – anywhere but in the mirror. They were too close – yet their reflections seemed miles apart. He felt uneasy. Kate had distanced herself from him and she stood, small in stature, but wielding an unspoken, unnerving power. All he wanted from her now was anger, but there was none. Unnecessarily, he adjusted his tie. 'Well . . . you knew that it was going to happen, didn't you?'

'Yes.'

'You knew what the score was?'

'Yes.'

'And you're not angry?'

'No.'

He couldn't take it any longer. Abruptly, he pulled away from the mirror. 'I'm . . . I'm sorry you had to find out that way.'

'Are you?'

His words had tumbled out – meaningless platitudes. Now he found that he had meant them. 'Yes,' he said with feeling, 'I am.'

'Good.'

'So . . . Kate . . . that's it, then, isn't it?'

'Not quite.'

'I beg your pardon?'

'I want you to do one last thing for me.' For the first time, Kate smiled, her full moist lips parting to reveal gleaming, perfect teeth. And for the first time, Steven saw something threatening – almost predatory – in her expression. He had never, he supposed, stopped to consider her beauty and its various components. She had always been just Kate. Pretty little Kate. An adjunct to his perfection.

'Oh!' Steven shrugged. 'Sure ... anything. What?'

Still smiling, Kate went up to him. In one swift movement, she put both hands to his neck and pulled. Hard. His tie; his uniform; his armour fell to the floor.

'Kate. . . !'

'I want you to make love to me. Just this once. Just once more.'

'But . . .'

'And then you'll never see me again.'

Steven stared at her, unable to fathom the expression on her face, nor the reason for her actions. Cute Kate had always been docile. Yet now, standing back from him, she was a creature alive with some strange passion; moved by some demon that impelled her to challenge him. Her expression, he now realised, was almost *mocking*. It excited him.

Kate saw his excitement. Again moving towards him, she smiled into his eyes and then sank to her knees. Her fingers, long talons newly and vividly burnished with red, teased him through the fabric of his trousers. He moaned gently, tilted his head backwards and thrust his pelvis forward.

'Buttons,' whispered Kate. 'I like buttons.' She started to undo them. 'Nothing sharp. Nothing to hurt yourself with. Nothing that can scratch you . . .'

'Kate!' Steven's eyes flew open, the momentary pain causing his sex to deflate in her hands. 'Your nails! Be careful.'

Kate smiled up at him. 'Oh, but I shall, my darling, I shall.'

Steven relaxed at her caressing tones, and smiled as she cupped his ball-sac in one hand and used her nails, gently now, to tease the area beneath it. 'Oh yes,' he sighed. His sex grew erect again, responding to Kate's other hand. 'Better. Much better. That's good.' His hands were now in her hair, rhythmically stroking the tumbling blonde mane almost as if he were trying to coax it, too, into life. He closed his eyes and rocked back and forth as her hand masturbated him gently. Then, as he lunged forward with increasing excitement, he moaned loudly as his cock sank into the warm wetness of her mouth. She took him deep into her – deeper than he'd ever been before. He was lost now, lost in the ecstasies of passion. His only thought was for his own pleasure – and for the satisfaction of having Kate on her knees before him.

But Steven couldn't see Kate's eyes. While her mouth worked rhythmically, automatically, the expression in her eyes was not one of unbridled pleasure, but of cool calculation.

Kate felt a tremor running through Steven's body, an involuntary shudder that heralded the imminence of orgasm. She backed off and got to her feet. With one hand gently massaging his cock, she stroked his face with the other. 'I want you to come inside me,' she whispered. 'I want to keep a part of you within me.'

Steven watched, eyes ablaze with lust, as she

removed her silk dress in one swift movement. She was naked underneath it. She smiled at him. Steven, unaware that, still half-dressed, he looked almost comical, mistook her expression for adoration. As Kate sank backwards on to the bed, he ripped off his shirt and fumbled at his trousers, wincing as the coarse material brushed against his erection.

Kate knew from experience that he would now lunge at her, that his only thought was to sink into her as quickly and as deeply as possible. He had never asked her what she wanted, or how she wanted it. Often he had plunged into her before she was ready, while she was still dry, causing her to wince with pain. But this time she had made herself ready; this time she had plenty of fuel with which to warm herself. And that fuel was anger. For the first time in her life she was using her anger positively, transferring it into energy. Sexual energy. And for the benefit of no one but herself.

Steven launched himself on to her. As his cock cleaved into her, brutally parting her lips, she grunted with satisfaction. Well-lubricated with her own juices, she was more than ready for him. But her eyes, like his, were closed. And her mind, like his, was focused entirely on her own satisfaction. As he thrust into her, Kate moved her legs from underneath him. And then his eyes flew open in surprise as she clamped them around his buttocks, forcing him more deeply into her, binding him to her and keeping him inside her until she was racked by the orgasm that had been prompted by anger, fuelled by deceit and finally released by the knowledge that

213

within the secret folded design of her sex she held the key to power.

Kate laughed out loud at the memory. Steven hadn't wanted to leave. He had said he'd made a mistake, that he really hadn't meant to dump her for Paola. What he had meant, of course, was that he'd never realised Kate could be so good in bed and that he wanted to sample a few more of her unexpected delights before dumping her. Kate had no doubt that he would, in the end, dump her. Lying back and stretching luxuriously, she thought back to their first meeting and the business acquaintance who had introduced her to the darkly handsome, dangerous Steven. 'Admire,' the acquaintance had said, 'but don't touch.' But Kate *had* touched. She had also fallen wildly in love with Steven – and fallen for the oldest self-deception in the world. Now, she merely smiled at her naively. But then, six months ago, she had decided that *she* would be the one to change him. She would love him unconditionally and he, in turn, would fall in love with her and abandon, forever, the string of women who had been his version of a love-life.

Silly Kate, she thought now. Imagine confusing love with sex. Smiling again, she reached for her wine glass. The cool liquid soothed her. It felt good, almost sensual, as she swallowed it slowly. Then she raised one naked leg and pressed the wine glass against it. That, too, felt good. She ran the glass slowly up to her knee, enjoying the sensation of the chill of the glass against the heat of her flesh. She was still high on the afterglow of sex. Smiling wickedly to herself, she dipped two fingers into the wine glass and pressed them against her legs. Her labia were wet already, sticky from the intermingling of her own juices with Steven's come. But the wine added a freshness and a momentary coolness. Idly, she wondered what it would be like to have someone pour wine all over her mound and lick it off. The very thought brought a rush of blood to her head – and a surge of excitement between her legs.

Kate sipped her wine again. There was no hurry for anything now. She felt relaxed, contented with the thought of sex, rather than the actuality of it. Then she frowned. It was Saturday night, and she and Steven had been going to the opera. Now, obviously, they weren't. The old Kate, she mused, would have stayed at home with a book or the television for company, not daring to venture out to such a public place, so patently on her own. But the old Kate was no more; she had been replaced, suddenly and dramatically, by a wanton creature faced with a world of possibilities. A world of sexual possibilities. The old, foolish Kate had been a slave to the myth – her high-powered career notwithstanding – that one day a man would sweep her off her feet.

Again she laughed out loud. It had taken her thirty-three years to realise the truth. She was an independent being, a sexual animal. She had huge reserves of sexual energy she was only just beginning to tap. And from now on she would dedicate herself, once again, to being swept off her feet. But this time there would be a huge difference: she would seek to be bowled over, not by love, but by the weapons that men carried between their legs. She wanted them to surrender those weapons to her; to feel them driving into her, relentlessly, powerfully, endlessly. She wanted to be fucked. She wanted to play men at their own game. And if the men she found were unable to provide her with what she wanted then she would have different men. More men. Any men. She would have as many men as she wanted. She could have several men at once; plugging her orifices and filling her with everything she had ever wanted. And even if they thought they were dominating her they would be wrong. They would be indulging in their fantasies. And Kate would be living reality.

She realised, with a start, that she had lost track of time. With an annoyed glance at the alarm clock, she rose from the bed and wandered, slightly unsteadily, into the bathroom. She had drunk too much wine. She had also lost some of the feeling in her legs. Her blood, her being, her very soul seemed now to be concentrated *between* her legs. Stepping into the shower, she welcomed the sharp needles of water on her face, her breasts, running down her back. She reached for the shower gel and began to wash herself. But not *there*. She wanted still to smell of sex. She wanted to go to the opera and still be aware of her body. She wanted to sit in one of the very expensive seats she had booked wearing a short black dress, a pair of shoes – and nothing else. She wanted to be dirty.

Verdi. She had never before wondered why Verdi was her favourite composer. Now, as she sat in the darkened auditorium, she realised why. His music was unbelievably, almost shatteringly sensuous. It teased the senses in a way that no other music did. It played with you. Listening to it with your eyes closed, thought Kate, was the next best thing to sex.

She wasn't quite sure at what point she realised it *was* sex. Somehow, her imagination had run riot and had interfered with the reality of what she was hearing. *Nabucco*, the tale of banishment from Israel, had become something else in her mind. The heart-rending, sometimes mournful, sometimes shudderingly climactic music had overtaken her senses and in her mind the virgins and the Hebrews were not mourning the loss of their homeland but were playing an elaborate courting ritual. Their sad voices, rising to a defiant crescendo, became instead the actual act of sex; quiet foreplay, gentle cajoling, sudden, violent penetration and then a rhythmic pounding that washed everything away except the glory of the moment.

Kate was swelteringly hot, both because the huge auditorium was jam-packed full, and also because she had worked herself up into such a state that she had become overcome by lust. Opening her eyes, she tried to focus on the stage. Instead, she looked down with horror at her skirt; it had ridden right up to her crotch. Her alarm was intensified by the fact that she could smell herself; sweat, sperm and her own juices, both old and new, contributed towards the heady, raw smell of sex that was suddenly overpowering. She felt at once exhausted, excited and embarrassed.

She also knew she was being watched. The seat next to her – Steven's seat – was empty, and on the other side was the aisle. But two seats away sat a man who was looking at her with undisguised lust. Catching his eye, Kate quickly looked away. Was this really her, she wondered? Had the demure, sensible, high-powered career girl Kate really been openly masturbating in a renowned, majestic opera house? Under her lashes, she looked back at the man. He was still staring at her. Boldly, she stared back. He was dark, extremely good-looking and had a wolfish grin on his face. As Kate met his eyes for the second time, his grin widened. It spoke more of arousal than of amusement. Kate flet a spasm of desire shoot through her. She was already so highly charged that she knew it wouldn't take much more to push her over the top. And then the music started again. It was the beautiful, haunting slaves' chorus that never failed to move her. It started quietly, like a smooth, tantalising caress. She knew it would get louder, more forceful, yet maintaining the same throbbing, sensual rhythm.

She closed her eyes again. She didn't know what to do: give in to her mounting pleasure or try to fight it. She wished she had something in her lap that would take her mind off her desires. Desperately trying to pull down her skirt, she brushed her hand against her sodden mound and realised two things: it was far, far too late to take her mind off sex – and she did have something to play with. Heedless now of the man near her, she parted first her legs and then swollen, tender lips. Her clitoris was already hard, and responded to her touch by sending a shuddering wave of ecstasy through her entire body.

The music was louder now. The slaves were rising up, their voices deep and powerful, calling out to her, filling her ears with their longing. Enveloped in a haze of lust, Kate knew she was with them now. But they weren't calling out for their native soil, they were calling to her. Free of their manacles, they were naked and all around her. Kate was turning in time to the music: at first slowly, then more quickly as urgency filled the air. Except she wasn't Kate any more, she was a virgin from the opera and the slaves were about to ravish her. Her white gown was torn from her body and there were hands stroking her: rough, calloused workers' hands. They were at her neck, her breasts, they were teasing her taut nipples. Then a hand went between her legs, stroking her clitoris and arousing her as she had never been aroused before. And she was begging them. She was begging them to mount her, to take her savagely with their oversized, engorged pricks. She was shouting at them to pound into her in time with the music, to rock back and forth, to match her screams of desire. They had swept her off her feet now; her legs were wrapped round the waist of the largest slave and his massive cock was scything in and out of her as she clung to him. And then the chorus reached its climax; a heart-rending, blissful crescendo that took over all her senses and then left her sprawling, exhausted, spent and satisfied.

At first Kate didn't know where she was when she opened her eyes. She blinked several times at the scene in front of her, unable to separate fantasy from reality. Then she realised she *had* been satisfied. The seat beneath her was damp, the hem of her dress was twisted and wet, and she felt an overpowering sense of contentment.

her briefcase; something to fantasise about; something to dream about until she became so bored and frustrated with work that she would reach for it and, simultaneously, for a telephone.

For Kate knew that she would soon be very bored. Her job had now taken on a new significance for her. Previously, she had relished donning a smart suit, travelling under the awakening streets of London and reaching her faceless office in the City. The anonymity of it all had pleased her. She had been doing what she had been brought up to do – to be dutiful, hard-working, and not to stand out. But now she knew she *deserved* to stand out. She was different. She wasn't just another stockbroker in just another city. She was Kate. Smiling again to herself, she crossed her legs. The pink paper in her lap unfurled and fanned out towards the floor. A few annoyed glances were cast in her direction and her grin widened. For some of the glances hovered for longer than was necessary. Kate was breaking the rules. As she bent down to pick it up she wondered how the people in the office would react to the sudden yet discreet change in her. For she had not been idle on Sunday. She had rifled through her wardrobe, fitting together outfits that she wouldn't normally wear to work: choosing more elegant shoes, deciding on more vibrant colours. And she had thought long and hard about her make-up. Steven had liked her without any. He had liked her to look fresh and innocent; hadn't wanted her to stand out. Now she understood why. Without make-up, Kate looked demure and merely attractive. With it, she looked sensational. She had the features and bone structure of a model: a perfect canvas waiting to be dressed. Well now that canvas *was* dressed.

Kate glanced up, as if by instinct, as the tube pulled into her station. Perhaps, she thought, work wasn't going to be so boring after all.

Outside, the grey and uninspiring weather matched the façade of the building where she had worked for the past four years. It was work she enjoyed; demanding, well-paid and interesting. Yet, just as her leisure time had been set aside to please Steven, so her work hours had been devoted to pleasing others. At Courtenay de Witt, brokers of the old school, women were expected to behave like Victorian children – to be seen and not heard. And they were rarely to be seen wearing scarlet jackets with black skirts.

'Kate!' Robert looked up in surprise as she entered the office and sat down, as she had for the past six months, at the desk next to his. 'You're looking . . . er . . . marvellous.'

Kate smiled sweetly. 'I thought it was time for a change.'

'Um . . . yes, indeed.' Robert looked uneasily to see if anyone else was watching. He liked what she was wearing; he had always secretly thought that Kate, were she to let her hair down a little, would look stunning. Now that she did look stunning, he felt it was inappropriate. Kate, suddenly, was noticeable.

Kate, depositing her bag on the floor and switching on her terminal, looked at Robert out of the corner of her eye. She knew the effect she was having on him and it amused her. Robert, like most of her male colleagues, looked as if he had been created as an unremarkable grey suit, and had chosen a face to match. And now he looked slightly disconcerted. Sex, thought Kate. It was that simple. She now looked like a person who knew what sex was all about. Robert, of course, was prone to bragging about his own sexual activities – they all did that – but on any social occasion he made a bee-line for the 'terrified of women' corner. Initially, Kate had thought he might be gay, until she had realised that they all did that in preference to being stranded – alone – with a member of the opposite sex.

Just then Robert interrupted her reverie. 'You're early,' he said. Then he blushed slightly as she looked him full in the face.

'Yes,' she replied. 'Early meeting.'

'Oh. Those new French clients.'

'Yup.'

'I hear Mark's going over to woo them.' Mark was the newest recruit to Courtenay de Witt's sales team. Smart and good-looking, he was younger than Kate – and more junior. This news about his client-wooing was not entirely unexpected to Kate. Before today, she would have accepted it with quiet resignation, as a fact of life in a man's world. But that was before today.

'Is he really?' replied Kate with a hint of a smile. 'That would be very nice for him, wouldn't it?' Then, looking at her watch, she got up, leaving Robert looking dumbfounded and slightly uneasy. Something, he thought, had got into Kate today. She definitely wasn't herself.

Kate strode into the meeting room. 'Ah,' said Miles Courtenay, the company's chairman, 'there you are.' He looked up without much interest and continued. 'There was really no need for you to come, you know. No need to trouble yourself with these Frenchies.' His blank expression changed as he noticed her bright red jacket. A small, troubled frown wrinkled his perfect, patrician features. Kate, he thought, was uncharacteristically and inappropriately dressed. He let his expression speak for him. He usually did, and especially where Kate was concerned. He prided himself on his tolerance of women. But he couldn't disguise his hatred of clever women.

Kate, however, was not to be put off her stride. She glanced sidelong at Miles, at his dark, attractive, supercilious face. Then she sat down and smiled at the room in general. The two other men present were staring at her as if they had just noticed her for the first time. Their expressions were an almost comic mixture of interest and suspicion. 'I thought,' said Kate to Miles, 'that as I introduced these clients to Courtenay de Witt, perhaps I ought to be the one to go to Paris and formalise the relationship.'

The brief ensuing silence was heavy with surprise – and disapproval. 'I thought,' said Charles Grant, the head of dealing, 'that you weren't keen on going . . . er, abroad.'

Kate smiled. 'I used to think so too. But I feel I've been rather unfair on everyone else' making them do more than their fair share. After all, I started on this project. It would only be fair for me to see it through.'

Miles indicated their junior colleague. 'We were thinking of sending Mark. It would be a good

225

opportunity for him. Y'know, cut his teeth on a blue-chip client.'

Kate looked at Mark. 'And what do you think?' she asked boldly.

Her question had caught Mark off-guard. True, he had been looking at her as she asked the question, but he hadn't been thinking about business. He had been wondering how on earth Kate had managed to escape his attentions thus far. Like many of his colleagues, Mark saw himself as a powerful sexual being. Yet unlike most of them, he had a personal history that would qualify him as such. He liked sex; he had been told he was good at it. And he wanted to have sex with Kate. Her sudden assertion of her position excited him. He liked assertive women. It was something he generally kept quiet about. 'I beg your pardon?' he replied, reddening slightly.

'I said what do you think about Paris? Are you desperate to go? I just thought it would make more sense if I went. After all, you don't know very much about Pharescault, do you?'

Miles Courtenay looked at her, aghast. It was for all the world as if one of the walls had just spoken.

'Kate . . .' began Charles.

But Mark interrupted him. 'No, she's absolutely right, Charles. Kate's the one with all the low-down on French pharmaceuticals. If I went, it would just mean Kate would have to spend long hours briefing me.' He paused and looked cryptically at Kate. 'And that would be rather a waste of time, wouldn't it?'

'Absolutely.' The vehemence of Kate's reply took Mark aback. He looked at her again. There wasn't even a trace of interest in her eyes. Where desire had been brewing in him only moments before, there was now disappointment. It was as if, in Kate's eyes, he didn't even exist.

'Although,' he added after a moment, 'it would, I admit, be a very useful experience.' He turned to Miles Courtenay. 'We couldn't, I suppose, go together?'

'Certainly not.' Miles was adamant. 'Complete waste of money. It's merely a case of flying over, getting the signatures, and flying back again. And as that's the case, I suppose *you* might as well go, Kate. Alone. Do you good to get a day out of the office.'

While this exchange was going on, Kate shot a sidelong glance at Mark. Had he noticed, he would have revised his opinion about her attitude towards him. His suggestion that they go to France together had prompted a vision in her head so strong and so sudden that she thought for a moment she was taking leave of her senses. Mark was good-looking in a way that, up until now, had not appealed to her. Short, blond and almost boyish, he was the sort of man whom she might have described as being sweet. But not now. Not with the vision in her head . . .

It turned out to be more than a day. Livid at Miles for treating her like a peaky child in need of a breath of fresh air, Kate deliberately organised the meeting for Friday. It would enable her to spend the weekend in Paris – to take in the sights, smells and sounds of that city and to shop for the sort of clothes that would suit her new image. But more importantly, it would mean that she could do exactly what she wanted for two days. And she had plans for those two days.

Yet those plans, after the meeting at Pharescault, went by the wayside. The company's chief executive, the Comte de l'Escault-Tonnère, had seen to that. Charming, debonair and evidently much charmed by Kate, he had insisted that she allow him to entertain her for the weekend. At first Kate had demurred, and then laughingly accepted after the Frenchman's repeated protestations. Paris, he had said, was no place for a beautiful girl on her own. Furthermore, it was crawling with tourists at the weekend. She would be much happier, he insisted, with him. His 'place in the country' would, he said with a smile, be much more appealing to Kate. And it would be a pleasure for him to cater to her every whim.

As they sped out of Paris that evening, she glanced at her companion out of the corner of her eye and wondered about his motives. His every action so far had been the act of a perfect gentleman. Furthermore, he was an aristocrat, immensely wealthy, and called the shots in the running of an international and highly respected pharmaceutical company. Yet there was something about him that puzzled her. He was, for one thing, dressed in black. His suit at the meeting had been black, and now he was dressed casually in the same colour. She had to admit that it suited him. The polo-neck accentuated the thick glossy black hair and the swarthy five-o'clock shadow. His eyes, Kate noticed with some surprise, were almost black as well. He was like a darker, more intense, far more attractive version of Miles Courtenay. His car, too, was black.

With a flash of white teeth and an amused grin, the Frenchman interrupted Kate's thoughts. 'May I ask, *m'selle*, what is troubling you?'

'Oh . . . I was just . . . thinking, that's all.'

'Very bad for you. It is the weekend. You are not required to think. You must enjoy. You must relax. You must do just what you want.' With that, the Frenchman deftly reached for the gear stick, changed up a gear and gunned the engine fiercely as they sped uphill. Mechanically, Kate looked at his hand. It was strong, with well-defined fingers and beautifully clean nails. And it was covered with fine black hairs. By comparison, the hands of most of the men she knew appeared somehow antiseptic.

'Actually,' said Kate, 'I was thinking that if I had been a man, would you have invited me to your home for the weekend?'

Again he flashed a brilliant smile at her. 'If you had been a man and I liked you, then, most certainly, yes, I would have invited you.'

'So you entertain a lot, *Monsieur le Comte*?'

'Please! No more of this *Monsieur le Comte* business. It is, as I said, the weekend. You must call me by my Christian name.'

'I don't know your Christian name.'

'It is Nero.'

'Nero?' Kate was surprised. Then she laughed. 'Of course. Nero. Black. What a wonderful name. It's . . . it's so unusual.'

'And you are Kate, yes? Another short name. I like short names. They suggest strength, don't they? Short and to the point.' Then he sighed. 'But, yes, Nero is unusual. And it suggests, as you say, blackness. It was a black day for my mother

229

when I was born.'

Kate looked over at him in surprise. His mouth had drawn into a thin, set line. 'A black day? Why?'

Nero was silent for a moment. Then, as quickly as he had become serious, he relaxed again. He waved a hand in a Gallic gesture. 'Oh . . . it is . . . not important. Perhaps I will tell you one day. But now I will tell you who you will meet at my house.'

When he had first told her that there would be other weekend guests, Kate had been momentarily disappointed. Then she had laughed inwardly. Just because a change had occurred within herself, it didn't mean that she necessarily radiated the freedom, the hunger, the *availability* she felt. Just because Nero had warmed to her didn't mean he wanted to ravish her. And he had, after all, just intimated that it was a matter of indifference to him whether she was male or female. Mark, she thought, would be livid if he knew what he was missing. Kate made a mental note to tell him.

'You will meet,' continued Nero, 'my family.'

'Your parents?'

Nero smiled. 'No, not my parents. My wife. And my oldest friend, Georges, will be there with, I think, his new girlfriend.' He frowned. 'Georges is always having new girlfriends. It seems that he can never find what he wants.'

Kate was silent for a few minutes. She was almost beginning to regret having accepted Nero's invitation. His insistence on asking her had not been due, she now knew, to sexual attraction – but she had flattered herself that he was intent on making sure she had an enjoyable weekend in France. Now she suspected that his only reason for asking her was to dilute a boring family weekend.

As if reading her thoughts, Nero cast her a knowing look. 'You are thinking, are you not, that it will be a boring weekend? It will not,' he continued adamantly, 'be boring. I am a perceptive man, Kate. I have a strong feeling that you are the sort of woman who will enjoy our family weekends.'

Again he flashed her a smile, yet this time it was without any trace of humour. It was almost threatening. Kate felt an involuntary shudder run down her spine. There was definitely, she felt, something odd about this man.

Half an hour later, Nero changed abruptly into second gear and threw the Porsche into a dramatic turn. Kate, who had been on the verge of sleep, was catapulted into wakefulness – and almost on to the floor. Instinctively, she reached out for support. Her hand found Nero's leg. She could feel the taut muscles beneath the expensive material of his trousers. In the darkness, she blushed. 'Oh! I'm sorry.' Grabbing on to the armrest, she pulled herself back into her seat.

Nero, rather to her surprise, patted her hand. 'Don't be,' he said. 'Don't be.'

Kate regained her composure in time to catch a brief glimpse of an imposing gatehouse as they sped up a long, winding drive. Finally, after what seemed like miles, they drew up outside a vast, crenellated sandstone edifice. 'So this,' said Kate, 'is your "place in the country"?'

'Yes. It is very fine, is it not?'

'Beautiful,' sighed Kate as she got out of the car. 'It's ravishing.'

And she could apply, she thought, the same words to Nero's wife. As a dark, silent man whom Kate took to be the butler ushered them into a hall so grand and sweeping that it could have been a church, a tall, elegant woman came towards them. She stretched her arms out towards Kate and smiled. The smile, Kate noted, didn't reach her eyes.

'So,' she said, 'you are Kate. Nero said you might be coming to us. I'm glad you did. I knew you would.'

'*Madame la Comtesse* . . .'

'Please! You are a family friend. You must call me Ghislaine.' Then, waving imperiously at the butler, she indicated Kate's suitcase. 'Fabian. Show Mademoiselle to her room. She is tired after the journey.' Then, turning back to Kate, she announced that they would all meet in the salon in half an hour. 'The salon,' she pointed with a talon-like nail, 'is there.'

Silently, Kate followed the butler up the wide curve of the grand staircase. As a greeting, the staccato-like welcome of the countess was, she thought, very peculiar. Cold. The woman had looked at Kate as if she had been a piece of meat rather than a weekend guest. And her eyes had bored into Kate's as if they had been looking for something. But even stranger had been the words 'I knew you would come.' Surely, Kate thought, the woman hadn't even known of her existence until Nero had phoned her?

After they had trudged for what seemed like miles along a high-ceilinged, chilly corridor,

232

Fabian stopped outside a door, ushered her inside and announced, unnecessarily, that this was her room. Then, as silently as he had appeared in the hall, he disappeared again.

The room was vast. It was also boiling hot – a welcome contrast to the rest of the château. An open fire was roaring in the grate, and two radiators beneath the enormous windows were belting out even more heat. The fact that the room was largely painted red added to the impression of an inferno. Kate shrugged off her coat and sat on the edge of the bed. It was king-sized. She smiled. Would she need this bed? Who did the comtesse think she was going to share it with? Half an hour later, Kate descended to the salon. The others were already assembled. The comtesse, again elegant, rushed forward and took Kate's hands. Kate nearly flinched: the comtesse's own hands were freezing, yet she didn't *look* cold. She was wearing an ice-blue strapless dress that fell simply and beautifully all the way to her feet. Her blonde hair was tied in a chic French plait and her eyes – the same colour as her dress – again bored into Kate's.

'Come and meet,' she said, 'our other guests.' Then she shrugged almost apologetically. 'We are a small party this weekend, but it is better that way. More *intime*, don't you think?'

They were also a strange party. All of them looked with interest at Kate, as if sizing her up. Georges, Nero's oldest friend, was as unlike her host as it was possible to be. Where Nero was tall, lean and muscular, Georges was fat and flabby. Elodie, his girlfriend, was also large, but in a voluptuous, Junoesque way. And her looks, in

233

contrast to the elegant setting of the château, were equally startling. She would not have looked out of place, thought Kate, walking the streets of the less salubrious areas of Paris. Her high heels, vivid slash of red lipstick and dyed blonde hair made her a most unlikely companion for these French aristocrats. They were all, however, charming to Kate. Very attentive. As drinks progressed to dinner and as a succession of fine wines accompanied one course after another, Kate began to realise they were being almost *too* attentive. Ghislaine seemed concerned that Kate wasn't eating enough meat. Nero felt she wasn't drinking enough. Georges said little, but watched her avidly, almost greedily. And Elodie, with her loud, flat voice, paid Kate so much attention that Kate became convinced that the woman was, if not a lesbian, than at least bisexual. She even touched Kate's legs during dinner, in supposed admiration of her dress. As Elodie's hands lingered, Kate became increasingly embarrassed. It was all so odd, she thought. So incongruous in the grand setting of this eighteenth-century dining room. The conversation remained on general topics; on business, on hunting in France as opposed to England, and on matters of taste and style. Trying to distance herself from Elodie, Kate looked to Ghislaine. The comtesse, straight-backed and rigidly formal, was an unsettling combination of ascetic and carnal. Despite the heat of the room, she looked almost blue with cold – an image fostered by her glacial eyes and her dress. Her face was expressionless, yet her mouth was open, ready to devour the piece of rare, bloody meat on her poised fork. In her other hand, in a strangely mannish and inelegant pose, she held a glass of red wine. Kate watched as she tilted back her head, drawing deeply on the ruby-red liquid. Nero, too, was enthusiastically chewing his way through the meat that Kate found indigestible in its rawness. He was also talking to Georges at the same time. Talking with his mouth full, revealing at once sharp, gleaming teeth and chunks of bloodied beef. Flesh, thought Kate. That was the word that stood out this evening. The women were all revealing much of it in their attire. The men were attacking it: everyone was devouring it. Fabian, silent in the corner, was carving more of it from the huge joint that he had wheeled in, with accompanying applause from the table, a few minutes before. The trolley, originally pristine with its white linen cover, was now a brilliant mixture of red and white. The white, thought Kate, for the pure of the untouched. Yet now most of it was impure: a patina of vibrant blood was slowly covering everything.

As she surveyed the room, Kate began to realise that she had already drunk a great deal and that her thoughts were becoming muddled. The room – imperial and imperious in its colours of red, white and gold – was slowly expanding and retracting as she looked at it. The ancestral portraits on the wall began to take on lives of their own. Where they had previously looked aloof, now some were smiling, others frowning. Several seemed to be looking both knowingly and approvingly at Kate. Then, befuddled by the wine, she realised that it was her companions round the table who were looking at her.

Approvingly. And knowingly.

Kate felt a frisson of fear charging down her back. Something was not right. Everyone's teeth were too white; their lips too red. Elodie, in particular, was looking somehow surreal. Her lipstick was now smudged; she was alternately laughing raucously and pouting sulkily. With each expression her lips seemed to take on a life of their own. Now they were a perfect O. Now they were drawn back, cleansed with a little pink tongue that darted back and forth. They were both alarming and inviting. Kate was at once attracted and repulsed.

Suddenly she pushed back her chair and stood up. Holding on to the back of it for support, she looked at Ghislaine and explained weakly, 'I'm sorry. I suddenly don't feel . . . don't feel too well. I think I'd better . . .'

'My dear!' Ghislaine was now all hostess; all concern. She too stood up. 'You poor thing.' She gestured at the table, still laden with food. 'I do hope we haven't overfed you. We are, I admit, somewhat greedy when it comes to culinary pleasures.' She approached Kate. 'Would you like some fresh air – or perhaps you would like to go to bed now? You must do as you please, you know. Make yourself at home.'

Kate smiled in relief. 'I think bed. It's been a long day and I think I'm just over-tired.'

'As you wish. Shall I come up with you?'

'No, no. Really. I'll be fine. And I'm sorry,' she gestured apologetically at the others, 'to spoil dinner like this.'

Nero, now also on his feet, gestured graciously back. 'You haven't spoiled it at all. On the con trary, your presence has enhanced the evening.'

Kate already felt better by the time she reached the dark, chilly hall. Silently, she cursed herself for her behaviour. No wonder they had all been looking at her so strangely. She was the odd one – they were just perfectly normal people, enjoying a sumptuous meal and a closer intimacy than was customary in England. Elodie, Kate felt, was just over-friendly. Any sexual undercurrents had been, surely, figments of her imagination.

Reaching the top of the stairs, she turned along the corridor towards her room and realised, with a pang of alarm, that she couldn't remember which of the many doors was hers. Panic again made her feel slightly dizzy and, in an effort to retain her balance, she grabbed at the nearest object – one of the many classical busts standing sentry beside the walls. As she groped frantically for a hold, she felt a part of the bust give way and, with an almost imperceptible creak, the wall behind it began to slide back. Righting herself and looking round in amazement, Kate saw herself on the threshold of a dimly lit, heavily draped room. Both curious and afraid, she stepped forward.

The room, she was surprised to find out, was a portrait gallery. In between heavily swagged curtains, great gilded portraits looked sombrely at each other across the room. Kate looked briefly around her and was puzzled to see that the secret door through which she had come appeared to be the only entry point to the room. She groaned inwardly. She had, she knew, stumbled upon a secret art hoard. Nero de l'Escault-Tonnere was a collector of stolen works: why else would his treasures be hidden away in this secret room? Miles Courtenay would be furious that she had sullied the spotless reputation of Courtenay de Witt by introducing Nero as a client – and delighted to be able to throw her out of the building as fast as he possibly could.

But, as she stepped forward to survey the paintings, she realised something altogether different. There was another, very good reason why these paintings were hidden, private. They were erotic paintings. For while the backdrops, the clothes and the furnishings on the canvasses spoke of aristocratic opulence, the poses of the figures themselves reflected the ultimate in decadence. Kate felt a frisson of excitement as she surveyed them. On her left was a man dressed in the glorious finery of the era of Louis XIV, with a long black wig and a heavily jewelled and brocaded coat. Yet his expression, unlike that of most paintings of the time, was one of pure, unadulterated joy. It was not difficult to realise why. His erect penis was sticking out of the folds in his frock-coat and was being both held and fellated by a woman on her knees in front of him. And that was one of the less explicit of the paintings.

Suddenly, Kate began to feel dizzy again as she looked around her. One wall was dominated by a huge canvas depicting what would normally be called a conversation piece, with many people sitting and standing in a social situation. But all the people here were in an explicitly sexual situation. In fascination, Kate approached the enormous, gilt-framed painting. It was, she noted, a pastiche of the Dutch School; the room and furnishings were plain to the point of starkness, and the clothing of the figures spoke of puritanism. Yet their actions were the opposite. They all, men and women alike, had exposed, oversized genitals, and they were collectively performing every sexual act imaginable. Beneath a plain table, a partly clad man was performing cunnilingus on a woman who was evidently in a state of blissful rapture. The man, in turn, was being fellated by another woman. Above and around the table were similar scenes of couples, threesomes and foursomes all in the throes of joyful, uninhibited sex. Kate, to her surprise, found herself slightly aroused by the scenes before her. Sex, for her, had never been a spectator sport, yet there was something about this painting that suggested the artist found it a beautiful experience that ought to be shared. He had managed to capture the exquisite agony of people on the verge of orgasm; he had managed to portray genitalia – male and female alike – as objects of great and rare beauty, and there was a lightness and a freshness to the painting. Kate had to fight back her desire to touch the canvas. Instead, she turned round and found herself in front of a portrait that looked, at first sight, as if it were by Rubens. A large, voluptuous woman was lying naked on a sofa in a room filled with flowers of all kinds, but it was one particular flower that formed the centrepiece of the painting – the woman's vagina. Again oversized, it was also over-painted, with subtle pinks and vivid reds contrasting the deep black of the pubic hair. And it was deliberately painted to look like a flower; like some sort of giant lily in full bloom. It was also giving of its nectar to another; to a woman, slimmer but still voluptuous, who was paying homage and squatting on her knees beside the sofa. Her beautiful and incongruously delicate fingers were playing with the flower, teasing the clitoris into hardness and darting into the vagina itself, parting the delicious folds of flesh and exploring its hidden secrets. The smaller woman herself was also getting satisfaction: the full, rounded pink cheeks of her bottom were fully exposed and she was squatting on what appeared to be a dildo. The dildo, somehow, looked like the stalk of another flower; rigid and proud, and painted with a delicate sheen that spoke of moisture flowing from her vagina above. Kate, still reeling from her discovery, nevertheless found the painting highly erotic.

'So! I see you've found our little art collection. Pleasing, is it not?'

Kate whirled round. 'Oh my God! Nero . . . I . . . er . . .'

'You got lost.' Nero, looking almost vampiric in his black dinner-jacket in the lush, red-hued room, was standing by the door. He was also smiling. He approached her. 'It happens, you know, in a house this size. People wandering into . . . strange rooms.'

Kate looked at him. What, she wondered, was this all about? Nero should be highly embarrassed, angry at Kate for stumbling on what she assumed to be his secret perversion. Yet he seemed complacent. She decided to challenge him. 'You knew, didn't you, that I would find this room?'

Nero laughed and shrugged. 'Non! That would have been far too much to expect.' Then he looked her straight in the eye. 'But we were going to show it to you later.'

'We?'

'Yes. We. My wife and I. Elodie. Georges.'

Kate suddenly felt a stab of fear. 'Why?'

Nero twisted his fingers in an elegant gesture. 'Because, my dear Kate, we knew you were one of us.'

'No I'm not! I'm not . . .' Kate looked around her, at the bizarre portrait gallery, at the same time remembering the strange, loaded atmosphere of the surreal dinner downstairs. 'I'm not,' she finished decisively, 'a pervert.'

Nero seemed to find that highly amusing. Throwing back his head, he let out a bellow of delighted laughter. 'Oh my dear Kate, you are so funny. You so *English*. So repressed.' Then he touched her very gently on her breast. The gesture, so intimate yet so casual, sent a jolt through her. Nero noticed. 'But beneath that cool exterior burns an inferno of desire, am I not right?'

Kate could only nod dumbly. She had, she felt, suffered a complete assault on her senses and suddenly felt exhausted. All she wanted to do was go to bed. 'Please,' she said, 'I can't cope with this right now. I feel . . . *odd*. Dizzy and elated, exhausted yet full of energy. I think I'd better go to bed.'

Nero noddd. 'Yes, I'm not surprised you feel like that. But it is, in general, a pleasant sensation, *non*?'

Kate looked sharply at him. How did *he* know what she was feeling like? Then she realised. 'You've drugged me, haven't you? You've given me some awful potion and now you're going to . . .'

'Ssh.' Nero patted her gently on the shoulder as he led her from the room. 'All we have done is give you something that will intensify your pleasure.'

'But I don't *want* any pleasure! How dare you!'
Kate snatched her arm away and stalked ahead
of him. 'It's like you planned this,' she said as he
approached her once more. 'But you *can't* have.
You didn't even know I was coming. I mean, for
God's sake, it was supposed to be a *man* coming
to sign the deal with you.'

Nero looked at her and shrugged again. 'So?
As I said, if I had liked him, I would have invited
him.' He looked shrewdly at Kate. 'Do you think
the man who was supposed to come would enjoy
it here with us?'

Kate turned on him. 'You mean a man would
have had the same treatment from you?'

'Yes. Why not?' Nero looked genuinely
puzzled.

Kate, now at the threshold of her own room
was becoming angry. Yet there was something
else beginning to eat at her. Jealousy. 'So I'm just
a body, am I? A body to be used for your
purposes. A receptacle.' She glared at him. 'A
collection of orifices. That's how you see me, isn't
it?'

'No. You are a person. You are a person who
feels. A person who wants and needs pleasure.'
He shrugged again. 'And you are a woman,
which pleases me. If you were a man that would
please me too.' He paused and looked into her
eyes. 'You find that odd?'

Kate found it more insulting than odd. She also
felt slightly revolted by the idea of Nero with
another man. No man, she felt, was capable of
arousing another in the way that a woman could.
Nero would have to be corrected in his mistaken
assumption. He saw the slight smile playing at

the corners of her mouth. 'You find it amusing, then?' he continued.

'No. I find it . . . interesting. And challenging.'

'So you would like to challenge me?'

'I'd rather interest you.'

They were standing very close now. Kate could smell Nero's breath as he spoke, she could see the healthy pinkness of his mouth and the gleaming porcelain of his teeth. But more importantly she could smell him – the feral, the animal smell of a man in the first stages of arousal. It excited her. So did the teasing word-play that was helping her, too, reach a state of sexual arousal.

'I thought you knew that you *do* interest me.'

Kate lowered the strap of her dress from one shoulder. 'Do you find me as interesting as your portrait collection?'

Nero's hand moved to her other shoulder as he manoeuvred her from the doorway to the bed. 'More so. My portraits are merely portraits. Dead things. You, my dear Kate, are very much alive.'

Kate looked into his eyes. While his tone was teasing, his expression was serious – almost threatening. She shuddered with a mixture of excitement and fear. She was on the bed now, flat on her back. Nero, still fully clothed, loomed above her. His hands, strong, beautiful and clean, were toying with her dress, and as he pulled it down over her breasts her nipples became taut with lust. Kate found his touch unbearably tantalising. It was exquisitely gentle – more of a sensation than a touch. She closed her eyes and let waves of desire wash through her.

'Tell me,' she said in a low tremor, 'about your paintings. Why do you hide them?'

Nero's fingers were now playing with her nipples. 'I hide them because we open the château to the public.' He bent his head to her ear. 'Even the French public would find them hard to digest, don't you think?'

Kate opened her eyes. Nero's dark brows and piercing black eyes were barely inches from her own. 'I think they would find them beautiful.' She shook as Nero's hand descended from her breasts to her stomach and then, agonisingly slowly, towards her sex. Kate had become hardly aware of the fact that he had managed to disrobe her completely. 'The flowers,' she continued through gritted teeth, 'are beautiful.'

Nero's voice seemed to become deeper. 'I agree,' he whispered. 'The *nénuphar* is the most beautiful flower of all.' As he spoke his hand found her clitoris and began to massage the erect, erotic stem. Then his fingers encircled the rosebud pink petals of her sex-lips and began, with excruciating slowness, to penetrate her.

Kate gasped and arched her back. She was beginning to find it almost impossible to concentrate on what Nero was saying. What he was doing to her had all but robbed her of the ability to speak normally. Yet she was aware that their strange conversation was an integral part of their lovemaking.

'What,' she asked through gritted teeth, 'is a *nénuphar*?'

Now Nero's head was between her legs. 'A *nénuphar*,' he whispered, 'is a water lily.' His hands were somehow all over her, pressing more urgently on her skin, stroking her and filling her with strange sensations. And he was speaking in short, staccato bursts, his tongue now forming a word, now darting forward to taunt her clitoris and tease her vulva. 'It is also . . . the slang word . . . for a vagina. A pretty word . . . is it not?'

Kate could only groan in reply. She could feel that she was soaking wet between her legs – and not just from the ministrations of Nero's expert tongue. Her own juices were flowing like a life force. Again, she started to feel delirious. But this time she wasn't sure if it was from the effects of whatever drug Nero had given her, or from the way he was going down on her. She didn't care. All she cared about was the exquisite pleasure Nero was giving her, the thundering sensations between her legs and the shattering orgasm that was sending spasms through her body.

She was so engrossed in her own pleasure that she didn't hear the door opening nor the gentle tread of several footsteps. Her mind was concentrated on her water lily – her *nénuphar* – and on the fact that Nero had stopped talking and was tasting the sweet elixir of her juices. No man had ever spent so long tonguing her. She was in heaven. Only after a moment did she realise that there was something wrong with the position of Nero's hands. No one, not even an Olympian sexual performer, could massage her breasts and her hair while their head was buried between her legs. A wave of panic shot through her and she opened her eyes.

The first thing she saw was the vivid scarlet gash of Elodie's mouth. The woman appeared to be completely naked and she was kneeling on the bed beside Kate. And it was her hands, their fingers painted the same red as her lips, that were massaging her body so gently, so softly – and in perfect imitation of Nero's touch. Kate opened her mouth in horror, yet before she could say anything one of Elodie's hands was on her lips.

'Hush, *chérie*,' said the Frenchwoman. 'You were enjoying yourself, *hein*?' She smiled tenderly at Kate. 'Why stop now?'

Kate turned her head, freeing her lips from Elodie's hand. She was wide awake now, fully conscious of all around her. The unexpected arrival of Elodie really threw her; left her feeling vulnerable and exposed – and curious. Half angry and half ashamed, she tried to draw her legs up, to curl out of her position of wanton desire. Yet her ankles were caught in the vice-like grip of Nero's hands. Still fully clothed, he was standing at full height, looking down at her with an inscrutable expression. 'Elodie is right. You were in ecstasies. You were enjoying your pleasure. Can you not enjoy *our* pleasure?'

Kate was caught between doubt and desire. She *had* been enjoying Elodie's skilled fingers; she had been delirious at the sensations Nero's finger and tongue had been providing. And she felt unfulfilled. She had been waiting in agony for Nero to enter her, to ride her hard and roughly. And she still desperately wanted to give him pleasure.

But she was confused – and someone recognised that confusion. A voice on her left suddenly distracted her from Nero's grinning face and Elodie's pendulous breasts and petulant mouth. 'Perhaps,' said the voice, 'our Kate needs time to get used to Elodie's divine touch? Perhaps she is unaccustomed to the delights of her own sex.'

Kate turned her head to find Georges standing on the other side of her bed. But it was a completely different Georges to the man she had been dining with only an hour previously. This Georges was naked and sporting the biggest erection Kate had ever seen in her life. Jutting out proudly from a heavy, hairy scrotum, it arched towards his rotund belly and stood glistening, powerful, red-veined – and ready. Georges noticed her expression and laughed delightedly. 'It is enormous, my *bitte*, is it not?' He stroked the head, causing it to spasm in excitement. Before Kate could reply, Georges knelt on the bed and started clambering over her. 'Worry not, *ma chérie*, it is destined for Elodie. Look! Her hungry mouth already open in anticipation.'

It was true. Elodie's eyes were gleaming at the sight of her boyfriend's prick and her tongue was moistening her lips in readiness for George's invasion. Yet those were not her only signs of arousal. In silent fascination, Kate watched as Elodie began to finger herself. Like everything else about Elodie, her pubis was larger than life. She was pouting open, her tender sex-lips standing swollen and puffed up with the blood of excitement. Between the folds, her clitoris was a solid throbbing knot, protruding proudly and begging to be touched. Kate had a sudden desire to touch it, yet years of sexual convention held her back; generations of social taboos stopped her from wallowing in the pleasure she knew she might receive.

Instead, as Georges knelt on her other side and Elodie lowered her head to his groin, Kate began to finger herself. Her hand was sharply smacked away. 'Enough!' It was Nero, still standing between her legs, and naked now. His nakedness was more pleasing that that of Georges; as Kate suspected, his body was powerful and finely honed. Where Georges had sagging, excess flesh, Nero had muscles. His prick, too, was different. Kate shivered involuntarily as she looked at it. It was sleek, rigid and perfectly sculpted. Nero bent Kate's legs so that her knees were pointing to the ceiling and, still standing, edged closer to her so that his rock-hard thighs pressed against her bottom. For one panic-stricken moment, Kate thought that he was preparing to enter her rear passage, to ravage her in a place where she knew it would hurt. But he just stood there, his towering, tantalising prick inches from her still-wet pussy. 'Watch,' he commanded. 'Watch Elodie and Georges.' His smile was both threatening and lascivious. 'You will learn something.'

Kate, still too stunned to say anything, did as she was told.

And she learned. She learned that it was possible to fellate a man as massive as Georges. Elodie's lips were stretched to straining point, yet she continued to take inch after inch of Georges's throbbing member into her mouth. The muscles of her throat were, Kate noticed, visibly expanding and contracting as she orally massaged the giant cock. Georges now began to thrust with his hips, to force his all into her willing mouth. Clumsily, he grabbed Elodie behind the head and pushed her further on to him. Kate was so close that she could hear Elodie breathing through her nose.

And then the full length of the gleaming weapon was buried in Elodie's face. Her chin, with each movement of Georges's hips, banged against his scrotum. Kate was not only astounded – she was extremely aroused. Yet she had no way of satisfying herself. Every time her hand went to her own pulsating vulva, Nero slapped it away. She pleaded for him to enter her, but he wouldn't. Only Elodie's own sex was near enough for her to touch. Yet still she couldn't bring herself to put her hands between the other woman's legs, to play with the damp, shiny petals so similar to her own yet so forbidden to her. Suddenly Georges pulled his cock free of Elodie's mouth. The sound of flesh meeting wet flesh was replaced by the laboured, gasping noise of Elodie fighting for breath. But it was clear she wanted more. She grabbed Georges round the hips and tried to force him back into her mouth. He needed no encouragement. Amply lubricated by Elodie's saliva, he slid into the tight sheath of her mouth and pumped back and forth, each movement heightening the sexual frenzy of the couple, and driving Kate into a state of impotent, desperate arousal.

Nero still held her ankles beside his thighs and next to her bottom. She was, from the waist down, immobilised. And still her hands refused to reach out for Elodie's sex. She tried to massage Georges's ball, to feel the passionate heat of his flesh, but again Nero stopped her.

'Please,' she moaned. 'Please Nero! Do something ... fuck me, for God's sake! I want you, can't you understand? I want you inside me!'

Nero laughed, a deep, guttural sound from

deep down in his throat. 'You want,' he teased, 'this?' As he spoke, he suddenly jabbed his rock-hard manhood against her throbbing sex.

'Yes!' she cried. 'But don't tease me. *Please*, Nero!' Her eyes were closed, her legs were quivering and her entire body was riven by frustration. She wanted to be filled. And still she was empty.

But Nero was enjoying teasing her. Repeatedly, he pressed the knob of his cock against her, occasionally into her, and then withdrew; playing with her, promising her, he was driving her mad with lust and demented with desire. Still with her eyes closed, Kate felt rather than saw Georges and Elodie change position beside her on the bed. She didn't want to look; didn't want to witness what would no doubt be the tumultuous climax of their desires.

And then Nero plunged. In one movement, he prised her legs further apart and entered her. Kate's whole body spasmed at the suddenness of it, and at the equally sudden, gloriously intense spasm of pleasure she didn't expect to feel. Nero uttered not a word. Like a finely tuned, well-oiled machine, he pistoned into her again and again, withdrawing almost completely with each thrust and then lunging back into her. For Kate it was complete ecstasy; each time he entered her it seemed like he was plunging deeper than any man had been before, and each time he sank into her depths his steely thighs smacked hard against the tender flesh of her bottom, making her feel like she was an integral part of a beautiful, perfect machine.

Nero's heaving shoulders lunged against her

still-bent legs, yet he remained in a semi-standing position. Kate wanted him to bend closer, to meet her mouth in imitation of the way his loins were meeting hers, yet his whole body remained between her legs. Kate didn't know if the effects of the drug were again washing over her or if she was simply stuck in the exquisite agony of being only semi-satisfied, but she was beginning, once more, to feel disorientated. As her eyes opened and shut in time with Nero's thrusts, she realised that someone was looming over her. In the flickering light of the room, she made out the flabby form of Georges and the silhouette of his erection. With horror, she knew that he was going to force himself down her throat, to ravage her mouth and throat, to inflict real pain on her. The muscles of her vagina clamped around Nero's manhood. The movement was made in fear, yet it drove both of them to further heights of desire. and then she realised that Georges was standing with his back to her and she saw, through the V of his legs, the willing target he was aiming at: Nero's mouth. She saw Nero's eyes glint with desire, saw him arch back and withdraw from her. And then he entered her again, this time with even greater force and a renewed hardness. And this time he did bend forward, but to Georges, not her, to encircle Georges's erection with his lips and to savour him just as he was savouring Kate.

Kate moaned. She had lost touch with her feelings – or had she? She was excited and revolted. She was being ravaged by a man she sought to please, yet he in turn was being ravished by another man. It was a situation so alien to her previous experiences that she had nothing to compare it with. She hardly knew what was happening. Her entire body was convulsed with desire, yet whose desire? Nero's thrusts had become less intense. He now seemed to be exploring her, massaging her inside – just as Georges was exploring Nero's mouth, massaging the pink wetness of his throat. The two movements were as one. Everything was as one. The rivulets of her own juices were the same as Nero's juices: they flowed from her sex; they flowed from his mouth; they lubricated the lascivious beast with three heads that they had created on this heaving bed of desire.

But there were four of them on the bed, four naked bodies seeking supreme satisfaction. Elodie was the fourth. Clever, experienced and patient, she had been waiting for this moment: waiting until Kate was so utterly consumed by the conflicting kaleidoscope of sex that she would be unable to resist. And this time she didn't – and couldn't – resist. She saw Elodie manoeuvring into a position above her, blocking out her view of Georges's writhing hips and then squatting above her face. As Elodie's quivering, moist sex loomed over her mouth, Kate knew she was about to experience the ultimate in sexual gratification. And it seemed so *right*. Nero was still pleasuring her, now bringing her to the brink of orgasm. Georges was still making love to Nero's mouth, sharing with him the ultimate taboo of man-to-man sex. But it was Elodie who now made the portrait complete. Drinking in the familiar, heady aromas from the secret folds between her legs, Kate began to taste, for the first time in her life, the juices of another woman. It was as if she had been performing cunnilingus all her life. Parting Elodie's swollen labia with her urgent tongue, she found the rigid clitoris and began to caress it. Then, matching Nero's thrusts into her own body, she let her tongue dart in and out of Elodie's sex. It was as if she was masturbating, being fucked and *being* masturbated – all at the same time. She licked again and again, her strokes becoming faster as Nero teased her towards orgasm; towards his own orgasm; towards Georges's and towards Elodie's. Once more, everything was as one, and the juices now running down her face became her own; the nector spattering on to her belly as Georges withdrew from Nero's mouth became the seed entering her as Nero himself ejaculated. Her body was the catalyst. Three people were joined together above it, and as it spasmed and shook with the glory of ultimate fulfilment so the others reached their peak of satisfaction and filled the room with a harmony of lust.

Passion spent and pleasure achieved, the others collapsed around her. Kate hardly knew what did and didn't belong to her own body. Everything and everyone was the same, each pulsing heartbeat matched the other and each body secreted the heady, animal aromas that come from secret places and linger sweetly in the aftermath of desire.

Yet there was a sound in the room that Kate couldn't place. As her breath came more easily, as the stroking hands around her subsided into stillness, the noise seemed louder. Turning her head towards the fireplace, Kate searched for its source. Her befuddled brain refused to take in

Then someone touched her and she screamed. She opened her eyes in panic and saw a face grinning at her. This face, too, puzzled her. It was a man's face, but she didn't know him. He was good-looking in a slightly effeminate way and, like Nero, had perfect teeth. Unlike Nero he had a gentle, kind face. Kate wondered why such a face should disturb her so much.

'I'm sorry,' said the man. 'I didn't realise you were sound alseep, but we're two minutes from Heathrow. Please,' he added with another smile, 'fasten your seat-belt for landing.'

Kate stared blankly at him. What on earth, she thought, was this stranger on about? Then, bleary eyed, she looked around her and remembered where she was. She was, of course, in the plane going back to London. The steward, lingering for a moment, looked on in amusement as she gathered her wits. 'You must,' he said, 'have had quite an exhausting weekend.'

If only he knew, thought Kate. If only he knew.

She cast her mind back to the bizarre events of Friday night at the chateau. She knew for sure that the orgy on her bed had not been a dream, for when she had woken up – alone – on Saturday morning, there were enough lingering reminders of the night before. The smell, for one thing. The musty, heady smell that still permeated her bedroom was the smell of stale sweat, of bodies that had mingled together. It was neither pleasant nor repugnant. It was just there. And then there had been her own body, still tingling with the incredible sensations of her night of sex. Her legs were sore, her neck was stiff, but it was the place between her legs that most reminded her of a night of frenzied love-making. Nero's pile-driving pounding had left its mark. She remembered the sight of him naked, the taut muscles and the rampant cock that had reminded her of a steely, indestructible weapon. How long had he fucked her for? Kate had no idea. All she knew was that she had enjoyed him more than she had ever enjoyed another man.

But if Friday night had been strange, Saturday was even more bizarre. Kate had descended to the ground floor of the château after a long, hot bath and a breakfast brought to her by the inscrutable Fabian. Seeing Ghislaine and Elodie in the salon, and feeling uneasy about meeting them after that extraordinary night, she had approached them with some trepidation. She needn't have worried. From their conversation, the previous night may not have happened.

Ghislaine, warmer and more welcoming than yesterday, had been full of solicitude about her guest's welfare. Had she slept well? Had she breakfasted to her satisfaction? Elodie too was different. Bubbly now where she had been brash, less tarty than the night before, she was full of girl-talk and bombarded Kate with questions about where she bought her clothes, where she lived in London, and where the best restaurants in that city were to be found. Kate, slightly nonplussed, had played along with them.

The whole day had continued in that fashion. Nero and Georges, returning from a tour of inspection of the chateau's parkland, took them all out to lunch at a nearby restaurant. The afternoon had passed in a leisurely fashion, with walks in the garden, words of praise from Nero about her performance at yesterday's meeting at Pharescault – yet not a word about her performance that night. During an even grander dinner in the chateau, when they were joined by two more French aristocrats and a clutch of obviously wealthy neighbours, the conversation became even more formal and revolved around generalities.

Nero was the consummate host; Ghislaine, expertly attentive to all her guests, talked, of all things, about her children. Kate was mildly shocked to discover that the two young Escault-Tonnères were in their early twenties. Old enough, she mused, to play the same games as their parents. But again she was having doubts about the reality of those games. Despite the soreness between her legs and the pungent smells of that morning, she was ready to admit that they had not been games but dreams – until the man on her left asked her what she thought of Nero's famed portrait collection. A slight smile played on her lips as she prepared to respond. But Nero, two places away, had also heard the question, and had noticed Kate's expression. Something impelled Kate to look at him before she replied – and his own expression wiped the smile immediately off her face. She had never seen anyone look so thunderous, so threatening. Turning back to her left, she replied that, yes, she was greatly impressed by the glorious paintings gracing the walls of the chateau. It wasn't until a few minutes later that she could steal another look at Nero. He was still watching her, and had evidently been listening to every word of her conversation. Catching her eye, he nodded and smiled curtly in approval. So it *was* all true, thought Kate. She hadn't dreamed of a sexual marathon, she had participated in one.

As she fastened her seat-belt for the descent to Heathrow, Kate examined her feelings about the weekend. Today, Sunday, she had been driven to the airport by Fabian, after fond farewells from Nero and Ghislaine, and entreaties to visit again. And still they hadn't mentioned Friday night. Ghislaine had even apologised that Saturday's dinner had gone on for too long, keeping Kate from the comfortable bed to which she no doubt wanted to retire. She had, eventually, retired – alone – to spend an uneasy hour wondering if she would remain alone. She did.

Why, she thought? Why the extraordinary, frenzied performance of Friday night? And why no mention of it throughout the remainder of the weekend? It was as if her hosts had two identities, as if they were split personalities operating on two entirely different, completely separate levels. Then, as the plane touched down, Kate felt a jolt totally unconnected with the reverberation of the wheels meeting the tarmac. The jolt was within her – it was a realisation that she too had a split personality. She, since her split from Steven, was two different people. She was Kate the capable stockbroker during the day, and she was an insatiable, sex-crazed siren at night. With a smile, she remembered that this was her own decision, that she had deliberately set out to lead a double life. She should, she supposed, find it flattering that the Escault-Tonnères had so quickly established what lay beneath her cool, calm exterior. Yet something about the weekend caused Kate to frown: had she been used by her hosts, or had she used them to satisfy her own urges? It had probably been a bit of both, but they had undoubtedly called the shots.

Suddenly decisive, Kate sat upright in her seat. Nobody, from now on, would call the shots. She would be the one to decide where and when she would indulge herself. And when she saw Nero again – as she would, business-wise, on numerous occasions – she would be more careful. But then again, she thought with a wicked grin, perhaps she owed him something. A foursome? Sex with another woman? But for Nero, Kate would have experienced neither. She felt a twinge between her legs as she remembered those experiences. Perhaps she did owe something to Nero. She would, she decided, find a special place for him in her favours.

A few minutes later she stepped confidently out of the plane thinking, with pleasure, of Nero and the future. Had she been a clairvoyant, pleasure would have been the last thing on her mind.

Mark was the first person she saw in the office as, the next morning, she entered the corporate finance department of Courtenay de Witt.

'Kate!' He appeared to be genuinely pleased to see her. Evidently he had not been with the company long enough to learn the art of treating women with certain suspicion and not a little contempt.

Kate couldn't help returning his cheerful grin. 'Hi! Good weekend?'

'Oh,' Mark shrugged eloquently. 'So-so. And you? How was the dashing French count?'

'Oh . . . dashing. Very formal, very correct.' She smiled again. 'And very rich. I spent the weekend at his château.' Seeing Mark's expression, she added quickly, 'With his wife and family.' She wondered what Mark's reaction would have been if she'd added, 'And with his cock buried inside me for half the night.'

'Oh.' Mark looked slightly peeved. He had, Kate remembered, hoped to do the Paris trip himself. 'Lucky you.' Then he looked, frowning, into the mid-distance. 'Doesn't he own the Château de Grassigny?'

'That's the one.'

'Fabulous art collection there. World famous, I believe.'

'It wouldn't surprise me in the least,' replied Kate as he walked towards her desk. 'It was certainly most . . . illuminating.' Mark, she decided, was an innocent. Charming, well-meaning, but innocent – and certainly not, in reality, the man she had fantasised about on Friday. That fantasy, that blatant, powerful vision, rather embarrassed her now, and more for Mark's sake than her own. And she really shouldn't tease him. He might, for one thing, develop fantasies about her. And she had enough fantasies of her own to keep her busy for some time.

Sunday night had been restful, but not idle. She had spent much of it itemising everything she wanted to experience sexually. The only problem, she now realised, was how? Looking around her at the bland occupants of Courtenay de Witt, she was fairly sure that – Nero apart – work and pleasure would be mutually exclusive. As she sat down at her desk she carelessly deposited her bag on the floor. Too carelessly, as it happened. The bag was open, and it fell on to its side, spilling its contents all over the floor.

'Bugger.' Kate scrambled to the floor and started picking up all her personal, essential items. She did so with some embarrassment. Men, she thought, didn't have this problem. Men didn't need lipstick, make-up, combs and all the other paraphernalia requisite to being a woman. Mind you, she reflected, how many women needed *three* lipsticks, several toffees, old eye-liner pencils, loose change in several currencies, and several loose business cards? Certain that Robert, on the phone at the desk next to her, was silently laughing at her, she blushed and swore that tomorrow she would buy a new bag. A smaller one.

In her panic, she failed to see one of the business cards that had ended up some way from the others. It was Mark, again passing her desk, who saw it lying on the floor. 'Is this yours?' he asked casually, bending to pick it up.

Kate turned and smiled gratefully. 'Oh, yes, I think it must be. I . . . I, er . . . dropped my bag.'

'Careless.' Mark looked at the crisp white card in his hand. 'Just as well you dropped it.' He grinned. 'It's not as if it's got "this belongs to Kate" stamped all over it.' With that he flicked the card on to Kate's desk and walked off.

Kate stared at the card. She had forgotten about its existence. Again, she felt a hot flush burning her cheeks as she remembered how it had come into her possession.

It was the card left by the man at the opera.

They met at the Ritz. Kate, feeling that phoning from the office would be, to say the least, wildly inappropriate, had phoned him from a call box. And even that had been difficult. She didn't know his name: he didn't know hers. Not a word had passed between them. Their voices would be those of strangers. The only way she could announce herself was as 'the girl from the opera'.

'Nabucco?' was the succinct reply.

'Yes,' said Kate. 'Nabucco.'

'Ah. I seem to remember that you enjoyed the performance.' The voice, deep, slow and well-modulated, matched exactly the chiselled, wolfishly elegant face of the man who had watched her bringing herself to a shattering orgasm. 'I certainly,' he continued, 'enjoyed your performance.'

'I thought you might have.' Kate was confident, in control. She had, after all, nothing to lose and everything to gain. She was speaking to the only person – apart from the occupants of the Château de Grassigny – who knew of her newly awakened, voracious sexual appetite. 'I wondered,' she continued, 'if we might meet.'

'I could think of nothing more delightful.' He paused. 'Tonight?'

Kate considered for a moment. Should she play hard to get? If so, why? She didn't want to be hard to get. That was why she was phoning him. 'Yes. Tonight would be fine.'

'Good. Shall we say the Palm Court at the Ritz? Seven o'clock?'

*

At quarter past seven Kate walked into the hotel and made her way through the sumptuous hallway to the gilded splendour of the Palm Court. It took her but a moment to identify the man from the opera. Smiling, she marched towards him as he stood up and extended his hand in greeting. They could, thought Kate, have been old friends meeting for a casual drink, such was the easy intimacy that somehow already existed between them.

'Hello,' he said. 'How nice to see you again.'

'And you.'

'Please,' he continued, indicating a chair, 'sit down and have a drink.'

'I see,' replied Kate as she saw the bottle of vintage Veuve Clicquot in the wine cooler beside him, 'that you're fairly confident about what I'm going to drink.'

He raised an eyebrow in mock amusement. 'I'm confident that you're the sort of girl who enjoys the good things in life, but I'll order orange juice if you prefer.'

Kate laughed. 'No thanks. Champagne fits the bill rather nicely after the beastly day I've had.' As if by magic, a glass, filled by a discreetly hovering waiter, appeared in her hand. She raised it towards her companion. 'To . . . to what?'

He returned the gesture and smiled. 'I was hoping you'd be able to tell me.'

Kate, enjoying the sensation of appearing close to someone whose name she didn't even know, shook her head. 'No. Not fair. You started this.'

'All right.' Again he raised his glass. 'To the future.'

'Whose future?'

He looked searchingly into her eyes. 'Yours.'

'And do you feature in this future of mine?'

'I might.'

'Mmm.' Kate twirled one long finger round the stem of her glass. 'Intriguing. Especially as I don't even know your name.'

'And I don't know yours.'

'There we are then. Stalemate.'

'Don't you think,' he asked, 'that's rather exciting? Not knowing each other's names.'

'It might make life a little difficult.'

'I prefer the word challenging.'

Nero, Kate remembered, had used that word. 'So you want to challenge me? Is that why you gave me your card?'

'I thought I might . . . offer you something. A challenge, I suppose, of sorts.'

'Even more intriguing.'

The man leaned closer to her. He was, she felt, very attractive. With his swept-back hair, widow's peak and piercing, deep-set eyes, he should also have appeared predatory. Yet, strangely, he seemed nothing of the sort. He made Kate feel safe. And it was, she thought, an even more peculiar situation.

'Not many girls,' he began quietly, 'would make such an exhibition of themselves at the opera. If we're talking intriguing, then *that* particular episode fits the bill, don't you think?'

Kate considered for a moment. 'No. Not really,' she said at last. 'Intrigue implies mystery. I don't think there was anything particularly mysterious about what I was doing.'

'Agreed. But I found the *impetus* behind it mysterious. Why that opera? Why the empty seat beside you? Why did you carry on once you'd become aware of me?'

'So you think I was doing it for your benefit?'

This time it was he who considered for a moment. 'No. I don't think you were. I think you were doing it entirely for yourself. The fact that I was aware of you made it only more exciting for you. I think that gave you a feeling of power. I think seducing me was the last thing on your mind.'

Kate really *was* intrigued. Whoever and whatever this man was, he was spot-on about her feelings that night. 'But I did, in a way, seduce you. You gave me your card.'

'Strictly speaking, I only gave you a piece of card with a telephone number written on it.'

'*Your* telephone number.'

'One of my telephone numbers.'

'My. How important you must be. Lots of telephone numbers. For lots of girls, perhaps?'

Her companion stopped with his glass midway to his lips. Again he looked deep into her eyes. 'Something like that,' he said.

'Don't you think,' replied Kate, 'that it's about time we stopped playing games?'

'Don't you like playing games?'

'I do. I love playing games. But they are all ultimately serious, don't you think? And then there has to be a point to them.'

Crossing his legs and taking another sip of champagne, he contemplated her again and appeared to come to a decision.

'Yes. You're right. There was a serious reason why I gave you my number, and there is a point to this conversation.' He paused. 'I want you to work for me.'

'To *work* for you?' Kate was stunned. Whatever she had expected, it certainly wasn't a job offer. She straightened her back, sipped her drink, and retorted defiantly, 'I already have a job, thank you.'

He took in her elegant pink jacket, Hermès scarf and short black skirt. 'A good job too, by the look of you. I suggest you keep it. Evidently it pays rather well.'

'It does.' Kate eyed him speculatively. She was beginning to think she knew what the point of this encounter was. He had more than one telephone number. He hadn't denied her accusations about lots of girls. And he wasn't asking her to give up her current job. The only thing he knew about her was that she was uninhibited. She felt a sudden rush of adrenaline – through fear, or excitement? – as she challenged him. 'You're a pimp, aren't you?'

As she said the words, she realised how inappropriate, how inelegant they sounded in the plush, hallowed confines of the Ritz. Her companion obviously thought so too. He laughed at her outburst, a deep, hearty yet friendly laugh. Then he gestured expansively around him.

'Are you trying to get us thrown out of here?'

'No. I'm trying to get you to the point, remember?'

At that he shrugged good-naturedly. 'So you are.' Suddenly he was serious again. 'Since you ask such a direct question, you deserve a direct answer. No, I'm not, as you say, a pimp. I am, however, in a strange position of having a large number of . . . of business contacts who are not averse to the company of beautiful, accomplished and intelligent women who . . .'

'Who like sex?'

'Yes. In a word.'

'So you're offering me a job as a high-class call girl?'

For the first time, the man opposite her answered her without a smile. Beating the nearby waiter to it, he leaned forward to refill Kate's glass. 'Actually, I'm not offering you anything at all yet.'

'I don't . . .'

'I mentioned a challenge, didn't I? That is all I can provide for you at the moment.'

'Supposing I don't want this challenge of yours?'

'You, if you remember, were the one who phoned me. That rather implies that you accepted the first challenge, doesn't it?'

Kate had to let him score the points on that one. Silently, she cursed herself for not playing more of the waiting game. 'All right,' she said, 'I admit that. So what's the second challenge?'

'Well, my dear. I can see that you're beautiful. I know that you're educated and intelligent. You're undeniably sophisticated. You ooze class out of every pore.' He bent forward again and smiled into her eyes. 'But are you any good at sex?'

Kate acepted the challenge. This man was every bit as sophisticated as herself, equally intelligent, and – more importantly – she trusted him. She didn't know why, but she had the distinct feeling that he was completely above board and that he would give her what he went on to promise: a great deal of money for discreetly 'entertaining' a few well-chosen clients. Furthermore, the fact that her sexual prowess would be tested by what he called 'his boys' rather than himself appealed to her. She wanted this man to be a friend and an equal. Attractive as she found him, she was not sexually attracted to him. Nor did she want sex between them to be an issue that could complicate their putative relationship. She found the nature of that relationship almost as arousing as sex itself.

And she turned on by the idea of 'the boys'. After they finished their drinks and left the Ritz, they crossed Piccadilly and went into the narrow maze of streets that housed some of London's most select shops – and most salubrious addresses. This was where the flat – her place of work if she rose to the challenge – was located. This was where the boys were waiting.

'You are really quite arrogant, you know,' said Kate as she followed him through the streets of Mayfair.

'Me?' Again the raised eyebrow, the look of mock amusement. 'Why do you say that?'

'Because you seem to have mapped out a new . . . a new interest for me all on the strength of a night at the opera when I got a little carried away.'

' "A little carried away". Is that what you call it?' He laughed good-naturedly. 'I would call it something else. But,' he added seriously, 'you must remember that I have a lot of experience in spotting new . . . er, talent.'

'Hmm. The girls. The lots of girls. Does each one have a different telephone number for you?'

'Yes. I operate a very discreet business. Nobody

has access to anyone else. That way nobody gets hurt.'

'And do none of them know your name?'

'No.'

'And you don't know their names?'

'Not usually, no.'

'But that's insane! How on earth do you communicate with each other?'

'You are the only person in the world who has the telephone number you called me on. If you end up working for me, that telephone will be your only means of contacting me. We don't need names for that. It always operates that way.'

'But what if *you* want to get in touch with *me*?'

'I shall leave a message at the flat.'

'The flat we're going to now?'

'Yes. Your flat.'

'My flat! Wait a minute! You don't think you can buy me, do you? Anyway, I've already got a flat.'

Her companion seemed uninterested in this piece of information. 'Presumably you go to an office to do your work during the day? Yes, I thought so. So if you get this job with me, the flat will serve the same purpose. Your place of work. Nothing more. You won't own it and I can assure you I'm not trying to buy you anything. I am intending to employ you, that's all.'

'This is all very clinical.'

'It's a business. You look like a business-woman.'

'I am.'

'Good. Then I think we understand each other.' With those words, he stopped outside an imposing, unmarked doorway.

'This is where I leave you.'

Kate felt suddenly uneasy. 'You're not coming in?'

'No. Why should I? I have no wish to watch you with the boys. I may deal in an irregular business, my dear girl, but I can assure you that I'm not a voyeur.' Then, seeing the faint doubt that marked her face, he reached out and patted her gently on the shoulder. 'You said you thought I was arrogant. I think a better way of putting it is that I know when I'm right. I know I'm right about you. You're a woman who has much to give. Go and give it. Go and get it. I'm sure you won't disappoint the boys. And they,' he added earnestly, 'most certainly won't disappoint *you*.' He made to leave her and then, turning on his heel, he smiled and said, 'Remember, you have absolutely nothing to lose this evening. But you do have everything to gain.'

Kate watched him walk away. She herself, she thought, could turn and walk away. There was nothing to keep her here. No one forcing her to ring the doorbell and enter a flat where a whole world of new experiences might open up to her. He was testing her, she realised. He didn't know her name and he had no way of contacting her again. He was also very clever. Evidently he did his business through trust and goodwill. She, in turn, already trusted him. She also felt well-disposed towards him. And she felt curious about what she would discover behind the door. Curious. Excited. And aroused.

She rang the doorbell. Her hand had hardly left the buzzer when the door opened. On the threshold stood the most glorious specimen of

271

manhood she had ever encountered. He was the colour of milk chocolate and his face, wreathed in smiles, was completely unlined and deliciously smooth. He was clad in jeans and a polo shirt, both of which, mused Kate, must have been outsized. For this man was huge. Not fat, just big. Very big.

'Hello,' stammered Kate, 'I'm . . .'

'I know who you are,' he replied, shaking her hand. 'I'm Rupert. Please,' he gestured, 'come inside.'

Wordlessly, he led her through the door and into the elegant, beautifully appointed ground-floor flat. The flat that could end up being Kate's place of work. Rupert ushered her into a drawing-room and gestured towards a chair. 'Do sit down. May I get you a drink?'

Kate, already slightly heady from half a bottle of champagne, could only nod slightly. For her eyes had already focused on the other occupant of the room. In contrast to Rupert, this man was both fair and short. Kate took in the delicate face topped by a shock of blond hair and the lithe yet muscular limbs encased in a scanty pair of shorts and a T-shirt. He smiled and approached her. 'Hello,' he said warmly. 'I'm Sebastian.'

Rupert and Sebastian. Kate nearly laughed. Two beautiful, well-spoken men. An expensive flat in Mayfair. Champagne. And seduction. Suddenly, the last thing she felt like doing was making love. Neither of these men turned her on. They were too perfect; they looked as if they had been created rather than born. Created from a blueprint of someone's idea of masculine beauty.

Yet it was as if they could read her thoughts.

Rupert brought her a glass of champagne and a tray of exquisite-looking smoked salmon. The three of them sat down, ate, drank and chatted. Like the man from the opera, the man who had brought her here, they both had the knack of making her feel totally at ease. They were also highly complimentary. Gradually Kate began to relax, to laugh at their ready humour – and to forget why she was here. Only when Sebastian commented that she looked tired did she remember. Tired meant bed. And bed meant that they were both going to test her.

They were too subtle for that. As if it were the most natural movement in the world, Rupert approached her, sprawled at her feet and removed her shoes. Seeing the startled look on her face, Sebastian grinned. 'Rupert's an expert at massage. You'll forget what tired means at the touch of his fingers. I promise you.' With that he left the room – and left Kate feeling, once again, slightly uneasy. While these two men displayed no signs of intimacy with each other, she somehow felt excluded, as if they knew something she didn't. But as Sebastian had promised, the touch of Rupert's fingers began to do strange things to her. At first he concentrated exclusively on the soles of her feet. Appearing to hardly touch them, he nevertheless managed to send little spasms, little pleasurable waves all the way up her legs. She sank deeper into the sofa, feeling herself relax, feeling her muscles give up all the tension that she hadn't even known they possessed. Then she closed her eyes and let her mind drift. It was bliss. Rupert made not a sound; Sebastian had gone; the only sound in the room was of her own breathing, and it was getting deeper and more gentle by the minute.

And still Rupert concentrated on her feet. Now they were soft and supple, sending sensations to the rest of her body. She had completely forgotten about sex. What Rupert was doing to her was infinitely more sensual, much more powerful and more completely absorbing than sex.

Then she opened her eyes and saw, greatly to her surprise, that Rupert was now massaging her calves. But so light was the touch of his hands that she was unaware of them. Rupert looked up at her. 'Shall I remove your stockings?' he asked. 'I know they're sheer, but even so they create a barrier. It's important,' he continued in his tantalisingly husky voice, 'that there's nothing between your skin and mine; nothing to interrupt the flow.'

Kate nodded in acquiescence. If Rupert continued as he had started, she was sure he would be able to remove all her clothes without her even noticing. She closed her eyes again and felt his hands reach upwards and under her skirt. With infinite patience and subtle expertise, he unhooked her stockings and began to roll them down her legs. He made no move to touch her between the legs. It was as if he were determined to avoid both her sex and the subject of sex. Kate liked that. Trusting completely in both him and the movements he made, she was able to close her eyes again, to let her thoughts wander once more. This time, prompted by the memory of his hands reaching the softer, more sensitive and fleshier area of her upper thighs, those thoughts became more focused. They turned to the subject of sex. She let herself fantasise about what the huge black man at her feet could do to her; about what she could do to him.

It was the latter consideration that drew her to make a decision. Suddenly she was on her feet and standing above Rupert. He was still curled at her feet, now holding the stockings he had so expertly removed. She looked down at him. Then she looked at his crotch. She could see no signs of arousal there. That he was sexually unstimulated both pleased and angered her: pleased her because he was putting her pleasure before his own; angered her because her awakening arousal had not moved him. 'Stand up,' she commanded. In one sinuous, elegant movement, Rupert got to his feet. Now he was looming before her, his chocolate brown eyes fixed on her own blue ones. He said nothing. He was waiting.

'Undress me,' she said.

Again his hands were on her body, touching, stroking, brushing different parts of her anatomy. Initially, he made no attempt to undress her. He circled her, still touching her. Now he was letting his fingers run through her hair; now he was massaging the back of her neck; now his hand was cupped round her buttocks. She closed her eyes. He made her feel like a sculpture, a precious work of art that he was treating with awe, that was so delicate it would shatter at the touch of rough hands. And then he began to take her clothes off. First her jacket; then her skirt. Now there was only her underwear, the delicate lace of her bra, panties and suspender belt. And suddenly there was nothing; nothing except Rupert's expert fingers massaging the secret areas of her body. He stroked her breasts, coaxed her nipples into unbearable tautness; he pressed his hand against her stomach, sending a fluttering sensation down towards the place that was now wet; he encircled that place with both hands – yet he didn't touch it. He was teasing her, and she could bear it no longer.

'Take your clothes off,' she said. 'I want you naked.' She watched as he divested himself of his shirt in one flowing movement. Beneath it was a magnificent, gleaming, muscular torso. Kate reached out to touch it. In imitation of his movements, she began with his nipples, her fingers fluttering against the wrinkled mahogany, soft against hard. Now they, too, were hard, and as she pressed herself against him she felt that his cock, still hidden beneath the rough denim of his jeans, was responding likewise. She felt it twitching against the material, straining for release, begging to touch the flesh of her belly.

And suddenly it *was* released. Swiftly, Rupert unbuttoned his fly and let his jeans fall to the floor. As he stepped out of them, his erection slapped against the fine line of hair that ran to his belly button. As Kate looked at it, it seemed to grow before her eyes, swelling and pulsating and stretching further up so that it rose beyond his belly button. Suddenly Rupert crushed her against him and she felt the rigid member against her own skin. It nestled there, hot and throbbing, jerking slightly in anticipation of what was to follow.

Rupert's hands were stroking her back now; her hands were at the back of his neck, the part of a man's body that always awakened her animal urges, the part that, to her, was an inexplicable source of delight and arousal. Now Rupert parted her lips with his bold tongue. Probing and tasting, he explored her mouth and let the champagne of their saliva mingle into a heady concoction – a foretaste of the more pungent juices that would emanate from a greater blending, a bolder probing that would soon take place. Now he was sucking urgently on her tongue, savouring it as if it were a nipple or a clitoris, worshipping it with his sensual mouth.

Kate moaned, her hips lifting and beating against his strong, taut body, beginning to beg for more of him, signalling her desire to be ravished by the cock that was still beating against her.

As if on cue, Rupert broke free from their kiss. At the same time, he traced the straining ridges of her spine with three long, languid fingers – and then brought them through her hair and down the centre of her brow. He let the fingers run down her nose, applying small amounts of pressure that became pleasure and transformed the beautiful fingers into elements of exquisite torture. Then he let them play on her lips until they were wet and lubricated and ready to slip into her mouth. Kate accepted them eagerly. Bigger and harder than his tongue, they also moved in and out with a rhythm more fierce and more suggestive of another, pounding rhythm. Kate licked them, savoured them and coated them with her saliva to prepare them for where she knew they would go next. For she and Rupert were working as one now, and as he withdrew his fingers from her mouth she shivered in anticipation as he ran them swiftly down the front of her body, between her breasts and across the gentle curve of her belly to her pubis and then directly, urgently and forcefully into her vagina. Kate moaned loudly as she felt their warm wetness probe deep inside her, nearly lifting her off her feet. She felt the muscles of her vagina contract against them as they drove into her. She was acutely conscious of her own juices now, of the slippery wetness flowing out of her and over Rupert's fingertips. She could feel her pleasure mounting, sensations rippling wildly through her body. It zigzagged through her nerves, limbs and glands – and then returned redoubled to her vulva and the muscular brown hand that possessed her.

Her body hot, her sex fervent, she felt herself poised on the edge, aflame and inflamed with desire. Still standing, she felt her legs begin to shake and give way. She was no longer relaxed, she was positively taut and tingling with desire; her entire body was straining for release. Again, Rupert was with her. As quickly as he had entered her with his hand, he withdrew and immediately cupped her buttocks in both hands. Then, lowering them to the top of her thighs, he started to lift her off her feet. Kate moaned again. She had lost control. She was completely powerless in his arms, and now she was being lifted against him. She grabbed the back of his neck with both hands and squeezed her eyes shut. She sensed Rupert moving his legs further apart, felt him achieving a sense of perfect balance – and then sighed in ecstasy as the rounded, pulsating head of his penis nudged against her quivering sex. Then it was still, ready and eager to plunge into her.

'Please,' she moaned. 'Please . . . do it. Now.'

Rupert obeyed her. In one slow, blissful movement, he lowered her on to him, burying his rampant cock inside her. Kate gasped as she felt him sink even deeper, even further into her. Her legs were now wrapped round his waist, and his hands, still supporting her buttocks, served only to force her further against tim. Kate, although totally at his mercy as she clung to him, felt as if she were the one in control; enveloping him with her limbs, she had the sensation that she was the predator, clinging voraciously to the creature whose seed she must suck.

And then Rupert's hips began to gyrate and she sensed his immensely powerful legs begin to flex and bend beneath her, letting his cock move in and out in the familiar thrusting movements that she had been aching for. Only after a moment did she realise that his whole body was moving, that he was walking out of the room and up some steps with Kate impaled on him. Moaning, she clung more tightly as she felt her breasts being crushed against his chest and the taut bud of her clitoris being ground against his steely pelvic bone. As he walked, his cock massaged her insides, moving both in and out and sideways, intensifying her pleasure, heightening her senses, increasing her lust.

Suddenly his hands were round her waist and he was pushing her away from him. Unwilling to relinquish him, Kate tried to press harder against him, but he was too strong for her. She felt a great emptiness as his cock slithered out of her and she fell backwards, moaning with frustration. For a split second she was suspended in the air and fear overcame her, blotting out the anger at his sudden and unwelcome withdrawal. Her eyes flew open and she let out another little moan – a sound that was stopped in its tracks as she landed on the soft contours of what she realised was a large, sumptuous bed. She lay on her back, surprised, disorientated, and looked up at Rupert. He was standing at the end of the bed, towering above her, glowering at her. His prick, now coated with her juices, jutted proudly against his washboard belly. Wordlessly, she spread her legs, knowing that he would launch himself upon her, once again sheathing his manhood inside her.

'Rupert,' she stammered, 'I . . . I want . . .'

'But it's not what *you* want that matters.' He was looking at her strangely now. 'You are here to serve me.' He looked at his sex with undisguised distaste. 'You've made me dirty.' His eyes met hers again, and as he spoke they took on a wicked glint. A look of challenge. 'Wash me.' he commanded.

As suddenly as he had pushed her on to the bed, he stepped forward, gathering her into his arms and swept her clear of the mattress. He carried her through a door which led to a luxurious bathroom, replete with every conceivable luxury – including a multi-headed shower. Bundling her into the cubicle, he pressed a button and suddenly water was all around them. It came from above, from below, and from all different levels of the walls around them. Powerful jets of water, stimulating and caressing all parts of their bodies.

Rupert pushed her against the side. 'Wash me,' he commanded. 'Wash me all over.'

Now Rupert was the work of art, the perfect sculpture that was to be worshipped. Kate started with his neck and shoulders, soaping them and creating a beautiful snowy lather in magnificent contrast to the smooth brownness of his skin.

Then the water came in cascades, washing away the soap and sending it swirling down the contours of his glistening, muscular body.

Kate worked her way down, following the rivulets of soap towards his cock. She soaped it, coating it and cleansing it, massaging his balls, enjoying the silky feel of the delicate skin. She felt his cock twitch at her touch, and then, as she lowered herself to a squatting position, she felt her own sex being massaged by a hidden jet of warm water from beneath. A completely new and not unwelcome sensation, it served to intensify her desire.

'You're clean now,' she said at last to Rupert. She wanted him in her again; she was again filled with the urgency of desire. She looked up at him and saw that his eyes again held that strange expression of contemplation, desire and distaste.

For a moment Kate thought that he was going to force himself into her mouth and start pummelling the back of her throat with his thick brown manhood. Lightning visions of that evening at the Château de Grassigny flooded into her mind as she recalled Georges invading Elodie's eager, pouting mouth. Kate knew that she wasn't capable of taking a man so completely that way. Not a man like Georges – and certainly not a man like Rupert.

Again it was as if he were reading her mind. Now his expression was one of tenderness as he reached down for her and gently pulled her to her feet. He bent his head and started kissing her. With his tongue probing gently and passionately, he then began to caress her again. Kate felt enveloped. This huge man was all over her, and he was turning her into a churning cauldron of desire. She was now at her height; she knew that if his fingers, now at the firm mounds of her buttocks, moved towards her clitoris that it would be over.

Rupert pulled gently away from her. Now their bodies were completely separate, yet the water cascading all over them served to unite them. The jets of water that were playing delicately on her breasts massaged his chest; the sweet softness of the warm liquid teased their private places; their bodies were wet and slippery – and aching for release.

'Turn round,' said Rupert.

Kate obeyed. She would accept whatever this man decided to do to her. As she turned, Rupert pressed lightly on her shoulders, bending her forwards, at the same time forcing her legs further apart and exposing her buttocks to him. His erection nestled briefly on the small of her back. Then it moved down, following the curve of her buttocks, pausing at the entrance of her anus. 'No!' she cried. 'Not there! Please, Rupert, not there.'

'No,' he replied from behind her. 'Not there.' Kate's flames of desire now flickered again as his cock found her other entrance. His long, stiff penis burrowed into the satin membranes of her vagina and she moaned as her awareness focused only on the long, sweet and total entry of his body into hers. Her flesh jumped around him as he pushed forwards, her inner walls twitched and caressed him of their own accord. She was only dimly aware of the discomfort of her situation, of her arms flailing wildly around as she searched for something, anything, to support her as Rupert's thrusts increased in their intensity and her legs once again became weak. Her love-juice was running freely, mingling with the water, seeping downwards in silvery, silent streams.

Rupert was grunting now, deep, masculine grunts that came from above her and that matched each powerful stroke of the marauding rod that possessed her. Kate wanted to cry out too; each penetration went deeper into her and forced her further forwards; now there was water in her eyes, in her mouth, and she nearly choked. She felt diminished as the man above her, gloriously upright and astoundingly powerful, forced her into submission. Totally at his mercy, she felt herself shift slightly in the swirling waters of the shower; shift so that one of the jets, surging up from below, began to lap at her clitoris. And suddenly Rupert didn't matter any more. Every push, every heave, every shove of his penis inside her was merely an adjunct to what was happening within herself. Hugely and completely, she felt herself climax, felt herself floating in a world of glory, a world of her own that was detached from the dark force over and in her. And then, somewhere within the swirling mists of water, steam and the fulfilment of her own desire, she heard Rupert cry out as he thrust one last time within her, as his balls tightened with the exquisite sensation of orgasm, as his seed spilled within her. So aware was she of the flow of water all around her, so attuned to the sensation of streams of liquid, that she actually felt him ejaculate, flet him inundate her body with rapture. She was still beneath him, but now she had his power. He slid out of her, vanquished, and she rose to her full height.

Shaking slightly, she turned to Rupert. He was

283

now supporting himself against the walls of the cubicle, breathless, smiling and satisfied. Kate looked at his cock. It was withering before her gaze; flaccid and diminished, it had lost its power. Experience told her that Rupert was now no longer interested in sex, and certainly not interested in her. As they looked at each other, now distanced under the same gushing torrents of water that had united them moments before, Kate remembered why she was here. Her own feelings of enjoyment and of satisfaction were irrelevant. Rupert had been testing her, testing her ability to satisfy a man regardless of her own pleasure.

Thus she was totally unprepared for what happened next. Rupert leaned forward and kissed her on the mouth. It was a chaste kiss; only his lips made contact, yet the lingering, feather-like brush of his mouth against hers, the wetness that suddenly joined them sent a small, erotic tremor through her entire being. And when Rupert pulled away his eyes spoke of solicitude. And so did his words.

'Now I've made you dirty,' he said. 'Now I shall wash you.'

Reaching for the soap, he massaged it into a frothing lather and began to spread it gently and generously all over her. Kate closed her eyes and let herself wallow in the unfamiliar sensation of a man who, sexually spent, seemed intent on pleasuring her further. Rupert seemed to realise that, while no longer at the height of ecstasy, she was still hovering on the threshold of arousal. She stood, slumped against the shower cubicle, revelling in the touch of his hands as they soaped her and softly worked their way down her body once more, providing sweet contrast to the sharp touch of the needles of water. Never had she thought it possible that a man could be so attuned to a woman's needs. And even when he reached the moist folds of her sex, he seemed to be in complete accord with what she wanted. Her swollen puckered lips, so recently invaded by his throbbing tumescence, had no need to be touched, yet her clitoris, still a hardened knob of desire, responded to his exquisitely gentle touch and in seconds he had brought her to another orgasm; not the shattering, all-consuming climax that she had just experienced, but a sweet tremor that washed through her so slowly that she was able to savour it as it transported her.

Afterwards he dried her. He enveloped her in a voluminous towel and slowly and with exquisite delicacy he massaged her tingling skin. She threw her head back, closed her eyes and let her thoughts wander. Was this what her clients would be like if she passed the test? Gentle and intent on pleasuring her as much as themselves? Was this what *all* men were like once they found themselves operating without normal social conventions, away from peer-group pressure and traditional role-playing? For if Rupert had in some way reduced her status, he had reduced his own even more. This was no sexual stereotype kneeling before her; this was a creature showing her, in the most revealing way possible, that he wanted to please her.

At last he was finished. He motioned for her to get to her feet.

'Rupert . . .' she began.

But he forestalled her. Putting a hand to her

lips, he smiled and told her to go through to the bedroom. 'You must be exhausted,' he said.

Kate dropped her towel and looked uncertainly at him. 'Is that it then?'

Rupert now had his back to her. 'No, not quite.'

'Oh.' Kate now felt mellow. Satisfied. Secure. She didn't feel like entering the uncertain territory of sex again. 'So you're coming with me?'

'Yes. But you go first. I've got things to do here.'

'What things?' Suddenly Kate felt vulnerable.

Rupert turned to her and grinned. He was holding a toothbrush. 'Am I not allowed to clean my teeth?'

Kate laughed. Then she looked seriously at him. 'Rupert, I can't believe . . . I mean I can't tell you just what it meant . . .'

But again Rupert stalled her. 'Go,' he said, gently shoving her towards the door. 'I think you're about to embarrass me.'

Embarrass him? Kate thought about that one as she stepped into the bedroom. Had he over-stepped the bounds of his role? Had he lost himself somewhere along the line? Had he actually fallen for her? Kate considered the latter point. All along, he had acted like her lover, like he had been making love to her for years than testing her sexual prowess. Even when he had commanded her to wash him, to soap his magnificent body, he had done it in a way that suggested it was for her pleasure rather than his. Kate, on the other hand, had been too overwhelmed by all he had done to her to even consider him properly as a person. She felt a stab of guilt.

Lost in contemplation, she walked towards the bed. Naked, deliciously warm and exquisitely clean, she stretched languorously as she prepared to climb on to it. Someone, she realised, had been in the room while she had been with Rupert. The lights were now dimmer than they had been before and lent the room a warm, mellow glow that perfectly suited her mood. She looked around the room, for the first time noticing the subtle colours and delicate hues of its furnishings and pictures. The room had an aura, not of sex, but of sensuality. And adding to that aura was a heady, almost arousing smell that hadn't been there before. She stood there, delicately wrinkling her nostrils as she tried to identify it.

On the other side of the room, the man standing in the shadows looked admiringly at her. Naked and assuming she was alone, her stance was a totally unselfconscious one; her lithe, athletically graceful body was at ease with itself and the stillness of her posture lent her a madonna-like serenity. The man felt a stirring in his loins. He moved towards the centre of the room and held out his hand. In it was a small pot. 'The smell,' he said, 'comes from this.'

'Sebastian!' Kate flinched and looked at him with a mixture of surprise, anger and embarrassment. The latter emotion eclipsed the others and, automatically, she tried to cover herself with her hands.

Sebastian laughed at her discomfiture. 'Embarrassed?' he teased as he approached her. 'Under the circumstances, that's a little unnecessary, don't you think?' Then, with an air of undisguised appreciation, he eyed her up and down. 'And,' he continued with a glint in his eye, 'it's not as if you've got anything to be embarrassed about.'

Kate looked at him. This, she thought, was unreal. She had just had sex with one of the most beautiful men she had ever seen, and now, here in front of her, was another of the species, practically *breathing* sex at her. Unable to think of anything else to say, she asked him what was in the pot.

'It's a sort of oil,' he replied. 'A body oil.'

Their eyes met again and then Kate returned the languorous, appraising look that Sebastian had just directed at her. Naked, he was as unselfconscious as she had been a moment ago. He was also, like her, unaroused. She liked that. It suited her mood – and the mood of the room.

'Whose body,' she said with a lazy smile, 'is it meant for?'

Sebastian grinned. 'Yours? Mine? Both of us? Does it matter?'

She shrugged. 'I don't know.' Then, feeling slightly unsure of herself, she indicated the room with a sweep of a hand. 'I'm just . . . well, just a bit new to all this, that's all. I'm not sure what's supposed to happen next.'

'What would you like to happen next?'

Kate thought for a moment. 'I'd like,' she said at length, 'some fresh air.'

If that remark surprised Sebastian, he didn't show it.

'Dressed like that?' he asked.

'I'm not dressed at all,' she replied with a grin.

'No. Nor am I. So that option's closed to us.' Sebastian put one hand to his head in a curiously childlike yet deeply endearing way. 'Unless,' he continued, 'we go on to the balcony.'

'The balcony? I didn't know there was one.'

Now Sebastian padded towards the huge

window. The curtains were fully drawn, and were billowing slightly in the warm, gentle breeze of the summer's night. 'Oh yes,' he said as he began to open them. 'It's rather wonderful and . . .'

'Won't anybody see us?' asked Kate anxiously.

Sebastian turned to her, his expression all innocence. 'So? It's not as if we're doing anything wrong, is it? All I want to do is massage you. The oil,' he indicated the pot he was still holding, 'is a terrific relaxant.'

Kate stared at him, not knowing if he was teasing her or being serious. This perfect specimen was intending to take her, naked as was he, out on to a balcony in central London, massage her with an oil whose smell she was already beginning to find erotically intoxicating, and pretend the whole thing was *ordinary*. There was certainly nothing ordinary about the way she was beginning to feel; about the sensations beginning to well within her. 'You're not serious,' she said, suddenly annoyed with herself for feeling aroused.

'I'm perfectly serious.' He pulled one curtain aside and opened one side of french window to its fullest extent. 'Look.'

Kate stepped forward and looked. For a moment she just stared at the scene before her and then she put one hand to her mouth. 'Oh. Oh my God,' she whispered. 'It's beautiful. I've never seen . . .'

'No. Few people have.' Sebastian's voice, also coming in a whisper, was closer to her now. She could feel the minty freshness of his breath as it caressed her ear. She didn't dare look at him: she knew without being told that he was standing almost close enough for the hairs on his legs to touch her own fine, near-invisible ones. She had thought Sebastian short: now she realised that he was exactly the same height as she was, and perfectly positioned to lean forward and mould his body into her own. 'It's not bad,' he continued, 'for a balcony, is it?'

It was, thought Kate, hardly recognisable as a balcony. It was more like some sort of hanging garden. While the whole area could not have been more than ten feet square, it was populated by the most exquisite vines, honeysuckles, exotic creepers and sweet-smelling flowers. Above her, she noticed, the area was actually covered by a glass dome, and she thought she detected glass behind the foliage on two sides. But the side directly in front of her was open to the elements: she could feel the breeze and could see the greenery wafting gently in its caress. 'It's extraordinary,' she said. 'Extraordinarily beautiful.' She stepped forward on to the warm, bleached-wood flooring and then noticed the only piece of furniture in the enclosed balcony room. It was a large, soft and extremely inviting day-bed. She turned and looked at her companion. He was still standing at the french windows, and was silhouetted by the light from the bedroom behind them. Another extraordinarily beautiful thing, she thought. His finely tuned muscles lent a pleasing and unthreatening definition to his slight shape. Then she sank on to the bed and looked at the flowers and greenery around her. Sebastian moved too – to the iron railing on the open side of the balcony. He stood there in contemplation while Kate looked at him – at the set of his strong shoulders and the firm, finely rounded contours of his buttocks. Again she felt a tremor run through her. She couldn't see if Sebastian was in tune with her; if he too was beginning to get aroused.

'Can't anybody see us here?' she asked after a moment.

'No. But they can hear us. There are other flats and houses around here.'

'But we're not doing anything wrong, are we?' She grinned at his back. 'So there's no need to be quiet, is there?'

'I s'pose not. But then I'm always quiet.'

'Why?'

'I'm not a very good conversationalist.'

'I didn't come here for conversation.'

'Why are you talking, then?'

Kate frowned at that remark. Only when Sebastian turned round after a moment of uneasy silence did she realise that he had been joking – and that he was in tune with her.

She gazed speculatively at him. 'It's like the Garden of Eden,' she whispered. 'But in miniature.'

'In miniature?' Sebastian was now standing directly in front of her.

She grinned at him. 'The garden, I mean.'

'Yes, it's quite enchanting, isn't it?'

'I'm not sure that's the word I would use.'

'Isn't it? What word would you use?'

Kate smiled lazily up at him. She was enjoying this. It was better than the Garden of Eden. 'It depends,' she said teasingly, 'which part you want me to describe.'

'You choose.'

'I think I'd describe the part that's closest to me

as excitable.'

Sebastian laughed, causing his half-erection to sway before her eyes. 'Oh,' he said after a moment of looking straight into her eyes. 'It can get a lot more excitable.'

'Oh good.' Kate shifted position so that she was lying on her side. She felt suddenly wanton, suddenly desperate for more sex. She felt the same as she had the night in the opera: completely shameless and utterly unsatiable. The episode with Rupert seemed like a distant memory now. Here, in this tiny, luxurious bower, in this secret garden with its intoxicating smells, she felt as if she were in her own opera or on some stage. And now she was ready to perform.

It was as if Sebastian could read her mind. He bent forward and picked up the pot of oil he had been carrying when he had so surprised her in the bedroom. 'You, on the other hand,' he said as he joined her on the bed, 'don't look like the excitable type.'

Kate put her tawny head next to his blonde one. They were now so close that their noses were all but touching. 'Oh, but I am,' she purred. 'I'm extremely excitable. It just takes the right sort of things to excite me.'

'Things like this?' Sebastian's fingers, warm and fragrant with the oil from the pot, played agonisingly gently on her breasts.

'Mmm. And things like . . .'

'Like that?'

'Oh! God! Oh Sebastian . . . '

Sebastian put an urgent finger against her mouth to quieten her. She wanted to bite it, so aroused was she by the sudden and unexpected accuracy of his other hand as it parted her sex-lips and found her clitoris. Yet no sooner had those fingers delved into her than they were gone, leaving Kate straining and arching her back with unfulfilled desire.

'How about,' teased Sebastian, 'things like this?' Now his talented hands played on her belly, massaging the aromatic oil over her soft skin. Kate groaned in pleasure and turned fully on to her back. She stretched luxuriantly, revelling in the warmth of the night, the gentle air on her warm body and the even more gentle, hugely erotic sensation of Sebastian's hands as they slowly turned her entire body into a cauldron of desire. For a moment she let her own hand play with his hair, running her fingers through the silken strands, pulling gently and twisting them around her fingers in time with Sebastian's movements. Then, as he moved further down her body, she stretched once more and reached over her head in a long, lazy arc. Her hands found the delicate petals of one of the climbing plants, and as she stroked their softness so Sebastian continued his tantalising ministrations, effortlessly turning her entire body into one glorious erogenous zone. His hands were all over her now, and as she again stretched in ecstacy, she felt him at her breasts again, touching the hard little buds and teasing them into straining tautness. As she began to writhe and moan, Sebastian again found her mouth – but this time with his own. He lay astride her, yet careful to keep his weight off her, and parted her lips with his ardent tongue. With exquisite tenderness he explored her mouth. His movements were rhythmic, reminiscent of another, more intimate exploration of her secret parts. With an urgency that matched his own, Kate responded, eagerly and hungrily kissing the man who was so slowly and so agonisingly bringing her back to the peak of pleasure to which Rupert had brought her earlier in the evening.

Yet Kate had forgotten about Rupert. Her senses were in the process of being so completely and totally assaulted that she had thoughts for nothing except the glorious present. Sebastian's mouth was on hers. His body was on hers: his fine, smooth skin was rubbing against her breasts and against her stomach while another part of him was edging towards her pubic mound with the gentle promise of fulfilment of the ultimate desire. But as erotic was the heady mixture of smells: the freshness of Sebastian's breath as he broke off from his kisses; the musky aroma of the oil that now coated them both; and the sweet, almost tangible aroma of the honeysuckle and the other plants that perfumed the night air with their aroma. Kate was in ecstacies: now pulling almost frenziedly at Sebastian's hair as he taunted her with his expert kisses; now reaching back to the plants behind her and weaving the delicate, silky tendrils between her fingers. She had completely forgotten where she was. London seemed a million miles away: all she knew was that she was floating in some nether world where sensation was all, where nothing could impinge on perfect pleasure, and where her whole *raison d'être* was to live for the glory of the moment that she hoped would go on for ever.

Sebastian broke the spell. Now with his mouth at her breasts, he broke off to chastise her for the increasingly loud noises she did not even know she was making.

'But we're not,' she gasped, 'doing anything wrong.' She managed a grin. 'That's what you said, isn't it?'

'Mmm.' Then his talented tongue moved even further down her body.

'Don't!' she moaned. 'Don't . . . do that. I can't . . . I can't bear it.' But she could: it was the most bearable thing she had ever experienced.

'Don't,' countered her lover, 'shout like that. The neighbours.'

'Fuck the neighbours.'

'I'd rather fuck you.'

'Do it. Do it then. Please, Sebastian.' This, she thought through her haze of desperate desire, was Kate speaking. This was Kate the stockbroker begging a stranger to screw her and satisfy her until she was completely spent. The thought flew from the befuddled brain as quickly as it had arrived. It didn't belong to the moment.

'Only if you promise me one thing.' Again Sebastain brought her back to her senses – or as near to them as she could get. He was stroking her thigh now, starting underneath her raised knee and stopping tantalisingly short of her soaking, willing sex.

Through her delirium of lust she told him she would promise everything and anything.

'I don't believe you,' he said with a wicked smile.

Kate pulled at the sprawling vine beneath her as she writhed in a mixture of ecstasy and agony: the former because of what he was doing to her; the latter because he wouldn't go any further.

'If you pull any harder,' continued Sebastian as

he tormented her, 'you'll pull the vines off and leave us in full view of the neighbours.'

'I don't care,' said Kate through gritted teeth as she wriggled again to his touch. She thought she really was about to go mad. Again she shouted at him, and this time his reaction was not to tell her to be quiet, but to reach under the bed and pull something out from beneath it. Kate looked on, bemused, as he unravelled a length of beautiful, shimmering green silk. For a moment fear flickered in her eyes. 'What ... what are you going to do to me?'

'I'm going to make sure you keep quiet.' With those words he dangled the silk over her body, letting the cool folds of material caress her, drawing the silk across her most intimate places with torturous slowness. She gasped as he teased the material over her damp sex and her hard, swollen clitoris. Again Kate moaned – even more loudly than before.

'See? You can't keep quiet, can you?' With that he approached her head again and kneeled over her. His prick, now fully erect and glistening with the oily nectar that covered them both, bobbed against her nipples. Kate reached for it and touched it as she had touched the petals and vines behind and above her, caressing and massaging it. It twitched in her fingers as she stroked up and down its head, from the proud glans to the soft, wrinkled scrotum. 'Do you trust me?' asked Sebastian as he looked into her eyes. His tone was as gentle as his expression.

She didn't even have to think about her answer. The look he was giving her reminded her of something, or of someone. For a moment she looked at him in bewilderment. Surely, she thought, she had met this man before? She knew him: his body, his voice and his features were as familiar to her as her own.

'Yes,' she replied. 'I trust you.' Somehow, she knew that he would do nothing to hurt her: all he was interested in was pleasing her and it surprised her to realise that the thought of being gagged not only pleased but excited her. The windows of the neighbouring flat were only about two feet away and Sebastian, she reckoned, was genuinely worried about their love-making being overheard. And there was something unbelievably erotic about making exquisite love in full hearing, if not in sight, of their neighbours. Danger, she thought, added an extra dimension to pleasure.

And so did the cool silk as he wound it around her. A frisson of excitement shot through her as she smelled the material. It smelled of Sebastian, of her juices, of the oil that coated their straining bodies. And it wasn't really gagging her; the way Sebastian covered her mouth with it served only to muffle any sounds.

When Sebastian finished, Kate found herself, to her slight horror, relishing the fact that she had let this man have power over her. She almost wished he had insisted on tying her hands as well – on fastening them to the vines behind her so that she became inextricably part of the vibrant, verdant foliage. She reached back again and gripped the fleshy stem of one of the vines as Sebastian used his tongue to trace a firm, fine line down the centre of her body to the centre of her soul. She gasped into her intoxicating silken bridle as, with astounding accuracy, he found her clitoris and nuzzled at it with his mouth, sending little electric shocks of lust through her. She felt her body tense and her hips buck as he savoured her juices. She closed her eyes and a vision came to her of her night at the opera, of the rampant slaves and the nubile virgins. Now she was both virgin and willing slave. Now she was willing Sebastian to enter her and give to her what she most craved.

In one quick, deft movement of his lithe body, he did exactly as she silently commanded. With both strength and tenderness, he mounted her, parted her legs even further and plunged gloriously into her. The moist folds of her labia welcomed him and the muscles of her vagina spasmed as he plunged into her depths. Almost involuntarily, her hands moved away from the clinging vines and went to his shoulders, down his back and to the muscled orbs of his buttocks as she urged him ever further, ever deeper.

He was a master of his calling. Relentless at first, he pounded into her as if his own pleasure was the only purpose of their congress. Then, just as Kate silently willed him to, he withdrew and nudged gently at her opening while teasing her clitoris with one eager, darting finger. Kate's hands left his body again. For a second they teased her own breasts, coaxing her nipples into increasing, unbearable tautness. Then, as Sebastian entered her once again, her fingers found the leafy, verdant growths behind her and she thrashed against them in a frenzy of lust. One hand dislodged some blossom and it floated down on to her face and her shoulders, cloaking her in delicious, fragrant petals.

She began to lose both her sense of time and of reality. All she knew was that she didn't want this coupling to cease. At some point Sebastian manoeuvred her on to her side so that they lay, still entwined, but in the intimate posture of sleep. When their eyes met Kate saw in Sebastian's what she knew to be in on her own: an urgency and a pleading; a desire for this never to end. She clung to him, trying to wrap her legs round him and to let him slide even deeper into her. As she did so, Sebastian started kissing her. It nearly drove her demented: her mouth was still bound by the silken folds and couldn't emulate their thrusting with a play of tongues. Instead, Sebastian kissed her on the nose and on the forehead. Then he dropped little butterfly kisses on her eyelids and, when his thrusts once again became more urgent, he nuzzled into her neck, forcing her head backwards. She clawed desperately at him, wondering if she would ever again experience a pleasure so intense.

She was only dimly aware of an extra pressure on the bed and of the strong hands at her shoulders. She wasn't even aware that her eyes were closed until a warmth enveloped her back and a voice whispered into her ear. Only half of her registered that someone had joined them on the bed.

She resisted but feebly – and only for a moment. Turning her head as she writhed in ecstacy, she saw the soft, chocolate eyes of Rupert gazing intently into her own. She caught her breath and the muscles of her vagina clamped round Sebastian's rigid cock as fear momentarily gripped her. Then, as Sebastian remained still within her, as he stroked her hip and uttered soothing noises, Rupert started whispering again.

'Relax,' he mouthed into her ear. 'Enjoy.' Repeatedly, he whispered the words and stroked her hair in time with Sebastian's caresses of her body.

Kate was trapped. Sandwiched between two powerful men, she was entirely at their mercy. There was no escape – and nor was there any desire to escape. Kate felt overwhelmed instead of overpowered. Overwhelmed by the situation, by the increasingly heady night smells; by the fresh, feral smell of three bodies conjoined; by the increasingly heady fragrances of the still, silent night, and by the loving, expert ministrations of the two men who were worshipping her body. Most of all, she was overwhelmed by what Rupert was now doing to her. Conflicting emotions surged and seethed through her as he ran one strong hand over her buttocks down to that secret, forbidden place where no man had ever been before; to the puckered rosebud of her anus.

As Sebastian began his slow, rhythmic love-making again, Kate wrapped her leg round his body, pulling him against her, urging him further into her, and opening herself to Rupert. She was both scared and excited, yet she also felt secure in her trust of these men. They wanted purely to pleasure her and to bring her to the very frontiers of desire. And now Rupert, as the head of his proud, erect manhood nudged towards her behind, was reaching those frontiers. Kate winced in pain as he forced his way into her. Pain, she had been told, was related to pleasure: now she knew the connection. She knew that the greatest pleasure could only be experienced after the knowledge of pain. For now Rupert's thrusts were relaxing her muscles, now the pain had evaporated and in its place was pleasure that mounted to unbridled ecstacy as she welcomed him into her. This, then, was the apex of desire; the zenith of pleasure. She moaned and bit the folds of silk in her mouth as she experienced a greater glory than she had ever known. She could feel both men inside her; they were thrusting in tandem as they penetrated her from two sides. She could feel the soft tissues inside her being caressed as Sebastian and Rupert worshipped her body with theirs. This Garden of Eden had lured her, seduced her and tempted her to do something she had never before considered. And of that she would be eternally glad.

For now something was happening to her. Her entire body stiffened and moved involuntarily as both men increased the speed of love-making, as they both groaned and buried their heads in her neck; one at the front and one within the tumbling tresses of her hair. She was dimly aware of a new spot being touched within the depths of her being as a wetness coated their sopping limbs, as she shuddered and reached out behind her when the pleasure became so intense that it turned into physical pain. Her flailing hand again found the flowers behind her and suddenly all three of them were coverd in cascading petals. Simultaneously, the twisting, writhing bodies on the bed erupted into a crescendo of desire and then subsided into a blissful stillness.

The last thing Kate was aware of was the sensation of completeness as, warmed by the bodies on either side of her, she was coaxed by the sounds and smells of the night into the welcoming arms of Morpheus.

Chapter Four

SOMEONE CAME TO her in the middle of the night. At first she didn't know who it was; at first she was completely unaware of *where* she was. Sebastian and Rupert had enveloped her around them as she slept on the balcony and later, she dimly remembered, they had taken her inside when the caress of the night breeze had cooled. Then she had slept again, a sleep induced by extreme fatigue, yet disturbed by the same events that had made her tired. She had been tested. She had been made love to as no one had ever made love to her before. Kate the stockbroker was appalled by what she had done in this house. Kate the uninhibited sexual temptress was proud; a dangerous side of her, a hitherto buried aspect of her nature had, from somewhere in the depths of her soul, risen forth to meet the cutting edge of carnality, and to rejoice.

Her sleep was disturbed. Someone was getting into bed with her. Someone with a lightness of touch that seemed familiar to her. Her befuddled brain cried out at the thought that, yet again, she would be required to perform, to play the game and, as she knew she had done, to win.

It didn't happen. A blond head settled next to her own. She moved away. A voice whispered in her ear. 'Shh,' it said. 'Sleep.' Kate still wasn't fully awake. The voice continued, a soft voice, lulling her back to the nether world of Lethe, to sweet sleep, this time to blissful, undisturbed unconsciousness. A tiny frown crossed her brow as she drifted away. She knew that voice, she knew that body. But she couldn't remember who it was. And then a voice, a different voice, told her it didn't matter. All that mattered was oblivion.

She awoke to the sun streaming through the bedroom window. She blinked as its rays danced over her eyelids, teasing her gently into consciousness. And then she saw Sebastian standing before her and the events of yesterday came rushing back to her. She lay where she was, unmoving yet stiffening in a mixture of embarrassment and shyness. Lust, she thought, had done strange things to her. She had been so uninhibited that she would have done anything Sebastian and Rupert had required of her. She *had* done anything they required – and she had loved it. Kate the prude of this morning rested uneasily with Kate the temptress of the night. She looked at Sebastian, smiling uneasily, and pulled the sheet against her breasts.

The Sebastian before her was the Sebastian whom she had met in the drawing room the previous evening. The blond, boyish Sebastian with the grin and friendly manner. He was even wearing the same clothes; a white T-shirt and boxer shorts. Through half-closed eyes, she examined him. This, then, was the rampant creature of last night. Yet now he seemed an almost sexless individual who was looking rather rumpled, somewhat lost.

He noticed her flickering eyelids and smiled. Then he yawned. 'I had to get up,' he explained, 'for work. I thought you might have to as well.' He peered through the swathe of muslin curtains. 'Nice day.' Then he turned back to her. 'Coffee?'

Kate was speechless. Here was the man who had taken her into the Garden of Eden, who had, with his friend, reduced her to a quivering mass of lust, and now he was talking about the weather and offering her coffee. She looked down at her body, then around her. Yes, she thought, I am awake. This is real. Sebastian was still standing at the end of the bed. 'Milk?' he prompted. 'Sugar?'

Kate was so stunned that she couldn't think of anything to say. Then she surprised herself. 'No,' she found herself saying, 'just black.'

Sebastian trotted out of the room. Kate peeled the bedclothes away from her and looked at her body. She didn't know what she expected to see. Her body looked the same as it always had, yet it felt different. It felt as if it were glowing with a new and powerful light. She covered herself quickly as Sebastian returned with two cups. He laughed when he saw her clutching the sheets to her chest. 'I know,' he said, 'I know just how you feel. You never want them to see you in the buff the next morning, do you? Well try not to mind me.' He leaned towards her. 'Here's your coffee. Black.'

'Thanks.' Kate took a sip. 'Mmm. Delicious.'

She didn't know whether to laugh or cry. She was being as crazy as he was. Then she looked up at him. 'What do you mean by "them"?'

'Mmm?'

'You said you never want "them" to see you naked.'

'Oh. My clients.' He sipped his coffee and sat down on the edge of the bed. 'He did explain, didn't he? About Rupert and me?'

'He?'

'Your . . . our . . . mentor, I s'pose you could call him.'

'Well, he said you were going to test me. To see if I could rise to your challenge. He didn't,' she added, 'mention who you were.'

Sebastian turned to her, a puzzled expression on his face. 'He *didn't* explain much, did he?' He looked into her eyes. 'Rupert and I are escorts. We perform for money. A lot of money. We deal with the very top end of the market.' He smiled at her. 'Just like you're going to do. Except you'll be called a courtesan. If you want the job, that is.'

'You mean I passed?'

'With flying colours. You were very instinctive. And you got the hang of it pretty quickly that you were the one with all the power.' From the tone of his voice, Sebastian may well have been discussing her learning to ride a bike.

Now it was Kate's turn to be puzzled. 'Me? The one with power?'

'Oh yes. Without a doubt. Remember, *you're* the one who has what others want. That gives you all the power. You just have to learn how to . . . how to play the game.' Then, in a brotherly fashion, he squeezed her hand. 'You didn't mind

305

about me gagging you – or about Rupert joining us, did you?' He grinned. 'You were making a hell of a racket, actually.'

'So you told me.' Then Kate was silent for a moment as she reflected on what Sebastian had said. It all sounded so *easy* so much fun.

Sebastian seemed to be reading her mind. 'If you're thinking that you're going to have a lot of fun doing this, then you're absolutely right. At this end of the market you get to indulge your every fantasy. Rich people,' he added reflectively, 'are usually very adventurous.'

Adventure. That, after all, was what she was after. Fun; adventure – and maybe a little danger? 'Are any of your clients,' she asked, 'ever . . . well, *perverted*?' She savoured the last word, testing it for weight, trying to decide whether or not it indicated a concept that excited her.

Sebastian laughed. 'Yeah, I guess so. Nothing too dramatic, though. Bondage is quite a common thing. There is,' he indicated the wardrobe in the corner of the room, 'a whole bunch of bondage gear over there. Whips. Masks and so on. Rubber fetish gear and, of course, leather.'

Leather. The smell of leather had always turned her on. When she was a girl she used to go riding and the smell of leather saddles, of sweat and the sight of men in their jodhpurs had, even then, done something to her. I really am, she mused, going to be able to indulge all my fantasies. Then another thought occurred to her. 'Why do *you* do this, Sebastian? You've got another job, haven't you? Didn't you say you have to get up to go to work?'

Oh yes, I've got another job.' Then he was

silent for a moment. 'I'll tell you why I do it. Firstly, the money. Do you know how much you can earn? A thousand a pop – and that's the absolute minimum. Secondly, I enjoy it. And thirdly, I love doing it for the experience of human nature.'

'You mean you see people at their rawest, at their most base?'

'Yes. Generally, although some clients . . .'

'Men?'

Sebastian grimaced. 'Only sometimes. I'm afraid I really don't like it. It's the only thing about this business that I can't seem to get my head around. Pity really.'

'Why?'

'It pays much better. I'm youngish, blond, y'know. They like that. Especially the closet ones. The cabinet ministers and so on.'

Kate started to giggle – and then stopped abruptly as she saw the expression on Sebastian's face. 'Don't you ever find it just a little demeaning?' she asked.

'Oh no. As I said, it gives you power.'

'You said it was always the women who had the power.'

'In most cases, yes. Not in the case of male escorts.'

'Because you're the one they want something from?'

'Absolutely.' Then he turned and, again in an intimate but asexual manner, he patted her arm. 'You, my dear, are going to have a great deal of fun doing this.'

*

As Sebastian got up to leave the room and get dressed, Kate remembered her strange, semi-somnolent experience that had both disturbed and enhanced the quality of her sleep. 'Sebastian,' she asked, 'did you come back into bed with me last night?'

Sebastian looked at her as if she were mad. 'No, of course not. Why?'

'I just . . . I just had this feeling that you did. To sleep. Not to . . .'

'To fuck. Don't be embarrassed about words. They're just words.' Then he grinned. 'And don't develop fantasies about the people you fuck with. They're just fucks.'

She took the job. Sebastian, consciously or unwittingly, had done her a favour. He had confirmed her initial feelings about the power balance in the game she wanted to play. He had also, before he left, reassured her about the clients she would meet. Only one in a million people are really perverted, really dangerous – and you might meet that one in the normal course of events. Very few of the rest of them even want to talk dirty, let alone play dirty. Most of them, he told her before she left the house, just want to talk big. Talk about big, boring amounts of money. And then give you some of it. A thousand pounds a go. Minimum.

Sebastian also appeared to have been deputed to provide her with the details about the flat. He gave her the keys. He told her it was hers for the evening only. He told her that she must call 'her number' every day to see if she had a client for that evening, in which case she would meet him at the flat. Kate didn't ask what happened in the flat during the day. And no, he said with a smile, neither he nor Rupert lived there. They had just come in for the evening. They had come to work. He shook her hand on the doorstep.

Mechanically, she held out her own hand, finding the incongruity of the situation both baffling and laughable. But she didn't laugh. This, she remembered, was serious business.

'Well good luck,' he said cheerily. Then he was gone.

Kate, too, departed in a rush. She had to go to work. To Courtenay de Witt, to her other life.

Mark was, again, the first person she encountered. She met him in the lift. 'Hi,' he said. Then he looked closely at her. 'You look . . . different.'

'Do I?' Kate grinned at his friendly face. 'I can't think why. I'm even wearing the same clothes as yesterday. Isn't that awful?'

'So am I,' confided Mark. 'But I won't tell if you don't. The stuffed shirts upstairs might think we'd been doing something naughty.'

'I can't think what you mean.' As soon as she had said the words, Kate cursed herself for being so prim. Mark, she was beginning to realise, was a bit of a breath of fresh air around here.

Mark laughed. 'Oh come on, Kate. Only dirty stop-outs wear the same shirt two days in a row.'

'Ah,' she teased him, 'but you're the only one wearing a shirt.' She looked closely at it. 'It *is* the same one as yesterday.'

Mark felt a flicker of hope. 'So you notice my clothes. That's a good sign.'

'I only noticed because . . .'

'Because what?'

'Oh . . . nothing.' What she actually meant was that she only noticed because the shirt he was wearing matched his eyes. Not that there was anything unusual in that. The unusual thing was that the eyes were uncannily similar to those of the man who wasn't Sebastian and who had joined her in bed last night.

Mark's eyes stayed with her throughout that long, tired morning. At one point they were opposite her own, across the table in the meeting room. She examined them covertly. And when she wasn't looking at them, they, did she but know it, studied her. Mark, she thought. Wearing the same clothes as yesterday. Mark was blond. Slight of build. He looked not dissimilar to Sebastian, the man who *hadn't* come to her bed. It was ludicrous, she thought. She'd had a vague suspicion that Mark fancied her, but to imagine that he knew anything about her personal life, about her whereabouts last night was simply ridiculous. No one knew what she had been up to last night. And then she recalled the expression on Sebastian's face when he had told her that she was lucky, that she, as a woman, was the one with power. Suddenly she knew that the man *had* been Sebastian; associating himself, again, with power. She smiled inwardly.

On the other side of the table, so did Mark.

She barely knew how she got through the day. All she wanted was to go home, to her *real* home, to soak in a hot tub and retire, alone, to bed. But she had to make the phone call. She had to let the man who had introduced her to the strange twilight world of sex for money know that she wanted to work for him. He would know by now that she had risen to the challenge his 'boys' had provided, but he didn't know that she was prepared to be challenged anew. To be screwed. Because now she knew exactly who would be doing the screwing.

When she eventually found time to call him, he appeared delighted at her decision. Would she care to meet to finalise arrangements? he enquired. At the Ritz again, unless she preferred somewhere else? No, she replied, the Ritz would suit admirably. So civilised. Exactly, she thought, like the decision she had just made.

The rest of the day passed in a haze of tiredness. She was almost unaware of half the things going on around her. Only one event registered in her mind. It concerned Pharescault and Nero de l'Escault-Tonnère. Nero. Nero who had played with her. Now she knew that was true. He had toyed with her, playing a game of cat and mouse. And she didn't owe him anything. Quite the opposite. She now felt he owed *her*. But Nero was a client of Courtenay de Witt, and it was in that context Kate was forced to think of him.

Miles Courtenay, so Kate was informed, had decided he was a bit 'iffy' about Pharescault. Typical, thought Kate. If a man had brought that client on board, he would be ecstatic. What he really meant, she was sure, was that he was a bit 'iffy' about Kate being in charge of such a major account. She could tell by the apologetic way Charles Grant, the head of dealing, was talking to her that he was thinking along the same lines.

'What Miles wants,' said Charles, 'is a complete

profile – past and present – of Pharescault.'

'But I *gave* him all that ages ago.'

'He seems to think there's something missing.' Charles spread his hands eloquently in front of him. 'Something about the distribution of shareholdings.' He noted Kate's mutinous expression. 'Look Kate, I'm really sorry, but you know what Miles is like when he gets a bee in his bonnet. I'm more than satisfied about the whole thing, but Miles, well . . .'

'Miles doesn't trust me to do a good job.'

'Miles is very old-fashioned . . .'

'Meaning that he'd prefer me to cook lunch for him rather than make a great deal of money for his company.'

Charles laughed. 'Since you mention it, yes. But as you say, you're making – and have made – a great deal of money for us. He's not unaware of that, Kate. I've been putting more than a few words in his ear.' He stood up. 'And I'll carry on doing so. Just prove to him that you're not going to lose a great deal over Pharescault, okay?'

'But I don't have *time* to go digging out that information all over again!'

'I know. I've thought of that. If it's all right with you, I think I'll ask Mark to do it.' He saw, again, her thunderous expression. 'At least, to help you do it. You know how keen he's been on this one all along, Kate. And he's young, you know. Quite green. It would do him good to work under you for a bit, to take direction from you.' A slow smile spread across Kate's face. Charles took it to mean she was pleased at his suggestion, at his flattery. 'So that's all right, then?' he finished.

'Absolutely. A marvellous idea.' It was certainly,

she thought an *interesting* idea.

Even more interesting was her meeting, the next day, at the Ritz. Again the man from the opera was waiting for her. Again he welcomed her like an old and valued friend. And again he declined to offer his name, or to enquire after her own.

'Anonymity,' he smiled, 'is the key. The more you know about a person, the more they acquire a personality.'

'Yes, agreed, but giving away your name is hardly unlocking your personality.'

'It proves you exist.'

'Oh come on!' Kate thought this was going a bit far. 'I *know* you exist. You're sitting opposite me. I'm sitting opposite you. We're talking, we're drinking champagne. Other people can see us. Of course we exist.'

'But, for each other, we only exist in this specific, minutely defined situation. We can't operate in another environment if we don't know who we are. Think about it. If you *really* didn't have a name, how would you identify yourself to other people?'

Kate wasn't impressed by that one. 'By my personality, or course. Your argument doesn't make sense.'

'Yes it does. I said that the more you know about a person, the more they acquire a personality. I know almost nothing about you. You know very little about me. That's the way it will stay. Almost, if you like, as objects.'

'I don't like being treated as an object.'

'Some objects are very valuable. Some people treat their objects far better than they treat other people.'

Prompted by his words, an image floated into Kate's mind. It was of herself and Rupert and Sebastian. They had treated her, with infinite delicacy, as a precious object. It was as if they had been worshipping her. And she had done the same to them. Objects. Objects of desire.

She took a contemplative sip of champagne. 'You're very clever, aren't you? I called you arrogant the other night. I think perhaps you are arrogant, but as I don't really know you I can't tell, can I?' She smiled at him. 'But your words are clever. You're telling me, aren't you, that the way to succeed in this job is to remove any notion of real people, and concept of personality, from the people I'm dealing with?'

'Something like that.'

'So why was I allowed to know Sebastian and Rupert's names?'

'You weren't actually. Those aren't their real names.'

Kate waved her hand dismissively. 'I'd already guessed that much, thank you. But they were still *names*. Why?'

'Oh, I don't know. Seemed like a good idea at the time.' Certainly was, thought Kate. The whole night had been an immensely good idea. She looked at her champagne glass, at her attractive companion, at the Rococo splendour of her surroundings. 'All this,' she indicated the room with a sweep of her hand, 'all this plushness. All this smart conversation and pseudo-philosophical banter is just a sop, isn't it? It's just a sop to make me feel I'm not actually just a tart who's going to earn lots of money for you.' The words were not prompted by their conversation, they were prompted by an earlier conversation, the one with Charles Grant. For Kate was beginning to feel that Courtenay de Witt, not this man opposite her, was playing her along. Of course this man was going to make money out of her. But he wasn't trying to steal her soul.

'I hope,' said her companion after a moment, 'that you don't really believe that. We're two civilised people having an equally civilised conversation, and I'm not trying to pull the wool over your eyes. I have no idea how much your clients will pay you. That's really up to you. And I don't take a cut from it.' He frowned. 'I thought Sebastian would tell you that. Evidently he forgot.' He looked her straight in the eye. 'The clients pay me a set – and separate – fee. What they give you is yours.'

'Oh.' Kate was pleased to hear that. It was, like everything else about this man, civilised.

'And as for your being a tart, you really couldn't be more wrong.'

'Sorry.' Kate's reply was sarcastic. 'I meant courtesan.'

'That, I suppose, is the official word. But it's still a long way from the truth.'

'Oh?'

He leaned closer to her. 'If you sell your body up against a wall for a fiver, then you're a tart.' Now he looked appraisingly at her. 'But if you're Cleopatra and sell it against a pyramid for the price of a country then what you are, my dear, is a diplomat.'

Chapter Five

DIPLOMACY. KATE WAS good at diplomacy. She already knew that. Her upbringing, her education, her job – all of them had trained her in the art of diplomacy. Diplomacy was playing with power. So was sex. Her sexuality had only been fully awakened – and there was a bitter irony – by Steven, the man who had so coolly and clinically dumped her. She had only been a pawn in his cynical game of sexual diplomacy. She hadn't seen herself as a player. Well, now she was. A player in an altogether more sophisticated game. What she got out of this game was entirely up to her. Money – money that she didn't even need – was a certainty. So was power. And, most importantly, so was her own sexual gratification. But that would depend on how she played the game.

She paced the drawing room of the flat. Here she was, awaiting her first client. She wondered what he would be like. Then she remembered that it didn't matter. He would, as a personality, be an irrelevance to her. He would probably bore her. He would no doubt bore *into* her. But she would be the one screwing him. She would be the one having fun. He arrived. He was foreign. That didn't surprise her. Most of them, she had been told, would probably be foreign. He was also very well-mannered and extremely polite. Would he care for a drink, she enquired? He accepted with alacrity. She fetched the bottle of champagne in its cooler. She herself wanted to drink a lot. She was, after all, nervous. But she didn't want her client to drink too much. All she wanted was to fire his eagerness for sex. She didn't want to diminish his ability to perform: to screw her. For she, ultimately, would be the one doing the screwing.

She was already excited. Just looking at him as an anonymous sexual performer made her feel hot. Yet she knew she had to excite him. She asked him about himself. He told her many things about his business, his travels, his importance. He was telling her that he was rich. He was boring her. He was getting excited. His own power excited him. That didn't surprise her. What did surprise her was that she was becoming even more excited – by her ability to excite him. She moved closer to him. He responded by touching her, very gently, on the face. Then he bent her head towards his. Kissing, she thought. I'm supposed to kiss this person. She did. It was easy. Their mouths met; his hungry, hers compliant. His tongue wriggled around, searching for hers, exploring the dark, plush cavern of her mouth. Kate saw herself almost as an observer, disassociated from the embrace in which her body was participating.

Then he pulled away. He didn't look at her as

317

he announced, in a gruff, almost embarrassed way, that he would kiss her somewhere else. With that, he knelt in front of her on the sofa, roughly pushed her dress up, pulled off her panties, and buried his head between her legs. Kate was more than a little taken aback. She hadn't expected him to move so quickly – and she hadn't expected him to be so rough. Yet his roughness only served to increase her fervour. She moaned softly. The man was eating her as if he were starving, lapping at her sex, darting inside her with his wet tongue, exploring that cavern as he had explored her mouth.

Kate moaned again and grabbed the man's head. He appeared to like that, and shoved his face further into her. She was desperate for him to find her clitoris, to massage it and coax it into begging, budding tautness, yet he contented himself with exploring and nibbling her outer lips, with lapping at her labia with his thick, urgent tongue. The sensation was pleasant – but not enough. Kate let go of the man's head and let her hands wander under her dress to her breasts; to the nipples that, instead, she coaxed and stimulated into hardness. Her actions soon made her desperate – in one swift movement she then pulled her dress over her head. She felt as if the man who was trying to pleasure her below was merely an adjunct to her masturbation session – an appendage that would soon find its true, primeval purpose. Again she started playing idly with her nipples, flicking them gently, teasing them into hardness, enjoying the sensation of playing with her breasts while this stranger was playing down below.

Then he lifted his head and saw what she was doing. Suddenly there was a glint in his eye. Hunger of a different kind. He tried to lunge at her, to lap at her breasts with his mouth. Kate quickly altered her instinctive reaction of self-defence into a teasing, coquettish gesture. The slap on the face became a gentle, finger-waving admonition and, in a sultry, husky voice, she told him to take off his clothes. 'You're still dressed,' she teased. 'I want you to be naked. I want you to be comfortable.'

He obeyed her. The glint in his eyes intensified as he stood up and started tearing off his clothes. Kate decided not to help him. Seeing this man stripping before her was a turn-on in itself – not because he had a particularly exciting body, but because it served as a reminder to Kate of her power, of the fact that she possessed what he so patently and impatiently wanted. As he pulled off one garment after the other, Kate began to play with her breasts with one hand and to massage her clitoris with the other. Yet she kept her eyes on his. It made, she thought, for a highly charged tableau; she, the temptress, teasing him with her enjoyment of her body and he the hunter, desperate to get at his prey.

Now he was naked. He bent down towards her but, again, she stalled. She pushed him back upright and stood in front of him, smiling into his eyes. She ran her hands over the back of his neck, down the sides of his back, and lightly massaged his buttocks as she began to kiss him; little darting kisses that teased him, pecked him, tantalised him. She could feel the head of his prick throbbing against her as she whispered.

'Not here. In the bedroom.' She was stroking his chest now, threading her fingers through the hairs that, she had been pleased to discover, were glossy and silken. 'It's warmer there, more luxurious. And I want this to last.' With that she broke away from him, picked up her champagne glass and put it to her mouth. She gazed at him over the rim as she drank deeply. 'Let's take this through with us.'

She had obviously made the right move. His excitement was increasing visibly. He murmured muffled endearments into her ear, into her hair and her neck as he followed her into the bedroom. Languidly, Kate sprawled on the bed and opened her arms to him. 'Come.' Then she parted her legs. 'Come to me.' In one frenzied leap he was on the bed, all over her. Then he started sucking at her breasts, nibbling at her nipples with his teeth, licking and sucking and at the same time massaging her breasts. Kate moved her head from side to side; if she had thought she would have to imitate sexual delirium, she had been wrong. She needed no pretence here. She moaned, more loudly this time. He took this as an invitation to move his hands further down her body, to massage between her legs. Kate gasped as his hand found her clitoris. So he did know she had one. His hand pressed roughly, almost too roughly right on its centre. Then he moved his hand up and down in an awkward, jerking movement. It was slightly slightly painful. And, as with Rupert on the balcony, it was also a strange and unexpected trigger to pleasure. 'Oh!' yelled Kate. 'Oh God . . . oh please .. . oh yes. No!'

320

But he was not interested in her pleasure, or even in her pain. He shifted position, moved both his hands, and his mouth came crushing down on hers. This time she responded eagerly. He found her tongue and caught it between his lips, sucking deeply and wetly. Again Kate touched him on the head, the shoulders and the back; confident caressing motions that urged him deeper into her mouth and caused his loins to tremble against hers. His thick cock was now pressing eagerly on her stomach and, slipping her hands between his body and her own, Kate reached for it. The feel of it, the texture and the hardness, were reassuring, erotic and pleasing.

At her touch on his sex, the man above her reared up so that his head was way above hers. The glint in his eyes was now wild, lust-crazed and unfocused. A spontaneous, feral roar escaped his lips as he snatched his penis from her grasp and plunged into her.

It was a strange coupling. She, groaning and writhing beneath him; he, panting and pistoning above her. He stabbed at her, then drew back and pumped with rapid movements at the entrance of her sex with the bulbous head of his cock. Kate forced herself to relax, to let him in. Then he was back inside and shafting her deeply again. This time, Kate was ready. This time, Kate enjoyed it. And this time, he climaxed after twelve short strokes. Kate felt him shuddering above her, felt him plunge one last time into her and shoot his seed. He moaned in ecstasy.

Then there was nothing but the sound of their breathing. His breaths came initially in short, sharp bursts as he fought to reclaim his strength, his power. Kate's were deeper and softer; relief mixed with a strange sense of victory. She pushed him gently off her, yet not away from her, and looked into his eyes. She smiled. So did he. 'That was ... that was *perfect*,' he sighed. 'You were perfect.'

Kate felt a sudden rush of pity for the exhausted man lying next to her. Gently, she touched his face. 'So were you,' she said. 'You were so ... so ...'

He took her hand and pressed it to his mouth. It was a sweet gesture. This man, she thought, might well be sweet. What a pity I neither really know nor care. For half an hour, he dozed beside her. Then, as if operating to the dictates of some internal alarm system, he got up and left the bedroom. Kate heard swooshing and splashing from the bathroom – and then silence as he returned to the drawing room for his clothes. When he returned, he was dressed. Kate the stockbroker wished him gone as soon as possible. Kate the seductress had other ideas. Kate the seductress hadn't yet had the pleasure of her own orgasm. She smiled and slowly, coolly, she propped herself up on one elbow and reached for her glass of champagne. 'Stay,' she entreated, 'stay.' Her pose was kittenish, her voice a low purr.

'I can't.' He sounded genuinely upset. 'I've got ... I've got to go.'

'Will I see you again?'

'I hope so. I hope for the night next time.' He threw an envelope on to the bed. 'In which case, there'll be more of that.'

'Oh you are *sweet*.' Kate hoped she wasn't

overdoing it. She wasn't. He looked at her in admiration. 'I hope there will be many more occasions, Cleo.' And then he was gone.

Kate waited until she heard the front door close behind him. Then she let out a whoop of joy and scrambled to the end of the bed where the envelope had fallen. Tearing at it with frantic fingers, she marvelled at its thickness. She lay on her back and let its contents spill all over her body. Then she started to laugh, a deep, throaty laugh of pure satisfaction. She most certainly hadn't sold her body for a fiver. She was anything but a tart. She had told him her name was Cleo – the man from the opera would appreciate that – and this huge, decadent, luxurious bed was her pyramid. And even if she hadn't sold herself for the price of a country, she hadn't done too badly. Where she had been naked a moment before, she was now wearing two thousand pounds. Some things, she reckoned, were even better than orgasms.

Chapter Six

TWO DAYS LATER, she met her next client. She opened the door to him – and to a strange sensation that she had met him before, that she knew who he was. He was tall, very tall, and exuded an air of supreme confidence. He appeared worldly in the sense that he was accustomed to bending the world to his will, that other people's rules didn't apply to him. Yet, like the man of two nights ago, he was charming, polite, and well-mannered. She wondered why such men had to seek illicit pleasures.

'I'm Jim,' said the man as she ushered him through the front door.

'And I'm Cleo.' So normal, so formal. So at odds with the reasons why they were both here. Yet she wasn't called Cleo and he wasn't called Jim. Somewhere in the back of her mind, she knew what his real name was. She had either heard it or read it somewhere. No matter, she thought. Names go with personalities. This isn't a personality. It's a client.

He was, however, quite interesting. Over

champagne he talked about shares, bonds and futures. It made Kate realise why girls like herself became courtesans. These rich, hugely successful clients didn't just want a pretty face; they wanted someone who could at least relate to what they were talking about, to the only things they were capable of talking about.

'You seem remarkably well-informed, Cleo. I was afraid I'd bore you with my conversation.'

'Not a bit,' laughed Kate. 'I read my *Investor's Chronicle* like other people read their Bibles.'

'Oh.' Jim was slightly taken aback. 'I didn't expect that.'

'What did you expect?' teased Kate.

'Well . . . I expected, of course, someone strong. Someone who knows what she wants. Someone who's not afraid of exercising her . . . her *control*, if you like.'

Kate was beginning to have an inkling of what was expected of her. This powerful City financier sitting before her may be powerful in the boardroom, but she suspected something else in the bedroom. Something that his wife – he was bound to have a wife – would balk at. She stood up, drawing herself proudly to her full height. She was five foot ten. A useful height for occasions like this. 'So you didn't,' she said with an edge to her voice, 'expect me to be able to understand the *Investor's Chronicle*, is that it?'

Jim squirmed in his chair. There was an element of delight to the movement – and a suggestion of self-loathing. 'No,' he said. 'Not at all. I fully expect someone like you to understand . . . everything.'

Kate was closer to him now, towering above

him as he sat, somehow diminished, in his chair. 'I do,' she replied. 'I understand everything.' She was behind him now, hovering over his head. Suddenly she tugged at his hair. He winced. In pain. In delight. 'But do *you* understand everything?'

'I . . . I don't know what you mean.'

'So you're stupid?' Another tug. Harder this time.

'If you say so, yes.'

'I do say so. And I want you to understand one thing.'

'What's that?' His voice had lost its confident, booming tone and was now quieter, less sure of itself. Whining.

Kate bent down and whispered in his ear. 'I want you to understand that you're mine. You belong to me. And as you're *mine* you'll do what I say, won't you? Won't you?' she repeated, this time tugging none too gently at his ear.

He squirmed again, relishing her harsh words, revelling in her superiority. 'Yes! Yes, I'll do anything you say. Anything.'

She moved again. Standing in front of him now, she looked at him with disgust. 'Stand up!' she barked. He obeyed. 'Strip!' Frantically, he began removing his clothes, revealing white, flabby skin and too much flesh. 'Stay there,' she commanded. Quickly, she moved to the bedroom and to the cupboard in the corner. Sebastian had shown her the contents of that cupboard. He had even had to explain to her the purpose of some of them. Inside was a plethora of equipment catering for every type of sado-masochism, every aspect of bondage – toys for dangerous games.

Quickly, Kate divested herself of her black sheath of a dress and selected a few items. The whip. The black leather hood. A leather garter and suspender belt. What else, she wondered? The little clamps, perhaps. They, Sebastian had explained, were for nipples. Little clamps to encase the buds and torture them, pull at them. Kate had been revolted at the idea, yet now, the thought of using them on this man amused her. She wanted to torture him. He was a symbol of male dominance in the City, the epitome of all she disliked. And today, especially, she would relish the thought of reducing that symbol to a quivering, supine, begging wreck and to salvage only her own pleasure from it. For earlier today Miles Courtenay had personally hauled her over the coals for what he considered to be inept research into the background of Pharescault. He knew as well as she did that Courtenay de Witt employed highly paid researchers. He knew that if any mistakes had been made, they would have been their mistakes. Yet Kate was a woman and the researchers were all men. Enough said.

Smiling to herself, Kate hastily put on her new outfit. The hood was uncomfortable. It would become extremely hot. Yet as she inhaled the smell of the leather, she felt a stirring in her loins. Leather. There was undoubtedly something erotic about it, and more importantly, it was *different*. It made her feel different about herself. It made her feel like a different person. She added the studded gloves to her ensemble. She didn't want to sully her own beautiful hands with the cringing creature next door. Beauty was not something he would appreciate. Ecstasy was another matter. So was exquisite pain.

Kate walked back through to the drawing room. She cracked the whip as she entered. 'Move!' she shouted. The sight of her, the sound of the whip, her commanding, strident voice had the desired effect. He nearly jumped out of his skin. His expression betrayed a mixture of terror and glee. Evidently she had got it right; this was what he wanted. The man from the opera had told her that vast wealth and sexual masochism often went hand in hand. She hadn't believed him. She had laughed at the image of hugely rich, highly successful men begging to be dominated by women. Now she wasn't laughing. Had she been a fly on the wall she would have been amused by the man in front of her, shivering with fear and anticipation. But she wasn't a fly on the wall: she was the lady with the whip, and she despised him. She despised him for his double standards, for the bombastic, bullying arrogance which she knew he would display in the office and for his pathetic need to be dominated in secret, in private, by someone who, once he had had his thrills, wouldn't exist for him. Kate laughed inwardly. Tomorrow, without difficulty, she could find out who he really was; she could expose him, sell her story anonymously. But she knew she wouldn't do that. She was just fantasising. Discretion was the major condition of her employment – and she had a great deal of respect for her employer. But more important than that was the fact that she wasn't interested in this man as an individual: it was what he stood for that interested her, that was even beginning to excite her. If he was indulging in his own private fantasy, then so was she. With each crack of the whip she was flaying an institution, not a man.

'Move!' She had hit him twice now; strokes that sounded harder than they really were. It was the 'thwack' of the whip that was the point of the exercise. It excited and scared him: it aroused her. This was a new experience for her – and a deeply pleasurable one. Jim hopped about, trying to escape from her. Yet the look in his eyes said 'more'. 'This way!' she commanded, pushing him towards the bathroom. 'You're filthy!' she shouted. 'You're filthy, dirty. What are you?'

'I'm filthy,' he whimpered, 'dirty.'

Now she had dropped the whip and had him by the hair. She shoved him towards the shower and bundled him into the cubicle. Then she turned the dial and there was water everywhere. He screamed. 'It's too hot!' he wailed. 'It's boiling!' He tried to escape from the jets of water, yet everywhere he turned there was more. The water came from above, below and from all around him. Kate knew it wasn't too hot, yet she turned down the temperature. She mustn't, she thought, get too carried away. She might end up *really* hurting him. And that wasn't necessary to fulfil her fantasy.

'It had to be hot,' she snarled, 'to wash away all those other women.' She glared at him through the slits in the hood.

'You've been with other women, haven't you?'

'No! No, I swear I haven't! I haven't!'

'Yes you have. You've been bad with other women. I can still smell them.' She looked around her and grabbed the back-scrubber from the shelf beside her. 'I'm going to wash them off you, I'm going to scrub you until you're clean and until you beg for mercy. You'll like that, won't you?'

'Yes! Yes, please!'

'But you won't like it *too* much, will you? Because if you do, I'll have to punish you again.'

'Yes! No!' he cried, almost delirious with excitement, not knowing what he was saying, just willing her to attack him with the bristles of the long brush. The bristles were softer than Kate had hoped, yet his skin was so raw from the water that they did- the job. She scrubbed his head, his hands, his shoulders and his back. In great parrying thrusts she attacked his legs, his feet and his buttocks. Then, as he squirmed and squealed in agonised delight, she concentrated on his genitals. His cock and balls were small, the former displaying only feeble signs of arousal. As she scrubbed them he closed his eyes and threw his head back, as if he were in the throes of orgasm. Yet his prick shrivelled in self-defence and his balls tightened as she attacked them. Pain and pleasure, she thought. He enjoys pain. It gives him pleasure. Not necessarily sexual pleasure. Just pleasure.

She began to feel herself becoming excited once more. She was completely in control. She could do anything she wanted to this man.

Now the brush was at the entrance to his anus. He squealed. Kate began to prod, to poke at the tiny puckered hole with the head of the scrubber. Kate shoved harder. There was no way she could get the head of the scrubber into him, but he was revelling in her every try. She noticed the beginnings of another erection and smiled to herself. She remembered that, long ago, Steven had once had a shattering orgasm prompted by her finger inside his bottom. Was this, she wondered, what all men were really like? Did they all have a secret, deep-seated desire to be penetrated?

'You're getting excited,' she shouted.

'Yes,' panted Jim. 'Yes . . . excited. Do it more . . . please . . .'

'No!' she screamed, withdrawing the brush. 'No! You're not allowed to get excited! Bad!' she yelled. 'Naughty! Not allowed.' He looked genuinely contrite, as if he were a little boy caught breaking a simple rule. 'Get out,' she continued. 'Dry yourself and get into the bedroom. You have to be punished.'

He perked up at the mention of punishment and rubbed himself furiously with the bath sheet that Kate threw at him. She walked into the bedroom ahead of him, cracking the whip as she went. I'm enjoying this, she thought. Does this mean this is my true sexual persona? Am I a power-hungry, lust-crazed dominatrix? She caught sight of herself in the mirror. No, she decided, this isn't really me, but I *am* enjoying it. And that's partly because I'm angry at what this man stands for. And anger can do funny things to you. Like fear, it makes the adrenaline churn through your body. It can sweep along other emotions in its wake, turning it into a melange of conflicting desires. You can wet yourself through fear, she reasoned, but the tiny wetness seeping gently through her sex had nothing to do with fear. It was due to that concoction of sensations welling within her. And sensation, she knew, was all.

He appeared at the bedroom door. 'On the bed,' she snapped. With alacrity, he jumped to her command and lay on his back in the middle of the bed. He looked at her as a recalcitrant puppy might look at its master, wagging its tail in hope, still eager to please. But in this case, his tail was his penis, and as he looked at her, at her hood, leather garter and the studded gloves, his semi-erection stirred again. He was waiting for her next command: he knew what it should be. So did Kate. She strode towards the cupboard once more, this time extracting two sets of manacles.

He saw what she was doing and could barely contain his excitement. 'No!' he screamed. 'Please! Don't tie me up . . . please don't tie me up! I'll be good . . .'

'Too late,' said Kate. 'And anyway you're not capable of being good.' She whirled round to face him. 'You're bad. You're rotten, through and through. Rotten to the core. And do you know what happens to people who are bad?'

His eyes were nearly popping out of his head now. 'They . . . they get punished,' he stammered.

'And how do they get punished?'

'They get tied up . . . and beaten.'

So she was required to whip him again. The thought did not displease her. She climbed on to the bed and shackled his wrists to the headboard. His ankles were more difficult. She had to pull his legs as far apart as they would go in order to tie them to the foot of the bed. Then she stood up on the bed, towering above him, relishing the total dominance she now had over him. She could do anything she wanted with him now. She could even leave the flat and abandon him there, manacled to the bed. The thought amused for one brief, wild moment. If she did that, he would regain his senses, his fantasy would fade and his alter ego, his 'true self' would re-emerge. That would be one humiliation. But she was happy to humiliate him in the manner he desired; that way she would have the opportunity to do it again – and again.

She picked up the whip and dangled it over him. Suddenly he looked more terrified than before. She didn't blame him. If she used the whip on his inert form she could inflict very real damage. She could damage him so severely that his wife would see; so severely that he wouldn't be able to work. That thought amused her. But that would not do. Instead she jumped off the bed and towards the dressing table where she had left the nipple clamps. She also picked up her hairbrush. That would do, she thought. She would spank him with that. 'Do you know what these are?' she asked, brandishing the clamps. She could tell by his expression that he genuinely didn't know. 'They're instruments of torture,' she explained. 'See? I put them on like . . . *this*, and suddenly you're in pain.' He howled as she attached them to his flabby breasts. Yet even as she clamped them on to him, she saw his nipples contracting – either in pain or with pleasure. It didn't matter. Now she went to work with the hairbrush, slapping him with resounding smacks, inflicting little blows that left white patches on his skin.

He hated it. Or perhaps he loved it. Kate didn't care. All she cared about was that she herself was beginning to love what she was doing. She watched him flinch and wriggle in pain. She saw him try to squirm out of the bonds that kept him tied to the bed, completely at her mercy. She was the all-powerful aggressor. Behind the hood she was anonymous, invincible.

Kate realised suddenly that she was beginning to fantasise. Behind the hood she could think what she wanted. The man before her had ceased to exist for her. Now he was just an instrument who would eventually play a part in her fantasy. She felt herself becoming wetter, felt her lips swell and her clitoris begin to harden. She felt wild and free and omnipotent. The latent exhibitionism that she had displayed at the opera was developing. Then, she had been both carried away and ashamed of herself. Now, she was simply carried away. At the opera, she had been embarrassed that the audience might see what she was doing. Now, her audience was spread-eagled on the bed before her. Trapped. Tied to her whims. Unable to extricate himself from her fantasy. She leaped on to the bed, suddenly more aroused than ever. Still spanking her captor, she crawled to his face and whispered in his ear. 'I'm going to suffocate you,' she purred. 'I'm going to make sure you can't breathe. I'm going to kill you.'

'No! No ... *please!*' Again his whole body shook. Again the near-tumescent prick bobbed against his stomach.

Positioning herself to face the end of the bed, Kate squatted over his head and cupped his balls in her hand. Slowly, she manoeuvred herself down on his face as the same time as she squeezed his balls. She didn't want him to give her head; she knew he wouldn't know what to do. All she wanted to do was to rub herself against him, to force his face to massage her wherever she wanted. She found her pleasure with the tip of his nose.

She could tell he was outraged. His whole body squirmed beneath her and she sensed him gasping for air. She raised her bottom slightly, lowered her head – and took him into her mouth. His cock was stiff now; not huge but fully erect. She let it massage her throat. She closed her eyes and sucked his glans within her, running her tongue in sweet caress around the sensitive tip. This was *her* fantasy. She could do what she liked. And this was not *him* beneath her. She had forgotten who he was. He was the possessor of a cock. That was all that mattered. She sucked gently, teasingly, intent on keeping him there and at the same time keeping him from coming until it should please her for him to do so. In her mind, in her fantasy, she saw herself bent over this man, using him to stimulate her body, knowing that he was powerless under her command. His manacles were almost irrelevant. Even if he had been free to move, he would still have had no control over his need for her.

Then she became enraged as she sensed the imminence of his orgasm. She let him out of her mouth in a flash. 'No,' she cried. 'That's not allowed! You've been bad. You're a bad boy. You can't do *anything* until I tell you.' To emphasise her point, she squeezed his balls again; harder this time, hard enough to make his erection subside and to provoke an agonised moan that became muffled as she savagely pressed herself to his face once more, drowning his protests. His tongue entered her. She hadn't expected that. It pressed a hidden button inside her. Now she was ready. Quickly, she pulled herself off him and rose to her feet above him on the bed. Her legs could hardly support her now, such was the heat, the rush and the power of the churning sensations at their apex.

It didn't matter. He thought she was quivering with rage. Again he became wildly excited. She started shouting at him, calling him a filthy bastard, a dirty swine, a stupid, ignorant, bad boy who deserved more punishment and greater pain. His face was scrunched up in anguished torment. As she lowered herself to her knees and pulled at the clamps on his nipples, he screamed that he couldn't take any more punishment, that he'd had enough. It was just what Kate wanted to hear. Her eyes closed behind the hood, her hands let go of his body, her sex descended on to his and her mind transported her to a place where, as she rocked up and down, she knew she was screwing the world.

He gave her a lot of money. She told him he would have to be punished for doing so. He smiled and said he hoped so. But she doubted he would come back. She had called him Miles.

Chapter Seven

'IT'S NOT THAT we think you've done anything wrong . . .'

'So what is it then?' Kate was so angry she lost sight of the fact that she was addressing the company chairman. She glared belligerently at him and waited for an answer.

Miles Courtenay was clearly taken aback by her anger. He wasn't used to being addressed in this manner even by his most senior colleagues – let alone by a woman who had, he firmly believed, been so keen to take on a major client that she had overlooked some essential background information.

'I don't see where I went wrong,' continued Kate, too impatient to wait for his answer. 'I acted on the information provided by the research department. I don't wish to implicate them in what is, after all, only a rumour, but . . .'

'But no serious corporate financier would go all out for a client of the magnitude of Pharescault without doing a little research of their own.' Miles's voice was harsh. His eyes ice-cold.

'I don't understand,' said Kate.

'Perhaps that's because you're not a serious corporate financier.'

'Miles,' interjected Charles Grant. 'Please. I think you're letting your emotions take control here. I realise you're worried, but as Kate said, it is, after all, only a rumour.'

Miles now directed his glare at Charles. 'And as you well know, in today's climate, any rumours of money laundering have to be taken extremely seriously. *Extremely* seriously.' He banged a fist on the desk in front of him. 'For Christ's sake!' he yelled, 'it now appears that the market was rife with stories about Pharescault.' He swung sharply back to Kate. 'Didn't you hear *any* of them?'

Kate, desperately trying to keep her temper under control, replied evenly, 'If I spent all my working life listening to stories I wouldn't have any time left to do my job.' She made a placatory gesture. 'I realise that if this is true – *if* it is true – then we will be party to some fairly serious charges of fraud . . .'

'And do you know what will happen to us?'

Kate tried valiantly to disguise her contempt for the man before her. She knew Courtenay de Witt would be fined massively. She also knew that wasn't Miles's main concern. He would probably, she mused, be blackballed from all his clubs. A fate he would consider worse than death. 'I imagine,' she said, 'that we'll be implicated but found not culpable. It's not as if this will set a precedent within the financial market.'

'It will,' replied Miles icily, 'set a precedent for Courtenay de Witt.'

Again Charles intervened in what he saw as more a clash of personalities than a corporate blunder. 'Look,' he said, 'Pharescault has had a blameless record for longer than anyone can remember . . .'

'Until that blasted Nero de l'Escault-Tonnère inherited the chairmanship.'

Kate wondered how many people were already talking about Courtenay de Witt's blameless relationship – until that blasted Miles Courtenay inherited the chairmanship. Miles's father, thought Kate bitterly, may have been, privately, an out-and-out misogynist, but at least he'd treated women with the consummate charm and deference typical of his generation. Not like his shit of a son.

'There is nothing,' continued Charles calmly, 'to suggest that Nero has anything to do with any . . . er, irregularities in the financial conduct of Pharescault.'

'Apart from the fact that he's a jumped-up little shit,' said Miles.

Snap, thought Kate.

Miles turned to her again. 'You've met him, haven't you? What's he like?' His lip curled slightly and he continued. 'You even spent a weekend with him, I gather. We don't encourage that, by the way.'

Kate ignored his last remark. It was totally untrue. Solely designed to wound. 'He is,' she replied, 'extremely charming. Chivalrous, courteous.' She wanted to add that he had a cock even bigger than Miles's ego. Instead, quite pointedly, she added, 'And so is his wife, Ghislaine.'

'Humph.' Miles, for once, was lost for a ready reply. He looked round to Charles. 'So what do you suggest we do?'

'Nothing. I suggest we continue as we are. Unless – or until – Mark comes up with something.'

Kate had to bite her lip at the mention of Mark. She, after all, had complained that she didn't have time to try to substantiate rumours of Pharescault's money laundering. Charles had already put Mark on to the case with her – albeit reluctant – agreement.

Miles looked triumphantly at Kate. 'I'm sure that boy *will* come up with something,' he said. 'He's extremely bright, that one.'

Any notions Kate might have had about Mark being a breath of fresh air had evaporated. It wasn't, she supposed, *his* fault that he was Miles Courtenay's blue-eyed boy, but that increasingly obvious fact was doing nothing to endear him to her. She wondered, momentarily, if she should offer to resign. Then she checked herself. That, no doubt, was what Miles was expecting her to do. He wouldn't dare fire her on the flimsy grounds he possessed: even he was conscious of Courtenay de Witt's appalling reputation as far as women were concerned. Firing her would do his image no good whatsoever. And image, to Miles, was all. She looked covertly at him and wondered, fleetingly, what would happen if she opened the door of the flat in Mayfair one night to find Miles standing there. The very idea, of course, was laughable. But what she would do to him wasn't. She would give him the same treatment as she had given the man who called himself Jim. In her eyes, they were one and the same.

Mark, to give him his due, was sympathetic. 'I'm really sorry about all this,' he said later in the day. 'Charles told me that Miles had a bit of a blind spot where you're concerned and . . . well, I don't want you to think that I'm trying to get one over you.'

Kate nearly said she doubted that was possible. Instead she looked at his smiling, apologetic face, but before she could reply an alarm bell rang in her mind. There was something about his face that didn't *fit*. That sort of face had troubled her before. She wanted to like it – but she found herself faintly repelled by an emotion she couldn't quite identify. 'S'all right, Mark,' she said at last. 'I know it's not your fault.' Then she grinned. 'I shouldn't have been so bullish about trying to bring Pharescault on board all on my own.'

'If it's any consolation,' replied Mark, 'I would have done the same thing in your shoes.'

'You nearly did.'

'Yes.' Mark smiled a tight little smile. 'I nearly did.'

Kate had the strong impression that he wanted to tell her something. His suddenly hesitant manner indicated that he was fighting with something, some sort of inner turmoil. The moment passed. 'You look tired,' he said suddenly. 'I hope you're not letting all this interfere with your sleep.'

If you spent, she thought, two nights a week having sex with strange men then you'd look

341

pretty tired as well. 'No, no,' she said. 'Late nights, that's all.'

Mark looked at her impeccable attire and grinned. 'At least you've been getting home at night.'

Kate returned the look. 'So, I see, have you.'

Their eyes met. Briefly and uneasily.

'Look,' he said, 'if I discover anything about Pharescault that really will get us into trouble, I'll come to you first. Don't think I'll go rushing off to Miles telling tales on you.'

'Thank you. That's kind of you.'

'Not at all. You are, after all, my superior.'

Kate's next night at the Mayfair flat was, initially, a troubling one. The pressures of the day refused to leave her. Charles was still being charming. Miles was still being vile. Robert, at the desk next to her, kept looking at her as if he knew something she didn't. And Mark was largely absent. For two days he had been attending a seminar on money laundering, an activity, as Miles had so rightly said, that was now endemic amongst clients of major City firms. It had become the white-collar crime of the nineties, largely unknown to those outside the City, often undetected by those within. Yet reputations and fortunes were, increasingly, being destroyed by it.

Kate sat, quietly sipping champagne, and contemplated her own position in the current case of Pharescault. There was nothing, *nothing* concrete to indicate that the French company was involved in illegal activities. Nothing that could damage Courtenay de Witt. Nothing that could affect her. Nero himself, of course, was a different matter. She already knew that he had a secret life, one that he neatly compartmentalised in his stunning, secluded country chateau. But did he have another life? A criminal one? Kate had talked several times to him on the phone. Business talk. Serious talk. And she had said nothing about Courtenay de Witt's current investigation of Pharescault. Nero must remain completely ignorant of it. It wouldn't do to alienate a client who may, in the end, turn out actually to possess the blameless reputation of which it boasted. And no mention was made of the bizarre events in which Kate had participated at the Chateau de Grassigny. She had written to Ghislaine to thank her for 'a delightful weekend'. Nero, in one of their conversations, had mentioned that he was glad she had enjoyed her visit. Would she come again, he asked? The tone of his voice had changed when he had uttered those words. Kate, suddenly hesitant, had replied that she wasn't sure. Nero had laughed his deep, throaty, undeniably sexy laugh and said that he *was* sure. Kate felt an unpleasant sensation running down her back. Nero, she felt, knew too much about her.

He was shortly to know more. It was he who was standing on the doorstep when she answered the bell.

'Nero!' Kate let her mouth hang inelegantly open, her shoulders droop as she slumped in surprise against the doorpost.

Nero laughed. 'I surprise you, then?'

Kate had to think quickly. She wasn't just surprised. She was shocked. Appalled. She drew herself to her full height. 'I . . . I wasn't expecting you, no.' This, she thought desperately, must be a ghastly mistake. A desperate, dire coincidence. She mustered a smile. 'And while it's nice to see you, I think there's some sort of mistake. This . .' she gestured inside, 'is a friend's house. I'm just . . . house-sitting. Would you,' she added, 'like to come in? I'm afraid my friend won't be back this evening so you'll miss him but you're welcome . . . a drink or something, yes?' She knew she was wittering. The words were just tumbling out of her mouth. This was worse than anything she could ever have imagined. Nero was standing on her doorstep. Nero was here to visit a courtesan. Kate was that courtesan. Had he known – or was it a genuine coincidence? Or perhaps it was a mistake. 'Or maybe,' she added hopefully, 'you've got the wrong address?'

Nero laughed again. 'No. This is the right address. And I have no interest in your friend. It's you I've come to see . . . Cleo.'

Cleo. So he knew about that. Reluctantly, she stood aside and let him enter. He looked admiringly at her as he passed into the hall. 'You look,' he said, 'expensive. Business must be good.' Again a little laugh.

They went into the drawing room. 'Since you're here,' said Kate through clenched teeth, 'you might as well have a drink.'

'Oh! I thought that since I'm here I could have anything I wanted?' He looked at her in amusement. 'And that's why I'm here.'

'How did you know?' asked Kate as she poured champagne with trembling fingers.

'Oh.' Nero shrugged dismissively. '*On circule.*

344

On rencontre des gens qui racontent des histoires.'

'And exactly what *histoires* have you been hearing?'

'Les histoires des grandes horizontales. That is what you call them in English, is it not?'

'I think you'll find that expression's rather old-fashioned.'

'And you're a modern girl, isn't that right, Kate? Or should I call you Cleo?'

Kate looked at him for a long, silent moment and then perched on the edge of the sofa. She dangled one hand in her glass as she carefully chose her words. 'What I do in my spare time, Nero, is entirely my own business.'

Nero perched on the seat opposite. 'Absolutely,' he said. 'I couldn't agree more. I am the same. I regard my private life as completely separate from my work.'

'Given the nature of your private life, that's probably just as well.'

'Oh Kate, you are so funny.' He took in the room in one sweeping gesture. 'You are living, as you say, in a glass house. I don't think you ought to be throwing stones.'

'Why are you here, Nero? Did you *know* it would be me?'

'I didn't *know*. But I was fairly sure. The person who described you was very accurate in his observations.'

'So you've come to taunt me, to expose me? You're going to go rushing off to Miles Courtenay to tell him what I do in my spare time, is that it?'

Nero looked put out. 'Why on earth should I do that? I don't think you've been listening to what I've been saying. This has nothing to do with business – or at least with stockbroking and corporate finance.'

'I'm not totally naive, Nero. I find it very hard to believe that you don't have some sort of ulterior motive.' Cat and mouse, she told herself. He had played with her previously. He was no doubt here to play with her again. This time for higher stakes.

'You don't trust me very much, do you?' Nero pouted like a thwarted little boy. It didn't suit him, thought Kate. Not at all. He seemed to realise this himself and changed his expression. Now he was the Nero of old. Slightly supercilious. Knowing. 'Look,' he said, 'I agree that when I found out – totally by accident I may add – that there was a lady answering to your description performing this charming . . . service, I was intrigued. I thought I had to come and see for myself that I had been right about you from the moment I first set eyes on you. That you were a true voluptuary.'

'I do this for money, Nero.'

Nero stood up and approached her. 'I don't think that's quite true, do you? You don't really need the money.'

'How do you know? I may have the most appalling debts for all you know. It isn't exactly unheard of for girls like me to go on the game.'

'You do yourself a disservice, my dear. "On the game" has dubious connotations.'

'And you think there's nothing dubious about this?'

'I think it's hilarious. You, as a stockbroker, perform a service that I require and for which I am sure you are sufficiently highly paid. And you, as a courtesan, also perform a service I require. The two can remain completely separate, can they not?'

Kate was beginning to feel disarmed by his proximity. She remembered their drive from Paris to the château. The power emanating from him. The smell of him. The little hairs on his beautiful hands. She wished he wasn't quite such an attractive man.

Now he was touching her face gently, looking at her with something approaching adoration. 'And there's another reason, my dear Kate, why I had to find out if this lady of the night was really yourself.'

'Oh? And what's that?' Kate could feel herself trembling. Damn. He would know why. He would know that she wasn't trembling in fear.

He was nuzzling at her neck now. 'That night, at the château, I suddenly realised that I felt more for you than just lust . . .'

'Liar!' With more strength than she knew she possessed, Kate pushed him away from her. 'You bloody liar! In the light of the way you demonstrated "what you felt for me" I find that extraordinarily difficult to believe.' She glared at him. 'I barely knew you, Nero. I thought I was being invited for a quiet weekend in the country and what did I get instead? Four sex-crazed fiends who drugged me and then gang-banged me!'

Nero laughed again. 'Gang-banged? What a quaint expression.' He looked her straight in the eyes. 'And it's an expression that implies brutality on one part and unwillingness on the other. That's not how I recall that evening, Kate.'

'All right! All right! I *enjoyed* it. I admit I enjoyed

it. I admit I was a willing participant. But don't try to pretend that you wanted anything other than sex. If you wanted anything more meaningful you wouldn't have taken along your friends. *And* your wife, for God's sake.'

'My wife,' said Nero, 'is incapable of achieving orgasm during intercourse, poor thing. She prefers to watch. So sad for her, really.' From his slightly disinterested tone, he might well have been talking about the peculiar fads of a recalcitrant racehorse. Then he addressed her directly again. 'But I agree,' he said, 'it was all too sudden. I myself would have preferred a more . . . a more civilised seduction.'

'Are you talking about me now?' Kate felt herself cast as the horse. The object of discussion.

'Yes.'

'So why the drugs? Why the suddenness if you didn't want it? And why, for heaven's sake, did none of you even *mention* what had happened that night. It wasn't exactly very fair on me, was it?'

Nero looked apologetic. 'No, it wasn't, I admit, very fair. But you see, I was not in control of the situation.'

'What do you mean? It was your house. I was your guest.'

'That may have been so, but I'm afraid on that particular occasion I was answerable to Georges.'

'*Georges*?'

'Yes, Georges. My friend Georges.'

Kate waved her hand dismissively. 'I am perfectly well aware of who Georges is, thank you. But why was he calling the shots?'

'Because I owe him many favours.'

'Oh great. So I was just a favour, was I? I thought you were trying to tell me . . .'

'Kate, Kate. *Please* . . .'

But Kate's thoughts were beginning to take her elsewhere. Nero owed Georges 'many favours'. Interesting.

'So what "favours" did Georges do for you that you are so indebted to him?'

'I hardly think that's relevant to—'

'I think it is. I thought you were trying to explain why your seduction of me – if you can call it that – wasn't quite right, why you had to kowtow to Georges.'

Nero, exasperated, poured himself more champagne with a flourish. 'I am not indebted to Georges. He's helped me make a lot of money, that's all.' Suddenly his eyes took on a dreamy, far-away look. 'And since my father died . . .' Then he stopped abruptly, remembering where he was, who he was with, why he was here. He stared at Kate again. 'But none of that, as I said, is really relevant.'

Kate thought it was. Extremely relevant and extremely interesting. So Georges had come on the scene since Nero's father had died. Nero had made a lot of money since then. And since then Pharescault was rumoured to be money laundering. All very interesting as far as she was concerned. But Nero was now looking speculatively at her. 'Georges – for whatever reasons – was in a position to, as you say "call the shots". You, however, are not. I have no need to explain myself to you.'

Kate smiled sweetly. She didn't want Nero to think she had been listening to, let alone inwardly digesting, his explanations about Georges. And Nero was right. She was hardly in a position to be making demands of him. Despite his protestations, she didn't trust him. He had the power to destroy her career. Power. There it was again. A strong word, a valuable commodity, a concept to be treaty with caution. She remembered another, equally valuable type of power. The one that had brought both of them to this flat tonight. The one that *she* possessed.

'You're right,' she laughed. 'You've caught me in a delicate position.' Then she put down her glass and indicated the door to the bedroom; There was no trace of amusement in her voice as she said, 'Shall we just get on with it then?'

Nero was appalled. She had meant him to be. His commanding look, his imperious tone completely vanished. Her brusque statement had offended every Gallic pore in his body; a body that, however peculiarly it interpreted notions of romance, evidently possessed them. 'Kate! Kate! I can't believe you said that. I'm not here to "get on with it". I know you don't believe me when I say that I'm genuinely drawn to you, but that is the case and you could at least do me the service of pretending to believe me and even to pretend to reciprocate my feelings.'

Kate laughed again, in genuine amusement. 'Oh Nero, you really are quite funny sometimes.' She went up to him and traced a finger over his lips. 'All that wounded pride. If you had a moustache it would be bristling with the indignity of it all.' Now she took her finger away, draped her hands round his neck and looked into his serious, dark, beautifully shaped face. If he really wanted to make love to her, she thought, he could. He would be more than welcome. Because she was desperate to make love to him. 'We find ourselves,' she continued, 'in a very strange position. You are visiting a courtesan. It is her job to make men feel special. Usually I know nothing about them and have to pretend to be interested in them. But this time, Nero, this time it's different. You know your courtesan; she knows you. And there is not an element of pretence, of play-acting when she tells you that there is nothing more that she would like to do at this moment than make love to you.'

'Kate . . .'

'Ssh.' Again she put her fingers to his lips. 'No pretending. This has nothing to do with anything else. Not with business. Not with your private life. I'm not pretending I'm in love with you and you're not in love with me. We're just two people who are wildly attracted to each other. Isn't that . . . isn't that just so *nice*.'

'So exciting. . .' He smiled into her eyes and ran his hands down the front of her jacket, stopping at the first button.

'So . . . liberating,' she whispered as he started undoing the buttons.

'So beautiful,' he said in awe as he stroked her breasts.

'So big,' sighed Kate into his chest. Then she looked up at him and smiled at the same time as her hand traced the bulge under his trousers, 'and so hard.'

They both laughed. Now the desire that had been mounting within both of them was overflowing into their every movement, their every gesture, their every word. They were both semi-naked as their lips closed together once more in a frenzied kiss. Kate was being driven crazy with desire by this man who was pressing himself agamst her; bemg driven crazy by his touch, his skin, by the very smell of him. She drew away from his mouth and pressed her fluttering lips against his eyelashes, against the sculpted bridge of his nose. With her hands she massaged the back of his neck, revelling in the feel of the hard flesh beneath the hairline, the promise of the power that lay in the strong shoulders below. Like an exquisite butterfly alternately flitting and landing on its object of desire, she let her lips travel up and down his face until she again came to his mouth. At first she kissed him softly on the very surface of his lips, travelling along the cruel yet voluptuous lines, mingling his wetness with her own. Then she felt him shudder and pull her closer to him with a firm, impassioned gesture. He crushed her mouth on his, forcing it open, finding her tongue with his own and toying with it, sometimes play-fully, sometimes fiercely until she too shuddered in ecstasy.

His hands were on her back now. He had already removed her jacket, now his expert fingers were undoing her bra, one hand curled up in the intricate lace of the garment, the other cradling her back and rubbing it in great, tender, sweeping motions. Each muscle lost its tension as the smooth palm caressed her skin; she could feel a tiny, delicious spasm every time his fingers encountered tautness and massaged away every sign of tension. She saw herself naked from the waist up, melting even further into his embrace as slowly they both sank to their knees. His mouth left hers and for one tantalising moment she closed her eyes and let herself fantasise about his next movement.

It was no fantasy. With the delicate yet desperate rhythm of a hungry fledgling, Nero's mouth closed over her left nipple, sending blissful sensations all over her, making her muscles tighten again in excitement. She felt hot now, slightly hazy. And strangely disembodied; conscious only of the slow, burning sensation enveloping her whole body. Her breasts swelled against Nero's face as he now nuzzled between them, and her clitoris, in unison with her rigid nipples, was tightening exquisitely. She cradled Nero's head to her, running her fingers through his thick, dark hair and savouring the delicious smell of his hair, the faint aroma of the vestiges of some dark, powerful scent and the stronger aphrodisiac of his maleness.

Kate imagined them as they were, two beautiful bodies in the throes of passion, kneeling against each other, his head under hers, her arms now stroking the tanned, muscular ridges of his back. She imagined them as an ode to Aphrodite, a hymn to Diana, a monument to Apollo and Artemis. The two of them entwined like lovers, engulfed in lust.

The slow, deliberate rhythm of Nero's love-making was doing strange things to her. She had forgotten about games; there was only one role she wanted to play now and she knew it would come naturally to her.

Nero helped her to her feet. He smiled into her

eyes. 'I think,' he said gently, 'it would not do to make love here.' He indicated the carpet. 'The knees. It would rub.'

'Like this, you mean?'

Nero moaned. 'That is not my knee.'

Kate gasped as he, in turn, touched her. 'And that . . . Oh my God . . . that is certainly not *my* knee.' She stood still for one short, beautiful moment as Nero's probing hand nestled against the fabric of her underwear, as one of his fingers rubbed against the silk and searched through the sheer folds of the fabric to the moist folds of her flesh and the erect bud, the little core beneath them. They stood there, boy and girl, man and woman, fondling each other in secret, forbidden places. And then they moved to the bedroom. In a frenzy of lust, they removed their remaining clothes, all the while staring at each other with an aggressive, animal hunger. Kate admired Nero's taut, muscular frame, his broad shoulders, his lithe hips and the coating of silken hairs on his chest that ran in a straight, enticing furrow to his sex. Last time, in a drug-induced daze exacerbated by the flickering firelight of her room at Nero's chateau, Kate had been unable to savour his body, to appreciate the beauty of his maleness and his manhood. Now she could look at him in all his naked and rampant glory.

And he was looking at her. She saw his tongue run across his lips in a gesture of pure animal lust as he gazed at her body, at the wayward, tawny hair, the jutting prominence of her glorious breasts, the gentle, alluring contours of her hips and the dark, moist mound that burned with desire between her legs. With the loping, predatory gait of a panther he advanced towards her. She caught her breath as a frisson of fear ran down her spine. Her own notions of power had disappeared. He was the hunter: she the prey. The willing prey.

She backed towards the bed as he suddenly lunged for her, his eyes narrowed and hard. Suddenly she was on her back on the bed. Strong arms grabbed her ankles and forced her legs apart. She closed her eyes as she felt his breath on her; a cool contrast to the churning heat within her. And then his tongue was in her, his warm, moist, prodding tongue plunging into her cleft. She gasped as it opened her, arousing her further. Preparing her. She opened her thighs further, letting him cover her sex with his mouth as his tongue continued its penetration of her damp, eager furrow. She moaned his name repeatedly. His name meant black. His head, nuzzling at the apex of her desire, was black. And then blackness itself overcame Kate as Nero's tongue lapped at her clitoris and induced a shattering, thunderous orgasm of delirious intensity.

Nero didn't move. It was as if he were drinking in her wetness, sating himself with her juices, savouring her nectar. She lay there panting, feeling delicious little spasms racking through her until she subsided and came to rest in a place called Nirvana. Nero's tongue kept her there, hovering on the edge of desire fulfilled and desire reawakening.

Kate wanted to be reawakened with his hardness. She forced his head away from her and cried out to him. He moved. She moved. And then they were in the middle of the bed, again on their knees, face to face. This time it was Kate who lowered her head. He was fully erect, straining and pulsating. It was terribly important to her that she pleasure him, that she try to do for him what he had done for her. She kissed his long, smooth cock, let her tongue wrap itself round the head and stroke it gently. Nero cupped the back of her head in his hands and she felt herself slowly pushed further forwards, felt his tumescence force itself upon her. Not yet ready to take him deep into her throat, she let her lips slide sideways down the glistening shaft towards the soft silken sac that encased his balls. With exquisite gentleness, she nibbled at the scrotum, letting her teeth both excite and frighten him with their delicate sharpness. She cupped the silken orbs with one hand; with the other, she explored the unfamiliar nether regions between his cock and his anus, the delicate territory where she could further fire his passion. She felt his sex hvitch as she explored with her tongue and fingers; now she could feel it flex against her cheek as she worked her way back up the shaft and once more took the head into her mouth. This time she was ready to take him in as far as she could. She felt his entire body tremble as she went down on him, moving both hands to his taut buttocks as she did so. His taste was delicious, strong and salty and diluted with little drops of viscous, vital pre-come. Nero kept his hands at her head as she sucked him, but let her find her rhythm until he felt himself completely sheathed within her welcoming mouth. Then he began to move his hips back and forth in time to some hidden tune within him, some wicked tempo that would result in a crescendo.

But Kate didn't want that. She sensed his mounting desire, his inevitable climax – and she didn't want her final solace to be cruelly denied her. She pulled back, hearing him gasp as her teeth played gently on the emerging shaft. His eyes were wild as they met hers – there was only one thing they could now focus on. Roughly, he pushed her on to her back. Willingly, she lay down. Instinctively, he straddled her. And wondrously, she felt her vagina blossom and flower in time to welcome his steely rod as it plunged into her.

She was asleep when he left. She hadn't meant to fall asleep, yet after their love-making a sense of total satisfaction, of sweet exhaustion overcame her. But her slumbers were not peaceful. Somewhere in her head a voice spoke to her. She knew the voice, but couldn't identify it. And she couldn't understand what it was saying. All she knew was that it disturbed her. Eventually, it woke her. In sudden fear, she reached out for Nero. He wasn't there. He wasn't anywhere in the flat. And soon she discovered there was nothing at all left to remind her of his visit. Not even an envelope. Nero had broken the rules.

Chapter Eight

TWO DAYS LATER Mark told Kate there was nothing wrong with either the financial or moral conduct of Pharescault.

'Are you sure?' she asked.

Mark looked at her. 'You sound almost disappointed.'

She was. She had spent a lot of time thinking about Nero since his visit to the Mayfair flat – and the one thing her thoughts always came back to was that she didn't trust the man. Not one little bit. She enjoyed his body, she even revelled in it. But his mind was a different matter. And she was now positive that, despite his protestations, it was uppermost in that mind that he now held sway over her. He had the power to wreck her career and she had no doubt that he would use that power if he saw fit.

To illustrate that, he had left her no money. It was his way of demonstrating that he didn't owe her – he owned her.

Kate looked blankly at Mark. She *was* disappointed, she thought. If she had been able to find damaging information about Nero his hold over her would be destroyed. She, instead, could destroy him.

'No, no,' she said quickly. 'Of course I'm not disappointed. Just surprised, I suppose. Miles seemed so positive. So, for that matter, did you.'

Mark smiled at her. 'Well I was wrong, wasn't I? And I'm glad. At least your reputation will remain unsullied.'

Kate smiled thinly back. If only he knew. If only he knew.

Mark pondered her strange expression. She had been so cool of late. While she had seemed to enjoy their light-hearted bantering, he knew that she now regarded him as a sort of 'boy next door'. She had remained unapproachable; impervious to his approaches, uninterested in his slightly clumsy references to sex. His feelings for her remained undiminished, but he knew she was the sort of woman who operated in a man's world – not a boy's one. Yet here she was looking suddenly vulnerable. Lost. Worried. 'Are you all right, Kate?' he finished. 'You look as if you'd seen a ghost.'

A ghost. No, she hadn't seen a ghost. She'd seen Nero. Naked, hovering above her, driving into her both tenderly and unremittingly while her juices had flowed out of her to lubricate them both. No, she thought, she hadn't seen a ghost, but she'd seen the face of the only man who could reduce her to a screaming, crying, quivering wreck. And the only man who had the power to destroy her.

She forced a smile. 'No, no, I'm fine, really. Just

a little tired – and a bit upset. Pharescault's my baby, as you know. I most certainly wasn't looking forward to telling Miles that it was spawned by the devil.' She paused. 'Have you told Miles yet?'

'No. He's away today. I'll tell him tomorrow.'

'Good.' As Mark turned to leave her she called out to him in genuine gratitude. 'And Mark, thanks. Thanks for doing all the work on this one. I really didn't have the time.'

Mark grinned back. 'No problem. It's a pleasure.'

A pleasure, thought Kate as he walked away. What did he know of pleasure? Did he know how closely it was related to pain? And pain was what she felt now. Something had gone badly wrong. Through her lust for power she had indirectly got herself into a position over which she had no control. Nero claimed he had no interest in informing anyone at work of her nocturnal activities. She half-believed him; she believed that her double life added, for him, an extra dimension to their love-making. And owning her would add another, even more dangerous one.

Lost in her thoughts, Kate sat motionless at her desk. What if she had uncovered information with which she could threaten him? She would, in fact, have been fucked in every sense of the word. If she had used that information to destroy him then he would have taken her down with him. If she hadn't used it, then Miles Courtenay would have destroyed her career. Fucked. Her only hope now was that she was mistaken about Nero – that he wasn't dangerous and that he wouldn't return to the Mayfair flat. But she knew that was a forlorn hope. Two nights ago he had left without giving her any money. He had broken the rules.

And to prove his point he returned that night and broke another rule. He didn't come alone. When Kate opened the front door it was to a smiling Nero – and an ecstatic Elodie and Georges. Worse, standing slightly behind them was a complete stranger. In that moment she decided that she hated Nero. She hated him for having the capacity to fill her with wanton lust, to impair her judgement and reduce her in her own eyes. She hated him for playing a different game. For breaking rules.

'Nero!' Again she felt like a hostess whose party had got out of hand. 'I, er . . .'

'. . . didn't expect to see me?' Nero laughed. 'Come on, Kate, you know me better than that. You know how much I enjoy seeing you. You know how much *you* enjoy seeing me.'

They were all in the hall now. Without her realising it, Kate had let them advance into the flat. The place felt hot, claustrophobic. Panic welled up within her.

'And Kate,' Elodie, again overly made-up like some grotesque caricature of a chorus girl, smiled her fleshy, full-lipped smile, 'you can imagine how excited Georges and I were when we heard about your new . . . career.' She laughed heartily, horribly. 'We knew we were right, didn't we Georges? We knew Kate was a true voluptuary.'

Georges was also smiling. 'We knew, *ma chère*, that you were one to appreciate *sensation*. And look,' he gestured around the room they were now entering, the plush, luxurious Mayfair

361

drawing room, 'where your love of sensation has taken you.'

He looked appreciatively at her. She felt a mild, unpleasant churning sensation in her stomach. 'Oh,' continued Georges, 'this, by the way, is Didier. Didier, this is Kate.'

Didier said hello. Kate returned the greeting through gritted teeth as she examined the stranger. He was tall and well-built; attractive in a boorish sort of way. Kate disliked him on sight.

In the drawing room, they made as if to sit down. Kate tried to pre-empt them. 'Look,' she said, 'I'm sorry but I really don't think you can stay. I think you've maybe misunderstood the situation. I can't deny what Nero has obviously told you, but this ... this operation is run on fairly strict lines.' She looked pointedly at Nero. 'I only entertain one client an evening.'

Nero shrugged. 'So? This time you can make an exception. We are all old friends, *hein*?'

'Not true, Nero. And if you don't all leave now I'm going to summon someone who will make you leave.'

Nero was delighted. 'Oh! So you have a bodyguard. My, you must be important.'

Kate looked at him. This, she thought, was the man with whom she had made love the other night. Made love, not 'had sex'. She knew she didn't love him – she hadn't even been sure that she really liked him, but she had, temporarily, trusted him. She had trusted him because she had wanted sexual satisfaction from him. Let that be a lesson, she thought. The trust should come first – and with no strings attached. But she had learned that lesson too late. 'No, she replied curtly, 'I don't have a bodyguard, unlike, so it would seem, the three of you. . .' She gestured towards the impassive Didier.

'Oh, Didier's not our bodyguard,' interjected Georges. 'He's a friend. He's also an actor, by the way.'

Kate missed the teasing tone of his voice, and the quick, loaded glance that passed between all four of her visitors.

'How very nice for him,' she continued, 'but as I said, if you don't leave—'

'Then you'll summon this "someone".' Suddenly there was a harder, more threatening tone to Nero's voice. 'And how much does this person know about you, Kate?'

'I don't know what you mean.'

'Oh dear. Perhaps you're not as clever as I thought. And you a stockbroker too.'

Kate had known exactly what he meant. A tremor of fear ran slowly through her. 'Nero,' she said evenly, 'are you intimating that you are not to be trusted? Are you telling me that you would go back on your word?'

'What word?'

'That you would not tell anyone what I do in the evening.'

Nero, now comfortably ensconced in the sofa, smiled up at her. 'I told Elodie and Georges. But only because I knew they were looking forward to seeing you again. Apart from that, no, I have no intention of telling anyone else.' He crossed his legs, leaving one elegantly shod foot dangling in the air – and one rather less elegant word dangling threateningly in the already charged atmosphere.

'Unless?' Kate said the word for him.

'So you are not stupid. That's good. I'd hate to have a fool looking after my business affairs.' Nero paused for a moment. 'Unless, my dear Kate, you decide that you'd rather not "entertain" us this evening.'

Business affairs, thought Kate. He's threatening you. You can threaten him. She opened her mouth to reply, yet the words didn't come out. You can't threaten him, her brain insisted. The rumours were unfounded. She put one hand to her mouth, stifling the little moan of despair that escaped. She was trapped, she thought, well and truly trapped.

Nero was watching her, enjoying the rapid eye movement that signalled her conflicting thoughts. 'You are thinking,' he said. 'You are thinking, perhaps, that you might not enjoy the four of us this evening?' Slowly, he stood up. 'But think again, my Kate. Think back to the evening at my chateau. You enjoyed that, didn't you?' He sighed. 'You English. You are so *English*. What happened to your expression "the more the merrier"? Why can that not apply to sex as well?'

Why not indeed? she thought. Because this is about to become sex under duress, that's why. This will be rape. Gang rape. Suddenly she felt powerless. She, the predator, was about to be eaten by her prey.

Elodie seemed to be reading her thoughts. 'It's not as if,' she pouted, 'you're going to be doing anything you don't enjoy. We're not going to *hurt* you.'

Kate looked at her speculatively. She believed her. Elodie and Georges, she mused, were truly obsessed by sex, by new experiences, by different sensations. They weren't evil. Nero, however, was a different matter. Was he not their passport to their flights of sexual fantasy? Was he not the one with the collection of obscene, pornographic paintings? Was he not indebted to them? She looked back at him and for the first time saw him as a truly depraved character. If there is any justice in the world, she thought, I'll get back at him one day. Somehow I'll get even. Then she looked away and into herself for strength. Distance yourself, she thought. Play their game, but play it as a character in their fantasies. Play it like a true actress. She turned to face them all and held up her hands. 'All right,' she said, 'I'm sorry. I'm being stupid. I'm just a bit overwhelmed to see you, that's all. And I'm just feeling a bit . . . a bit vulnerable.'

'Oh Kate!' Elodie was all solicitude. She leaped up from her chair and came towards Kate. 'There is no need to feel threatened. Please.' She put one arm around Kate in an intimate, friendly manner. Despite herself, Kate felt reassured. Elodie was as tall as she was, and much bigger. Her voluptuous curves, encased in clothes slightly too tight for her, lent her a certain warmth, a quality of reassurance. Kate smiled uneasily at her. In a way, Elodie was quite refreshing. Rarely had Kate met anyone who carried her sexuality so overtly and so confidently. The woman positively oozed licentiousness. Yet something about her suddenly occurred to Kate. Elodie, she remembered, could be fun. At the château, on the Saturday, she had been hugely entertaining. *Let's pretend*, thought Kate. Let's pretend she is being fun. My entertaining friend.

'So,' continued Elodie, 'I think we should all perhaps settle down and have a drink, *hein*? Then, perhaps, we might go out to dinner. Come, Kate, let's go and raid your kitchen.' Wordlessly, Kate followed Elodie into the kitchenette. Dinner? Elodie's suggestion had really taken her aback. Mechanically, she retrieved glasses from the cupboard while Elodie made a quick and expert examination of the fridge.

'Laurent Perrier!' she exclaimed. 'Vintage too. You have very good taste, Kate. The boys will appreciate that.'

Kate couldn't help smiling. 'The boys.' She remembered the last men who had been introduced to her as boys. There had been nothing remotely boyish about what they had done to her.

And they had done it after drinking vintage Laurent Perrier.

She watched as Elodie opened the champagne and foraged around for something to eat with it. 'You are not,' she said, 'much of an eater, are you Kate? There is only one little pot of caviar in this flat.'

Kate had to laugh. 'This isn't my home, you know, Elodie. I don't actually come here to eat.'

Elodie too laughed. 'Of course. I forgot. You come here to work, *non*?'

Kate was silent for a moment. 'Doesn't it . . . doesn't it even surprise you? What I do, I mean.'

Elodie turned round in surprise. 'No. Should it? If anything, it encourages me. Like Nero, I find you English so . . . so *silly* when it comes to sex. You are being sensible, I think, opening yourself up to new experiences like this.' She looked pensive for a moment. 'But you won't do this for long, will you? You are discovering yourself, are you not?'

Without waiting for Kate to reply, she nodded to herself and continued, 'And when you have found what you are looking for, you will stop, yes?'

'How,' replied Kate, 'do you think I'm going to find what I want when you lot barge in here with the intention of raping me?'

Elodie laughed, loudly and uproariously. 'Rape you? What are you thinking of?' Then, again, she was serious. 'Do not underestimate your own sex, Kate.'

'Meaning?'

'Meaning that the first time I saw you I knew you wanted to experience something you would not dare to initiate on your own. Sex, I mean, with another woman.'

Kate chose not to reply to that one. It struck a chord too deep within her for her to dare respond. 'But what about Georges? And Nero? And this . . . Didier person?'

'Georges is my boyfriend, Kate. He is as open about sex as I am. Nero. . .' Elodie's eyes hardened as she mentioned his name, 'Nero . . .'

'You don't like Nero, do you?' Kate surprised herself by the question. Even more of a surprise was that she knew her suspicion was correct.

'Nero,' replied Elodie, 'is a *difficult* man. Very moody. Very, how do you say, volatile. I think it is because of him that poor Ghislaine . . .'

But Kate didn't want to hear about poor Ghislaine. 'Elodie, this isn't a game, you know. Nero has got me in a very difficult position. If I don't do what he says, then he could lose me my job. He could expose me, ruin my life.'

'Well,' said Elodie brightly as she picked up the champagne glasses, 'you'd better do what he says then, hadn't you?'

She did. Over drinks in the drawing room, she made a special effort to please Nero. Soon she forgot she was making an effort. When Nero wanted to be nice, he was charm itself. When he was in a good mood, he no longer looked depraved, the hard lines on his face became character lines and Kate, despite her better judgement, found herself being drawn to him all over again. This man, she thought, may well be the devil personified but he's an angel in bed. His words are sometimes rough, but his caresses are tender. He may be using me but he can also make me feel needed and wanted. As she fell gradually under his spell she found it more and more difficult to remember that she was acting a part.

She would probably never understand Nero and his motives, but she reckoned she now had the measure of Georges and Elodie. They were sex-crazed. They thought she, Kate, was a 'true voluptuary', but she knew she had nothing on them. As another bottle of champagne was opened and consumed, she also found herself warming to them, and to Elodie in particular. The woman was, if nothing else, brutally and disarmingly honest.

Little by little Kate was beginning to enjoy the game again. It was so divorced from reality that even thinking about it gave her a frisson of excitement. Two lives. A double life. Pretending, play-acting and power – all mixed up together in a potentially lethal cocktail. It was interesting, intriguing – even exciting.

Only when they went out to dinner did she have a chance to talk to Didier. Mellower now, she was prepared to revise her initial impression of him. In the flat, she had noticed him laughing uproariously with Elodie. Boorish or not, she thought, he evidently has a sense of humour.

He did. As food and drink relaxed all of them, Didier began to regale her with extremely funny tales about his experiences with English people. He had the gift of being amusing without being patronising, of making serious points dressed up as anecdotes. And like the others, he was adept at playing the game of pretending that this evening was nothing more than a reunion of old friends.

'So what,' asked Kate at one point, 'brings you to England?'

'Oh,' Didier made a dismissive gesture, 'business, I'm afraid. Boring business.'

'Acting? Acting doesn't sound boring to me.'

There was a brief silence broken by Elodie as she coughed theatrically and touched Kate's arm. 'Didier only acts part-time, Kate. It's a sort of hobby for him. The rest of the time he's in business.'

'What sort of business?' Kate knew that Elodie's interest in "business" started and stopped with that one vague term. She wanted to know more.

But Didier's business appeared to bore him as well as Elodie. 'Just very tedious business, I'm afraid.' His eyes took on a new look, almost a glint, as he addressed Kate anew. 'Not nearly so interesting as my acting.'

'So tell me about that then.'

'Your interest in cinema,' teased Georges, 'must be very limited if you've never seen Didier on screen.'

'Not fair, Georges,' said Didier. 'Remember, Kate lives in England.'

Kate smiled gratefully at him. 'Yes, it's sad how few French films are shown in this country.'

'But on the other hand, a lot of mine are very popular in America.'

'Really? But I thought...' She stopped and looked at her companions. Something was wrong. They were smiling cryptically. They were teasing her. Nero, silent at the head of the table, caught her eye and very slowly and equally deliberately he took an oyster from his plate and swallowed it. Then, still focusing on Kate, he licked the empty shell. When he put it back on his plate a thin sliver of moisture ran out of his mouth. He caught it with his tongue, licked his lips, and then smiled innocently at her. Kate looked from him back to Didier. 'You make,' she began, 'rather specialised sorts of films, don't you?'

Didier laughed. 'Specialised. Yes. I like that term. You could say they're specialised.'

'But they have another, more accurate term?'

'Yes.'

'Which makes them illegal in England?'

'Yes.'

Kate was at once fascinated and repelled. Here, sitting opposite her in one of London's most fashionable restaurants, was a pornographic film star. He looked, she thought, so *ordinary*. His conversation was ordinary – no, more than that, it was civilised. She remembered that she had at first thought him boorish, and rather resented him for being nothing of the sort.

Didier smiled at her. 'You are thinking, are you not, that I am really quite ordinary?'

'Yes, actually, I am.' But she was also thinking about something else. Something that she had never dared to admit – not even to herself. With a huge effort, she forced her attention back to Didier.

'But you must remember,' he was saying, 'that I also find you quite ordinary.'

'Is that supposed to be a compliment?'

He laughed. 'Yes, in a way it is. What I mean is that you don't look like—'

'Yes, I know what you mean.' Kate looked at him, her face devoid of expression. At least she hoped it was devoid of expression. She hoped it didn't betray what was going on in her mind. What's it like, she thought? What on earth is it *really* like? Surely it must get boring after a while. But surely, in the beginning, it gave you a tremendous high. An experience like no other. A tiny, involuntary shudder passed through her body as she considered the implications: a sort of immortality; a weird kind of power. Power over the people – the *truly* anonymous people – whom you were going to sexually arouse. The people you would never even see.

'What's it like?' she asked, suddenly unable to stop herself.

'What's it like to be filmed having sex, to know that thousands of faceless people are going to watch you, to see you, to *salivate* over you?'

For a few seconds, the table was silent. It was Elodie, as usual unable to contemplate silence or control herself when she was excited, who blurted out a response. 'Well,' she said dabbing at her luscious red lips with a crisp linen napkin, 'tonight you are in the lucky position of being able to find out *exactly* what it's like.'

Fantasies. Who were these people who had suddenly appeared in her life to indulge her fantasies? How did they *know* what she was really like? At the Chateau de Grassigny they had ravaged her on her bed and she had loved every minute of it. They had anticipated little desires that had only flickered through her consciousness at odd moments in her adult life – and that she had always dismissed as curiosities or even latent perversions to be quickly and guiltily suppressed. And yet these people had awakened them and satisfied them. They had even left her alone to come to terms with what she had experienced; to view them as simply *experiences*. To forget about them if she so wished. And now they were back. Back to seduce her anew and let her live out her odd, exhibitionist fantasy – at a price. And that price, because of Nero's knowledge of her, would be both her complicity and her silence. By the end of the meal, she realised she was willing, even eager, to pay that price.

Elodie took charge when they returned to the flat. Kate was now more drunk than mellow and surprised herself by how easily she let herself be led by the Frenchwoman. While the men settled down with their cognac in the drawing room,

Elodie ushered Kate into the bedroom. Vague, dream-like thoughts and sequences floated through Kate's mind. I am with a woman, she thought. Only women know what it's like to be a woman; only they know the secret desires, the secret thoughts and the special, secret ways that they like to be touched. The last time – the only time – she had been with Elodie it was as part of a frantic, communal coupling. Now they were on their own.

'Now that we are on our own,' said Elodie with a smile, 'we can do what we want, *hein*?'

'I . . .'

Elodie put one long, commanding finger against Kate's lips. 'Don't tell me,' she said. 'You may not think this is what you want, but it is what you need. Believe me.' Suddenly she turned away towards the bathroom. 'I am going to massage you, *ma chérie*. Take your clothes off while I go to find some oil.'

Kate did as she was told. A massage. Elodie was right. It was exactly what she needed. Despite her slight drunkenness, she still felt tense with excitement and apprehension. She also felt tired. For the last few days chaos had reigned within her mind. Conflicts in every area of her life had conspired to rob her of complete peace of mind. A massage would help restore the balance.

She was almost asleep when Elodie returned. Naked, face down on the bed, beginning to float away in relaxed, happy contemplation of strong hands kneading out the knots in her muscles, she almost resented the reality as she felt Elodie clamber on the bed. 'I don't think . . .'

'Ssh. You are not required to think. Thinking is

not good when you are being massaged. Just because you've got a good brain doesn't mean you have to use it all the time.'

What a liberating idea, mused Kate as she felt Elodie's deft, oiled fingers at the back of her neck. I don't have to think. Moments later, she didn't even have to tell herself not to think. All she was suddenly capable of doing was *experiencing*. The fingers had expertly ironed out the creases in her neck and her shoulders; the tension in her upper back had completely evaporated. And Elodie was mouthing soothing words that drifted dreamily into Kate's consciousness. 'You are so smooth,' she whispered, 'so sleek, so sensitive. It is a pleasure to touch such unblemished skin. You have the beautiful skin of a beautiful woman. There is nothing like it in the world. Nothing like it . . .' The hands moved skilfully and artfully down Kate's body. The pleasure of the massage was intense, yet it had nothing to do with sexual pleasure. The hands, now at the back of her thighs, made no move to explore the area underneath them but carried on down, down and down, bringing Kate with them, gently coaxing her down into an area of her mind she didn't know existed; a place where she found perfect peace, a fusion of her body, her mind and her soul.

She was hardly aware of Elodie's instruction to turn over. Languidly, rousing herself only briefly, not bothering to open her eyes, to break the spell, she obeyed. The hands touched her face. Elodie's hands were large and strong yet her touch was exquisitely delicate as it caressed Kate's forehead, her temples and all the areas of her face where previously unnoticed muscles spasmed and released their tension. This, thought Kate, is bliss. Heaven. Perfect pleasure.

Only when Elodie's hands descended to Kate's breasts did she realise that the pleasure could be intensified. So relaxed was she, so uncluttered was her mind that her entire being was instantly and overwhelmingly receptive to this new idea. The idea of sex. Elodie's touch on Kate's breasts was like an electric shock, it sent a chain of reactions pounding through her body and alerted every pore, every follicle and every gland to a new and delicious presence. As Kate's nipples hardened into spikes of eroticism, so her thighs parted further and her mouth opened into an 'O' of pleasure. Elodie remained at her breasts. Her clever hands caressed them gently. These could be *my* hands, thought Kate ecstatically. Every movement Elodie made was the movement Kate would have made; every cupping gesture, every idle tracing of a finger, every little flick of a fingertip: they were all commands from Kate's own brain. It was as if she and Elodie were one person.

Kate groaned again. 'I want . . .' she began.

'Ssh. I know what you want.' And as Elodie said the words so her knowing hands snaked all over Kate's smooth, brown body and her head descended to take the taut bud of a nipple in her mouth. Kate shuddered in ecstasy. This, she thought, was total arousal. For the first time in her life she acknowledged that women have a different arousal system from men, that the signals are more subtle and the clues less obvious. But Elodie was solving all the clues. And suddenly Kate was no longer passive; she found within herself a desperate desire to respond, to give as well as receive.

The understanding between them was unspoken. Kate's sudden movement meant that they were now side by side, and that her mouth was mere inches from Elodie's. She had never kissed a woman before. It wasn't, she discovered, much different from kissing a man. But it was more gentle. Elodie's mouth as soft as the petals of a flower. Her tongue, on the other hand, was as strong as a man's and as it parted Kate's lips it explored with a familiar and divine energy. As they kissed, their bodies touched in other places. In every other place. Elodie's nimble, practised fingers darted all over Kate, kneading and massaging the softness of her flesh. And then they were parting her thighs even further and one urgent finger was exploring her wetness. They broke free from the kiss and Elodie slowly travelled down Kate's body, licking, touching and pressing in just the right places as she went until her platinum head had replaced the hand between Kate's legs and her talented tongue was lapping at the deep, moist valley.

The tongue slipped inside and Kate went suddenly rigid. Her back arched and she felt herself poised on the brink of a cataclysmic eruption. Wanting yet not wanting fulfilment, aching for yet desperate to prevent the explosion of molten lava that threatened to boil through her veins, Kate heard herself whimpering.

'No . . .' she moaned. 'No, Elodie . . . don't do this . . . don't do this to me. *Please*. I can't stand it. . .' But Elodie carried on, greedily and voraciously lapping and probing at the burning channel of Kate's sex. Now she was at her clitoris, teasing the rigid, straining bud, nibbling at it with impossible gentleness. Kate wriggled beneath her, madly excited yet deeply frustrated. Again she wanted to reciprocate, to rouse herself from the groaning passivity of her position. And again Elodie understood. She raised her head from Kate's swollen, streaming sex and, more aggressively this time, pressed her entire body against Kate's. Their mouths met again, mingling together and creating juices to make a strong, powerful female nectar of unparalleled sweetness. Their breasts meshed together, softness seeming to multiply against softness until their nipples touched and a sharp, electric jolt passed between them. And further down, Kate experienced a new sensation that eclipsed anything she had felt before. Elodie was rocking her pelvis against her own. Automatically, as if it she had been doing this all her life, Kate parted her legs further and then lifted them up, wrapping them snugly round the other woman's waist. Her movement enabled them to rub together even more closely. Mound of Venus against Mound of Venus, they were, thought Kate in a flash, *humping*. This is something you can't do with a man, she realised. He can't rub his clitoris against yours, he can't *understand* what it's like. And then her mind was diverted again as Elodie over-whelmed her with the multiple sensations of their coupling. The mouth on hers was greedy, avid and voracious; the breasts nuzzling against her own were urgent, superbly fruity, wonderfully and exotically pendulous. Kate clasped her hands around Elodie's buttocks – they too were ripe yet at the same time tight and muscular. What she felt was an essential oneness with the sacred female shape; a feeling that mounted and soared as she realised that this time there was no holding back. The hard nuts of each clitoris, their swollen, melting vulvas pressed one final time against each other and then there was an ache of such intense pleasure that it crossed the threshold into pain. Kate cried out as her limbs started to shake uncontrollably, as Elodie began to thrash and writhe on top of her with the intoxicating force of her climax and as the two vaginas, operating as one, clenched from within and sent one last momentous ripple through their heaving, spasming bodies.

They lay silently for a moment. Words, as they had been all along, were irrelevant. Instead, when they had finally sobbed out their pleasure, when the frantic turmoil of limbs had subsided, they kissed again. This time there was no urgency in the play of their tongues, it was a leisurely, unhurried kiss that spoke of tenderness rather than carnality. It was the perfect kiss.

'A perfect finale!' said a voice from somewhere Kate couldn't identify. In one lingering movement she drew her lips apart from Elodie's and, still with her eyes closed, wondered if she had, through this excess of passion, been physically transported to somewhere else. Somewhere where voices praised her, where her bountiful love-making was appreciated as something beauteous to behold.

She opened her eyes and, just as her orgasm had shot through her like piercing lightning, so normality revisited her spirit. In a flash, she remembered where she was and who she was with. She turned to Elodie. The Frenchwoman still had her eyes closed; her face was a picture of contentment; her smile one of utter bliss. Then she looked towards the end of the bed and at the men standing there. One of them, Didier, was holding a video camera. As Kate looked straight into the lens the tiny whirring noise that she had been unaware of ceased and complete silence echoed round the room. A strange, ominous silence. A silence alive with promise.

Kate lay back against the pillows. 'You filmed us,' she said in a small voice.

Beside her, Elodie raised herself to her elbows. 'Yes,' she said dreamily, 'they filmed us.' Then she looked down into Kate's eyes. 'It intensifies the passion, does it not? To know that someone is watching, someone is filming, that our every movement and caress is being kept forever.'

I didn't even know, thought Kate desperately. I wasn't aware they were filming. And I didn't *need* anything to intensify my passion.

Where a moment ago she had felt elated, indescribably contented, she now felt ashamed, angry. She really was, she thought, a 'true voluptuary', a creature of the night, a being devoted purely and exclusively to the pleasures of the flesh. She looked down at herself, at the hot, tender skin that tingled to the touch, at her still-swollen sex, her nipples that had hardly retracted since Elodie had so joyously coaxed them into proud, passionate points. And then she looked almost dumbly at the men standing before her. What she wanted, she thought with a mixture of amazement and disgust, was *more*. She was insatiable, a body driven solely by its appetites, a carnal creature hungry only for sexual sensations. Each of her recent experiences had taught her things; things that she thought she could control. She had believed herself to be the mistress of her own destiny – but now she had met her nemesis. Her lust had robbed her of the very control she had thought she was exercising. And now she didn't care.

She stretched luxuriantly, knowing that all eyes in the room were on her. She arched her back and folded her arms behind her head and closed her eyes in concupiscent contemplation. 'I want,' she whispered, 'to live out my fantasies.' And then she called out that she wanted Didier.

She saw the smile on his face. She saw him pass the camera to Nero. And then she watched him strip. Her eyes took in his whole as he threw off his clothes. He was broader, altogether bigger than she had first thought. And he was hairier. She looked at him as if from a great distance, as if she were an actress watching herself on film, as if she were no longer inhabiting the present. And then she heard the hum of the camera as Nero stepped towards her, as fantasy merged into reality.

'Play with yourself,' he commanded, 'while Didier *se branle*.' Kate lifted her knees, exposing her still moist vagina for the camera. She closed her eyes and pressed the flat of her hand against her sex. She smiled as she gently parted her lips, rubbing her clitoris at the same time. She was still aroused, still ready – and now waiting for some-thing more than the touch of her own fingers.

'Good.' Nero's voice seemed to come from miles

away. 'Keep smiling and then look at Didier. Look at him as if you can't believe the size of his cock.'

Kate looked. She saw him masturbating the rampant rod that only moments ago had been flaccid. His lack of arousal had annoyed her. She had seen the straining crotches of the other two men and had been angered by Didier's seeming disinterest in her performance with Elodie. Perhaps, she thought, he needs a camera to arouse him. Covertly, she looked at the lens, the electronic eye that excited her more than the eyes of her companions. The dark eye that she would perform for. The anonymous eye that would watch Didier penetrate her with the prick that seemed to be growing as he masturbated. She could believe the size of his cock. But only just.

'Get to your knees as Didier approaches.'

Kate obeyed, noticing, as she got up, that Elodie had left the bed, left the room. And so had Georges. 'Where's Elodie?'

'Shut up.' Nero's face had disappeared behind the artificial eye and his voice seemed to come from the camera itself. She was a machine. Obeying the commands of another machine. And she was loving it.

Now Didier was in front of her. He presented his proud sex for her to worship.

'Suck,' the camera commanded.

Kate opened her mouth, moistened the head with her tongue and started to draw the shaft into her. She had been ordered to do it, and she *wanted* to do it.

'Take it further in.' She tried to swallow the monster in its entirety, but started to choke well before he had crushed his pelvis against her mouth. 'Come on, more!' said the voice. Again she tried, this time feeling strong hands at the back of her head; Didier's hands, forcing himself further and deeper into her straining mouth. She thought she would suffocate and, just as panic began to seize her, she felt Didier withdraw. His cock slithered out of her mouth, allowing her to take great heaving, rasping breaths. The camera came closer to her face.

'Good.' Nero chuckled mirthlessly. 'The camera never lies. Didier is like a donkey. Kate cannot take him in.' He was silent for a moment as Kate regained her breath. Then he ordered her to try again.

She was desperate to try again. She was performing in her own fantasy. She wanted to be a good performer. This time she was told to let him in and out, to let the camera capture her moist lips coaxed to their fullest extent by his hugeness, to record the dribbles of saliva that flew out of her mouth as he pummelled to her throat and back. Again Didier's strong hands were at her head and she was bobbing up and down, gradually taking more and more of him into her. Triumph eventually overcame pain and discomfort when she realised her face was buried in his groin – that she had taken him all in.

Then, on command, he withdrew. Kate felt her mouth a vacuum, saw herself as a helpless fish, begging for yet denied of its sustenance. And then she saw Didier tremble as his scrotum tightened and he came. Kate marvelled at the jets of semen that spurted forth, and yet she was disappointed. She had wanted him to stay in her mouth, to offer her his seed, to nourish her with the warm, salty liquid. As Didier closed his eyes in ecstacy, Kate reached out as the fruit of his lust touched her breasts. Gently, she rubbed the white pearls into her skin, moisturising herself with the precious liquid. She too closed her eyes. She had been frustrated by his climaxing while denying her of her own orgasm, but she knew there was more to come. She knew that the camera hadn't finished its work.

Nor had Didier. As she was told to lie back again and open her legs she realised why men like Didier did what they did. They were a breed apart. They had a power to rival that of the opposite sex. As she lay back on the pillows she could think only of his erection – his continuing erection. His ejaculation of mere seconds ago had not diminished it. There it stood in front of her, still pulsating, still throbbing – ready to penetrate her other orifice. She couldn't wait.

'Wipe your breasts,' urged Nero. He threw her a handkerchief and she ran it across her chest, cleansing herself of the stickiness, wiping away the seed. Again she felt powerful. Didier was still erect because of her; because of her ability to arouse men beyond the normal boundaries of desire. If this man was exceptional then so was she.

She was told to lift her legs in the air as Didier prepared to mount her. She snarled aggressively as she did so, mouthing obscenities at him, urging him to pound into her. She had experienced tenderness with Elodie and she didn't want it any more. She wanted him to come to her with brutality, to lay his heavy body on her, to force himself into her. She wanted all of him; his smell, his sex, his seed.

She saw herself as the camera saw her: as a slut, a wanton, shameless *thing* who only existed for the purposes of sex, who only stirred to life at the prospect of relentless, unremitting sex. Somewhere in her head a voice denied this, but she didn't listen to it. She refused to believe that this wasn't really her, that she wasn't like this. She paid little heed to the voice that cried within her and told her that she had gone too far, lost control of herself and made the biggest mistake of her life. All she cared about was the blank, inanimate eye of the camera lodged between her legs and the other eye, the winking slit at the head of Didier's penis, which would soon plunge itself into her willing softness.

'Enter her. Slowly. I want to see every fold of her skin, every movement.'

Didier spread his own legs wider and lifted Kate's so that they encircled his torso, so that her feet were digging into the small of his back. She could hardly bear the tension. She clenched her vaginal muscles, trying desperately to control the spasms that were already beginning inside her. I'm being filmed, she said to herself. I'm living out my innermost, dirtiest, most secret fantasy. And I'm loving it. The other voice inside had lost the power of speech: instead it cried great, wracking sobs in unison with the heaving of her body as she tried to control herself, to save herself for the pleasure to come.

Now, at last, he was entering her. As if in slow motion, Didier poked gently at her sex. Already open, she felt herself blooming like a flower displaying itself in its full glory, enticing him, inviting him. Her soft flesh welcomed him, folded around him in a dizzying embrace. Yet he would not go further. Groaning now, screaming at him, she tried everything to make him sink right into her. She pressed against his back with every muscle in her legs, pummelled his torso with her clenched fists, but still he played with her. For a moment he withdrew, letting the camera capture her hungry, dilated sex in all its heaving readiness.

And then it was satisfied. In one sleek, strong movement, Didier merged with her, entered her and filled her completely. She let out a long, deep sigh that bordered on a scream. So hard was his initial thrust that she imagined herself disappearing between his hard, rigid body and the soft, yielding mattress. She didn't care. There was only one part of her that mattered now, and it certainly hadn't disappeared.

It was the centre of everything; of her soul, of Didier's being and of the whirring, clicking, probing attentions of the camera. She gripped Didier joyfully as he rode her, savouring his savage thrusts, crazed by the sensations welling at her core. And she let herself imagine. She imagined what it looked like, this glorious beast with two heads, rocking up and down to the most blissful rhythm of all. And then everything was blocked out of her mind except the thundering force of her orgasm as it rushed through her, making her clench and spasm against Didier as he pounded into her like an automaton. As she lay pinioned beneath him, writhing in the agony of ecstasy, she was only vaguely aware of the camera at her head, recording her in the throes of complete abandonment. As abruptly as he had entered her, Didier withdrew and raised his powerful body higher on his elbows. His face, too, was scrunched up in an expression that indicated the imminence of his orgasm. And then it relaxed above her as he let out a cry and released his liquid all over her body. She lay there, feeling him spurting over her, revelling in the sensation of being inundated and intoxicated by sex. She could *feel* sex all around her, she could smell sex in the air, the heady smell of her own sweat and the glorious man-smell of Didier. And then she rubbed a finger on her belly, coating its tip in the warm, viscous fluid of Didier's life force. Sensation is all, she said to herself as she opened her eyes, put her fingertip to her mouth, and smiled a beatific smile to the camera above her. Then she tasted sex. She has tasted it before, and loved it. But this time, as her breathing returned to normal, as Didier disappeared and as the camera recorded its final, awful truths, it tasted different. It tasted bitter.

'Be careful,' said a voice above her, 'about choosing your fantasies. They might come true.'

Chapter Nine

KATE WANTED TO die. She hoped that she might actually be dead and that her liberated soul was looking down on her lifeless body in sad contemplation of its ruination. Except her body wasn't ruined. It was washed, scrubbed and refreshed by what little sleep she had been able to summon. And now, like an automaton, it was heading towards the City, taking her to work as it had done on countless previous occasions.

It was her soul that was ruined, she thought. The little, vital part of her that dictated her self-esteem and her *raison d'être*. As she trudged along the concourse towards the offices of Courtenay de Witt, she realised that she now knew she had only one specifically defined reason for existing. She existed not as a person but as a gap surrounded by nothingness and to be filled by everything. That was, she supposed, what she must always have wanted. It had taken her so long to get there because she had let her intellect interfere, had let herself pretend that she had a brain to rule her body and dupe her into thinking she could exercise an element of control over her life. Steven had known what she was really like. Why hadn't she stayed with him? Why hadn't she let him use her as the sexual object she really was? Why had she thought she deserved anything better?

Now she only deserved to die. No, that was wrong. She didn't deserve anything – the term implied some sort of reward. There was nothing to reward her for. Other people took their rewards from her. She had become their plaything and their trophy. And Nero's toy.

Her naively almost made her smile. Her ridiculous, infantile notions about being in control of the situation amused her. Nero had been twirling her round his little finger since the day they met. Wrapping her around him. And like a vagina welcoming the ardent thrusts of a penis, she had let him in, welcomed him into her warm embrace and let him drive into the very core of her being and reduce her to nothingness. Her search for sexual liberation and gratification had been nothing of the sort: it had merely been a protracted exercise in subjugation, a confirmation that nothing about her mattered except what was between her legs.

She now belonged to Nero. He had told her so. The others had left before him and he had told her that he now owned her. He had even looked at her pityingly and said he'd never met anyone who could so easily and quickly let themselves fall under his spell. She had wondered why he needed people to fall under his spell, why he needed to control people. And then she had looked at him and, in an instant, she knew. Nero de l'Escault-Tonnère was evil. He was morally bankrupt. But he didn't need Kate to aid him with that particular aspect of his unsavoury life. He needed her to help him with a more sophisticated form of evil: his professional conduct in the world of international finance.

She looked him in the eye and knew. 'So Mark was wrong,' she whispered to herself.

'Mark? Who's Mark?'

'Oh . . . no one.'

'Like you, then. A nobody.' Then he had come closer to her and sat on the edge of the bed. 'Do you know, my Kate, why I need you to be mine?'

'No.'

He smiled down at her. 'Oh, but I think you can probably guess. You are not a fool – at least where it comes to business. I'm afraid your sexual conduct leads one to suggest otherwise. Talking of which . . .' he paused in mid-sentence and let one hand snake down her naked body towards her sex. She closed her eyes. Not more, she thought. I can't. Not again. Not with him. He stopped at her pouting entrance and gently inserted two fingers. She was still so wet, so well lubricated that the sensation was not unpleasant – just unwelcome. 'Do you know,' he continued, 'what they call this?' His fingers were teasing, prying, exploring. Yet something suggested that, while he was in her sex, he wasn't thinking about sex.

Kate shook her head. 'No. I don't.'

Nero chuckled and withdrew his hand. With a handkerchief and a curiously disinterested gesture, he wiped her juices off his fingers. 'They call it insider dealing.'

389

Kate didn't think that was very amusing. She didn't reply. She just stared into his predatory, gimlet black eyes and waited for him to come to the point. He stared back, amusedly awaiting the results of her befuddled thought processes. It didn't take long to dawn on her. Her eyes widened in horror as she realised the other meaning of his double entendre.

'Yes,' he smiled. 'Insider dealing.' He examined the hand that he had just withdrawn from her. 'It has to be done delicately. Discreetly. It has to be done so that only the people involved know about it. And it can only be done, of course, by people who have access to it.'

Again he smiled. Kate felt sick to the bottom of her stomach. Nero had access to her, to every part of her. And she had access to the City, to financial markets and share dealings. She was in a position to feather nests – Nero's nests – through the strictly illegal process of insider dealing. If she was found out, she would lose her job and probably her freedom. And she couldn't refuse to do it. Nero owned her.

'Oh,' he added. 'And just in case you should refuse to do anything I want you to do. Just in case, during the day, you feel that you don't have to obey me, you may care, *ma chérie*, to cast your mind back to this.' And with a little triumphant smile he held up the video cassette that recorded the final humiliation of Kate and the ultimate debasement of her spirit.

And after that, remembered Kate with a shudder as she entered the lobby of Courtenay de Witt, he had given her instructions about how she was to manipulate the market and promote the value of Pharescault's shares. She would also launder money for him. She would promulgate one of the biggest financial scandals the City had ever seen. It was possible, Nero had mused, that she would be found out one day, by which time Nero himself would have vanished into another identity. Still, he had smiled, it was worth the risk, wasn't it? Opting for the possibility of being exposed as a criminal rather than the certainty of her 'little film' finding itself in the wrong hands?

Kate sighed heavily as she stepped into the lift. She would obey Nero. She knew she would: she didn't have any choice. He had covered his criminal tracks so well that no one in the City could damage him; no one could substantiate the rumours that had got Miles Courtenay in such a flap. It was ironic, thought Kate: Miles had been worried that Kate's supposed incompetence would damage the company's reputation. Little did he know that she might one day be branded far more than incompetent – and that she could scar Courtenay de Witt's reputation for ever. That, she supposed, would be a victory of sorts. A hollow one.

'Kate?' She turned in the direction of the voice as, two minutes later, the lift reached her floor and she stepped out. She saw Mark, hovering uncertainly at the door to the next lift. As she smiled weakly at him his expression changed into one of undisguised concern. 'Kate! Are you all right? I thought as you weren't in yet you must be ill.' He paused. 'You *are* ill, aren't you? You really shouldn't have come in, you know . . .'

'I'm not ill, Mark, just tired.' And if you make

one more joke about me being a dirty stop-out, I'll wallop you, she thought.

But she had underestimated him. He came up to her and put a friendly arm around her shoulders. 'Well, you certainly look as if you need a little support. I wouldn't say you're tired; I'd say you're about to fall over. Come on, O walking wounded, I'll escort you to your desk.'

'I really don't need . . .'

'Shut up. I know exactly what you need.'

Someone had said that to her before. She couldn't remember who it was. It had been on a different day, in a different life. And it hadn't been at all what she'd needed.

'You need,' continued Mark, 'some good news.'

'This isn't my office—' she began.

'No, it's the meeting room. We need somewhere private to talk.'

Kate looked sharply at him. Panic seized her and she felt a sudden build-up of tension at her shoulders and neck. Had she been found out? Had her discreet double life been rumbled? She almost hoped so. So much of her life had already been taken out of her control that she was beginning not to care about the rest of it. But as she looked at Mark, at the powerful yet gentle profile, she suddenly had a vision: a vision of the man who had, in her dreams, slipped into bed with her after her night with Sebastian and Rupert. The man, she realised with a jolt, was Mark. The man who, in her dreams, had been kind to her, had stroked her, and hushed her into a peaceful, safe sleep, had been Mark. She didn't know whether to laugh or cry. Mark, surely, was the boy next door, the sexless but friendly colleague whom she had come to regard as a breath of fresh air? And then he caught her eye and she realised, for the first time, what her subconscious had been trying to tell her. This was a man who cared. He cared about her not just as a friend. His eyes, those windows of the soul, informed her of that.

For a brief moment, as they stared at each other, Kate wanted to fling herself into his arms, to confess all and to tell him that she no longer wanted to play her game of danger and lust, of pleasure and power. She wanted to burst into tears and plead with him to help her extricate herself from the mess she now found herself in. Yet something held her back. Somehow she managed to control herself as a little voice in her head told her that, whatever happened with Mark, he must never know of her evening activities. For she wanted more than his arms around her: she wanted all of him – and that included his respect.

The moment passed. Mark, as if surprised and discomfited by what he read in her eyes, ushered her into the small room they used for departmental meetings and closed the door. 'Coffee?' he asked, gesturing towards the percolator.

'Please. I think I need kick-starting.'

Mark poured them both a cup. Kate watched him and smiled as she saw him pour just the tiniest amount of milk into hers. How sweet, she thought, he's remembered how I take it. He remembers things like that.

Then he sat down opposite her and there was nothing sweet about his expression. 'Kate, I've discovered something ... something very serious.'

She betrayed none of her inner turmoil as she stared him straight in the eye. 'Oh?'

'Yes. Very serious indeed. It's about . . . you're friend Nero.'

My friend Nero. If only you knew. But a faint ray of hope dawned in the battered horizon of her mind. 'D'you mean he's not squeaky-clean after all?'

Mark smiled. 'Not even remotely. In fact I would go as far as to say that he's carrying so much dirt I'm surprised he can walk.'

You said I could hardly walk just now. Is it obvious that I'm carrying dirt as well?

'Kate? Are you listening to me?'

Yes she was listening. But she didn't know if she wanted to hear. It was all going to come out. Nero. Georges. Didier and God knows who else. And me. If you expose them you'll expose me. She looked at him fondly. I'll miss you, she thought. 'Yes, I'm listening,' she said.

'Good. Because this is all going to come as a bit of a shock to you.' He took a deep breath and a fortifying sip of coffee. 'You remember that I spent a lot of time trying to find out if the rumours about Nero de l'Escault-Tonnère and Pharescault were true?'

'Yes.'

'And you remember that I failed?'

'Yes. My short-term memory is rather good, actually.'

But Mark missed her feeble attempt at sarcasm. He appeared to be looking within himself rather than at her. 'Well, the reason I failed is because I was looking in the wrong place.' Kate leaned forward across the desk. She was beginning to feel alive again. She was beginning to feel a rush of adrenaline. 'Go on.'

'Well, I wouldn't have even suspected anything were it not for Miles's reaction when I went back to report that I had come up with zilcho. I thought he'd be pleased – which he was. But then I mentioned that while Pharescault and most of its subsidiaries were above board, there was one privately owned company that I couldn't find anything on. A company wholly owned by Nero's family.' He looked Kate straight in the eye. 'It's called the Banc de Motte.'

'*What*? Nero owns a *bank*!' Kate was aghast. 'But . . . but why didn't I know?'

'Because it's got nothing to do with Pharescault. And because it's based in Lichtenstein.' Mark shrugged. 'And because it wasn't, as I'm sure you can imagine, very easy to find out who owned it.'

'So how did you find out?'

Mark grinned disingenuously. 'By accident, actually. But that's another and very long story – and not really the point.'

'So what is the point?'

'I'm getting back to that: Miles's reaction. He went completely white when I told him Nero owned the bank. He was pretty quick at disguising it, but not quick enough. Talk about alarm bells – they were ringing like mad.'

'You think that Miles . . . ?'

'I'm not telling you what I think, Kate. I'm telling you what I *know*.' Mark took another deep breath. 'Of course, Miles then went on to berate me for wasting everyone's time by poking my nose into affairs that had nothing to do with me –

or indeed Pharescault. He said the private companies of the Escault-Tonnères had nothing to do with the public ones.'

'Well, that's true.'

'I know. And I wouldn't have gone any further but for the fact that Miles looked like he'd seen a ghost when I mentioned the bank. That's when I did a bit more research and . . .'

'Mark, are you trying to tell me that Miles is involved in some way with Nero? Because if that's the case, I just don't believe it. You remember how furious he was with me the other day when he suspected that Nero had been laundering money? He was apoplectic – and adamant that we should find out the truth. That's not the behaviour of people who are implicated themselves.'

'I agree. What set me off was that Miles obviously didn't have the *faintest* idea that Nero owned the Banc de Motte – he was as shocked as you were. More so actually.'

Kate was beginning to get his drift. 'Yet he knew of the existence of the bank? And presumably it's a tiny affair?'

'Exactly. It was more than a little peculiar.'

'So you went and did a little more research—'

'And tried to establish a connection – a direct financial connection – between Pharescault and the Banc de Motte.' His voice hardened slightly as he added, 'And a reason to connect Miles with the bank.'

Kate just looked at him. Her heart was palpitating and she could feel a sheen of moisture on her forehead and palms. 'So what,' she whispered, 'did you find?'

Mark paused and then spoke slowly and deliberately, as if testing each word for its weight, its conviction and its importance. 'I didn't find anything that I can prove – yet. But I did discover that a transfer of shares in Pharescault didn't go where it was supposed to go. It went, via a hugely elaborate system, to some unknown destination in Lichtenstein.' Kate held her breath as he continued, even more slowly, 'And I also discovered that a transfer of funds from Courtenay de Witt went, through an even more elaborate system, to the same destination.'

'And that transfer . . .?'

'Was authorised by Miles.'

They spent a further hour huddled together in the meeting room. As each minute passed, so Kate's mood lifted. Her earlier, seemingly terminal despair evaporated and she felt a new life force surging positively through her veins. She also found it difficult to focus her entire attention on Mark: half of her was listening and replying to what he was saying, the other half was considering his extraordinary revelations in the light of her relationship with Nero. She now had ammunition against him. And as she and Mark talked an idea began to form in her head about how she could use it – to devastating effect.

'The problem is,' said Mark at one point, 'it's going to be rather difficult to prove anything against Miles.'

Kate still found it hard to believe that Miles Courtenay was siphoning money out of Courtenay de Witt and into, probably, his own pockets. 'Are you *sure*,' she asked for the umpteenth time, 'that Miles is really involved in fraud. It's so ... well, it's just so unlike Miles.'

Mark looked at her. 'How do you know what Miles is really like? How, for that matter, does anyone know what anybody else is *really* like?'

Kate averted her eyes. 'So it's going to be more difficult to get the dirt on Miles than it is on Nero, is that it?'

'But if we can implicate Nero, can't we then get Miles?'

Wonderful, she thought. Two birds with one stone. The two birds she hated most.

Mark shook his head. 'I don't think so. I really think Miles's astonishment at finding out who owned the Banc de Motte was genuine.'

'What a very stupid man he must be,' mused Kate. 'But,' she added, 'how do we know Nero doesn't know about Miles's illegal activities? He must know about everything that passes through that bank. Especially transactions that large.'

'Mmm.' Mark reflected on the figure he'd mentioned to Kate: a million pounds that had disappeared from Courtenay de Witt and ended up, he was sure, at the Banc de Motte. 'You'd have thought he would know, wouldn't you? But if he *did* know, then why not get Miles to trade illegally for him? Why not *use* Miles?'

'Maybe he isusing him. Blackmailing him or whatever.'

'Oh come on, Kate, that one just doesn't wash. If Miles was being used by Nero, he'd hardly instruct us to move heaven and earth to try and dig out the dirt on him, would he?'

No, thought Kate, he wouldn't. 'So it's all just one big coincidence, then?'

'Looks like it.' Mark gestured round the room. 'But not that big. The financial world is, after all, a very small one.'

But Kate didn't believe in coincidences like that – not where Nero de l'Escault-Tonnère was concerned. Where Miles was blustering and stupid, Nero was clever and cunning. He must know all about Miles, she thought. But getting Miles to launder money for him would be too risky. Much better to use someone else. Much better to use someone he thought he owned completely. Using me, she reflected, gives him two bites at the cherry. Two ways to suck the blood out of Courtenay de Witt. But not any more.

'So what do you suggest we do?' she asked.

'I've been thinking about that. This is too big for us to handle, Kate. Too dangerous. I reckon we go to Charles and tell him.'

'But what about the *proof*?'

'We'll get it,' he replied confidently. 'It'll just take time.'

But time was something Kate didn't have. In no time, *she* would be laundering money for Nero – and that would inevitably come to light in the search for proof to nail Miles. And so would every ghastly sordid detail about her private life. Time was most definitely not on her side.

'I suggest,' she said, 'that we wait.'

'Kate! Don't you realise how serious this is?'

Kate looked coldly across the table. 'Of course I realise how serious it is. I just need,' she continued, 'a day.'

'What for?'

'To do my own bit of research.'

'But . . .'

Kate stood up. 'A day, Mark. That's all I need. Please.'

With a puzzled frown creasing his brow, Mark looked up at her. 'All right then, a day. And then we tell Charles. But I can't think what you'll be able to achieve in a day.'

Kate used the rest of the morning to formulate her plan – a plan which, however she looked at it, could backfire on her because of one ghastly reason – the existence of the video of her torrid couplings with Elodie and Didier. If she had enough information to ruin Nero, then he had enough to ruin her. And if she dragged him down, he would take her with him.

That was one way of looking at it. The other was that Kate could ruin Nero so utterly and completely that his life would be all but over. He and his family would doubtless be incarcerated for years and the exalted name of the de l'Escault-Tonnères would become a synonym for scandal and fraud. Kate, on the other hand, would be humiliated, dragged through the gutter press, and no one in the City would dream of employing her again. But she would survive. Nero wouldn't. Her hand was stronger than his.

Her other option, she knew, was a simple trade-off. She wouldn't betray Nero: he wouldn't betray her. But that would necessitate her explaining her life to Mark, something she was loath to do. It would also be a compromise – and Kate hated compromises. She also hated the thought of not being able to implement the other, equally satisfying part of her plan.

And there was the final option – the rogue

hand. The one she felt she ought to try because of a tiny, niggling suspicion at the back of her mind . . .

At lunchtime, she phoned, as she did every day, the man from the opera.

'Cleo! How nice to hear from you.' He always said that. And he always called her Cleo. He had thought the name, and its inspiration, hilarious. 'How are you?'

'I'm rather exhausted actually.'

'Oh dear. And I'm afraid you've got another client tonight. It's—'

'It's the same man who came the last time. And the time before.'

'Yes.' The voice on the other end of the line sounded amused. 'You must crtainly be doing something for him. It's a bit odd, coming this often.'

On another occasion, Kate might have laughed at his choice of words. This time there was no room for levity. 'That,' she said, 'is precisely what I want to talk to you about.'

'Oh? In what way?'

Kate took a deep breath. 'When Sebastian told me how this . . . this system runs, he mentioned that all the clients were vetted.'

'Yes.' The voice was more guarded now.

'In what way are they vetted?'

'Very thoroughly, in fact. We check their credit worthiness, their background to some extent and, of course, we make absolutely sure they aren't in the black books of any other, similar agencies.'

'I'm impressed.'

'So you should be. We run a very sophisticated

operation. And we look after our employees.' He paused for a moment. 'But of course we can't guarantee that something won't go wrong. Has something . . . happened?'

'You could say that. I'm suspicious that one of my clients has lied about his name.'

'They all lie to *you* about their names. You knew that. It's better that way. But they can't lie to me. The system would find them out.' He paused for thought. 'They can't just pick a name out of a hat, and it's highly unlikely that anyone would go to the trouble of matching himself to someone else's credentials just to . . . well. . .' He trailed off, failing, for once, to find a polite euphemism for his trade.

'Unlikely, but possible,' countered Kate.

'Well. I suppose it *is* possible . . .'

'I think it's happened.'

'What makes you so sure?'

'I'm not sure. I just have this niggling suspicion that if this client had given you his real name it might have rung a bell. A warning bell.'

'So what, my dear Cleo, is the name?'

'Comte Nero de l'Escault-Tonnère.'

There was a sharp, almost agonised intake of breath at the other end of the line. The sound of a warning bell.

Chapter Ten

SHE WAS READY when the doorbell rang. Ready and waiting. She had spent the last hour in the Mayfair flat, finalising her plans, preparing to do to Nero what he had done to her. She smiled at the prospect. Thanks to the man from the opera, the prospect looked a great deal more attractive than it had earlier in the day. She had been right to suspect that Nero would be devious in every area of his life; right in her supposition that he would cover his tracks in everything he did. But now she had uncovered them. Now she was the huntress and he was her prey. She held all the cards. Once again, she had the power.

She smiled as she answered the door. So did Nero. She was charming to him as she ushered him inside and offered him a drink. He was polite to her. They chatted, made small talk. She could tell from the expression in his eyes that he was enjoying toying with her. She hoped he couldn't read the expression in her eyes. He was playing a waiting game. So was she.

He broke first. 'You seem,' he said, 'to have

accustomed yourself to the idea of me.'

'I beg your pardon?'

Nero shrugged in a boyish, self-deprecating manner. Kate knew that gesture. He was shrugging himself into his attractive mode as easily as one could don a new outfit. She had fallen for it on every previous occasion. This time, she noticed that it fitted him very badly. And neither did it suit him. 'I expected,' he continued, 'that you would not be very *sympathique* this evening.'

'Why?'

'Oh . . . perhaps because you are now required to do everything I say. Because I now have total control over you.'

Kate smiled at him. 'Has it ever occurred to you,' she said coyly, 'that the idea might excite me?'

Evidently it hadn't occurred to him. He looked quite startled. 'I did, I suppose, entertain the hope that you might one day realise that it would be in your best interests to obey me but . . . but I'm glad that you have decided to enjoy it.' He looked at her again, that proud, arrogant and supercilious look she knew of old. 'It is a strain, is it not, for women to pretend they have control over every area of their lives?'

Yes, thought Kate, it's a strain. But it's not a pretence. She uncurled herself from the sofa and went over to sit at Nero's feet. She looked up into his eyes. 'You've relieved me of a burden,' she said. 'I no longer have to pretend.'

Then she started to stroke his feet through the supple kid leather of his shoes. 'You own me. It hasn't taken me long to get used to the idea.'

'And so you will do anything I say?'

'Yes.' Careful, she thought, don't push it. 'But

Nero, you now have the power to put me in prison if I ... if I do your bidding in the stock market. I don't want to go to prison. Am I not in one already? Isn't that enough for you?' She could tell by the sudden movement of his feet, the subtle change in his expression, that he was becoming excited.

'You won't go to prison, Kate. You're far too useful to me. I'll look after you. You have no need to worry.'

But *you* do, she thought. You have no idea just how much you have to worry. Now she snaked her arms round his legs and rubbed her face against his trousers. 'Good,' she purred. 'I'm glad that you're going to look after me. I need it.' She started to move further up his legs. 'I want it.'

He wanted it too. She could tell by the sudden dreamy look in his eyes. In one leisurely movement, she put a hand to his crotch. He groaned slightly and leaned back in his chair.

'No, Kate,' he said without much conviction. 'Not now. We have many things to discuss. We must discuss how you are going to ...'

'Why not later?' she replied. 'We have all the time in the world. Why not let me satisfy you first?' Deftly, she pulled down his fly and let her talented fingers caress his half-hard member between the folds of his underwear. 'You may know exactly what I want, but I also know what you want.' A blow job, she thought. That's what he wanted. All men were the same, putty in your hands at the prospect of fellatio. Nero was no exception. He closed his eyes and parted his legs further as she gently massaged him to full erection. Then she leaned forward and licked the bulbous head with her soft, lapping tongue. Delicately, she poked it into the tiny hole at the top, the little winking eye from which she could coax a torrent of milky fluid. But she didn't want to. Not this time. That wasn't part of her plan.

While Nero's excitement mounted, Kate herself remained completely unaroused. She had too much to think about, too much to plan. She needed him even more aroused. She needed to get him and hold him at the point where his brain melted completely into his groin, at the point where men thought themselves at their strongest – and women knew them to be at their weakest. Slowly, she began to take his shaft into her mouth. She had always liked Nero's prick. The first time she had seen it, she had likened it to a rocket; smooth, sleek and powerful. She enjoyed the sensation of having such a weapon in her mouth, of sheathing it in her warm, moist embrace. Of capturing it completely.

Nero was getting restless. His breath was beginning to quicken. So, she suspected, was his pulse. She let him out of her mouth and then stroked his cock with her hand. 'Nero,' she whispered, 'you need to take your clothes off. You need to be all the way into me. You can't do it like this. Come,' she stood up and gestured towards the bedroom, 'let's do this properly.' She could tell from his expression that he was annoyed, that he disliked having her interrupt his thoughts, interrupt her delicate ministrations. Yet he complied with her request. The thought of burying his cock deep into her throat was enough to make him obey her. With an impatient grunt, he got to his feet and started to rip off his clothes.

Kate did likewise, discarding them as she made her way to the bedroom.

She was already naked and on the bed when he entered the room. Crouched on all fours, she was acting the part of a bitch in heat; hungry, sluttish and animalistic in her wantonness. It wasn't a difficult part to play – all she had to remember was what she had done when she had taken leave of her senses and let herself become the main player in a grotesque, debauched, *video-taped* tableau.

Nero looked at her in appreciation. He liked seeing her like that, her mouth greedily hanging open and her eyes fixed admiringly, hungrily on his proud, stalwart rod. As he moved towards the bed, Kate hoped that he wouldn't want to touch her sex. She was still dry, unaroused, and for the first time totally unmoved by the beauty of his body and the sudden, overpowering smell of him.

She needn't have worried. Nero was fixated on one thing only, on the prospect of letting her throat milk him dry. Kate's eyes lit up as he stopped at the end of the bed and motioned for her to crawl towards him. He stood, tall and majestic, his manhood echoing his stance, confirming his position as the all-powerful male subjecting the acquiescent female to his will. Kate knew that was how it looked. She was pleased. It was how she wanted it to look.

She fellated him as if her life depended on it. She flicked her tongue over the head of his swollen glans, loving it, caressing it, urging it to an even greater fullness before taking it into her mouth. When Nero cupped her head in his hands she knew it was time to let him slide in and savour the differing textures of her mouth. Gripping the shaft with both hands, she played his penis like an instrument, fondling the base with her strong hands while enveloping the pulsating purple head with her moist, teasing lips. She let him explore her mouth, guiding him with her tongue into the hidden recesses and down towards the darkness of her throat. When half of him was inside her she started a slow, rhythmic sucking in unison with the gentle squeezing of her hands on his balls. She heard him moan with pleasure, a sound so low and deep and sensual that it made Kate realise that she too was beginning to get aroused. She was far from being in the throes of sexual abandonment, but she was conscious of a rush of blood to her groin, a tiny pulse in her vulva and an infinitesimal hardening of her clitoris.

But Nero's pleasure was all. Stopping now and then, letting him slide out and licking him with excruciating tenderness, she then sucked him back in with a voraciousness that surprised even herself. And then she increased the tempo of the beautiful tune she was playing on him. With her mouth and throat fully extended, she accepted him eagerly, coating him liberally with her saliva, letting him lunge ever deeper, ever harder.

He started to come when he was right at the back of her throat. Kate thought she would suffocate as she felt a final stiffening of his cock, as it flexed itself in readiness for the great jets that were welling up from his tightened balls. She felt Nero's entire body tremble as he thrust savagely into the back of her mouth and let loose the first drops of semen. And then he came in a flood, spasming and shaking and crying out the wild, primeval call of an animal at the height of his being. Half-smothering from the length of him, Kate tried not to drown in his juices. And as she swallowed them, she recalled yesterday and the bitterness of Didier's seed. Today the taste was bitter-sweet.

Releasing Nero from the warm embrace of her mouth, she looked up at him, at the ecstatic expression on his face, and quickly scrambled up from her kneeling position. With great gentleness, she pulled him on to the bed. Nero's legs gave way and he sank gratefully on to the soft, welcoming mattress. He looked dreamily at Kate.

'That,' he said, 'was the most . . . the best . . .'

Kate stalled him by placing a tender hand against his lips. 'Ssh,' she said, 'it was a necessary way for you to release your tension.' Then she pushed him lightly so that he lay in the middle of the bed on his chest. 'Now I'm going to show you another way.' She reached over for the jar of oil on the bedside table, dipped her fingers into the liquid, and straddled Nero's back. He groaned again at the first touch of her fingers on the back of his neck.

'Just,' he whispered, 'like Elodie.' As he said the words Kate could feel the knots of tension on his muscles begin to unravel, and sensed him sinking deeper into the mattress. Good, she thought, if I can do it as well as Elodie then I'm going to succeed.

Kate found that she was beginning to enjoy herself. Furthermore, she was beginning to become aroused again. She had never massaged anyone before and as she kneaded Nero's broad, tanned back realised what a highly erotic experience it was. And it helped that Nero had a beautiful body. It was blemish free and had hair in only the right places. The sculpted, oiled muscles began to gleam in the soft light and gradually the man-smell of Nero mingled with the aroma of the oil and wafted through the room. Kate found the smell intoxicatingly sensual. Nero, she was delighted to notice, appeared to find both the smell and the massage intensely soporific. She lightened her touch and watched his eyelashes flutter and then finally close as he surrendered into the arms of Morpheus.

Scarcely daring to breathe, Kate remained motionless for at least a minute. Then, taking care not to disturb Nero, she climbed off the bed and went quickly about executing the final part of her plan.

Ten minutes later she decided she no longer had any need to be quiet. And Nero, she reflected gleefully, was about to have a very loud and rude awakening. She smiled and lifted the whip. It came down gently but right on target – right across the middle of Nero's back. She saw his body flinch as his brain was snatched out of sleep to send messages screaming all over his body. The message that reached his mouth was loudest. Kate had never heard a man cry out with such force. It was a bellow of rage more than agony. Nero didn't know what was happening to him. She hit him again, this time with even less force. The thought of what she could do with the instrument was far more pleasurable than any actual pain she inflicted. She didn't want to hurt his body. She wanted to hurt his mind.

Nero tried to escape. Kate saw his legs strain and his arms try desperately to give some sort of protection to his exposed back. Yet it was impossible. She had done her work well. Nero's hands were securely manacled to the bed head, and his feet, completing a four-pointed star, were tied to the end of the bed. He was trapped.

Kate watched in amusement as he tried to register the fact. As he turned his head towards her she watched several expressions cross his face in quick succession. Discomfort was followed by bewilderment; disbelief succeeded anger. And it gave way to fear as the reality of his situation dawned on him, as he registered the apparition in front of him. Kate rather regretted the leather hood Sebastian and she had giggled over when he had shown her the 'box of tricks'; it disguised the look of pure triumph on her face. Yet combined with the other leather accoutrements it could only enhance her status, her new role as a dominatrix over the man who had sought to ruin her life. The man who hated dominant women. The man who was about to be ruined by her.

'Kate!' She could see the whites of his eyes. 'What are you *doing*? What . . . what is all this . . .?'

Kate looked down at him and smiled at his gibbering fear. 'Isn't it obvious? I'm flogging you. This,' she pointed with one long, gloved hand, 'is a whip. In French you call it a *fouet*, which is, I think, much better as that word echoes the noise of the whip when it connects with its target as you . . .'

'*Kate! No!*' Nero pushed with all his might

against his bonds as the whip came down again. This time, quite deliberately, Kate missed him altogether. The threat was enough. *'Please!* What are you doing? Have you gone mad?'

'No. I think you're the one that's mad. You're so crazed with your lust for power that you've finally cracked.'

'I don't know what you mean.'

'Oh, don't you? Well never mind, I'm sure you'll remember once we start playing the truth game.'

'The truth game?' Nero was squirming now – and mainly with indignity. He flexed his muscles, wrenching ineffectually at his bonds.

'There's simply no point,' said Kate mildly, 'in trying to squirm your way out of this. You thought you had me under your thumb. Now I've got you under mine. In fact I've got you tied to my bed, and I've got this *fouet* in my hand and I'm going to—'

'No!' Nero saw the raised whip and flinched in agonised anticipation. But this time Kate was more interested in her pleasure than in anything he felt. She let the whip land gently on his back and ran it slowly and sensually down his body, drawing the tail of it through the cleft in his taut, muscular buttocks. Nero winced. Was he, she wondered, enjoying that particular sensation? She certainly was. She found Nero's buttocks extremely attractive; she imagined the whip was her hand, gently caressing them. Yet she decided to use her hand for an even greater pleasure. In her right hand she was holding the whip. Now, with her left, she was stroking her furrow, pressing the warm leather of the glove against her entire sex. It was just an experiment. Just to see if Nero's indignities could do anything for her. They could. Rubbing the little nub of her clitoris, she decided that this was going to be a new experience in pleasure for her. Intellectual pleasure. Sexual pleasure. Total pleasure.

'The truth game,' she reiterated. 'I think it's time to play it.'

'What . . . what is it?'

'Oh, it's very simple. It's not unlike the game you played with me yesterday.' She moved to the bedside table and bought out a small, square electronic box. Turning back to Nero, she took in his terrified expression and laughed. 'It's all right, this isn't an instrument of physical torture.' She paused, considering. 'Actually, it's far more effective than that.'

'What is it?'

'It's a quid pro quo. Yesterday you made a tape of me. Today I'm going to tape you. Just your voice. I'm going to ask you a few questions, and if I'm not satisfied with your answers I think you can probably guess what I'm going to do to you . . .'

She switched the micro-cassette into recording mode and stepped closer to him. 'Tell me,' she said quietly, 'all about the Banc de Motte.'

'*What!*'

Mental torture, thought Kate, is far more satisfying than physical.

'You heard. The Banc de Motte. Your bank – or perhaps I should say money-laundering operation – in Lichtenstein.'

'I don't know what you're talking about.'

'Oh dear. Well perhaps this will jog your

413

memory.' Again she wielded the whip. Yet even before she had time to use it, Nero broke down and confessed all. Like all bullies, he was a coward. He couldn't bear the thought of pain. So he told her every minute, complex and damaging detail about the Banc de Motte. The cassette recorder, like the video recorder of yesterday, silently recorded it all. It would need, thought Kate, some judicious editing later on – she would have to erase the crack of the whip. But not from her memory.

'And now,' she said, 'you can tell me all you know about Miles Courtenay.'

'Miles Courtenay?'

'Yes. Miles Courtenay. My boss. Your accomplice.'

'He's not my accomplice!'

'But you knew he was siphoning money from Courtenay de Witt through your bank?'

'Yes.'

'Tell me about it. Tell me how much. Tell me how long it's being going on for.'

She didn't need the whip to extract that information out of him. He seemed to despise Miles as much, if not more, than she did. And the information he had on the man was highly satisfactory. And deeply, terminally damaging.

'But Miles didn't know that you owned the Banc de Motte?'

'No.'

'So why didn't you tell him? Surely you wanted to become a client of Courtenay de Witt so that you could blackmail him to do your dirty work for you?'

'That,' said Nero furiously, 'was the idea. Until you came along.'

Kate paused for thought. Some careful editing would be needed here. And some careful questioning. 'So you thought that if you could find a way of blackmailing *me*, then I could do the dirty work and you would *still* have Miles to fall back on if anything went wrong. Very clever, I must say.'

'You were too good an opportunity to resist. Too much of a coincidence. Your ... ah ... nocturnal activities placed you right in my hands.'

Kate clambered on to the bed and stroked Nero's buttocks with the soft, sensual palm of one of her gloved hands. Then she turned her hand over and started pumelling his tender flesh with the sharp, shiny studs on the back of the glove. Nero howled. Then, when she stopped, he raged at her through gritted teeth. 'You seem to think you are so incredibly clever, my dear Kate. No doubt you are getting a thrill from this ... this ridiculous position you are temporarily putting me in ...'

'What makes you think it's temporary?'

'Because you forget that I possess a tape as damaging to you as you seem to think this one will be to me. If you destroy me, rest assured that I shall destroy you.'

'Mmm.' Kate ran her hands over him again. Softly this time. Really, she thought, he does have the most beautiful body. She felt herself becoming hot. Lying down on top of him, she pressed her warm flesh against his and whispered into his ear. At the same time she rubbed herself against him, feeling the mound of his hard buttocks against her own soft, yielding mound.

415

'No, Nero, you're quite wrong. You can't damage me at all. You seem to forget that you have a very . . . a very *memorable* name.'

'So? What's that got to do with it?' Nero spoke through gritted teeth. Kate wondered if he was becoming aroused again. His body was squirming beneath her. She felt he was trying to escape from her. They both knew he couldn't. Kate was in a position of supreme power. Kate was enjoying herself.

'Your name has a lot to do with it, my dear Nero.' She bucked savagely against him, fucking him. Fucking him mentally and physically. 'The name of Nero de l'Escault-Tonnère rings a few bells with my employer.'

Again Nero squirmed beneath her. A squirm induced, she guessed, by abject terror. 'I didn't . . . he doesn't *know* my name. He couldn't possibly. I gave a different name . . .'

'Yes, you gave Miles's name, didn't you? A nice touch, that one. Nice to get Miles's name on the books of a courtesan agency. Useful if you wanted to damage him. My employer, of course, could find nothing against Miles – at least not then. And if he'd asked me to describe you he would have got a passable description of Miles, wouldn't he? You're the same age, you look not dissimilar and you're both . . . you're both. . .' she stopped as she ground herself against him, as her breathing became irregular: she could feel her sex swelling and the beginnings of the tiny yet blissfully satisfying orgasm that had been welling up within her. She both wanted and didn't want sexual release, but she did want to demonstrate her absolute control over this man. And part of that control was using him as her sexual toy. Her moment had anyway arrived – there was no way she could stop herself now. With a final thrust she rammed her sex against him and screamed into his ear, 'And you're both,' she yelled, 'devious, evil, conniving, *absolute bastards!*'

Nero hated what she was doing to him. He hated it more than he had hated anything in his life. He knew what she was doing; he was aware that she was abusing him doubly, and he was powerless to stop her. He was also powerless over the erection that was now throbbing between his stomach and the mattress. He hated himself for that erection.

He tried to hit Kate with his head. It was the only part of his body that he could move and he butted it backwards, attempting to hit her in the face as, momentarily off her guard, she collapsed on top of him. He nearly succeeded.

Breathless and still shaking from her climax, Kate hastily crawled to the other side of the bed. 'Naughty,' she said. 'You tried to hurt me. That's not allowed.'

'So what if I have a memorable name? So what if I gave Miles's name? I still have the tape, you stupid bitch! I can still ruin you.'

'No, Nero. You're the one that's ruined, and do you know why? Your perverted, crazed sexual urges have ruined you. You couldn't appear at a London courtesan agency under your real name, could you? That name means too much to them. That name is mud. In fact,' she paused and looked down at his prone body. He had relaxed somewhat. Good, she thought, I'll catch him completely unawares now. She walked to the cupboard. 'In fact,' she continued, 'it was remarkably stupid of you to approach an agency again. Your sexual urges, as I said, have got the better of you. But when you found out that this talented new courtesan was *me*, you just couldn't resist, could you? And that, my dear Nero, has been your downfall.'

'You're talking rubbish. You know as well as I do that anonymity is the name of the game. Your "employer" would never reveal your clients' real names to you.'

'No, you're quite right, he wouldn't. I guessed. I guessed that someone as evil and perverted as you would have played this game before. I guessed that you would have caused trouble, even that people would be after your hide. And it didn't take us long to find out that "Miles" was in fact yourself. That Miles was Nero.' She was standing over him now, at the side of his bed and level with his buttocks again. He couldn't see her. 'My employer,' she added, 'was very interested to hear that. I gather he's got a score to settle with you. I gather you did something unpleasant once. Something dark, like your name. Something evil. What was it, Nero?'

Nero didn't respond. He lay face down on the bed, motionless, silent – and waiting in trepidation. He knew now that Kate was the one with the power. Kate knew all about him. But did she really, he wondered, know what had happened to the girl she was talking about?

He gritted his teeth. 'It was ... it was an accident, Kate.'

'Of course it was.' Kate's voice was heavy with sarcasm. Now she came nearer to Nero.

'Accidents have a nasty habit of happening, don't they?'

Nero didn't respond. The implication of her words was not lost on him.

'It would be most unfortunate,' continued Kate, 'for an accident to happen to you, wouldn't it?'

'What . . . what sort of accident?'

'Oh . . . I don't know,' said Kate airily. 'A lot of things can go wrong when people start indulging in their own private fantasies.'

'Being tied up by you is hardly my private fantasy.'

'So who *would* you like to be tied up by, then?'

'I don't,' replied the prostrate Nero, 'like being tied up at all.'

'Oh, what a shame. And here I was thinking how sweet you looked.' She did, in fact, think he looked sweet. The rippling muscles of his back were still straining for release from his bonds; his buttocks were clenched and his thick black hair was now in uncustomary disarray. He was a mixture of boyishness and rampant masculinity. He was also hers. Hers to do with as she pleased.

Yet she had already had her pleasure and slowly but recognisably it was dawning on her that she had now had enough of playing the game. She had reduced Nero to a cringing, supine creature and that fact no longer gave her any pleasure.

She walked round the bed and looked at his face. It was scrunched up against the pillow dike a child's; the thick, soft lashes that she had once found so attractive were squeezed together and through them she saw, to her surprise, the slow welling of salty tears. Suddenly she stopped and listened. The only noise in the room now was the sound of Nero sobbing: quiet, desperate sobs that came from deep within him. His whole body was heaving, being torn apart by their force. And Kate knew that he was crying because she had reduced him so completely, humiliated him so deeply that something within him had broken.

She felt suddenly sick. For a moment she was completely paralysed by an emotion she couldn't identify. Nero was now oblivious to her. She suspected that if she undid the handcuffs, unbound his feet, then he would curl up into a foetal position and cry even harder. She had destroyed him. She had destroyed him professionally, emotionally and mentally – and it merely made her feel sick. She backed away from the bed, thinking for a split second that she might actually retch, vomit out the whole ghastly, sordid saga of Nero. Obliterate him from her memory.

She went into the bathroom, rinsed her face under the cold tap and looked at herself in the mirror. She couldn't at first identify what she saw. And then, at last, she noticed it: something that had long been missing. It wasn't easy to spot but it was *there* – she could see it deep in her eyes, firmly rooted at the window of her soul. It was, she knew, called peace.

She left the bathroom, quickly slipped into the jeans and T-shirt she had kept for this occasion, and, with one last, thoughtful glance at the crying man on the bed, she went into the drawing room.

'Well?'

She walked towards the sofa. 'It's over,' she

said in a small voice. 'I've done what I came to do.'

The man from the opera stood up and smiled at her. 'So now it's my turn.'

'What . . . what are you going to do to him?'

'Does it matter?'

Kate thought about that for a minute. 'Yes. It does matter. I trusted you the minute I saw you. I thought you were a force of good.'

He smiled sadly at her troubled face. 'I haven't done you much good, have I?'

Again Kate considered. When her answer came, it surprised her. 'Yes you have. You've . . . you've let me exorcise my demons. You've let me live out my fantasies – and my fears.'

'You could have done that yourself.'

Kate smiled wryly. 'I know that now. But I didn't know how to do it then. I thought it was all about power.'

'And isn't it?'

She knew he was teasing her but she didn't care. 'Oh no. It's got nothing to do with power. Or control. Or domination. It's about,' she pointed at her stomach, 'it's about what's in here. The *feeling* inside. The way you see yourself. That's what it's all about.'

'And how do you see yourself now?'

Kate grinned hugely. 'Differently.'

They looked at each other for a moment and then he walked towards the bedroom. He stopped at the door. 'If I'm a force for good then I assume Nero must be a source of evil, is that it?'

'Yes. Something like that.'

'Good and evil cancel each other out, don't they?'

'I . . .'

He opened the door. 'Goodbye, Cleo.' Then he too grinned. 'As diplomats go, you're about the best I've ever met.'

Kate stood still for a moment. Should she, she wondered, follow him into the bedroom? Or should she leave this place and never return?

The choice wasn't hard.

She never saw the man from the opera again. She did, however, receive a final communication from him. Two days later a small parcel was delivered through her letterbox. It contained a video – and a business card. But this time the business card was blank.

Chapter Eleven

MILES COURTENAY'S SUICIDE made headline news. His disgrace, on the other hand, was not aired in public. Charles Grant, the new company chairman, decided that Courtenay de Witt could easily ride out the losses he had incurred. For all of their sakes, he pleaded, the facts of the case should remain secret.

It wasn't difficult to keep them secret – few people knew them. And only one person knew them all.

'There's something,' said Mark to Kate as they walked out of Charles's office, 'that you're not telling me, isn't there?'

'Mmm?' Kate, feigning disinterest, didn't look round.

'Come on, Kate. Don't play games with me. You marched into Miles's office yesterday after your "day's research", and half an hour later Miles resigned. I simply don't believe one day was enough for you to trawl through the records of God knows how many dodgy holding companies to get incontrovertible proof against him. You must have had something else – what was it?'

It was a tape, she thought. A tape from which she had edited Nero's angry roars but left his damning, damaging evidence against Miles. The look on Miles's face, she remembered, had been priceless – and pathetic. She had destroyed him as she had destroyed Nero. Yet victory over this man had left her with the same bitter, sick feeling as before. Never again, she thought. No more dangerous games. No more wielding of awful, destructive power. No more negativity. 'All right,' she said quietly. 'There *was* something else. I found out . . . something else about Miles.'

Mark looked at her in silent contemplation for a moment. 'And Nero?' he asked. 'What did you tell him to make him disappear off the face of the earth?'

Not this man as well, thought Kate. Don't let me tell him things that will make him hate me. I just want to forget. She squared her shoulders. 'If I tell you then I'll be telling you things about my past that I'd rather forget. It's all . . . it's all a bit unpleasant.' But not all of it, she said to herself. Not the voice of reason that I didn't heed. Not the blond head that I imagined on the pillow beside mine. Not the person who had kept her sane.

She looked at that person. In one brief, reckless moment, she nearly told him. Instead, in a quiet voice, she said, 'Please. Please can we just forget. Can't we just start again?'

'Start what again?'

Kate looked at him with a half-smile. 'Our . . . our friendship?'

They cemented their friendship that night. For

424

both of them it was like a homecoming; there were none of the awkward fumblings and uncertainties of a first, feverish coupling. Instead, after a leisurely dinner they returned to Kate's own flat – not that faraway den of vice where she had left Nero and her previous life – and made sweet, leisurely, languorous love.

Mark pulled off his jacket and tie the minute he sat down on the sofa. It was a gesture so natural that neither he nor Kate stopped to consider that he had done it without invitation. He needed no invitation. Kate, returning from the kitchen with two glasses of brandy, smiled down at him.

'I had a dream about you,' she said before she could stop herself.

'Oh?' Mark grinned. 'I'm flattered. And I'm glad it wasn't a nightmare.'

'A nightmare?' Kate was surprised. 'What makes you say that.'

'Well,' said Mark as she sat down beside him, 'I always had a feeling that . . . that you disliked me somehow.'

'Why?'

Mark shrugged. 'Your attitude, I suppose. You used to be so . . . so dismissive. So superior.'

'Oh. Well, I suppose I felt . . . somehow threatened by you. It wasn't easy for me when you came on board.'

'You mean a young, thrusting man to fight off.' Mark's lips began to curl at the edges in a slow, seductive smile.

'Something like that.'

He leaned closer to her. 'And do you still think that?'

But Kate was now thinking about something

else. As he came closer she noticed the dark-blond hairs of his chest underneath the half-undone shirt. She was thinking how much she wanted to touch them. She extended a hesitant finger.

Mark took it in his hand and brought it to his lips. 'Do you still think,' he said as he kissed it, 'that you ought to fight me off?'

'Actually, I was wondering if you were still young and thrusting.'

They both laughed. Then, in the muted light of Kate's drawing room, they found the missing pieces of each other's lives.

Later – much later – Mark stirred and turned to Kate. 'What,' he said, 'd'you suppose we should do with Pharescault now? Now that Nero's gone.'

Kate considered that one for a moment. Then she grinned to herself. 'Oh,' she said lazily, 'bugger Pharescault.'

Midnight Starr

Dorothy Starr

Acknowledgements

'Not Just a Pretty Face' first appeared in *Erotic Stories*, 1992; 'A Pet for Christmas', 'The Man in Black' first appeared in *Forum*, 1992; 'Hand in Glove', 'Sweet Saint Nick' first appeared in *For Women*, 1992; 'Merry Christmas, Mister Lawson', 'Quiet Storm', 'The Old *Uno Due*', 'Stranger Than...' first appeared in *Erotic Stories*, 1993; 'Perfecto' first appeared in *Forum*, 1993; 'Studies in Red' first appeared in *Ludus*, 1993; 'Pretty Young Thing' first appeared in *Women on Top*, 1993; 'The Fruits of Learning', 'The Gardener's Boy', 'Finders Keepers', 'Condition Orange', 'Crème de la Crème', 'Thirty-Six Hours' first appeared in *Erotic Stories*, 1994; 'A Thing of Beauty' first appeared in *Loving*, 1994.

Contents

Merry Christmas, Mister Lawson

THEY WERE PAYING her triple rate for Christmas Eve. Triple rate and reduced hours ... and there was no way on earth she was earning it!

The Logicorp Party had been such a sedate affair that the fall-out of canapés, crisps and other assorted mess was minimal. To Nattie Romaine, it almost seemed like cheating to take the extra money, but as the company's Japanese masters had no idea of what constituted a proper seasonal bash in the first place, and were prepared to pay top whack to any person who'd come in and clean up afterwards, how could a poor hard-up student resist? Especially a student who'd nowhere to go on Christmas Eve anyway.

Under normal circumstances, Nattie would've told them to shove it. But circumstances weren't normal this year, and when the domestic supervisor had said, 'Any chance you could do Christmas Eve, Natalia?', Nattie had grimly confirmed she could.

To be alone and sulking tonight was ideal. She'd purposely not gone home for Christmas, so that she and Andy could celebrate together. But now *he* was celebrating with somebody else, and she didn't want to celebrate, full stop. Not with family, not with friends, not with anybody! At the moment, her happiest thoughts came from here; from the necessary part-time cleaning job that topped up her meagre student loan.

Here comes the best bit, she thought, as she pushed open the door to the division head's office – the luxurious acre sized enclosure that was the domain of Mr Jared Michael Lawson, the sexiest thing on two legs that Nattie had seen in a long time!

Very few cleaners got to meet the owners of the offices they tended, but Nattie was lucky. Not only was Mr Lawson fabulously tall, dark and handsome, he was also a workaholic. Nattie's shifts alternated between early mornings, and evenings from seven until nine, but even so Mr Lawson was often at his desk while she worked. There was one particular instance she had special cause to remember: one glorious, blessed-by-heaven dawn . . . But it was no use getting into *that* now, or she wouldn't finish dusting before midnight! This is such a horny-looking office, Nattie decided, throwing her back into her hoovering and wondering if Mr L. ever thought of her as a person. He always seemed too busy even to notice her presence.

The man had beautiful taste, there was no denying it. The room was as cool and smooth as he was, with a massive antique desk that added just the right amount of classy yet rough-hewn ruggedness, it had the same tough, matter-of-fact edge that its owner possessed in abundance. There were no tacky Christmas decorations in here either, and not a single empty glass from the party – even though Mr L. did have a well-stocked drinks cabinet for entertaining his VIP visitors. This suite needed even less cleaning than the rest of the floor, but that didn't stop Nattie expending far more time and energy in it than she had in any other office.

When she'd finally dusted and polished the main area to perfection, she turned her attention to the adjacent 'executive' washroom; one of Mr Lawson's hard-earned perks. It was here that she'd had her 'particular instance', she recalled fondly. As she began scrubbing the sink with cream cleaner, she permitted herself a little memory.

She'd come in very quietly that morning – still half-asleep, to be honest – and just assumed that it was the security man who'd opened up and switched on the lights. It was only when she'd padded almost all the way across the office and heard the sound of running water from the washroom, that she'd realised it was Mr Lawson who'd beaten her into work yet again.

He'd been standing in front of the wash-basin, unconsciously posing like a pin-up in just the skimpiest of black, thong-like underpants. He'd been splashing water over his chest and under his arms, and as his flight bag had been open beside him, he'd probably just got in from the airport.

Nattie had crept away then, and started on somebody else's office, but the image of that long, bronzed body – clad only in the sauciest of undies – had haunted her brain ever since.

She'd thought of him during lectures, on buses and while buying her modest amounts of shopping. She'd filled every idle minute with that picture of him, made it the focus of her frequent masturbation sessions; even – to her great shame – used the sight of it to concentrate her pleasure while Andy had been making his rather abbreviated and unthrilling love to her.

Was that why they'd split? Andy hadn't been the most perceptive of men, but she wondered if on some subliminal level he'd become aware of his rival in her mind. Maybe so . . . But that was still no excuse for him dumping her just before Christmas. She was willing to bet that Mr Lawson wouldn't have been such a rat to whatever lucky woman *he* was involved with. Putting down the lid of the lavatory, Nattie sat down, stuck out her legs and leaned back. It was Christmas after all, so she decided to give herself a present: a beautiful Mr Lawson fantasy.

Slowly opening her mind, she coaxed the man in question inside. She saw the brown limbs, the tight, muscular bottom, the bulge in those teasing black briefs . . . but the quality of image wasn't clear. The light in the bathroom was too harsh and intrusive, bouncing off the tiles and hurting her eyes. With a sigh, she got up, flipped the switch, and settled down again in the darkness.

In her fantasy, it was slushy romance that initially held sway. They were in a restaurant, dining intimately, with champagne, roses, significant looks, the full bit. Mr Lawson was all smiles, sweet words and compliments . . . Presently, he was escorting her to his limousine and helping her inside it – but with lots of little fondles in the process. Sly gliding strokes tantalised her breasts and bottom; gropes, to put it bluntly . . . In her dream, Nattie's expensive designer frock was so exquisitely sheer and thin that his fingers burned warm where they touched.

In real life, she knew very well that Mr Lawson was a sophisticated and discerning man with

434

impeccable manners; but in fantasyland it was perfectly okay that he behave like an adolescent sex fiend and feel her up at every available opportunity. Within seconds of the car moving off, he was peeling down the top of her cocktail dress and baring her soft warm breasts.

Cocktail dress? Nattie asked of her dreaming self, knowing she'd never actually worn one and probably wouldn't ever want to. In the same way that she'd never ever bother to put up her soft blonde locks in such an elaborate and soignee hairstyle.

But it didn't matter how well-groomed she looked, Mr L. seemed intent on changing all that. Within seconds her hair was down and he'd uncovered her breasts and nipples. Her dark pink nipples that were already as hard as cherry pips. She could easily imagine how his cultured fingertips might feel on her skin, but to make the experience more valid, she unbuttoned her overall, pushed her T-shirt up to her armpits, then cupped her bra-less breasts in her hands. Squeezing herself tightly, she caressed her stoney nipples with her fingers, just as an experienced lover like Mr L. might do. Or Jared, as she liked to think of him at moments like these.

As she stroked and aroused her own breasts, her mind showed Jared overtaking her; moving further ... He was sliding up her skirt now, running it smoothly over her silky stockings and her even silkier legs. The action was so suave and accomplished that the thought of it, plus her own tender touches at her nipples, made the heart of her sex moisten freely. Jared's phantom fingers slid with sure, practised ease into her frilly, figured satin panties, then delicately stirred her hot flesh.

Wriggling on her impromptu throne, Nattie

longed to recreate *everything* with accuracy: to smoothly unclothe her own sex, then caress it elegantly to pleasure with her fingers. But her tight denim jeans made things awkward, and meant she'd never match the sleek grace of Jared.

Nevertheless, she tried. Skimming down the zip, she opened up her frayed but serviceable denims, inveigled her fingers inside them, and then into her just-as-tatty knickers.

Just as she was about to dive deeper and seek out her clitoris, a noise in the outer office stopped her dead. Desire itself didn't die, but for thirty long seconds her limbs and her body were frozen. There was somebody moving about out there. At the any moment she'd be discovered skulking in her hideout, possibly in the act of masturbation!

As she sat on the toilet, immobile and with her fingers still trapped inside her clothes, she had a flash of quite startling lucidity. The steps outside were uneven and hesitant – not a bit like Mr Lawson's usual confident strides. Yet she still knew it was him. She also got the definite impression he was drunk. As if to confirm her suspicions she heard an angry, muttering voice, then a stumble and a colourful curse.

What the hell was going on? She could imagine anybody getting slightly tiddly on Christmas Eve, even a smooth operator like Mr Lawson. But falling down drunk? Solitary Christmases were for romantic lovers like Natalia Romaine, not for debonair ladykillers like Jared Michael Lawson. Especially as there was a silver-framed photograph of a woman in a prominent position on his desk – an object that Nattie had always studiously ignored.

Even as she thought of the frame, there was a crash, a splintering, and the word 'bitch' perfectly enunciated in his deep-dark, bitter-chocolate voice. 'Bitch,' he growled again as Nattie finally pulled her hand from her jeans and tugged her T-shirt back down to her waist.

'Dammed fucking bitch,' he elaborated with a good deal more violence.

Nattie was behind the bathroom door now, and observing him through a convenient crack between door and jamb. As he swore, she flinched, but then calmed again. He obviously hadn't the slightest awareness of her presence, because he was sitting in his huge, leather covered chair, his long legs stretched and spread, and his straight body tellingly slumped. The silver-framed picture was lying on the floor some feet away, and on the desk before him was a tumbler full of amber fluid that Nattie assumed to be whisky. 'Bitch,' he reiterated, his anger, sorrow, disappointment or whatever seeming to combine with the liquor in erasing his extensive vocabulary.

'Don't need you, you know,' he muttered on, pulling at the buttoms of his shirt. His jacket was already on the floor not far from the picture. 'I can make my own fun . . .' He giggled then – the sound strangely sexy and boyish – and started struggling with his elegant, crocodile-skin belt and the zip of his dove grey trousers.

Holy Christ! though Nattie wildly, recognising immediately what her idol was up to. The very same act that she'd been about to perform.

Beneath the grey designer tailoring were plain dark briefs, but Nattie didn't get much time to study them. Almost immediately his equipment was on view. His penis; so superbly stiff and furiously red with its swollen and shiny-slick glans. She sighed, then wished she hadn't, terrified that the man outside might be sober in an instant if he heard her.

Oh God, Mr Lawson, you're beautiful! she thought breathlessly when the immediate danger was past. He was entirely absorbed in his own self-pleasure now; his eyes were closed, his breathing was heavy and he seemed oblivious to everything else in the world but the long bar of flesh in his fingers.

Nattie felt her own sex ache as her fantasy made careful love to his. The woman who'd ditched him or whatever must be mad! she thought, gaining a comforting new perspective on her own recent letdown. If she'd lost a man like Mr Lawson at Christmas, she really would be unhappy. Instead of feeling just mildly upset over an insensitive twerp like Andy.

What's more – she told herself philosophically – if she'd been out celebrating with Andy tonight, she wouldn't have had chance to see this!

Mr Lawson was in motion now, writhing in his deep, executive chair, his lean body bucking, his tanned hands a masturbating blur. He was groaning too; not flinging insults to his silver-framed betrayer anymore, but simply encouraging his own randy efforts with an evocative catalogue of grunts, sighs and broken, unintelligible words.

Andy would have come ages ago, observed Nattie, almost dispassionately. Her ex had a problem with pre-emptive spurting, whereas Mr L. seemed to be going on forever! His erection was invulnerable to his own ferocious fingers. He was wrenching at his flesh like a sex-crazed maniac, his chest awash with sweat and his angry red shaft all coated with the silver of his juices.

Is it the booze? Nattie wondered. Was he so aroused, so hard and so pissed that ejaculation and orgasm were impossible? It certainly seemed so. But

438

if that meant she could watch him for longer, there was no way she was about to complain!

'Oh God,' he moaned, more delectable than ever in his torments. His heels were dragging on the carpet, and he was tossing his head from side to side, dishevelling his usually-neat curls. 'Oh God,' he gasped again, licking his lips, his whole lean face stretched taut in an agony of pleasure. 'Oh, please! I can't—' he babbled, then suddenly his lust-darkened eyes snapped open and his grimace seemed to soften to a smile.

Nattie saw him settle back down into his seat, his cock still rampant, but his body a little more relaxed. It was as if he'd found an agreeable solution to his problem and was gathering his wits for his final implementation.

'Okay . . . Come out. You're going to have to help me with this.' He was looking straight down at his penis, and jiggling it playfully, but his voice was pitched towards the doorway.

If anyone had asked her, Nattie would've sworn that her heart stopped beating then. But nobody was asking her anything, and a moment later Mr Lawson repeated his order, his voice ragged and uneven as he started panting and gasping again.

'Come out. I know you're in there.'

He'd find her eventually, she realised, so there seemed no point in lingering. She pulled up the zip of her jeans and stepped out of the bathroom and the shadows.

'Now how did I know it was going to be you?' he asked, his lazy smile widening and his fingers still toying with his cock. 'You're the girl who always watches me, aren't you? The shy girl . . . The pretty one who never says a word.'

Even though she could move, Nattie couldn't

speak. Dumbstruck she walked towards him, her eyes locked tightly on that rosy pole of manflesh and the narrow brown hand that gripped it.

It was a time for neither debate or explanation. Nattie remained rapt and silent. Mr Lawson said simply, 'Please. Will you help me?'

Driven purely by instinct, she started pulling off her shabby working clothes. This god needed a woman's body around him for his pleasure. And though she recognised her many shortcomings, when it came to the moment she was a female with the necessary anatomy . . .

When her T-shirt came off, he smiled in approval. When she stumbled, struggling out of her close-fitting jeans, he laughed softly – though his brown eyes were benign, not mocking. When she was nude, he reached out towards her, his expression full of raw, burning hunger and his prick pointing straight towards her pussy.

A few moments ago, she'd been bemoaning her own lack of grace, but as Mr Lawson took her hand and helped her to straddle his lap, Nattie found a new and hitherto unknown source of poise. Astonished by her own lithe confidence, and the smooth way her limbs meshed with his, she moved over him, tucked his cock into her body and slid down on it slowly and sensually.

They both sighed as he bucked upwards to fill her completely. He, because she was so obviously the comfort he sought; she, because she'd never been so stretched and so pleasured. Mr Lawson felt vast inside her: his penis so alive, and so hot. His hands closed tightly on her buttocks; first to hold her and soothe her, then to move and guide her in pursuit of the optimum sensation. Her sensation as well as his . . . Without thinking, she leaned forward and

440

braced herself, one hand on his muscular shoulder. The other hand slid quite naturally down to her sex, a fingertip settling delicately on her clitoris to compliment the fullness in her pussy.

'Yes!' mouthed Mr Lawson, the heat in his eyes telling Nattie that he liked what she'd done.

Strangers, yet bonded, they rocked and writhed and swayed together in the cradle of the big leather chair. Nattie had never consciously employed sexual skills before, but now she discovered that she possessed some. Clamping her internal muscles around him, she caressed Mr Lawson with her body and almost shouted with triumph when he whimpered and struggled in response. His large cock seemed to swell up inside her, reaching inwards and bringing pure, bubbling joy to every deep-seated crevice and niche. In a frenzy, she rubbed and pummelled at her clitoris to the rhythm of his pleasure-crazed lunges. For what felt like hours they cried and squirmed and sweated together. Their bodies were mated as if they'd been loving each other for decades, and intended to go on for decades more . . .

But at length the sweet moment came. Nattie's orgasm seemed to fall from the sky like a star, dropping downwards in a glorious incandescent blaze and melding with Mr Lawson's rising surge of release. He cried out hoarsely, then silenced his own mouth with hers, pressing their lips together in a long wet kiss that sealed and perfected their climax.

'I imagine you'll be expected at a party or something now, won't you?' he asked quietly, a good while later. The force of their pleasure seemed to have burnt off the effects of the alcohol somehow, and his voice sounded normal and controlled.

Nattie was lying in his arms now, draped across

his knee, her naked body moist with his semen. Still overwhelmed, she shook her head – unwilling to open her mouth, re-establish hard reality, and highlight the disparity of their lives.

When he spoke, his soft, rich tones were tentative. It seemed unthinkable, and incredible, but to Nattie it almost sounded as if he were pleading.

'I don't suppose you'd consider coming home with me for a fireside feast, would you?' he asked.

'Champagne, nuts, cheese, mince pies: you know the sort of thing . . .' As she sat up straight, to look at him, she caught the tail-end of a glance towards the fallen photo-frame.

'Okay, I admit it. . .' he said, sounding momentarily bitter. 'It was originally planned for somebody else . . .' He paused for a second, as if shaking off a demon, then gave Nattie a warm, open smile, 'But right now, I'd much rather share it with you.'

It was totally crazy, but the decision was effortless. 'I'd love to,' she whispered, then daringly pressed a kiss to his cheek.

Her acceptance seemed to galvanise him. Matching her kiss with one of his own, he urged her up on to her feet, stroking the curve of her hip as he did so. His eyes went dark, then bright with a fresh, new burst of desire; but he grinned in an attempt to contain it. The word 'later' hung delightfully in the air between them, and he pushed his slightly-rising penis back into his briefs, zipped his trousers, then stood up beside her.

'Get your clothes on, pretty girl, and I'll rustle up a taxi.'

Wondering where her knickers were, Nattie watched him run his fingers through this crisp dark hair, then efficiently put the rest of his clothing to rights – no mean feat after she'd rubbed her seeping, sweating body all over him.

As he reached for the telephone, he hesitated. 'Just one more thing,' he said thoughtfully, and Nattie bit her lip, wondering if he'd just changed his mind.

'Merry Christmas, Nattie,' he whispered in her ear as he pulled her still only half-covered body back against him.

So you *do* know my name! she thought happily, pushing her breasts against the cotton of his shirt and realising – all over again – that it was the magical night before Christmas. In spite of his casual mention of nuts and mince pies and stuff, what'd happened in the big leather chair had made her forget the festivity of the season.

But now, held tight in such strong, gorgeous arms, she did remember – and her feeling of goodwill to all men could've lit up every street in the city. 'Merry Christmas, Mr Lawson,' she murmured as she pressed her bare belly against his groin.

Well, at least she knew what to give him as a present!

The Fruits of Learning

I NEVER REALISED I could be this happy, thought Madeleine blissfully as she accepted a peach from Delrina's golden bowl. Laying aside her book, she bit into the fruit's velvet skin, and as its ripe, sweet taste exploded on her tongue she sighed with pleasure, and felt the peach-juice dribble over her chin and drip down on to the slope of her breast. Licking her lips, and taking another large bite, she lolled back amongst the silk-covered cushions, closed her eyes, and remembered how she'd come to this place . . .

It'd all begun when her father couldn't pay the Prince's tribute.

The shame had been terrible, but there'd been worse to come when the Royal Chamberlain had suggested a solution. Madeleine hadn't known which to fear the most: year after year of debt and dishonour as her family struggled to find the money, or the total surrender of her body when she entered the Prince's service.

Madeleine had heard tales of such delicate arrangements, but had always dismissed them as hearsay. The ageing Prince was noted for his over-developed sexual appetites – especially where younger women were concerned – but it seemed preposterous that he could have her by command. Didn't he keep his Byzantine houris for such loathsome purposes? There were three pampered, licentious women, often glimpsed frolicking in the verdant palace gardens, their voluptuous, satin-skinned bodies lightly clad in tiny scraps of cloth of gold. Surely such beauty as theirs was enough to satisfy his Highness's needs? What could he want with a skinny, bookish virgin?

Still, the sacrifice had to be made – it was the only way to avoid Papa's ruin.

Though innocent in body, Madeleine well knew what passed between men and women. An intelligent girl, as well as pretty in her own fragile way, she'd deduced a great deal from her studies of literature and biology. To reproduce, it seemed, a man and woman must couple, and in this joining lay the ultimate pleasure. The touch of a man was supposed to be all that a women might crave, but for her own part, Madeleine was doubtful. She found the notion of a naked man fondling her and mounting her repellent. She knew that in this respect she wasn't like most girls of her age, but she couldn't see any way to change what she felt.

Nevertheless, despite her terrors, Madeleine was aware of her duty. When the day of her summons to the palace came, she followed the Royal Chamberlain without protest and tried stoically not to dwell on her fate.

At the gate of the sumptuous women's quarters, she was met by the Prince's three beauties.

'Don't be afraid, little one,' said Delrina, the tallest and most lovely, giving Madeleine a smile of great

445

sweetness and understanding. 'You'll be safe here with us. And you'll find a new way to be happy.'

Madeleine would have liked to dispute this, but Delrina's gentle charm *was* soothing. The Byzantine woman had eyes that were warm as brown velvet, and her mouth was soft and rosy. Her long, glistening black hair was crowned by a pretty, gilded cap, and like her companions, Nadia and Laurelina, she was sublimely curvaceous, and graced with proudest and lushest of bosoms, a tiny, tiny waist, and hips that flared elegantly yet ripely beneath the frill of her pleated silk skirt – the only garment that covered her body.

Nadia and Laurelina – blonde and redheaded respectively – were both equally enchanting and both wore the same bizarre outfits. They seemed bright-eyed and happy, and not the slightest bit troubled by their captivity. When she looked at them, Madeleine felt confused. She should have despised them for their willing submission, yet all three women had a strange and seductive effect on her, and their presence made her feel quite relaxed. She was still nervous of what the future might hold for her, but her new companions made the fear a little less.

'Come, we'll show you our sanctuary,' said Nadia gently, her green eyes glinting. She took Madeleine's arm and, as they walked, the tip of the concubine's uncovered breast brushed lightly against Madeleine's elbow. The tiny, bouncing contact produced a frisson of intense sensation, and Madeleine felt her whole body turn quivery and glowing. The relaxation she'd felt increased to a strange, heavy lethargy, and her own breasts seemed to swell and start aching. Her simple, woollen gown seemed suddenly too tight and in her belly there was a long, low stirring.

Shaken, she allowed the three young women to lead her down an exquisitely decorated corridor and into a room of yet more opulence and refinement. Elaborately embroidered hangings covered all four walls – except where there were a series of tall, well-filled bookcases and leaded windows trimmed with multicoloured glass – and underfoot there was a thick Persian carpet. The centre of chamber was furnished not with the usual wooden chairs and tables, but with a number of deep, upholstered divans, strewn with cushions and long, satin throws. Through two open arched doorways beyond, Madeleine could see other areas of equal luxury: an inner garden with a marble-lined pool and playing fountain, and a huge, airy, blue and gold tiled bathing room. The air in the chamber was fresh, and circulated freely, yet carried the perfume of roses and musk.

'This is our haven,' murmured Laurelina, gesturing towards the centre of the room with a toss of her burnished red hair.

'Our sanctuary,' whispered Nadia, pressing her breast more closely against Madeleine's arm.

'Our school of love,' finished Delrina with a slow sensuous smile, taking her place at Madeleine's other elbow, as between them, she and Nadia led their charge towards the bathing room. 'This is where we were taught the arts of love by the women who came before us, and they in turn were taught by the those who preceded them.' Reaching out, she touched Madeleine's blushing cheek and let her hand trail slowly downwards, 'This is where you too will learn many skills and accomplishments . . . but not necessarily for the pleasure of the Prince.'

Not sure what the other woman meant, Madeleine

allowed herself to be led into the bath-house.

Aren't they his servants? she wondered. His mistresses? How is it that they all seemed so powerful?

As the women undressed her, Madeleine began to shake more and more. First her dress, then her undergarments were peeled away from her pale, waif-like body; as each item of clothing was discarded, all three of the women examined the lightly freckled skin that was revealed. Madeleine's cheeks turned from blush pink to deepest, ruddy crimson as the secrets of her flesh were explored.

She moaned as Delrina took hold of her breasts, one in each soft-skinned hand, and seemed to weigh them and assess their tender firmness. She whimpered and swayed on her feet as Nadia's nimble fingertips slid into her furrow and travelled over each fold and indentation. She cried out hoarsely, and almost fell, as Laurelina drew a single hot fingertip between the cheeks of her bottom, then pushed wickedly at the most-forbidden entrance.

'Please,' begged Madeleine, with no real idea what she asked for as the the three women continued to probe her. Their slender fingers traversed and rubbed until her poor body was melting with excitement. She felt embarrassment and shame, but within and beyond it she felt the dawning of an amazing new knowledge.

For what seemed like an age she was pinned at the centre of a triangle of beauty, her naked female shape its prime focus. Then, as first Delrina, then Nadia and Laurelina withdrew, she cried out at the loss of their touch.

'Come, we will bathe you now,' said Delrina, taking Madeleine's hand in her own, then leading her towards the scented pool.

Used to the spartan facilities of her family's ordinary home, Madeleine was stunned by the richness around her. The slowly lapping water was deep enough at one end to stand in, although the women chose the shallower area in which to carry out their intimate ablutions. Flinging off their skimpy clothing, they joined her in the pool, and set about their task with a gentle enthusiasm. Stirred as she was by the way they'd caressed her, Madeleine accepted everything in a pliant, dreamy silence.

Once again their fingers searched her naked body this time coating it with a dense, creamy lather that slithered like an unguent across her skin. The thick white foam was scented with almonds, and every place it touched seemed to tingle. Madeleine sensed that this too was part of the preparation for pleasure; that within the soap itself there was some esoteric ingredient that aroused her to a heightened sensitivity. She felt herself leaning heavily into every stroke of the washcloth, constantly wishing it would go further and further. Her wet thighs slid apart with little conscious effort, and she sighed when the cloth went between them.

She knew now that a crisis of some kind was approaching, an unknown pinnacle of physical sensation. Every part of her was filled with a deep, sweet yearning, laden with a hunger that she couldn't quite define. Maybe this was the 'desire' the books spoke of: the rapture, the very transports of passion? It seemed almost incomprehensible that she should feel it with these women when the idea of a man made her shudder, and yet somehow she was helpless to resist.

'Surrender, my darling,' murmured Delrina, sliding the washcloth back and forth with great purpose. 'There's nothing to fear from your body.' As the dark woman pressed harder, the others also moved in close: each attending to a different part of Madeleine, and touching her where they'd touched her before.

Suddenly, a feeling like no other seemed to burst between Madeleine's twisting thighs. Heat, lightness, and a great and euphoric rush of pleasure. She could feel the very quick of her womanhood throbbing, yet the awareness of it seemed to speed through every bit of her, from her top of her head to the tips of her toes.

'Yes! Yes!' chanted Nadia and Laurelina in a chorus as Madeleine collapsed in their arms. She could no longer support the weight of her body and would have sunk beneath the water without them.

'That's the first lesson,' she heard Delrina whisper, then heard no more as the second one began.

By nightfall, Madeleine had caught up with the learning of a lifetime. Her three new friends had brought her time and time to that indescribable peak, and on each occasion the means had been different.

Lying naked on her divan, with her skin polished and gleaming, Madeleine tried to separate each instance of 'the moment' – but her pleasure-drugged mind wouldn't work. She seemed only to recall one, long lambent sequence of bodily enjoyment and sly caresses in all her secret places. When it was over, they'd dried her tenderly with a soft linen sheet, glazed her skin with a blend of sweet oils, then fed her a meal of fresh fruit and mild cheese, all washed down with a heady, spiced wine. After only a few mouthfuls, she'd been sleepy.

Alone now, with Delrina, Nadia and Laurelina retired to a large, shared divan of their own, Madeleine found herself suddenly wakeful and thinking.

Would the Prince expect such liberties from her? Or would he simply require possession of her hymen? She trembled, imagining his gnarled old fingers and his lined and wrinkled mouth doing the things that her companions had done to her. Would she not cringe with distaste if he sucked on her breast, or thrust a bony digit roughly inside her? Would she not die a thousand, shameful deaths if he caressed the velvet cheeks of her bottom, then probed her tiny portal with his tongue? And what if he asked the same of her? Oh, no, it was too horrible to contemplate.

Yet her companions must do such things for him, and they seemed delighted with their lot. They didn't lie awake and worry – although as Madeleine had *that* thought, she realised they weren't sleeping.

On the large divan, a few feet from her own, there were the beginnings of motion in the shadows. Three sets of smooth, naked limbs were combining, and three voices were sighing and gasping. With a sense of fascination, Madeleine realised that her companions were pleasuring themselves: both individually, and presently, in ensemble. Forgetting her worries, and forgetting sleep also, she let her fingers find the cleft of her sex.

The next day passed strangely contentedly, although not in the manner she'd expected.

After being left to bathe alone, and fed again on a delicious light meal, Madeleine was surprised when the women didn't touch her. She'd anticipated further lessons and further touching, and been perplexed when none were forthcoming. Instead, Delrina had led her to the bookcases, and encouraged her to choose the choicest volumes.

'All these books contain knowledge that will help you with your duties. You must read, so you'll know what we know.'

Loving books as she did, Madeleine had soon forgotten her disappointment. The private library was a wondrous hoard of knowledge, and as arousing in its way as the long, shared hours of yesterday. Each book was a classic of pornography. As she read – and read and read and read – Madeleine soon grew both learned and fevered. Every picture seemed to remind her of the touch of Delrina's lips, or the way Laurelina's fingertips could seek out, and find, the most discreet and receptive of pleasure-nodes, then tantalise them to the very edge of madness. Every line or paragraph of uncensored prose seemed to conjure up the taste of Nadia's sweat.

When evening came, Madeleine could recall little of the day. Her mind was a blur of sensual images, and her slender body a furnace of desire. A great well of heat that didn't even cool when finally the dreaded summons arrived.

This time, their bathing was even more scrupulous than yesterday, but in the water there were only acts of cleansing. In a daze, though feeling far less fearful than she'd expected, Madeleine let the other three adorn her. Washed and creamed with oils and lotions, she lay back and let Delrina trim her fluff of pubic curls, then daub her folds with a gentle, perfumed rouge. She allowed her nipples to be coloured too, then be painted with more oil so they'd shine. The last refinement was a diamond in her navel.

When her face too had been delicately painted, she let the women dress her in the same golden garments that they wore, and brush her brown hair to a glossy, rippling fall.

'The Lady Madeleine, my Lord,' announced Delrina at the door of the Prince's chamber.

Bowing low, Madeleine stepped forward, feeling more defiance – and desire – than fear now. Yes, she'd give herself to this ancient, lusty sovereign; but she'd use *him* to satisfy *her* rising appetites just as he'd be using her to slake his own.

'I am yours, my Lord,' she said boldly, speaking the words just as she been instructed. Then, with all the grace she could muster, she lay back on the silk divan before him and bared her treasure to his old, but piercing eyes.

Not daring to look at his face now the moment of surrender had arrived, Madeleine shivered as she heard the sibilant rustle of his heavy, brocade-trimmed robes.

'How lovely you are, my young one,' he murmured. 'How precious and how deliciously ripe.' His quavering voice had a soft, kindly ring to it – and as she absorbed this, her revulsion seemed to lessen. Perhaps there would be *real* joy here after all?

'Let us begin,' he said quietly, when what felt like an age of time had passed.

Eyes tightly shut, Madeleine heard more rustling, then felt the heat of a body close to hers. Gentle hands parted her thighs, and shuddering wildly she tried to relax.

Open ... More and more open ... She could almost feel an alien flesh touch hers ... Bracing herself for the Prince's rigid penis, she cried out when the kiss of contact came.

Crying again, and feeling something quite different to what she'd been expecting, Madeleine let her closed eyes open, and got the most beautiful and unexpected of surprises.

She saw power and eroticism in the Prince's aged face, and the light of simple pleasure there too. The surprise was that he was seated on his throne still, with his stately robes thrown negligently open and his penis clasped tightly in his fist.

When as his old eyes fluttered closed in rapture, Madeleine felt her own flesh leap and judder. Smiling, laughing, almost crying, she looked down towards the apex of her thighs . . . and saw Delrina with her red mouth hard at work.

Still smiling now, Madeleine took another greedy bite of her peach.

'I only want to *see* your beauty, gentle Madeleine,' the Prince had said later, 'and to see you learn the joys of pleasure from my darlings.'

The old man she'd so feared didn't want to touch her at all, she now realised. All he wanted was to watch as his women made love to her. A simple privilege she was happy to permit him. Plying her with wine afterwards, and looking fondly on her flushed and sweating body, he'd said that she need only stay at the palace for a little while longer, then she was free to leave, with her father's debts paid.

But do I want to leave? Madeleine pondered, chewing her mouthful of succulent peach-flesh and starting to wriggle against the satin of her cushions. Now that all's well, and I understand what the Prince *really* needs, it might be nice to stay here and enjoy his wondrous library; to fully savour the delicious fruits of learning.

Madeleine smiled happily as she considered this,

but before she could reach for her book, or even take another bite of peach, both the book and the fruit were quite forgotten.

Closing her eyes, she arched languorously on her bed of silken comfort, and as the peach slipped and fell from her fingers, a darting tongue lapped her breast clean of its juice . . .

A Thing of Beauty

IT WAS THE most beautiful thing I'd ever seen, but all it made me do was want to cry. I ran my fingers slowly over the lace, the boning, and the tiny appliqué flowers, and wondered what on earth had possessed me to buy something so ridiculous, so expensive and so useless. It was too late now, the time for sexy lingerie was long past. Not even a pure silk, gunmetal blue basque could salvage the ruins of my marriage.

I'd sent for it on impulse, from a flyer that'd fallen out of a magazine. It was one of those 'today's woman' glossies that I'd bought for an article on 'Putting the Spice Back into your Relationship'. I was clutching at straws really – doubly so in the case of the basque – because I don't think I've ever finished one of those oh-so-helpful articles. They all seemed so unreal and pretentious, as if they were written for tall blonde superwomen who wouldn't have problems in the first place, and probably wore slinky undies anyway.

Even so, I'd sent for the basque, strangely inspired because it looked so pretty, and because the model wasn't blonde, and even looked a little bit like me. She was more eye-catchingly glamorous, of course, but the raw material was the same. Straight nut-brown hair, medium figure, blue eyes. I was quite good-looking in my own way too.

Not that Mike had noticed lately . . .

Oh, he'd never been cruel or unkind to me, and I don't think he had the time to have an affair – he was too busy and preoccupied with his work. It was just that he'd stopped really looking at me, stopped meaning it when he kissed me goodbye every morning, stopped having either the interest or the energy for anything more than the most perfunctory and uninspiring lovemaking.

It hadn't always been like that. We'd been desperate for each other when we'd first fallen in love. I'd bought pretty undies then too. I remembered the gorgeous white lace bra and knickers I'd worn under my wedding dress – and the frenzied fervent way that Mike had stripped them off me. Then he made love to me, murmuring 'Jenny, oh, Jenny, I love you' as our pleasure rose up and overwhelmed us.

Somehow, though, apathy had crept in. I couldn't quite remember when the wildness had gone out of what happened between us in bed; when Mike had stopped reaching for me so often; when his being self-employed had started meaning self-absorbed; when I'd started reading voraciously, taking evening courses, and buying five packs of Marks & Spencers knickers instead of sheer satin and frills.

The blame was shared, I knew. Mike had lost sight of his home life in his desire to develop his business. But it was me who'd felt resentful, sought distraction, and hadn't tried to understand. When I'd wanted romance, I'd turned to my imagination instead of to the man I loved. The daydreams had turned into hastily scribbled-down stories that I'd polish up at my creative writing class. We'd both of us turned in on ourselves, instead of reaching out to each other.

It was only when I realised that my so-called love stories were always pretty lacklustre that it dawned on me how truly drab my own love story was. I'd been looking for a picture of an ideal hero, but I'd found no-one amongst the sleekly groomed male models in my magazine. I wanted him to be sandy-haired, handsome but not clichéd, quite beautiful but in a rugged sort of way. He had to be tall, and wear glasses, and – I realised suddenly – look exactly the way Mike had looked, in the early happy days of our marriage.

The revelation left me shaking, befuddled, cor~fused. Which might account for me thinking that the purchase of a single set of overpriced lingerie could solve matters. The flyer had fallen out of the very same magazine I'd been seeking my dream man in. But when the basque had arrived, so had the tears. For a while I sobbed furiously at my own futility and silliness, then decided to make the best of things. I'd get my money's worth out of all that extravagant satin!

In the old days, Friday had always been our best night – the night when the pure physical fireworks had gone off and our lovemaking had always hit its highs. Armed with gladrags, I tried to recreate the same conditions. I went mad on a special dinner, bought a wine we both liked; even took an afternoon off work to preen and pamper myself. I blow-dried my hair, waxed some bits of me and rubbed perfumed body cream into others. I did a special, but subtle make-up that ought to withstand the rigours of being ardently made love to. I made myself as beautiful as I could, then I put on my basque and its matching panties, some sheer, finely-seamed stockings, my best robe, and waited . . .

And waited and waited and waited.

At first the anticipation was lovely. It was so exciting to be building myself up to such heights again – waiting for my handsome husband with desire and sex on my mind. Sipping a glass of wine, I found myself filled with arousal for the first time in ages, my body tingling in its elegant silk and lace casing, longing for the moment when Mike's strong hands would release me from its sensuous confines. I began to re-live some of the memorable moments of our former lovemaking: the times we'd clung to each other, sobbing with pleasure, vowing to love one another always, and always with the same sweet passion.

I remembered one Friday when Mike had kissed every inch of my body, making me whimper with longing before finally ravishing me. He'd always been a good lover, always thoughtful, watching out for my satisfaction almost above his own. At least that was how it'd been in the beginning, before we'd begun to retreat to opposite corners of the universe. I stroked the cool, steely-coloured satin that shaped me, and made a conscious vow. Tonight, we'd pull ourselves back together again. If I wanted it hard enough I could get it. I breathed in, fluffed my hair, and checked my seams. I *could* make Mike start looking again!

Another hour, and another glass of wine later, I was feeling less optimistic. I was also feeling foolish, staring glumly at myself in the mirror, dressed up as a high-class tart for a man who probably wasn't interested. My suspenders looked stupid. My pushed-up bosom gross. My panties were too see-through, too sleazy, too little and yet far too much.

By ten, it was obvious he wasn't coming home, and just as the tears began, I got the call. 'A business meeting.' 'Don't worry.' 'I'll get a Chinese.' 'Don't wait up.'

It was only what often happened, but this time, done up in my beautiful things, it hurt a hundred times harder. 'I said, 'Yes.' 'It's okay.' 'No worries.' but inside my heart was dying. I put down the phone, scraped the ruined dinner into the waste bin, and drank another glass of wine in one long swallow. I could have finished the whole lot, but I even felt too miserable to get drunk.

In the bedroom, I unhooked, unlaced and unsuspendered myself, then cried again over my beautiful shimmering basque; so perfect, so seductive . . . and so pointless.

Bawling like a baby, in despair, I pushed it roughly in the drawer so I didn't have to look at it. I struggled into a serviceable cotton nightie, brushed my teeth, and crawled into bed, not expecting to sleep, but surprisingly, nodding off after a few cheerless minutes.

I don't know how long it was before the dream began. It could have been moments, or it could have been hours. I only knew that somehow I'd travelled in time, and gone back to those wonderful days – especially those Fridays – when Mike and I had been so close.

I could feel his warm body lying along side mine, his front against my back, like spoons. He felt so strong, and I felt so secure. I snuggled myself to his shape, then smiled with joy in my haziness. The way Mike pressed himself to me let me know that

460

we really were back in those glorious, desire-filled times. He was naked and my nightie had crawled up over my hips; I could feel how he wanted me. How he needed me. And in an instant, I realised how much I'd never stopped wanting him.

Sighing, I tried to turn over, but he held me still, kissing the back of my neck, his lips firm and moist against my ear. His arms came around me, and his hands caressed me, travelling slowly over my finely quivering curves. Their progress was sweet and familiar, yet strangely and poignantly tentative. I felt him asking silently for my permission ... and my forgiveness. I could swear I felt tears on the side of my neck – and not mine because I was too excited. Turning my face, I kissed the edge of his jaw, then pushed my body backwards against him, granting the permission he craved. With a low groan, he began to explore me, seeking out my warmest most sensitive zones, then finding them with sureness and skill. His fingertips travelled to all my softest chinks and crannies, then dabbled and dipped and stroked, making me whimper and squirm with delight.

Oh, it was so good, so real. So like those wonderful nights in the marvellous first months of our marriage. I *was* crying again now, but with pleasure, as Mike's fingers took me soaring to the peak. Once. Twice. Three times.

While I was still in heaven, he gently rolled me towards him, and on to my back, then moved his long, warm body over me. I was eager and shamelessly wanton, parting my thighs and pushing myself at him – making the way smooth and easy for his manhood.

As he entered me, he kissed me too, taking my lips with a slow, reverent beauty. I cried out and he

461

seemed to drink the sound straight from my mouth, to feed on it in the same way that his lips and his kiss nourished me. The famine of our love was over, and ravenous, we dove into a feast. I sensed Mike trying to hold back, trying to prolong the experience for me, but the need in us both was too great.

After just a few minutes we were shouting, crying, clinging to each other; clutching madly at each other's backs as an implosion of ecstasy engulfed us. Bereft of magic and oneness for so long, we were both swept away by the force of it. I wanted to talk and laugh, to reassure Mike and thank him, pledge that whatever happened in the future, we'd never drift apart again – but within seconds I was sinking fast into sleep. The last thing I remember was tears again. Mine trickling happily down my cheeks, and Mike's against my neck as I held him.

The next morning I awoke still full of happiness. I was filled with questions too, and puzzlement over the irony of timing. Just when I'd thought my last try had failed, it seemed that I needn't have tried anyway. Mike himself had made the first move.

I wanted desperately to ask some of those questions, but instead I let them wait – while we made lazy, wordless, Saturday lie-in love, and our bodies said everything for us.

'Why now?' I asked finally, when Mike brought me coffee in bed, and a rose still dewy from the garden. 'Because I saw this,' he answered sheepishly, picking up something from a drawer he'd just pulled open. 'I saw it poking out, and when I realised what it was, I realised you hadn't given up on me after all . . .'

In his hands he held my pretty blue basque, and

as I watched him, he stroked its delicate, flower-trimmed panels, then held it out shyly towards me.

'Will you wear it?' he asked, his voice rich with a dozen other questions as he waited for me to take it from him.

'Yes, I will,' I murmured, reaching out, 'I'll wear it whenever I think we need it. *Either* of us . . .'

He smiled as our fingers met across the lace, his face bright with love and relief.

Silk and satin aren't the only things of beauty . . .

The Gardener's Boy

ENGLAND IS A STRANGE old place: wonderful, fascinating, but strange. And I think I found the very strangest part of it, that summer when I stayed at Flitwick Hall.

I was running away, really, running as far and fast as I could from heavy emotional troubles. So that beautiful and magical house, far away across the Atlantic in England, seemed like just the kind of hideout I needed.

The invitation to visit the Flitwicks, my English relations, had been around for years. I'd always wanted to visit them, but until that summer I'd never had the chance. When I finally turned up, it was purely a spur of the moment thing, and consequently the house was all but empty. There was only a skeleton staff in residence, to take care of one nutty, reclusive old great-aunt I'd never even known that I had.

My troubles? A man, naturally, and the heartache of love turning bad. Ellery and I had been a hot number for a year, a solid couple so I thought, but one day we'd suddenly started arguing, then realised we weren't a number after all. The parting had been acrimonious, and I'd left with my soul feeling bruised. Two days later I'd also realised I was pregnant – from a meaningless, pleasureless encounter just hours before our final bitter fight.

Now Marylou Deschanel is no coward, I'll tell you, but this time I took the easy way out. I booked straight into a clinic and had an abortion, then went searching for my distant English roots in an effort to diminish the aching void.

Flitwick Hall was the prettiest place you could imagine – a mellow, gilded fairy-house that seemed to glow in the high summer sun. It was still and quiet and tranquil, yet it had a strange air of sexiness about it too; a muted brooding magic that soon set my recovery in motion. Although I've a feeling *that'd* already started when I got there.

Aunt Deebee was a frail old thing, who rarely, if ever, went outside. Even so, she seemed happy enough in her own way: all alone in her cool, shady parlour, smiling fondly at her albums of photos, and reading letters that were yellowing with age. I liked her very much, but all the same I was happy to be left to my own devices. I didn't think Aunt Deebee would understand me . . . because I couldn't really understand myself.

How the devil could I already be feeling horny again, after everything that'd happened with Ellery? I was though . . . Sex seemed to obsess me. I'd started maturbating only days after my surgery, and on the train that'd brought me down from London, I'd caught myself checking out the various travelling males. There'd been one who'd particularly turned me on. He'd been dark, and young, and really, really cute, with long hair and a deeply sweet expression. He'd looked up too, and caught me staring, then smiled the most dazzling, delicious and downright pussy-melting smile that I'd ever seen in my life. I'd been just about to say 'Hi', when the train had pulled into the station, and after everyone had finished hassling about with luggage my sexy-looking dreamboat had gone.

He was a wonderful fantasy though; and as I wandered aimlessly around the gardens at the Hall, his image kept returning to my mind. Especially when I found the little summerhouse . . .

It was a kind of ornamental cabin – what the architecture books called a 'folly' – about a mile from the Hall itself, and hidden away in a thick stand of trees. Sitting pretty in a tiny clearing it was like a gingerbread house straight out of Hans Christian Andersen, and it had a porch and its own enchanted oak tree. I'd never seen a place quite as lovely. As I lay down out in front of it to sun myself, I kept thinking of my dream guy from the train.

I imagined him coming through the trees towards me, emerging next to the oak, then kneeling down on the deck beside me. He'd start touching me and he'd be gentle. His fingers would stroke and smooth and heal. They'd find their own way to all my wounded places, then restore me with the pleasure of good sex.

I had my eyes tightly closed, but with my inner eye I could clearly see him smiling. *His* eyes were brown as autumn leaves and as bright as the brilliant summer sun. As my own hands settled lightly on my body, I could've sworn I saw him wink to urge me on.

As I stroked myself my fingers turned into his, and when they went between my legs, I gave a sigh. I couldn't believe how comfortable it felt. All the guilt about feeling sexy after losing my baby had disappeared, and the hot sensations felt honest and wholesome again. As I quivered, I thanked my secret lover.

'Oh, yes! Oh God, yes!' I gasped, then came with a supernatural quickness. It was a rich, rounded, almost earthy orgasm. I was drowning in a deep well of pleasure with a stranger's handsome face in my mind.

When I'd calmed down, I decided it was time to make tracks back to the Hall. But as I brushed down my skirt and stepped in my shoes, I felt a powerful sensation of being watched, an awareness so strong it gave me gooseflesh. I looked around, but there was no-one in the glade, and no-one hiding out amongst the trees. The whole neighbourhood of the cottage was deserted; so, as I made my way back towards the big house, I decided I'd had a little too much sun. Or too much of something else just as warming.

I didn't mention my spooky feelings to Aunt Deebee, but when we talked a while that night, she looked at me, her blue eyes suddenly sharper. 'Now don't forget to wear a hat in the sun tomorrow, my dear,' she said, her voice kind of vague and dreamy-sounding. 'We don't want you seeing things, do we?'

I told her I was usually okay in hot sun, but next day, I found a battered old sunhat in the cupboard, and put it on before I ventured outdoors. It was a pretty thing with a big round straw brim, but it didn't make the slightest bit of difference . . .

I still saw things.

When I arrived at the summerhouse, there was a sleeping figure lying out in the glade: a young man with shiny dark hair and smooth, bronzed skin. Most of which I could see, because he was naked as the day he'd been born!

I didn't say anything. I hardly dare breathe. He was lying on his front, taking the sun on his broad, gleaming back, and his ass was the finest I'd ever seen. His face was turned towards me, pillowed on his muscular arms, and there was a naughty little smile on his face, as if he knew he was being admired, but wasn't letting on.

The *really* crazy thing was that he looked exactly like my Adonis from the train. Younger, maybe, and rougher somehow, but the resemblance was truly amazing. And I couldn't hell? but think about his dick.

Would be be big or small? Wide or slender? Circumcised or a natural un-cut? Jesus, my thoughts were outrageous! But I couldn't stop myself . . . All I could do was imagine him turning over, stroking himself lazily – then getting hard. And as I thought *that*, his eyes fluttered open.

'I . . . um . . .' I began nervously, then shut up. Because my nature boy was getting to his feet . . . and he wasn't a boy after all. No way!

Before me stood a big, beautiful, grown-up man with a swaying sex that was long and already half-hard.

'Pardon me, ma'am, but I didn't think there'd be anybody here today.'

His voice was as pretty as his click. Very polite, very English, but not the kind of English I'd expected. It was a soft, very sonorous voice, kind of rich and countrified, and laced with an echo of the land.

'I just arrived. I'm staying at the big house. I sort of found this place yesterday and thought I might spend some time here,' I babbled, wondering why I was explaining myself to a bare-assed man.

'Beg pardon,' he apologised again, although he

didn't make a move to get dressed. 'I hope I didn't frighten you, ma'am. I'm the gardener's boy, ma'am, and it's my break . . . I was just having a quick forty winks.'

I wasn't quite sure what 'forty winks' was but I couldn't stop staring. He was a god; a hunk; totally drop-dead gorgeous, with the body of an athlete or a boxer, but the face of an angel of love. His cock was the ultimate in pure maleness; standing up like a club now, thick and dark.

'Sorry about that, ma'am,' he murmured, looking down, 'but I don't often meet pretty women in the woods.'

'It's . . . er . . . It's okay,' I mumbled like a dummy, wishing I could say that it was far more than 'okay', and that he could flash a treasure like that at me anytime. 'I'm Marylou Deschanel, from Portland, Maine, and Mrs Flitwick is my aunt, twice removed.'

'Sean Collyer, ma'am,' he answered, nodding his head respectfully – which looked incongruous with a hard-on that size.

I had to admire the guy though; not only for the beauty of his body, but also for his lack of inhibition. Most American men I know would have been blushing beet red and covering themselves up with their shirts. But not my bare-bottomed Brit. He just stood there in all his rampant glory, and I wished to hell I dare reach out and touch.

'I'd best be off then, Miss Deschanel,' he said, his voice as unperturbed as his attitude, 'I wouldn't want to disturb you any more.'

Some disturbance, I thought, watching the long easy swing of his click as he bent gracefully and reached for his clothes. I'd never have thought putting clothes on could be as sexy as stripping them off, but somehow this Sean changed my mind.

469

Even though his underwear was absolutely the weirdest . . .

First, he pulled on a thick, creamy-coloured vest, sort of woolly, with long sleeves and buttons. Then came his underpants, which were full-length 'combination' affairs in the same chunky fabric, but looked as horny as the skimpiest of jockstraps. Especially with a big erection inside them!

'Look, Sean,' I began, feeling bold enough to use his first name, 'you don't have to go on my account. Please stay . . . We could talk a while.'

My rough, outdoors-man just smiled – the same smile that the guy on the train had smiled, the grin that made me hot – then flicked his braces neatly up over his shoulders and pulled on a dark linen waistcoat. The heat of the day was stifling already, yet his heavy clothes didn't seem to bother him one bit.

'Best not, ma'am,' he said sturdily, and touched his fingers to his forelock just like the farmboys in the stupid old movies. Then, before I could protest, he was leaving, his long, easy stride taking him away so fast that I wondered if I'd just imagined him.

Maybe I *had* imagined him? If I had, I couldn't forget him. Inspired by his example, I peeled off my T-shirt and skirt, and just left on my tiny white panties. As I applied a coat of sunblock, I conjured up those long capable-looking fingers of his, and pretended it was him working the cool, creamy goop across my skin. I knew he'd be able to reach all the awkward places: the middle of my shoulders, the slope of my back, and the round, curvy cheeks of my rear.

Rolling on to my front I imagined him dealing with the easy places too, his fingers palpating the tips of my breasts and filling them with pleasure and heat. I could almost feel those fingertips sliding down me, then slipping lower and toying with the folds of my sex. He'd slide one finger right into me, one manly elegant finger, and twist it till I wailed with delight.

Without thinking, I made thought into deed, using my own hands to act out the fantasy. Pushing my hand into my panties, I stroked my own flesh with intensity. I rubbed harder than a gentle gardener ever would. Fingering with rhythmic swirling's, I brought my body to a fine burning climax, as a pair of brown eyes seemed to watch. Their pupils widened as my body bucked and heaved, then darkened as I groaned in release.

The sensation of being watched was so intense that I soared a second time, when usually it only happened once. My legs waved, and my butt bounced. As I came with a cry, I saw a tiny flicker of movement to my right. It was just a change in the pattern of shadows, or a breeze in the trees, but I prayed it was my handsome gardener's boy.

I didn't venture out until after lunch the next day; and when I did, the heat lay heavy on my back. I could hear bees droning in the long grass, smell the scent of the pollen-filled flowers, and I felt so full of the simple joys of living that when Sean wasn't waiting by the summerhouse it hit me like a cruel, hard shock.

I'd been so sure that he'd be there – either naked or clothed – that his absence hurt me far more than anything Ellery had ever done.

I tried to pull myself together . . .

Yeah, I'd had some fun yesterday, but that was no reason to get uptight. Sean was a worker on the estate, a guy who'd just happened to take his clothes off. He and I weren't a number, any more than Ellery and I. There was no way my handsome Sean had let me down.

Shucking off my vest and skirt, I sat down on the porch and applied some sunblock, still wishing for a pair of male hands to spread it. I'd decided to leave off my panties today, and so when my body was coated I stretched out naked, and surrendered to the mercies of the sun.

For a while I just toasted, letting the golden warmth soak into my bones I forgot my worries and I forgot my disappointment, and I hardly even noticed going to sleep.

I awoke in the coolness of a shadow, and felt my body being oh-so gently fondled. Someone was applying more sunblock for me, slicking it thicking over my thighs and my ass.

Sean! I thought joyfully, but when I rolled over I got one helluva shock. I was alone, the porch was empty, and the extra sunblock only existed in my mind.

I felt giddy for a moment, disorientated and deeply off-balance. It was impossible to believe he wasn't with me, and just when I managed to accept it, I just as quickly realised that he *was*!

The gardener's boy leaning nonchalantly against the side of the oak tree, a slow, sassy smile on his face.

'No drawers today, ma'am?' he enquired and nodded in the direction of my pussy.

'Er . . . no,' I answered, still bemused. So he *had* seen me yesterday after all . . .

'You were watching me – yesterday . . . Weren't you?' I demanded, sitting up, and trying desperately not to grab for my clothes. *He* hadn't been embarrassed naked, so goddammit, neither would

I! I was proud of my body, and I liked it- and I wanted *him* to like it just as much!

And he did.

'You're a beautiful woman, Miss Deschanel,' he said, ambling towards me from the deep shade. 'A man'd have to be six feet under not to look at you.'

Just the way he said it set a light in me, and when he dropped down to his knees, then reached out and laid a hand on my breast, it wasn't the hot sun that made my body glow.

Everything seemed to happen naturally, as if I'd been waiting for his fingers all my life. Or at least since long before my 'troubles'. Somehow, it was as if Sean knew exactly what ailed me and touching was his way to make me well. There was no roughness about his hands, none of the hard skin that a manual labourer should have had ... His caress was as light as thistledown and as cool as a shaded mountain pool. His fingers cruised across me like an unction, a blessed balm against the heat of the day. As he stroked me, his huge brown eyes held mine. They were soul-dark with some ancient, rustic mystery, something primitive I couldn't comprehend. I'd been with some sophisticated men in my time, but this fey country boy with his subtle smiling strength had more charisma than them all put together. Mad to get him, I cried out and strained my body close to his.

'Hush, ma'am,' he whispered against my lips, his fingers sliding slowly into my sex. My softly gorged, slippery, needful sex ...

With no guidance from me, he found my sweet-spot immediately; the minute patch of skin beneath the head of my clitoris that was so sensitive I could hardly bear it touched.

'Hush, ma'am ... Rest easy ... I've got you ..'

he mumured again, as I screamed and went rigid in his arms while a starburst of an orgasm consumed me.

It was impossible how quickly I'd come. And how strongly. He'd done next to nothing and I was in heaven, yet with other men it had often taken hours.

Slumped like a rag-doll against him I tried to recover and to think. I knew nothing about him, but I'd trusted him completely; he'd taken hold of both my body and my heart. My sweat had soaked clean through his undershirt, and my sap was dry already on his hand. I'd behaved madly, badly and riskily, yet I was certain I'd done the right thing.

'Are you all right now, Miss Deschanel?' Sean enquired as I looked up into his eyes. His olde worlde formality was so endearing, it made me want even more of him. I wanted him out of those clumsy woollen trousers; out of those boots; out of those wacky 'drawers' of his. I wanted him as beautiful and naked as he had been yesterday, but with his long, lovely dick deep inside me – as the true, final proof that I was cured.

'I'm great, Sean. I'm fine. But I could be better . . .' I gave him my most come-on look, 'That is, if you kinda get my drift?'

He didn't need asking or telling. With a bewitching, almost edible smile, he started unlacing his stout boots, and in no time at all he was wriggling his way out of his underwear – his sun-browned body primed for action.

Boy, how I wanted him! How I wanted *that*. Leaping up, and reaching for his hand, I nodded towards the door of the cottage. Now the crunch had come, I really *did* feel bashful. I didn't think I could make it in the great outdoors, at least not on our very first time.

I hauled at his hand, but Sean wouldn't move. He stood stubbornly on the porch, rooted to the spot, with an expression of real fear on his face.

'What's the matter?' I asked, feeling a little spooked myself. Sean was tough and rugged, genuinely and fundamentally strong, yet suddenly something had fazed him. Something about going 'inside'.

'I can't go in there, Miss Marylou,' he said, his deep voice barely a whisper.

'Why not?' I persisted. The summerhouse was so cosy and so cute.

'Because I can't,' he answered simply, 'I have to stay outside . . . I can't go into any kind of dwelling.'

'But that's n —' I began, only to lose the thread in an instant when Sean picked me up in his arms. Holding me as if I weighed nothing, he carried me across to the big oak tree and set me down on the turf in its shade.

'We'll be safe here, my sweeting,' he said softly, lying down beside me, his hands already moving on my flesh. 'Nothing can harm us out here.'

I forgot my objections. I almost forgot my own name. Sean's lovemaking was so complete, so delicate and so caring, the fact we were outdoors in the open air seemed irrelevant. I felt his fingers in my furrow and his mouth on my breasts, sucking one, and then the other till I moaned.

When I could bear no more, and I was clawing at his body like a mad thing, he gently parted my legs and slid into me, his possession as smooth as in a dream.

Inside me, he felt hard and massive, like the limb of a tree, yet there was no discomfort, no awkwardness and no pain. He moved like a wildcat gliding sleekly through the forest, or a stream flowing unstoppably to the sea. He did not displace or force or exert, but his sex seemed to fit into mine the same way the air we breathed hugged the soil beneath my back.

Our union was timeless, effortless, and ineffable, and when I soared I thought I'd never come down. But as I clung to him, and felt the pleasure start to shake his mighty frame, I was shocked when Sean pulled himself free of me. I protested, clamouring and grabbing at him; then he replaced his rigid cock with two strong fingers and I came again, far harder than before. With his essence pulsing out across my thighs . . .

'Not inside . . .' he gasped, his handsome face ruddy and contorted, 'Oh, no, not ever inside . . .'

It didn't make sense – but neither did getting laid beneath a tree in the sunshine by an Englishman I'd only known a day. With a sleepy sigh, I gave up trying to think about it and just enjoyed his silky semen on my skin.

When I finally woke up again, Sean was gone, but there was a bunch of wild flowers lying in my lap. Their scent was heady and vital, golden and romantic, and I felt more cherished than I had done in years. I missed him but I loved the things he'd done . . .

'I met your gardener's boy today,' I said to Aunt Deebee over dinner. 'He seems like a really nice guy.'

'Who?' my aunt said, her voice all reedy and shocked.

'Sean. The gardener's boy.'

'Oh. Oh, my goodness . . . Has he come back?' Her lined face had a trancelike expression on it, yet in the soft light she looked lovely and quite young.

'Yeah. Has he been somewhere?'

476

The last time I saw Sean was when I came here to be married. I was twenty-two. I met him in the woods again and again. But it had to stop, because I really loved Ernest, my fiancé, and being with Sean was very very wrong . . .'

It didn't make a lot of sense then, but afterwards, I kind of got the gist. My handsome young Sean had been killed several centuries ago, shot because a daughter of the house at the time had been crazy enough to smuggle him inside. Her father had gone berserk when he'd found Sean naked in her bedroom. He'd used a blunderbuss to turn him into a ghost!

It seemed I was just the latest in a long line of Flitwick women who'd seen 'the gardener's boy', but when pressed for more details of her sighting, Aunt Deebee had turned decidedly coy.

Had all of us *felt* as well as seen him?

The weirdest thing was that I wasn't even scared, just disappointed, because I supposed I'd lost him now. Illusions tend to vanish when you know what they are.

I didn't take my clothes off the next day. There didn't seem an awful lot of point. I just slithered the old cream on my face and arms, then lay down to doze in the sun.

The tremors woke me up very gradually. Cool, probing fingers were sneaking along the inside of my thigh, and heading boldly for the furnace of my sex.

It's a dream, Marylou, I told myself. The sun's too hot. You should've worn the hat again. You're hallucinating.

When the fingertips dove deep into my womanhood, I kept my eyes scrunched resolutely

477

shut. When the pad of a forefinger danced lightly on my clitoris, I still didn't dare take a look. What was happening to me was probably all a fantasy, but if it was one I wanted it to last.

Suddenly, though, I came, and felt my shaking self held tight and sure and safe – against a familiar, solid, man-smelling body that protected me with a tender loving care.

'But you . . . you're . . .' I stammered, as I finally met his big brown eyes.

'Yes, I certainly am, Miss Marylou,' said Sean Collyer – the apparition – very softly. 'But I couldn't let a lady down, could I?'

'No, you certainly couldn't,' I said happily in answer, and started tugging at the buttons on his fly.

Finders Keepers

Dear Jeremy,

I can't thank you enough for handing in my pendant. You can't imagine how much it means to me. A money reward seems sordid somehow, so may I treat you to a night out instead? I've enclosed details of where and when we can meet, and I look forward to showing my appreciation: my PROFOUND *appreciation.*

Anna Caspell (Mrs)

When he'd first read the letter, Jem Hathaway had been disappointed. The pendant he'd handed in must've cost a fortune and he'd been hoping for a cash reward. It was a bit of a mystery how a thing so obviously expensive had turned up outside his scruffy dump – the house he shared with half a dozen other guys, all equally as hard up as he was – but he hadn't asked questions, just dropped it in at the local police station. He was puzzled too, by the bobby-on-duty's reaction. The man had grinned broadly. No, he'd smirked from ear to ear as if someone had cracked a dirty joke, told Jem there was a reward, then nudged his mate behind the

479

counter in the ribs, muttering what sounded like 'jammy young bastard'!

Jem had wondered what the man found so funny, but in a police station he didn't like to ask. He just hoped the reward would be decent, because his meagre giro went nowhere. He'd been out of work for several months now, and jobs were getting scarcer all the time. Even a fiver would make life easier.

A couple of days later the letter had arrived, and it'd seemed that all he was going to get was a night out with an over-fussy, middle-aged widow – a reward that'd be over in a few hours, and probably a pain while it lasted. After a bit of thought, he'd told himself not be such an ungrateful swine, and decided the poor old biddy must be lonely.

But now, when it came to it, money was the last thing on his mind. Staring across the busy hotel foyer, he felt like pinching himself. There was a woman sitting waiting on a velvet-covered chaise-longue, about five yards away from him: the most beautiful woman he'd ever seen. She wore a black, heart-shaped pendant around her long, slender throat, and she was in exactly the right place at exactly the right time. She could only be Anna Caspell (Mrs).

Why didn't I realise? thought Jem, feeling numb: that fancy, flowing handwriting; the sexy pink notepaper; the heavy flowery scent he'd smelt when he'd opened the envelope. They'd all pointed to someone a bit special.

But even so, he'd never in a million years have imagined her as special as this. With hair like a living flame; dark, hungry eyes; and a red-stained, supermodel mouth. Mrs Caspell's 'look' was both chic and outrageous. She wore crimson leather from throat to toe: a boxy, wide-shouldered jacket, a skimpy bra top, and a short, tight skirt. She was sitting down, but Jem guessed she was tall, and made all the more so by high, spiked-heeled shoes in the same red leather as her clothes. What he was looking at was a total fantasy, an archetype, a woman who was beyond his wildest longings, yet living, sensual and vibrant. He'd only seen her fifteen seconds ago, but already his young cock felt as hard as a poker.

Cursing his nerves and his randiness, he swallowed hard, then strode across the foyer. Aquake inside, he held out the single scarlet rose he'd brought her, then told the apparition his name: Jem. The rose had been a daft impulse but, crazily enough, it worked. Mrs Caspell sighed softly, then smiled with a unfeigned pleasure and gestured Jem to sit down. Heads turned all across the foyer when she leant across and kissed him on the lips with a pressure that was slow and inquisitive.

When she broke away, Jem still couldn't speak. Stunned, he listened to her charming and poised introduction, and her thanks for his recent good deed. His heart went 'boing' inside him as she said his nickname, her soft voice husky and breathy.

Oh, shit, she'll think I'm an moron! he thought, hating his disabling shyness. Tongue-tied, he tried to focus on the one thing he did have going for him: his looks. He might be a stuttering nerd at times like this, but at least he was easy on the eye. His hair was thick, dark-brown and shiny. His skin was smooth and blemish-free, and his features were almost classical – large hazel-gold eyes, lips that were full, firm and sculpted.

In spite of his stupid misconception about Mrs Caspell being fair, fat and forty, he'd still dressed with the intention of impressing her. His suit was a pale biscuit colour and his shirt and tie two shades darker. It was only cheap chainstore gear, and the suit was second-hand, but with a bit of care and attention, he could wear it and feel he looked sharp. In the midst of Jem's sartorial ditherings, a waiter appeared. Swiftly and politely, the man placed a bottle and two glasses on the low table before them, and was gone again in an instant. Mrs Caspell poured the wine herself, skilfully filling each glass without spilling a single drop.

Jem took his drink and tasted it cautiously. It was a fantastic vintage he was sure, but he wasn't in fit state to enjoy it. He was dizzy and light-headed already; his heart pounding, his stomach fluttering, and inside his best, and only pair of pure silk boxer shorts, his prick was so hard it was hurting! Nearly sick with desire, he put his glass down and edged closer to the woman beside him. Then, without stopping to ask, or even think, he slid his arm around her sleek, narrow waist.

What the hell am I doing? he asked himself, shocked by the rashness of this move. He almost leapt clean out of his skin when Mrs Caspell smiled in approval, went 'Mmm', and moved in tight against his body. Almost dreamily, he stroked her smooth, bare midriff, and wondered if he'd ever be able to speak. It was hard to believe he'd thought meeting this woman would be. a chore, but still he couldn't relax. Raw, white need raced through him its painful flames stoked by her fingers. Long and graceful, they felt like thistledown wherever they touched him; questing slowly from his forearm to his thigh, and making his skin burn like fire beneath his suit.

They were supposed to be having dinner soon,

but Mrs Caspell seemed to be in no hurry. 'Let's freshen up in my suite first, shall we?' she murmured, squeezing his leg. As she led the way towards the lift, her perfect bottom swaying like a salsa, a light went on in Jem's brain. It suddenly dawned on him what 'profound appreciation' might mean.

It couldn't be true! 'The older woman' was his all-time, ultimate masturbation fantasy; the dream of his nineteen-year-old life. And it was happening here and now for real.

'Jem,' she murmured as the lift door closed.

His name seemed to fall from her dewy, red lips and settle on his prick like a moth. A single, simple syllable, it acquired an almost physical substance – a resonance. It coiled around his prick like wet silk and then danced along his whole twitching length. 'Jem,' she whispered again, then slid into his arms and made him hers.

This time it was Jem who did the kissing. Mrs Caspell's mouth opened wide beneath his, inviting him to drink from its moistness. His tongue dove in deep as she moulded her body to his, and like a lost boy he rubbed himself against her. Then stopped dead.

Oh God, his hard-on! He tried to pull back but Mrs Caspell wouldn't let him. Locking her hands in the small of his back, she worked her pelvis to and fro against his, massaging the thick bulge of his cock with the curve of her leather-covered belly.

In her suite the kiss continued. Jem had never wanted any woman as much as this, and quite obviously, she wanted him too. There was lust in the air all around them, but in a low seductive whisper, Mrs Caspell insisted they slow down and pace themselves. 'The longer the wait, the sweeter the fuck,' she promised, her mouth moving softly on his neck.

Jem nearly came on the spot. He'd heard women swear before, plenty of times, but he'd never heard one so beautfiul say 'fuck'.

But shock piled on shock. With a deftness that left him reeling, Mrs Caspell unzipped his fly, flicked open his boxer shorts, and eased out his heavy young cock. He yelped out aloud as she fingered his hard flesh: assessing the thickness and the weight of it, and scrutinising its long jutting shape.

How on earth could she think of waiting? Jem felt his entire body gather itself to plunge. He wanted to tip her on to the bed, bear down on her and tear off skirt and her panties. She'd be ready, he could tell. He didn't have all that much experience, but he knew she'd be wet, lush and open. Almost beside himself, he lurched forward – but Mrs Caspell only shook her head, tut-tutted, then tucked his penis back into his shorts. As she zipped him up, he was torn between relief and unbearable frustration. He'd been terrified of coming in her hand; yet her touch was so divine he could've wept. Without thinking, he gasped the word 'please'.

'Don't worry, Jem.' Her smile was slight and tantalising. 'It'll be soon. But first we've got to build up your strength.'

Their dinner was magnificent – doubly so when a four-course square meal was so rare for him – but Jem barely tasted a thing.

It was Mrs Caspell that he hungered for. His entire groin felt swollen and bloated, and he could do nothing but grit his teeth, and hold on grimly; waiting for the moment when she set him free from his stiffness and his misery. When she pressed her napkin to her tinted mouth and decreed that the meal was over, he sighed out loud with relief; then looked away from her low sultry laugh.

When they entered the suite, Mrs Caspell excused herself immediately and left Jem alone with his erection. He decided to follow her example and 'freshen up' in the second of the suite's ritzy bathrooms.

Fifteen minutes later, he returned to the bedroom, naked, harder than ever, and very nervous. Mrs Caspell was still 'freshening', but he could see she'd returned to the room in his absence.

The bedlinen had been meticulously turned down, and the pristine white area at 'his' side exposed. Mrs Caspell's attention to detail was strangely exciting and Jem's cock twitched at the thought of it. Was she this thorough in her lovemaking?

The only trouble was . . . in this situation there was one detail *he* should've attended to.

It would never have occured to Jem in a million years that he'd end up in bed tonight, so consequently he'd not brought protection. Anxiety started to wilt him, but as he looked around his eye lit on a sight that made him sigh with relief. Mrs Caspell had left a discreet but familiar box on the bedside table. A box with its lid flipped open to show the small silver packages within.

Jem prised out a condom, and studied its slim, distinctive shape. His free hand drifted automatically to his cock, and he felt a jolt of sensation in his loins. In his imagination, his searching fingers became Mrs Caspell's – examining him neatly and surely as she rolled down the skin-sheer rubber over his raging, ruby-tipped shaft.

Biting his lip, he abandoned his prick and tried to calm down. 'Cool it, Jem,' he admonished in a whisper. 'You haven't even seen her naked yet.'

Sliding on to the bed, he pulled the sheet up over him and savoured its smooth texture on his skin. The comfort and opulence of the room seemed just as much a fantasy as Mrs Caspell herself was, but as he lay there, his thoughts took a bizarre new turn.

By all that was natural and normal, he should be imagining Mrs Caspell's unclothed body now, but suddenly he saw the broad, grinning face of the bobby who'd taken in the pendant. The laughing policeman with his eyes that were salacious and knowing. 'Jammy young bastard' the man had mouthed – as if he'd seen the future and this very moment.

Suddenly, there was a small sound somewhere to Jem's right. Hardly breathing, he turned his head slowly on the pillow.

Swathed in what looked like cobwebs of creamy silk lace, Mrs Caspell was walking, almost floating towards him. When she reached the bedside, she eyed him speculatively, then shrugged her shoulders and let her soft, filmy garment fall away.

Jem felt like crying again, and this time, to his horror, it really happened. The woman before him was perfect. His complete, fully functioning dream. Her body was mature, yet delicate and slim; her skin was immaculate; her large, rounded breasts were crowned with the pinkest of nipples that were exquisitely puckered and stiff. At the apex of her long, sleek thighs, she had hair that was silky, lush and thick, a bouquet of blondish-red curls.

Jem blinked furiously to clear his tears. She was all he'd ever wanted, everything he'd ever yearned for. His problems seemed to fall away like mist, as if just one night with this fabulous woman might sustain him for months, even years to come. He lay completely still and passive while she threw back

486

the sheets, climbed on to the bed, and knelt beside him.

At first, she just studied him, her eyes glittering and dark. Then she started touching him, exploring with her long, tapered fingers and praising every feature she encountered. She enthused at length about his strong young physique, his smooth skin, and his hair. She admired his neck, his arms, his thighs and his hard, flat belly.

But when she reached his aching, straining cock, she seemed to find a whole new vocabulary, describing it with a eloquent lyricism, and an earthy and full-bodied directness.

Jem was stunned. He'd jumped a mile when she'd said 'Fuck' – and now she was saying ... saying everything! But it sounded more like poetry than a description of a man's naked body.

When the inventory was over, Mrs Caspell lay back and flexed herself slowly like a cat.

'Would you like to make love to me, Jem?' she asked. Her voice was calm and quiet, yet her question felt more like an order.

Obediently, he began kissing and licking her breasts and she hissed 'yes!' between her teeth in approval. After a moment, she whispered that he should bite her nipples, and he complied just as quickly, without question.

As his teeth closed lightly on her teat, he felt her pushing his hand to her cunt. Guiding him to a place that was already wet, and as molten as a furnace. A place where he first dabbled tentatively, then probed with more fervour, rubbing at the pearl of her clitoris.

Jem's caresses were blind guesswork, but happily they seemed to be the right ones. Mrs Caspell whimpered and squirmed as he suckled at her breast, her hips rising keenly to his touch. After a moment, she stilled, then jerked once, twice, three times in his arms, sobbing long and loud as her body thrashed and turned in its climax. Jem could hardly breathe or think. His only awareness was feeling. The tip of his manhood . . . Beneath it, satin flesh jumping madly.

Everything went quiet for a while, then Mrs Caspell started pushing at his head. With both hands, she urged him imperiously downwards, and Jem trembled when his lips met her belly.

As he kissed her smooth, white skin, he found a tiny scar just below her navel. Tracing its shape with his tongue, he wondered what'd happened there, and hoped it hadn't been too painful. When he moved lower, and nuzzled at her thick pubic floss, she generously drew apart her thighs and showed him her rosy female treasure.

Just inches from his nose, Jem saw curlicues of ruffled, swollen flesh, and a landscape that was glistening with her juices. At its heart was the minute, mysterious portal that would soon expand to receive him, and sliding his hands gently beneath her, he lifted up her body to his mouth and put his tongue to the membranes of her sex. She rippled like a wave as he licked her, and when he stabbed hard and quickly at her clitoris, she cried out in an extremity of pleasure.

Mrs Caspell wriggled and heaved but Jem held on tight. His tongue rode her deep, moist valley and he felt a great, almost terrible excitement. Her taste was rich and pungent, and her nectar flowed freely across his face, smearing his cheeks and his chin as her body arched up from the bed. He furled his tongue-tip, stabbed again, and her shouts turned to harsh, ragged screams. She was incoherent, but he didn't need words. He sensed her whirling on some hidden, inner fulcrum, lost in a free-soaring orgasm as her body throbbed and leapt against his mouth.

When Mrs Caspell's eyes fluttered open, she smiled radiantly and Jem knew he'd not been found wanting. He'd been tested, yes, but he'd passed, and passed well. Stroking his sweaty hair, Mrs Caspell whispered that it was 'his turn now' and with his desire for her racing through his veins. Jem rolled over on to his back in readiness.

Then blushed like a shoolboy.

His prick was standing straight up from his groin, stiffer than ever and waving very slightly in the air. The head of it was red and distended and pre-come ran out thickly from the tip. Tossing back her touseled red hair, Mrs Caspell hunched over him, and lowered her soft lips to his flesh.

Incredible!

Her mouth was a sucking well of heat, a hot liquid sheath that enclosed him in a way he'd only dreamed of. He felt engulfed by her, consumed by her, his penis both devoured and renewed.

She held him like that for long, long seconds, then relaxed her lips and took him in deeper. Deeper and unbelievably deeper, traversing his whole contained length with the tip of her amazing wet tongue.

It was like floating on a raft of sheer bliss, and Mrs Caspell's oral skills seemed boundless. One minute, she'd graze him with her small white teeth, the next, she'd hollow her cheeks and suck like fury until Jem thought his brain would explode. Teasing without mercy, she backed off again and again – just before the point of no return – leaving him balanced on an edge so critical that he pleaded and begged for release. Shouting mindless gibberish, he stared down from a mountaintop of rarefied sensation at the wildest, and most colourful of sights. A pair of glossy-painted red-stained lips sliding slowly on his purple-veined cock.

As her mouth worked, so did her fingers: stroking his thighs, jiggling his balls, dipping down into the cleft of his buttocks to tickle at his dark little opening. When she touched him there, Jem's eyes bulged. He bucked like a bronco on the bed and almost threw Mrs Caspell off his crotch!

After what seemed like a millenium, she planted one last kiss on the fat pink tip of his prick and licked up its round pearl of juice. Then she slid back on to the bed at his side, threw open her long, pale thighs, and pulled his body determinedly towards her.

The transition between suck and fuck was effortless. Even his usual disaster area – getting the condom on – was as smooth and co-ordinated as a dance. Between them, he and Mrs Caspell encased him in the microfine sleeve, then with a single guiding touch of her fingers, he plunged to his utmost inside her, and lodged deep in her moist clinging vale. As he plumbed her, he held his breath, scared that even a sigh might dissolve his perfect dream. But when Mrs Caspell gasped voluptuously beneath him, the fantasy stayed solid around them, and he felt her breath like a zephyr on his neck.

Her flesh was like hot liquid velvet, with an inner grip so snug and form-fitting that their bodies seemed machined to fit each other. Entranced, Jem just lay there and let Mrs Caspell – his goddess – work her magic. He felt her hands settle softly on his back, then slide lower and cup the cheeks of his bottom. As her fingers kneaded and pounded him, she started rocking her pelvis to their rhythm – creat-

490

ing a pleasure for herself out of his. Jem wanted to shaft her like a madman, fuck her like an animal, but somehow he managed to restrict himself, using slow, measured shoves that steadied his race towards climax.

But not, alas, for very long. It was their first time together, and Mrs Caspell was his ultimate and definitive dream. The faster he plunged inside her, the more she rose to meet him – a challenge for his every frenzied stroke.

She's fucking *me*! Jem thought in wonder, breathing hard against her sweat-sheered neck. He felt her juddering and contracting around him, and like a comet wreathed in white fire and glory, his climax roared towards him from the heavens.

When it arrived, Mrs Caspell made it welcome. 'Fuck me! Oh God, fuck me! I'm coming!' she shouted as she writhed beneath his weight.

And fuck her he did. Thrusting in with all his young strength, he matched her fierce cry with his own.

'Anna!' he screamed, as a heavy, beating pulse fluttered wildly in the warm depths that held him.

Jem couldn't tell whether the rhythm came from Anna's flesh or his – he didn't care. Their ecstasy had made them into one . . .

Sunshine was streaming into the room when Jem woke up, but it wasn't the light that'd roused him. Blinking and scrabbling around sleepily, he realised to his sorrow that he was alone. Mrs Caspell had gone, and left only her sweet perfume to console him.

'No!' he cried, sitting up, his heart a cold empty void.

When had she left? Where had she gone? Could

he catch her if he ran outside now? Naked . . .

What would happen to him, he wondered, if he didn't find her? One night with Mrs Caspell had been more reward that he could ever have hoped for, but suddenly it wasn't enough. 'No!' he shouted again, then froze with the words on his lips.

On the pillow next to his – in the dent where his darling had slept – was an object that was small, pink and square: a sheet of writing paper, folded in a neat little package. Shaking like a leaf, Jem picked it up, and as he unfolded it, out fell her pretty black pendant.

Dearest Jem, said the flamboyant, looping script.

> *You can keep this now. I shan't need to 'lose' it anymore, because I've found what I wanted.*
>
> *Sell it if you like. Buy some new clothes . . . You'll need them. I'll be in touch with you later today, and we can discuss a more permanent arrangement.*

Yours,

Anna

Yelling and laughing like a fool, Jem leapt out of bed and raced at top speed for the shower. Once in it, he started soaping his smooth body jubilantly, and working up a rich frothing lather – especially around his newly-hardened penis.

As he rubbed, he thought of the black heart, the pink note, and the angel who'd left them beside him. 'Finders keepers, Mrs Caspell,' he gasped, as his semen spurted thickly in her honour. 'And if you want to, you can keep *me* forever!'

Condition Orange

IF YOU'RE SHY, DON'T APPLY!
Wanted: stylish young man with good body for
undraped studies. Excellent remuneration.
Apply – with recent photograph – to Miranda
Scott, Box No. 1717.

Pip ran his finger around the rim of his glass, and
wondered what a lady photographer might look
like. Over the last few hours he'd pinned a hundred
different faces to her voice – but he didn't think any
one of them was right. She sounded sexy, but there
was an edge in there somewhere, an emotion he
couldn't quite define. Perplexed, he considered a
second drink, and wondered what she'd think of
him. Obviously the polaroid he'd sent had made a
good impression – she must've phoned him within
minutes of receiving it. But the photo had been
taken for a giggle, at a party, what she'd think of the
real Pip was debatable.

He was a young man of medium height – a dark
young man. He had dark hair, dark eyes, and dark
skin. His slightly swarthy skin was a legacy from his
beautiful Lebanese grandmother, and a casual

493

summer work as a gardener meant he was the same toasted brown all over. Even the naughtier bits had been evened out in seclusion, but for this job he wished his physique was more developed and chunkier. Still, Ms Scott must've liked what she'd seen; and as he adjusted his behind on the bar-stool, and felt his orange alert turning into red, Pip wondered if she fancied his cock. It *was* a good long size, he reflected, and it had been standing up in the picture.

It was trying to stand up now, but for photography that could be a problem. He was aware of certain laws about the condition of a male pin-up's penis, and he didn't think his present state complied. Perhaps he'd better have another drink and hope that alcohol would make his stalk droop.

He was just about to signal for the barman when the back of his neck prickled strangely. He didn't exactly know how he knew it, but Miranda, the photographer, was here.

But when he turned around, he nearly fell off his stool. Miranda Scott was indeed quite unlike any preconceived picture he'd formed. She wasn't arty, she wasn't 'media' and she wasn't even carrying a camera. What she did have, beneath her leather encased arm, was a shiny-black motorcycle helmet. His photographer was a 'hell's angelette'!

Dressed in black leathers from head to foot, Miranda was leanly-built woman of medium height, and of an age he couldn't put his finger on. As Pip watched, transfixed, she pulled off her butch looking gauntlets and ran her fingers through her slickly-cropped, tawny-coloured hair.

'Er ... Hi,' he answered at last, dropping down on to his feet as he remembered that it was customary to stand for a lady, even if she was one of the least ladylike he'd ever seen.

'I'm Philip Taylor-Kay,' he stammered, holding out his hand, 'My friends call me "Pip" . . . and you must be Ms Scott?'

'Call me "Scottie".' She took his hand in one that was still warm from her glove. 'That's with an "i" and an "e" by the way. I'm pleased to meet you.'

He tried to meet her eyes, but found it difficult. Hers were cool and steel-grey, their chilliness at odds with her heated skin. He felt that peculiar tingle again, the frisson he'd felt just minutes ago, but it faded when she smiled at him amenably.

'Would you like a drink?' he asked, feeling he should at least make an effort to get to know her. Somehow, though, this 'Scottie' didn't look like a someone who wasted time on meaningless pleasantries. 'Thanks, but no thanks,' she said crisply, stuffing her gloves into her pocket and whizzing down her jacket's hefty zip, 'I've got a bottle of gin in my room . . . Why don't we go up and get to work?'

'Er, yes . . . Fine . . .'

He was already following her as he spoke, still stunned by a momentary vision. The sight of a tender, dark-tipped cone beneath thin white cotton. For just a second, as she'd turned, he'd seen the body beneath the jacket, and a bra-less breast beneath the ultra-thin cloth of a T-shirt.

Scottie said little in the lift and Pip was glad of it. He didn't feel capable of conversation, and Scottie didn't have to speak anyway. Her body had its own unique language.

She stood with a straight back and her legs apart and braced, a stance that added inches to her height. To Pip she was utterly beautiful, just his type. She was the hard bitch; the amazon. Like the girl in *Terminator Two*, or Ripley, the Alien's adversary. She wouldn't flutter or flirt, or play silly girl games, yet she wore a brilliant Russian Red lipstick on a mouth that clearly meant business. He wanted her so much he was aching.

As she let him into her room, it occurred to Pip that this was a rather odd location for a shoot. Didn't photographers work in studios with spotlights and backdrops? But when she shucked of her tough, leather jacket, and abandoned her helmet, all questions dissolved like a mist.

What he'd thought was a T-shirt was in fact a skimpy white vest and her figure was more curvy than he'd expected. Her arms and shoulders were wiry, but her breasts were rounded and high, her waist narrow, and her hips had a soft sweet flare. Her legs looked almost endless in their glistening leather carapace and the double stitched line of her fly seemed to signpost the direction of heaven.

'Make yourself useful then,' she said, raising an eyebrow at his dithering silence. 'Fix us both a drink.' She nodded in the direction of the mini-bar, and the green litre bottle that stood on top of it. 'Mine's straight gin. You can please yourself, there's plenty to choose from in there.'

As he fiddled with glasses and ice, Pip watched her make the room into a studio. In a few mintues, she had fluffy white towels spread all over the bed and its headboard; and around that, at carefully paced out distances, she set a number of small, directable lights. On an occasional table she laid out an impressive selection of cameras.

The bed was now an intimidating zone of radiance, a hard white circle that made Pip dry-mouthed and nervous. At any moment, he'd have to shed his clothes before Scottie – and reveal to her his stone-hard erection.

He'd not intended to have another drink, but now he needed one. He didn't like gin but he poured himself some anyway. It smelt silvery and resinous, and to disguise its distinctive flavour he rummaged in the mini-bar, found a small can of orange juice, and topped up his glass with that.

'Orange ... Hmm?' murmured Scottie, looking up from her viewfinder. 'Good idea. Sloosh some into my glass too, will you?'

As he passed the drink across, Pip caught a strange expression on her face. For an instant, she appeared deeply unhappy. Sad, but wry too. Resigned; as if she were trapped in some cycle of sorrow that no amount of attitude could break.

'Cheers!' she murmured, her voice light and neutral as she tapped her full glass against his. 'Let's get to work, shall we? We'll start with a few shots *avec* clothes and work our way down to the skin.'

The modelling, when it came, was easy. Pip was amazed. He stood against the bed, he sat and he lay on it, and felt so comfortable he forgot his erection. It was only when Scottie touched him there – and he nearly shot through the roof with the pleasure of it – that he remembered the problem of his stiffness.

'Very nice,' she murmured softly, her fingertips lingering while Pip just shook. 'Shall we get a little closer to it?'

In an instant she was peeling off his clothes. First, she knelt down to remove his shoes and socks – her brow on a level with the swelling bulge in his chainstore Armani trousers – then she rose again to ease off his jacket. Pip stood still, a frozen mannequin, his arms moving limply at her bidding. He felt completely helpless, undermined in a way he'd never been before. He was rampant, yet unmanned by her slight, strong body and her sharp, very feminine fragrance – a pine soap, and something more musky; something quite basic and female, the hot distinctive smell of her natural scent.

Did she want him? Did his emerging young body arouse her? It was difficult to tell because she seemed so focused – but her nipples were pushing hard through her vest, and they seemed darker then they'd looked to him before.

The next pose was blatantly sexual. She made him lie on the bed, one hand inside his half unbuttoned shirt and the other lying draped across his groin. As she fiddled with her camera, and made the final adjustments to her lighting, he could feel his cock hot and throbbing through his trousers. He tried not to press down and stroke himself, but there was a riot in the hard flesh beneath; a craving. His 'condition orange' was a full red alert now, and he had a terrible, precognition that long before the rest of his clothes came off, his body would erupt and betray him. Every snap, snap, snap of her shutter seemed to impact directly on his penis.

She took another long sequence of shots, and then, to rearrange his limbs more precisely, she climbed on to the bed with him – and for this she kicked off her boots. Her white cotton socks were as innocent as a schoolgirl's, and for some indefinable reason the sight of them made Pip's cock leap. He could hardly keep still. He wanted to bend down, peel off those dainty white socks, then press his lips to her soft, slender feet.

'Right, Pip, take your clothes off and let's go for it,' she said suddenly, her voice no longer so controlled and silky. As she stepped off the bed, she appeared – for an instant – to sway.

Under any other circumstances, Pip would've leapt to her aid, worried about that moment of weakness and the strange, sad look that haunted her; but now all he could feel was an intense, excited embarrassment. His cock felt huge to him, enormous. It might please her; or she might be furious, because his stiffness would ruin her pictures.

Tentatively, he slipped off his shirt, and tossed it aside, then fumbled with the buckle on his belt. After a few seconds it yielded, but already there was sweat beneath armpits and a hot flush rising up his throat.

'Don't worry . . . Take your time,' said Scottie. She sounded calm, but there was noticeable hardening of her nipples and pinkness on her smooth, pale cheeks. She was breathing more heavily too, her small breasts rising and falling beneath the cling of the thin white vest. Perspiration was visible at her hairline, the slick of it shining on her throat.

As he stood up, and slid down his trousers, he modestly turned his back. With his fingers poised in the waistband of his briefs, he sensed her studying the shape of his buttocks, her eyes casting heat across his cleft.

'Come on, don't be coy . . . I want to oil you.'

'Oil?' he asked blankly.

'An essential ingredient in skin shots, Pip, my dear,' she purred, a rich sensuality replacing the transitory impression of ennui. There were several plastic bottles already on the coffee table, and a porcelain bowl, and as he watched her, she began pouring and mixing. 'Pants off, please,' she said emphatically, nodding at his skimpy tan briefs and the gross bulge distending the front of them.

When he tugged off his knickers, his erection bounced up like a sapling, its tip reaching out to Scottie. 'Is . . . is this a problem?' he asked, glancing downwards. He was felt like a horny adolescent caught wanking, but bizarrely it only made him harder.

'Not in the slightest,' she answered, still blending. 'A big stiff prick is an asset. I don't shoot for commercial circulation ... so anything and everything goes.'

His disappointment must've shown on his face. He was unemployed and he'd been anticipating the 'big break'.

'Don't worry. I'll mention your name in the right places.' Absorbed, she ignored both his face and his frisky erection. She was busy measuring out a minute amount of a substance from a smaller, brown bottle. When she was satisfied with her quantities, she swirled her potion with a flourish; even from halfway across the room, Pip could instantly smell its aroma.

The fragrance was sharp, sweet, deliciously and voluptuously fruity. It seemed to flow straight in through his pores, and caress both his heart and his gonads. He felt mellow, marvellously warm; his spirit at peace and his shyness a long-forgotten memory. He shivered with a deep erotic anticipation as Scottie approached him with her bowl, then trickled its contents on his chest. As the oil oozed slowly across his pectorals, she started spreading it and kneading with her fingers.

'What's in it?' he murmured, closing his eyes, not embarrassed now, but suffused with a lovely relaxation. f ler fingertips moved strongly but were also exquisitely gentle, their action setting fire to the fragrance. 'I can smell fruit,' he said breathing deeply and almost floating away.

'The carrier is a mix of almond, wheatgerm and walnut, but the ingredient you can smell is orange oil. Pure and essential ... Fruit for the brain.'

'Smells fabulous,' Pip murmured, shimmying helplessly as she sleeked the oil in long, efficient strokes across his ribcage and belly, then spread it out tormentingly over the creases of his groin and his thighs – avoiding his cock completely. In a ferment, he wondered what orange would do to him there. But he found out almost immediately when Scottie recharged her hands with oil and gently took hold of his stiffness. 'Oh God,' he whispered as her fingers slithered and slid, and his flesh seemed to swell and tingle. 'If that's what orange oil does for you, please, give me more!'

'Orange oil,' she intoned, her fingers still skilfully pumping him as she began a list of the oil's sovereign attributes. 'Good for skin conditioning, for relaxation, for muscular aches and pains . . .' She paused then, delicately caressing the tip of him, and when she spoke again her voice was sombre, 'Orange oil . . . Beneficial also for depression, hopelessness and lack of joy.'

The bleakness of her words seemed to fracture his drifting euphoria. Puzzled, he looked up, then said the first thing that came into his head. 'But I'm not depressed. I'm having a great time!'

'It's for me, Pip,' she said grimly, 'and don't ask why because it's too complicated.'

He persisted. 'Why? Why do you need it?'

She seemed not to hear him. Abandoning his long swaying penis, she stood up purposefully, wiped her hands on a towel and reached for one of her cameras. 'To work now, Pip . . . Let's do it!' Her spirits had obviously lifted and her movements were neat and animated, but there was still a faint shadow in her eyes.

The poses that followed were outrageous and made Pip forget all his questions. In a thick miasma

501

of orange, she arranged his body into shapes that would formerly have shocked him, and placed his hands on his flesh in ways he'd never have placed them himself. One half of him cringed, thinking of the images they were creating, while the other half quivered with pleasure. When she quietly ordered him to climax, he obeyed in an ecstasy of willingness.

Through the confusion of his own release, he sensed that Scottie too was gradually growing more sensitised. When she finally laid down her cameras, he was shocked that she didn't invite him to kiss her. He'd been so sure she wanted his body; so sure that they'd end up making love.

'But Scottie,' he protested as she started to stow away her gear. 'What happens now?'

'You get dressed. I pay you. You leave,' she said flatly.

'But what do you do?'

She paused again, her body quite still, her pale face washed of emotion.

'I put away my equipment. I masturbate. Then I leave.'

It sounded so stark and soulless, and Pip's body tightened with anger. Somewhere in the oil's soporific sweetness was an element that also sharpened the senses. Without knowing why or quite how, he knew that someone had hurt her; crippled her need for people; detached her in a private world of warped and sterile pleasure. It was obvious that she used the powerful effects of odours to help her fight her malaise, but he saw now she couldn't prevail – not on her own.

'Let me do it,' he said, rising from the bed, his naked thighs sliding with the oil. His cock was already resurrecting.

'Do what?' Her grey eyes were narrow and he sensed the stark damage inside her.

'Let me touch you. Give you your joy . . . Please, let me try?'

'Why should I? When I've paid you I don't owe you anything.' She was reaching for her jacket now, and presumably her wallet or chequebook.

'Why?' he mused, the citrus odour still at work on his spirits and his cock. 'Well, because I want some joy, and I don't think I can get it from anybody but you.' He was in front of her now, his hands and his penis reaching out. 'Please, Scottie, please! Forget my fee! Just let me stay here and touch you.'

'What the hell,' she said her voice still heavy yet carrying just the slightest spark of hope. With a small fated sigh, she leaned in towards him, pressed her breasts to his hard oily chest and encircled his waist with her arms. 'What've I got to lose . . . Let's fuck!'

Pip remember those words the next morning as he awoke in her bed and alone.

It hadn't been an easy task, bringing Scottie to joy. She'd been wary and tense, almost impossible to soften and please. But he'd persevered, smeared her body with warmed oil from his, and eventually he'd broken through her barriers. With a fund of patience and skill he hadn't even known he'd possessed, he made her sob and writhe, then jerk wildly in a hard-won climax.

After that they'd flowed together more smoothly and Scottie had relaxed and smiled – and come again on his fingers and his tongue.

He'd hoped against hope that it'd all meant something to her, but somehow her absence this morning was no real surprise. Especially not after what he'd discovered while she was showering and he'd got up to nose around . . .

It was all down to the orange and the gin, he thought bitterly. Just a fantasy, an essential oil trip.

In low spirits, he washed away the last trances of citrus from his body and dejectedly climbed into his clothes. She'd left his money, plus a massive tip, on the pillow, but knowing what he did now, the cash only made him feel sleazy. He wished she'd left him the orange oil instead.

Nobody seemed to take any notice of him in the hotel foyer, a young man in last night's crumpled suit. He put his head down, walked straight ahead . . . and was just about to step into the revolving door when Scottie stepped out of it, a newspaper in one hand and a twirling set of keys in the other.

'Where the hell are you going?' Her voice was angry, but in her deep grey eyes there was fear. And hurt. And an almost choking disappointment.

Pip froze. He'd made a huge mistake. A gigantic one. Not last night, but this morning.

'I thought that was it,' he said quietly, while his heart screamed at Scottie to listen. 'I saw the money and all your stuff gone. I thought you'd gone too.'

'I only went to stow my gear in my panniers, and get a paper. I was coming back to take you to breakfast.' She was starting to smile now, and her pale face was brightening and warming. 'I thought we might discuss another shoot . . . or several.'

Pip didn't want breakfast. He was hungry, but not for eggs or toast. Wasting no time on speech, he took a step forward, put his lips against hers, and used the pressure of his hands on her leather-covered bottom to pull her close and let her know what he needed.

'Scottie, you know the next time we "shoot",' he

began as their mouths drew apart.

Should he mention it? Let her know that he knew? He decided 'Yes' – because honesty was the best base to build on. 'The next time, do you think you could actually put some film in the camera?'

For several long moments her face remained blank and expressionless, and Pip was thrown back to a time beyond confidence, beyond pleasure, beyond nakedness and pure orange oil. But then she laughed – and laughed and laughed – her sleek head falling backwards as she chortled. He'd discovered her sly, kinky secret, but happily it didn't seem to matter. 'Okay, then, just for you.' She leaned close again and kissed his cheek, then smiled archly, her power back on line. 'Now, shall we eat?'

As they walked arm in arm towards the dining room, she seemed to muse a moment, then turned to him. 'I think we'll try a different oil next time too,' she said, her voice so much softer and more resonant. 'I might not need orange any more.'

Pip knew she wouldn't need orange oil, but as he escorted Scottie proudly to their table, he seemed to smell the faint ghost of it anyway . . .

A round, sweet fragrance, fruity and revivifying, the ineffable aroma of joy.

Crème de la Crème

'*WHAT SORT OF* fantasies do you have, Pandora?'

Jake Mallinson cursed inwardly at his perennial and insatiable curiosity. It was probably going to screw up his chances with the most interesting woman he'd met in ages!

'Mine? What on earth do you want to know about *my* fantasies for?' Pandora studied him obliquely across the outlandish sketch she'd just drawn. 'It's yours that're important ... You're the one who's paying for this.' She tapped the paper before them for emphasis.

'Yes, I know that.'

Jake thought furiously. How could he prise her secrets from her? He had to know more – she was driving him crazy! 'But I thought I might get some sexy new ideas from you,' he improvised, 'for the apartment, that is ... You're the interior designer, Pandora. You're the one with the creative mind.'

And the delicious body! he added silently, eyeing her elegant curves and the way her clothes hugged them so faithfully.

She'd changed her outfit since earlier in the day – when they'd surveyed his new flat – and was now wrapped in chic off-white from top to toe. A fine cream sweater shaped to her high, rounded breasts and a pair of milky, jeans-cut trousers embraced the contours of her legs and hips. This was the first time Jake had gotten a close look at Pandora's opulent undercarriage, and he'd discovered she was no less delightful below than above. Her hips were womanly yet lithe, and her backside pure heaven: tight, muscular and utterly curvy. For perhaps the hundredth time, he considered the mysterious vee of her groin, and wished his fingers were beneath that tantalising, double-stitched seam. His mind flashed back to one of his own recent fantasies – the lady rubbing herself madly for his amusement – and the picture was so graphically clear that he nearly came right there in his shorts.

Did Pandora masturbate? She was a healthy, vibrantly sensual woman who often worked closely with men. Surely she had a strong sex-drive? Surely that drive needed satisfying?

An uncomfortable thought suddenly occurred. Maybe Pandora was refusing his non-professional approaches because she was already involved? Because she was getting regular sex with somebody else?

'Maybe you don't need to fantasise,' he ventured.

'And what do you mean by that?'

'Well . . . If you've got a boyfriend and he's giving you plenty, you won't need to dream about it, will you?'

'Who'd go out with me?' She turned slowly in her seat, then nodded towards the substantial-looking hickory walking-stick that was propped discreetly against the bar. There was a bitterness in her beautiful eyes, and Jake realised that although he'd clean forgotten her infirmity, it was impossible for her to do the same.

'I would!'

He tried to put something more thah desire in his voice. He'd only known her a few days yet he wanted to . . . he wanted . . .

What the hell did he want? He did physically lust for Pandora Jackson. More perhaps than for any woman ever. But half-hearted as it sounded, he also wanted to be her friend. His own occasional feelings of isolation were bad enough, but how much more 'different' must Pandora feel when she so obviously considered herself flawed?

'Jake! We've covered all that ground already—'

'Okay! Okay! Okay! I'll leave it. But I'm still interested in your fantasies.'

'All right then, although I can't think why I'm telling you,' she said slowly, then paused to take a sip of her drink. 'I only came here to discuss the commission. And anyway . . . you'll be grossly disappointed, I can tell you that for a start!'

'No way!'

'Don't be so sure. My fantasies are old-fashioned, Jake. And boringly conventional.' She shrugged dismissively. 'I like romance: soft lights, lingerie, sipping champagne. A man who's gentle and gentlemanly; who'd treat me like a lady . . . A man who'd treat me as if *this* didn't exist!' She touched her leg, the one that was stretched out awkwardly, and not as straight and relaxed as the other.

Jake moved uncomfortably. He was ashamed to say that all he could think of was what was *between* her legs, not the legs themselves. 'But surely they can fix it?' he asked in an attempt to distract himself. After all, with orthopaedic surgery being so miraculous these days, she shouldn't really have to stay lame.

'You don't understand, Jake, do you? This is "after", not "before". They've fixed me up as much as they could. I've had umpteen bonegrafts. I've got a dozen steel pins in my thigh. I nearly lost the whole bloody leg!' She patted the stiffened limb which looked quite slender, shapely and normal in her elegant, flattering trousers. 'This is the best it gets. Ever . . .'

But it shouldn't matter, thought Jake, soaping his own sound, unblemished body. He was in the shower now, in his hotel suite. Though it was over two hours later, he was still brooding about Pandora, her dreams, her untreatable leg, and the lack of men who'd look beyond a slight but strangely appealing limp and see a truly remarkable woman. He couldn't believe he was the only one to whom it didn't matter? The problem, he suspected, was bedded in Pandora's own mind. She questioned her own sex appeal, and Jake wondered if someone had let her down.

'But not me, lady!' he proclaimed aloud in her absence.

I wouldn't let you down, he told her across the gulf of the glittering city. I'd treat you like a queen. If you'd give me half a chance – or even a quarter! – I'd lavish you with all the romance and tender loving care you can handle. And then some!

Under the teeming shower, through the steam and pine-scented foam, Jake let Pandora's sweet dream become his.

He saw her boudoir, self-designed in a romantically antique style, its decor subtle with many shades of iridescent cerulean blue. In the centre of the room stood a old-fashioned brass-railed bed; in it lay Pandora – eyes closed and apparently sleeping

509

– her fine body clad in ivory silk, blatantly sensual in its attitude of repose. The blue pillow was swathed in the luxuriant fall of her brindled red-gold hair, and her pale face was relaxed and softly smiling. To be fair to her, he pictured in the slight irregularity of her leg, and some scars clearly visible through the silk. In a moment of seriousness, he examined his reactions – and found only tenderness and a strong urge to nurture. That, and an overwhelming need to see what else lay beneath that thin gown. The hot sexy thing that was covered – for the moment – in delicate pure silk-satin and beneath that, graced with the soft living fur of her sex. Jake could see the faint dark shadow of it, mysterious beneath the fabric that gleamed across her loins.

She was sleeping, yes, but she was waiting for him. A magnum of Champagne stood in a cooler by the bed, and alongside it were two fine crystal goblets. A mound of caviare lay temptingly over cracked ice, its tiny black globules looked fat and sexy. Soured cream and crackers were arranged close by. Oysters were unnecessary, Jake decided. He was already aching with lust.

In his solitary shower, he tried to conjure the tangy salt roe on to his tongue, the fizzing Champagne, the tart richness of the cream. Then, in an imagination within that imagination, he strove for the flavour of Pandora's sex.

In his mind's eye, the dream-dreamer stirred and the silk tightened across her intoxicating form. Moaning, Jake worked up a thick lather and took his prick in his foam-covered hand. In reality she wasn't here to make things happen, so he'd have to to do the business for himself . . .

Slowly, so slowly, he moved his fingers over his trembling erection. There was plenty of time; he mustn't spoil it.

'Jake?' the apparition spoke and he went winging back to his dream. 'Jake, is that you?'

The strange, dark eyes fluttered open, and Pandora drew herself gracefully to a sitting position. Jake's flesh leapt as the silky nightdress, caught beneath her body, slid down and exposed one full milk-white breast.

'Oops!' she exclaimed, placing one long hand artfully over the bared globe. Her lacquered red nails looked stunning against the pure white skin beneath. Minx that she was, she let her rosy, puckered nipple peep between her first and middle fingers, and in a blatant gesture she tweaked her own body, drawing out the teat as if she were offering it to Jake's lips.

Which, as controller of this little fantasy, Jake decided she was! Within the fantasy, he strode forward, his whole attention fixed on that nub of pink flesh. Well, perhaps not all his attention. He had a little to spare for nipple's gorgeous twin, so clearly visible beneath the thin satin that covered it.

'Pandora,' he murmured, leaning over to fasten his lips around the exposed jewel, while his fingers found its silk-covered mate.

She was hard with desire for him, the tiny crests protruding insolently into his mouth and fingers. He sucked – and pinched – and she moaned incoherently, wafting her slim, lightly-clothed body against him. Immediately, the dreaming Jake dressed himself in a robe as insignificant as her nightdress. If romance was the keynote, a little mystery on his side wouldn't go amiss either.

Bemused, he leaned back against the shower wall distancing himself from the fantasy for a moment although continuing to stroke his cock.

'Hang on a minute, Mallinson,' he instructed, laughing out loud at himself. 'Who the bloody hell's fantasy is this anyway' I ought to spread her and fuck her, and be done with it! What's all this pussyfooting around in aid of? She isn't even here!' Yet, irresistibly, he had to believe she was.

'Get with it, Jake,' he told himself, taking a firm hold on both his prick and his mind. 'At least this way, I get Pandora. If I'm going to get her, I might as well make it as nice for her as it is for me.' Locking all the sensual seduction paraphernalia firmly back into place, he set his internal camera rolling.

Body, silk, silk, body; the sandwich was certainly arousing enough for now, especially while he was nibbling Pandora's nipple and getting a succession of gutteral moans and involuntary writhings for his efforts. Oh God, if this was what she was like when he sucked her breast, what would she be like when he went down on her? The temptation to splice straight to *that* sequence was almost painful.

But he resisted. There was plenty of time. He wanted this to last and, inexplicable as it seemed to his insistent prick, he wanted the non-existent Pandora to enjoy herself too. One last pull on her delicate breast-tip, and he released her, then moved up to place a kiss on her cheek, 'I'm getting too excited, honey,' he whispered out loud. 'Shall we have a glass of Champagne to cool off? I don't want to come too soon, Pandora. I want this to be really special for you. I want to give you a hundred orgasms before I even have one.'

'You're an ambitious man, Jake Mallinson,' she murmured with a smile, 'but please feel free to try!' Pulling back, Jake admired the perfect shape of her breast as it glistened under its coating of saliva. The sheen accentuated the magnificence of the proud

512

high curve, and made the swollen nipple look unbearably lewd.

That's it! thought Jake in his shower, enjoying the water cascading down his body. I'll drink Champagne from her breasts! And maybe . . .

Assessing the seductive banquet, he imagined the oceanic flavour of caviare combined with the taste of Pandora herself – the rich lusciousness of cream blending delicately with her smoky juice. Dropping his prick, he toyed for a second with spinning the shower dial to cold. It was all too vivid; his flesh was twitching madly, he'd erupt any second if he didn't hold back.

Back in his fantasy, he poured a brimming flute of Champagne and offered it to Pandora's Russian Red mouth; then watched the sexy undulation of her throat as she swallowed the sparkling wine with unashamed relish. God, everything about her drove him wild!

Topping up the glass he offered her more, and when she'd drunk her fill, he took a few sips from the selfsame glass. Setting it aside he prepared her a caviare-loaded cracker, then topped it with a little cream.

'Mmmm,' she murmured suggestively as she swallowed the titbit.

'More?' he enquired, poundingly aroused again.

'Yes, please!' purred Pandora, and Jake complied, his cock pulsing as he daubed on far too much cream and it seemed about to fall on the sky-blue sheet. Like a flash, Pandora caught the overflow and took it to her lips, pushing three fingers into her mouth and sucking them obscenely.

'You're a filthy woman, Pandora Jackson!' he growled, dragging her hand from her mouth and feeding her the second richly topped cracker.

Again, she swallowed it in the rudest way imaginable, then licked the slick of cream from her perfect cupid's bow lips in a long, sensuous double swipe of her tongue.

'And you're a damn fool, Jake Mallinson,' he told himself back in the real world. 'You'll hit the tiles with your come any second if you go on like this.' Before he could think twice and stop himself, he flicked the thermostat to blue – then yelped and yowled as the icy water pummelled his erection into submission. He let the cold water stream over him for a minute, then brought the flow-heat back to 'moderate'. Looking down, he saw his cock was flaccid again. 'Okay then, super-tool,' he told it, 'let's start again, shall we?'

'Aren't you having anything to eat?' enquired Pandora when he returned to her. She was lolling back against the pillow again now, her body succulent and her pose inviting. Jake was glad he'd designed her gown a shade too tight.

'I'm saving my appetite,' he replied, his gaze fixed on the shaded delta of her near-visible pubic curls.

'Aren't you even the tiniest bit hungry?' she teased.

'I'm bloody ravenous, you saucy whore!' he told her as his erection resurfaced after its dowsing – and in the sybaritic fantasy, he closed in on their banquet. His mind was full of outrageous ideas; naughty schemes to employ the various ingredients. The only trouble was . . . Pandora wriggled so much when he played with her that food and fine wine would end up all over the place. He'd better find a way to curb her wigglings, delicious as they were, and make sure that everything he applied to her slim white body went exactly where he wanted it to!

Instantly, his imagination produced the answer –

a dressing-table drawer half-open, and hanging from it a number of long silk scarves. He checked out the brass head and footrails of the luxurious bed; it was conveniently just the right size.

'You're a feast, Pandora,' he murmured, worrying her neck with a few exploratory nibbles while his eager hands enclosed her silk-covered breasts. Cupping and lifting, he kneaded them in a distinct circular motion, and Pandora made a low, feline sound in her throat. She liked her romance a little on the rough side, did the good designer, and Jake was more than happy to oblige her. He squeezed the heavy orbs, as if testing for ripeness, and her bottom moved rythmically against the mattress.

'Yes, lady, you're a feast,' he repeated, 'juicy . . . soft and tender. I'm going to devour every scrap of you!' he nipped at the upper slope of one breast and she whimpered. 'But first you need trussing!'

'Jake! What're you doing?' she demanded, a thin streak of panic in her soft harmonious voice.

'Just whatever I want! And you're not going to stop me, lady! Now stretch your arms back across the pillows, and spread your legs. Wide!'

Enjoying his own chauvinism, yet knowing in real life he probably wouldn't get away with it, Jake slid down the tiles to sit – his own legs outstretched – in the shallow water of the shower trough. It was going to be a zonker of a climax when it came; he'd be a fool to be standing when he lost control of his limbs!

He closed his eyelids against the light, warm stream and saw Pandora behind them, spread-eagled and ready to be tied.

The scarves, of course, were precisely the right length. It was a simple matter to secure her and he lavished her bad leg with special and caring

attention. Caressing it gently as he positioned it, he
bent over her ankle, her calf and her knee in turn, to
lay his mouth against each long pink scar. There
was no fear in her eyes as he did so.

'What now?' she asked huskily, licking her lips
again as if she knew how much it excited him.

'I'm going to taste you, Pandora,' he said bluntly,
moving to sit beside her, 'I'm going to get this pretty
thing out of the way,' he ran his hand over the silk
at her flank, 'and I'm going to eat you.'

'Do it then!' she taunted, flirting her crotch
towards him, seemingly unhampered by either her
bonds or her lameness.

'In my own time, sexy lady,' he said, trailing his
hand lightly across her belly. 'A perfect meal should
be savoured. Every mouthful appreciated to the
utmost. So I'm going to consume you very slowly,
Pandora. Inch by delicious inch . . .'

'Just so long as you get there eventually,' she
murmured, feigning nonchalance although Jake
could see a pulse beating furiously in her neck.
Tempted, he pressed his lips to the throbbing place
and sucked a small patch of skin into his mouth. He
considered love-biting her, then decided not to.
He'd save his lips and tongue for more succulent
places. He pushed up the white silk skirt and
bunched it roughly at her waist.

Just the sight of her was a banquet!

Pandora's thighs were long and slim – and even
the damaged one was relatively unmarked. Her
belly was smooth and softly rounded, and her sex
exquisite, lush and mouthwatering. Her feminine
hair was full and flossy, but not so dense that he
couldn't see the sensual blood-filled lips it guarded,
or the small delicate bud of flesh he'd soon be
teasing. The temptation to place his hand at her

crotch immediately was enormous.

But he didn't. It was to be a long, slow meal. Circumspection was especially necessary, Jake decided in the shower. His tool was rampant again only moments after its icy dowsing. In the fantasy, he threw off his imaginary robe, placed a single kiss on Pandora's trembling clitoris, then, ignoring her moans and entreaties, returned his attention to her breasts.

The elegant silk nightdress fastened down the front – as far as the waist – with a set of tiny ribbon bows. Jake undid these slowly and meticulously, but left the satin draped across Pandora's heaving curves until the very last second. Only then, and with a good deal of flourish, did he bare her.

Her nipples were like small, pink stones crying out to be fingered.

'Beautiful breasts,' he murmured, praising the sight he'd never truly seen. 'I'm going to bathe them in Champagne.'

'Don't you d—' Pandora yelled, then squealed as half a flute of chilled fizz was trickled over the entire surface of her chest.

The Champagne went everywhere – soaking the sheets and the silk gown as well as the sumptuous body it was aimed at. But enough remained on the twin targets to leave them moist and glistening, and a siren call to Jake's ravenous mouth. Leaning naked across her, he made his tongue flat and broad and spread the vintage wine all over her nipples and areolae, then continued over the full beautiful sweep of each engorged breast. He washed her creamy skin with Champagne, and every long stroke made her purr with pleasure.

'I'm all sticky,' she complained, not really complaining at all.

'You sure are!' said Jake, his fingers inside her at last. Pandora strained at her bonds, her pelvis rising to him as he dabbed gently at her clitoris, his mouth still glued to one breast.

She was already wet: deliciously slippery and perfectly primed for a long smooth ride. There was nothing to stop him sliding straight in her to the hilt.

But that wasn't the way Jake wanted it to be. They'd strayed from the 'romance' remit somewhat, but as Pandora was so vociferously pleased with the situation, it didn't seem to matter.

We're running something of mine now, thought Jake ruefully, pulling slowly on his rod as the water flowed around his submerged backside. The warm rippling sensation was like a subtle caress and he wriggled in the warm, barmy swirl and watched his prick jerk accordingly.

Yeah, we're running something of mine, he observed again. But God knows what! His phantom fingers flickered Pandora's sex, noted the oiled silk texture of her juices, and seeded the craziest idea. He eyed the Champagne again, then the caviare, and finally the cream.

'What on earth are you up to?' whispered Pandora huskily, her body moving involuntarily under his gentle fondling. 'For God's sake bring me off, you tease! Look, Jake, either suck me or screw me, but whatever you do, do it now!'

'Such impatience,' he taunted, aping Pandora's soft, humour-the-client-he's-paying-a-fortune tones, but secretly thrilled by her earthy demands.

'Jake!'

'Okay, lady. Just you lie still there. I want to try something.'

Amazingly, she obeyed him, but it seemed to cost her some effort. He watched for a moment as she bit

518

her velvety lower lip and scrunched her eyes tight shut. In no way a cruel man, Jake decided it was time to stop the teasing.

Holding open her pillowy blood-filled labia, he took a heaped spoonful of the soured cream and dropped it – in a single dollop – directly on to her clitoris. It oozed slowly down over the fruit-red tissues of her sex, clinging and shimmering deliciously. He added more and more until her whole vee was covered and he could see it bubbling in the pulsing mouth of her vagina.

'You dirty beast,' she chuckled, opening her eyes to see his trick – although Jake suspected she'd already sussed exactly what he was up to. 'I hope you're going to lick that off!'

'Try and stop me, lady. Just try and stop me . . . ! Within seconds he was crouched between her wide-open legs and perusing the lovely cream-coated sex in between.

Hmm . . . The idea of taking her seized him. Reaching over and supporting Pandora's head for a couple of seconds, he first kissed her on the mouth, then slid the satin pillow from behind her neck and repositioned it under her bottom. She bounced and whimpered when he took the opportunity, while he was in the vicinity, to finger the tender rose of her arsehole and slither some cream down deep along the groove.

'Don't . . . Oh God . . . Yes!' she babbled, 'For Christ's sake, get on with it!'

She was perfect now; perfectly positioned, perfectly ready. He dabbed on another spoonful of cream; then, grinning his wickedest grin, he flung the spoon away and tipped the whole dishfull straight on to her crotch. She moaned as he massaged it into the pretty reddish curls, her cries getting louder.

He murmured his response, playfully teasing her slippery labia. Irresistible!'

With that he placed his face between her legs in search of nectar and ambrosia. His goal arched towards him, a heavenly cup offered to his hungering mouth as Pandora's slim hips hovered inches above the blue satin. The tastes and the textures were so sublime that Jake devoured the contents of her sex, and while tongueing her, mixing the cream with her musky and abundant juices. Pandora mewled as he gently lapped and by the time he'd blended the cocktail to his liking, she was screaming; her frantic voice ringing out in extreme and tormented ecstasy.

Using his curled tongue, Jake scooped up a great swirl of cream-thickened juice and anointed. her clitoris with it. Then, with a murmur of 'beautiful, beautiful, beautiful', he enclosed the tiny organ in his lips and sucked as if it were the source of life itself. Pandora's body arched like a bow, went rigid, and, as Jake pressed his whole face into her sex, he felt her vagina pulsating wildly against his chin.

'I'm coming! I'm coming! I'm coming!' she keened in a long, rising wail – and as she did, Jake's own loins were consumed by the same fabulous fire.

'So am I!' he sobbed in wonder, as his vision of cream and flesh and silk dissolved and he watched his semen – his own cream – trickle slowly down the tiles and merge with the burbling swirl below.

'Bon appetit, Pandora,' he murmured. Resting his head back against the shower wall, he dozed off as the water beat relentlessly down on his slack, sated body.

It was the phone that pulled him from his sudden slumber. Leaping clear of the still teaming shower, he dragged a towel round his hips, ran, and grabbed up the receiver just in time.

'I thought you weren't going to answer,' accused Pandora, her slightly flummoxed tone making Jake wonder if she hadn't wanted him to.

'I was in the shower . . . But it's okay. How can I help you?'

'I . . . I've . . . I've been thinking about what you said about the commission . . . and . . . er . . . *us*. I wondered if you'd like to come over to my place for dinner? It's only a scratch meal, but . . . Well . . . I really think we should talk.'

'Great! Wonderful! I'd love to!' Jake couldn't tell which was thudding the hardest: his heart or the blood in his reborn erection. 'What's on the menu?'

'Nothing too fancy, I'm afraid,' came the soft strangely excited answer, 'I thought we'd start with crudites and sour cream dip. Does that sound okay?'

'Oh, yes,' murmured Jake, his eyes closing in ecstatic expectation, 'Oh God, yes it does!'

Thirty-Six Hours

THIRTY-SIX HOURS. It was all we had. I didn't know how to tell him . . .

I could see him beyond the barrier, his face alight with smiles. How could I kill that joy by telling him how soon I'd be gone again?

'Aura! Aura, baby, here!' I could hear him calling. See him angling his way forward from amongst the waiting throng. And for perhaps the thousandth time since we'd met, I wondered what I'd done to deserve such a prize.

Davy Hashimoto . . .

I could feel my strong, soldier-girl's knees go weak as he darted forward to meet me. My beautiful little Davy, my helpmeet, my lover . . . and my very best friend in the world.

'Oh, baby, it's so good to see you!' His arms were already around me as he spoke, and I was wrapped in his warmth and his fine, male scent. I could well imagine the envious look of my fellow female squadmates . . . Even some of them men would be jealous.

My lovely Davy the sculptor. How I'd longed to be with him again! I still couldn't figure out why I called him 'little'! He was five eleven in his socks – when he wore them – and strong and fit, if a touch on the skinny side. His body was sleek and powerful . . . as a man, he was more than substantial. Far more! I felt my own flesh twitch and moisten. Soon, McCarthy soon! Use a bit of that military training of yours, woman . . . Contain yourself!

'Hello, there, stud, how've you been?' I enquired, back in command as I pulled away. Well, a sort of command. I could feel that old familiar heat down below. The hot, dark need I always felt if Davy was anywhere near me.

'Fine, honey.' His thick lashes flickered, shading those long brown eyes of his: mysterious, artistic, all-seeing eyes. Half-Japanese, and wholly and entirely beautiful. 'But I've missed you! I've missed you so much! Oh, my, do you look good!'

As an artist, he should've known better, but my beauty was in his beholding eye, I suppose, not mine. I was just an average-looking lady squaddie, not a dog, but not spectacular either. Davy was the one who looked stunning. And he'd made such an effort today, bless his heart! To welcome me home, he'd made a genuine, concerted effort to be tidy.

'Come on, hunk! Let's go home,' I murmured, conscious of how time was whizzing by, and how this man who did his best work in the raw – both as an artist and a lover – had managed to look so great in his clothes today, in my honour.

His shirt was baggy and a little crumpled but the soft, raw silk was pristinely, immaculately white. His jeans were old and faded ones, but freshly washed and patched. He'd even managed to find a halfway decent pair of sneakers to put on. At home he usually went barefoot . . . and bare anything else if he thought he could get away with it.

Temptation attacked in spades as we moved through the malls and walkways in the direction of our communal flat. After all these months, all I really wanted to do was touch him; fondle that perfect arse in those tight, pale jeans; take the soft little cotton tie out of his hair and push my fingers through the whole, thick, black-silk mass. I wanted to stroke his toffee-brown skin; caress him everywhere; kiss his eyes, his mouth, his belly and his superb young cock. I wanted to devour him, consume him, feast on his sexy beauty. Fill myself with his flesh, his come and his love . . . Fill myself so choc-a-bloc with him I could survive another ten months.

'So, what've you done? What've you sold?' I enquired as we entered the huge, long studio that made up most of our home. It was polite conversation time. We never jumped straight into bed, no matter how much we wanted each other. We'd been together a fair while but there was still a small sweet shyness between us, a freshness that kept things exciting.

I even blushed when we faced one of his finished sculptures together.

'Not this one,' he said quietly.

I could see why. It was me. My body portrayed faithfully by hands that knew it so well. My face suggested and embeautied by hands that moved with equal skill over both clay and my own human flesh.

'You've flattered me . . .'

'No . . . Not at all, love. Clay doesn't lie.' He smiled, and I saw his long fingers flexing. Was it me he wanted to smooth them over? Or was it the simulacrum . . . the sculpture? I felt nervous; wanting but ridiculously scared. My whole body

524

was aching now. My panties were wet. Yet I still wanted it to be Davy who asked; Davy who started it; Davy who led me to our bed.

I suppose it was to prove my femininity. I wanted to take orders, not give them; respond, not initiate. Here with him, I was just Aura – not the high-flying super-efficient Squad Sergeant McCarthy.

'What's in the fridge then?' I asked, changing the subject, shying away from decision. 'What've we got to eat and drink?' I walked through to the kitchen nook, intensely aware of Davy just behind me: silent, light-footed and lithe.

'I made some stew,' he began, biting his lip when I turned around in horror. 'I thought we could just heat it up . . .'

I groaned. I hardly dare open the refrigerator. There was just one manual skill that Davy had never mastered – cookery.

There was something hideous in a casserole on the second shelf. It probably *could* be heated up, but it certainly couldn't be eaten!

'Oh, Davy!'

'Yeah, I know . . . It's gruesome! Shall we go out for a pizza?' That questioning note in his voice, and the sweet boyish smile that went with it, just melted my heart. I could eat *him*, never mind his dreadful stew!

Suddenly I felt hot and shaky, unbearably excited. I thought about what I'd just thought . . . and I knew I'd never felt hungrier. To find a scrap of control, I reached into the fridge and took out a bottle of Astrapure. My lips were parched but they needed to be soft and moist and pliant. I popped the cap and "lugged some of the fizzy water straight from its plastic bottle. I couldn't stall any more; I took another long drink, then put the water aside.

525

Turning to Davy, I wiped my mouth. I was still starving, and he'd never looked more appetising.

'Yes. We can go out, if you like. . .' Of its own volition, my hand floated out and settled on the crotch of his jeans, 'Or I could have a little snack first . . . It's up to you.' Please, Davy, I begged silently. Make *this* decision for me. Read my mind.

'Oh, yes, baby, yes!' he crooned, throwing back his head and closing his eyes as I squeezed him. 'Oh, yes, my love . . . my love, my love, my love . . .' His full crotch bumped into my grip, flaunted foward . . . and my decision was made for me – wonderfully.

A supplicant in khaki, I fell to my knees as Davy slumped back against the fridge door and spread his long lean legs to brace them.

'Do it, Aura! Do it!'

Euphoric, I leapt to obey. I flipped open his belt buckle, then unfastened his button-front jeans. Beneath the denim, his red cotton jock was hugely tented and a patch of dark, spreading moisture said everything I wanted to know. I looked into his face – and his eyelashes fluttered. Soft and black and heavy they signalled 'Go on! Go on!'

My fingers shook as I slid down his underwear and eased out his shivering cock.

Oh God, how I'd missed him! Missed this! His beautiful flesh, so stiff and rosy, the fat tip bulging and glistening. Veins throbbing beneath the velvet shaft . . . Totally alive . . . Primally male . . . The body of the man I loved.

With a great surrendering sob, he pushed his hips forward. His prick touched my open lips and I took the velvet knob inside my mouth and raved it all wet with my tongue – loving his salty man-taste and his long, soft whimper of pleasure.

His strong sculptor's hands closed tightly round the back of my head, and I revelled in being forced to take more. His glans probed my throat ... His pubic fluff tickled my worshipping face ... The clean scent of lemon filled my head ... That, and something more ancient and insidious: the heavy musky smell of an aroused, sweating man. My man.

Holding him as deep as I could without choking, I flirted and probed and worked him. My tongue went wild and my hands slid around his beautiful arse to pull him in closer than ever.

'Oh God, baby, I've missed you,' moaned my sweet pumping echo – wagging his lean flat hips as my fingers found the seam of his jeans. He couldn't last long; I could almost hear his semen churning. It was ready to rise, and I wanted it! I wanted his taste and his ecstasy. The sound of his breaking voice as he screamed out aloud in his climax.

Come, baby, come! I urged him, the words ringing silent in my head as I darted and dove with my tongue.

With a great, great cry he answered and obeyed, filling my mouth with his creamy heat, and his slippery silkiness ... His smooth male liquor nourished my loving heart and fed the soul that adored him.

'Oh dear, now what've we done?' he said a few minutes later, as we lay cuddled together on the kitchen floor; arms around each other and backs against the refrigerator door as we studied the results of what I'd just done.

Uninhibited as ever, Davy flipped at his softened prick with one slender, elegant forefinger. 'Not much use to you for a while yet, babe,' he observed, his dismay only feigned as he leaned inwards to kiss my neck, 'but not to worry, I've still got these—' He wiggled *all* his fingers in a way that made me quiver from head to foot. 'And this!' Like a demon impish boy he stuck out his wet pink tongue . . . and one particular part of me quivered far more than the rest.

'Maybe I should have a snack too,' he murmured, tugging at the belt of my fatigues . . .

'How long have we got, babe?' he asked at last. It was the question I supposed he'd been wanting to ask since I'd first appeared through the customs barrier; the one I least wanted to answer.

We were still lying on the floor, but in the studio den now, naked, snuggled in blankets and surrounded by the remnants of several large pizzas. 'Thirty-six hours.' I glanced up at the clock on the wall, and hated what I saw. 'Well, more like thirty now.'

'Oh God.' There was pain in his eyes, but then, being my sweet amenable Davy, he smiled.

'Do you think you can survive on my cooking tomorrow?' he asked, quirking his fine black brows as he shimmied free of his blanket. His body was so brown and strong, his cock so proud and rising. Suddenly, my own body felt very hot, very hampered, and much too covered up . . .

'There's always the pizza-on-wheels-man, honey.' I wiggled my way out of my woollen cocoon and edged closer to his naked male shape. 'But why?'

'Because, my love,' he said softly, reaching for me and letting his hands close gently on my breasts, 'with only thirty-six hours for this, we haven't got time to go out!'

Hand in Glove

One night in July

ALL WORK AND no play makes Jack a very tired boy . . .

J.J. massaged after-bath rub into the muscles of his shoulders and chest, and sighed. Tension popped beneath his fingers; knots of it nagged at his arms and back. His whole body was a great mass of aches.

That's the last time I put so much into one lousy job, he told himself, stretching hard then letting go in a release so delicious he almost came. He rolled his head from side to side, shrugged, then grinned. Okay, so he always put all of himself into everything. But at least next time, Madam could come round herself and ask him nicely!

There was no point letting *her* wind him up again. Because, one: the job was done now; two: in his heart of hearts he was actually grateful to her – *very* grateful. She'd handed him the biggest break of his whole career. Finally, three: he didn't like admitting it, but in a strange screwed-up sort of way he really got off on her! He'd never experienced anything like it before; he'd been aroused for the whole four weeks he'd worked on this job. Pushing his wet hair out of his eyes, he sighed again; a puzzled and worn-out man.

The night was hot, far too hot, so J.J. stayed naked. Wandering through into his lounge-come workroom, he studiously avoided both the sheaves of drawings strewn across every available surface and the glowing screen of his computer, and padded over to the sideboard to look with real happiness at his small but carefully chosen selection of bottles.

He never drank while he was designing – sobriety gave his work a keener edge – so this first drink afterwards was pure heaven. It always seemed doubly strong! After four interminable weeks slaving over Chantel Lindsey's darkly moody film sets, this one shot of icy single malt packed all the punch of every drink that J.J. had ever taken.

Up yours, Chantal! he toasted silently as the whisky slithered down his throat like velveteen fire. Next time, lady, have the grace to meet your drone in person!

The set he'd designed for her was good – an Oscar winner? – but even now, he still couldn't figure out why he'd worked himself to a standstill for a woman he'd never met.

Chantal Lindsey – the creative despot of her own red-hot production company – was demanding and brilliant, and absolutely specific in her written instructions. But she was never available in person. J.J. had always worked hand in glove with his producers before Ms Lindsey's non-presence, plus her stream of tersely pithy faxes and the imperious notes she'd scrawled on his early sketches, had really pissed him off!

Yet that same resentment had been the grit in a pearl; Madam Chantal had fired up his visionary juices and the outcome was the finest work he'd ever done.

Sipping his Hebridean nectar, J.J. reached back to knead his aching shoulder. God, that Chantal was such a ball-breaker!

What I need now, he observed sagely, is to give her a damn good grudge fuck! Especially as I've lived like a monk for the last month . . . Drink wasn't the only thing he'd had to give up.

Already partially aroused, J.J. set his mind to the possibility of sex; reviewing his possible bedmates as he topped up the level of his drink. Although unattached at present, he had several womanfriends he could ring and take out for the evening. Women who'd be more than happy to drink with him, eat with him, then, later, without question or embarrassment, let him take them to his bed.

It'd be a rip-off though. What the hell good was he to a woman right now? Self-absorbed and strung out, he'd nothing to give. Okay, so he could get an erection – he'd *already* got one! – but getting it up and keeping it up didn't automatically make the earth move.

Even so, he was still unbearably randy . . . and getting more so by the second. Damn you, Chantal Lindsey! he cursed the faceless woman. It's your bloody fault! I could die for a fuck, but I'm too screwed up to go and out and get one!

But he didn't have to go out and make like a superstud, did he? He'd got privacy, comfort, his own right hand . . . And, goddammit, he *was* supposed to be creative!

You're the designer, J.J. old son – design a fantasy! Design yourself some sex.

Settling carefully into his chair, he shimmied down so his buttocks were slightly spread. The leather seat felt exquisitely chilly against his bare behind, stark and sweet like the touch of a mystery woman. He used his mind to make the seat her hands, then wriggled deeper to make her caress him.

Taking a long pull of whisky, he swivelled the chair so he could put his glass aside. Re-adjusting his position, he pushed down, splitting himself a little more, and his cock reared up like a great red prong, raunchy and magnificent, right in the centre of his eyeline. Placing his hands palm-down on his lean brown thighs he teased his stiffened-flesh by denying the contact it ached for.

'You've got a beauty there, J.J.,' he murmured, clenching his groin and loving his own rod as it waved before him like a thick, lengthy reed.

She'll love it too, said a voice inside his head. A voice that was his own yet transformed by his need and a growing sense of excitement.

She? What 'she'? As his head grew light and his breathing laboured, he searched his mind for a partner: a cool goddess for his heated solitude. No face appeared, but suddenly it didn't matter; content with her anonymity, he took his shaft in his hands and began, slowly, to pump.

Deep in the luscious depths of the experience, everything was right on target; yes, even at this very first stage. J.J. had never had hang-ups about masturbation; he enjoyed it thoroughly and did it often. To him it was a celebration of his own sensuality that brought scope and richness to all other sex. He watched the long slide of his hand on his cock; the skin was still dry to the touch as yet, creating tantalising friction between fingers and shaft. Shaking slightly, he set his mindfilm running and drew upon the imagery of his recent designs. As his eyes closed, he waited for a woman to appear in his set . . .

He was alone in the middle of his own creation, the dark monochrome alley that still flickered on his computer screen. It was somewhere on the outskirts of a sprawling futuristic city, and deserted. Twilight gleamed greyly, and the faint thud-thud of hard rock music told him he was near an entertainment area. He felt excellent now: strong and sexy, ready for anything, and deep deep into his fantasy.

'Hello, J.J.'

A woman's voice: commanding but not strident, powerful yet soft as silk. In the dream, he froze in his tracks; in reality his cock leapt and he gripped it just under the crown to tame its volcanic arousal. He mustn't come yet. There was still a long long night ahead . . .

'Stop right there,' said the unseen woman. She was in shadow, but J.J. could make out a tall, slim, dark-clad form. 'Stand against the wall. Completely still. Put your hands behind your head.' Because it was a dream, he obeyed without question, and the woman moved partially into view.

His fantasy was skilfully lit. He could see a s lender neatly-curved body a grey leather suit . . . but no face. 'Mystery Woman' wore a sleek, *haute couture* garment that was as fine and tasteful as she was. This was class he was dealing with: hard, chic class. An indefinable resonance told him he ought to know her, though there was still no recognition. Her features remained frustratingly in shadow, veiled in a grey far darker than that of her suit. Only her voice defined her as beautiful . . .

'Well, what have we here?' Her drawl made the

hairs on the back of his neck stand up one by one and his prick throb slowly and painfully. The very words seemed to dance along the whole pulsing length of him . . .

She was standing in front of him now, her face still obscured, and he jumped in both body and penis when she pressed her leather-gloved hand to his groin. He groaned long and low as she squeezed him.

'Silence!'

The single quietly-spoken word synchronised perfectly with her left-handed slap across his face. The pressure on his cock and balls stayed precisely the same, his sex delicately vised between her grey-clad fingers. In reality, J.J.'s hand fell away as his prick quivered ominously.

'You will not speak in my presence,' she went on as she released his genitals, her tone honeyed and deceptively conversational. In the dream *she* had every right to command, and had J.J. no option but to obey. 'Press your back to the wall. Spread your legs slightly. Lift your buttocks. Bring your crotch towards me.'

Simple commands. Short, to the point, no compromise. In the dream, J.J. complied without question; back in the reality of his room, he shuffled his naked bottom deeper into the leather-covered chair, dilating his anus to kiss the smooth cold hide. Why is it, he wondered as his cock swayed and trembled, why is it I get off on her ordering me around? Why the hell do I love it so much?

In both worlds his thighs twitched . . .

'You may take your hands from behind your head,' she said pleasantly. Dream-time J.J. let his arms flop, his hands hung loosely by his denim-clad haunches. 'Now. . .' He could hear her smiling.

'Unzip your flies, push down your underpants, and expose your prick and balls.'

'Lady—'

Smack! His face flamed again.

'Shut the fuck up and do it!'

Still the same satin-soft voice, and in his imagination he hurried to do its bidding. In both worlds his eyes watered from the slap, but in the here and now he laid a hand carefully on his prick again. Testing. Assessing. As he squeezed cautiously a drop of juice swelled at the tip and, working with the slow craft of a surgeon, he spread the fluid down his shaft and began – with equal precision – to work the moist surface skin over the hard inner core.

Still dry though . . .

Reaching for his drink, he took a long sip, swirled the smoky fluid in his mouth then swallowed. Releasing his tool, he put the fingers that'd held it into his mouth. His own slight saltiness lingered a second then submerged into the taste of the Scotch. Sucking hard, he coated all four fingers in whiskified saliva and took them, glistening to his cock. The trace of spirit made his taut flesh sting and J.J. rolled his hips, savouring the sensation as his mind reeled out the fantasy.

The teeth of his imaginary zip bit nastily into his balls; his jeans were too tight to expose him comfortably and his tender, swollen testicles were forced up against the root of his prick. He was mortifyingly rigid and the woman's hidden eyes homed in like lasers. Then, as if dream-thought summoned dream-reality, a bright narrowly focused light was shining directly on his tense, shivering organ.

'A beauty,' she murmured.

That's what I thought, echoed real J.J., gingerly stroking the real flesh.

'Rub it, J.J.'

'But—'

'Do it, J.J. Wank yourself or I'll hurt you again. Down there. Now do it!'

Rock and roll, my queen! thought J.J. as real and imaginary hands fused and launched into furious movement.

There was no time for exactitude now. Hugely turned-on, he pumped himself like a madman, wrenching the skin back and forth over the solid rod within.

'Holy shit!' he hissed, his teeth locked in a death-like rictus as he leather-clad fingers reached out, laced with his, and rode the length of his tortured, blood-filled pole. Fire tore down his spine then shot out of his prick as semen; he watched – from a million miles away – as fine stings of it arced high in the air, then hit the woman's dark skirt and trickled slowly towards its hem.

'Rock and roll, rock and roll . . .' he whispered again, thrilling to the tremors that rippled through his belly and thighs, and the feel of his now ultra-sensitive prick contained within their joined hands.

When his eyes fluttered open, he looked dazedly around. Where was she? His grey woman with her gloved hands and her slim, spunk-splattered skirt?

But there was no sign of his goddess. The room was unchanged. Except for . . .

'Oh, my God!' he said softly as he espied the computer monitor. Filaments of come were rolling down it, pale against the shades of grey, their whiteness warm on the cool dark background of Chantal Lindsey's deserted alley.

It was so like his design it was frightening! Even the lighting was just as he'd imagined.

'She's around here somewhere,' the young PA had said, then scuttled away, as if she were as spooked as J.J. was by this shadowy, menacing alley.

Where was she, this hellcat who'd domineered him into creating this, and done it without one single instant of personal contact? Where was she, this Chantal Lindsey? And why, in this familiar alley, was he looking for someone else?

Suddenly he shuddered in delicious disbelief. Christ, he was erect! Any minute now there'd be a spotlight.

'Hello, J.J. . . .'

So soft and husky. Déjà vu grabbed him by the heart, throat and balls. It couldn't be! *She* couldn't be! It'd been a drunken vision. A wanker's mindgame!

Yet the voice spoke again . . . and was real. 'This all makes me feel as if I know you.' There was a faint movement in the shadows, a gesture that seemed to encompass the whole of their surroundings.

Then, to J.J.'s horrified joy, the discreet figure stepped forward, stealing his sanity with a chic dark suit with the soft gloss of leather and a pair of long, slim, immaculately begloved hands.

He hardly dared look at her face . . . but he did.

She wasn't particularly beautiful. Her even features, framed in a sleek cap of dark hair, were unremarkable apart from a pair of large, luminous light-dark eyes that glittered coolly in the gloom.

But it was her hands that held him hopelessly bedazzled. His stiffness magnified to a state of real pain; he wanted to fall forward, double over himself, clasp his aroused agony in his own shaking hands.

She was reaching out now; a greeting, presumably, as she moved towards him. 'Congratulations, J.J., this's exactly what I wanted.'

This? The set or the meeting? She looked down thoughtfully at her fingers as if knowing what they'd done.

Please! Yes! No! Pleading silently, J.J. followed her glance.

If that hand touched him, that hand in its thin leather glove. If it ever touched him he'd come. And she'd know.

Trembling, aching, wanting, he lifted his arm, extended his fingers and . . .

Sweet Saint Nick

TALK ABOUT GETTING an eyeful!

Lying in a Casualty Department, wearing an eye patch, a party frock and a cloud of Shalimar wasn't quite what I'd expected of a 'girl's night out', but as it was supposed to be the season of good cheer and all that, I was trying to look on the bright side.

Mainly because there *was* one . . .

Closing my eyes – the good one and the one still stinging madly – I conjured up the last thing I'd seen with 20/20 vision.

Father Christmas's willie!

Well, not exactly the equipment of Old Saint Nick himself, but the large and rather beautiful tool of 'Big Saint Nick – The Lady's Christmas Cracker' who'd bared his all for us with a good deal of groin-thrusting flourish, and given me a smack in the eye with his G-string too!

God, it'd hurt! Like hell! But even so, I couldn't forget the view . . .

I'd been rather dubious about a male stripper outing, seeing as I was currently off men, but when Big Saint Nick had prowled on to the stage, I'd changed my mind pretty fast, then said a great big thanks to Janie for getting us a front-row table!

Technically, he'd kicked off his act in a Santa suit, but the beard, hood and skimpy red tunic were soon history, and he was treating us to far more than the average Chnstmas Cracker: a pelvis packed with power, swirling and thrusting like a tribal warrior's. His G-string was red velvet, minute but bulging, and had a fluffy white pom-pom bobbing and bouncing right where the action was!

It was all very tacky, but endearing somehow; personally, I couldn't imagine getting a better Christmas box than his!

Not that the rest of him wasn't just my type. Long black hair tied in a pony-tail, and a muscular, golden, but not too massive body that moved as if classically trained to dance. A nice face too: dark, naughty eyes, and an even naughtier mouth. One that seemed to be smiling specifically for me. It could've been wishful thinking, but it was *our* table he chosen for his *coup de grâce*.

And why, still starkers, had he leapt so quickly to the aid of the woman his scanties had wounded? Janie and Sally and Louise had fussed and panicked while he'd gone and got dressed; but it was he, not them, who'd brought me to the hospital and it was his soft white handkerchief I'd clutched to my tear-stained face all the way.

His name, funnily enough, really was Nick; and as the injury to my eye was quite minor and would have no lasting effects, I was secretly quite happy he'd twanged me. If he'd stay a while longer I'd be even happier!

'Carrie? Your friend's here to see you,' said the nurse who'd treated me. When I'd blinked and focused, the man at her side still looked good to me, even through only one eye!

540

'How're you feeling?' he asked, a delicious combination of contrition and machismo in one spectacular package.

'Oh, not so bad . . .'

No, not bad at all, seeing that face, and thinking of the even better body that went with it. 'There's no permanent damage. It hurts a bit, and I'll have to wear a patch for a day or two and use some drops, but otherwise I'll be absolutely fine.'

'Look,' he said, then grinned sheepishly because 'looking' was a sore point for me, 'I feel responsible. I want to be sure you're okay. The doctor said they'd given you something for the pain and it'd make you woozy. The least I can do is drive you home.'

' 'S all right. Don't go to any trouble,' I said, not meaning it. I was starting to feel spaced out. Sort of floaty and floppy and in need of a body to cuddle. There was no-one at home since Harry'd left, so why not accept? Season of goodwill and all that. It was time I had some goodwill. And he was gorgeous. *All* of him . . . It was easy to remember what was under that lambswool sweater, and more especially under those tight blue 501s!

In that fleeting moment, it'd been the nicest cock I'd ever seen: dark and hefty; thick and swingy and perky. Concentration was tricky at the moment, but it seemed to me he'd been rather perkier than he should've been given the laws on public decency and all that Mary Whitehouse-type stuff!

The thought of him getting a hard-on – right there on the stage, and for me – made me giggle insanely.

'Are you sure you're okay?' His handsome face creased in a worried frown. There was a thin film of oil still gleaming on his cheekbones and I thought of how it'd shone on his chest and his thighs . . . Oh God, even his cock had been oiled!

541

'Carrie! Are you all right?' he persisted.

I was well out of it. I'd only seen his tool for a split-second, but in my imagination it reared up and pointed in my direction; thick-veined and throbbing, oil glistening along its chunky length and glinting on its swollen, circumcised head.

'I'm fine.'

Lord, that stuff they'd shot me was strong! In my mind's unhampered eye, Nick was crouched over me, nude, erect and godlike, and just about to drive in right between my thighs. I could see him sliding, feel him moving, and my body went loose and wet.

I shook my head wildly to clear it, then spat out a foul word at the intense jolt of pain *that* caused.

'You're not fine at all, are you?' His hand was holding mine now, and his voice was firm, kind and utterly meltingly sexy! 'I don't want to hear any more about it. As soon as the doc gives the word, I'm going to drive you home and take care of you!'

'Okay, Santa . . . You win!'

I didn't try to shake off 'woozy' this time. I was all in favour of woozy if it kept my sweet Saint Nick at my side and gave me such outrageously detailed visions! My eyelids – both covered and uncovered – fluttered down, and behind them Nick was dancing again. In my bedroom, stark naked, heavily oiled and rampant, he moved far more explicitly than he'd done for his public audience. His long tanned hands traced his long tanned thighs, then he cupped his sex and pulled and squeezed and wanked and offered the whole thick clublike mass of it to me.

'Oh, yes . . .' Wanting, my free hand rose up and reached out. Then it was taken determinedly in his.

'You rest here,' he said as I blinked in disappointment at his fully clothed body. He was frowning again and looking at me with a sharp, narrow-eyed expression that made me wonder if he'd sussed my craziness.

'Rest here.' He squeezed my hands. 'As soon as I get the go-ahead, I'll take you home.'

'Mmmm . . .' I was drifting again, the images not purely sexual this time, but cuddly and comforting too. My eye twinged briefly but then decided to settle.

I waited. I rested.

This is mad! I thought later, slumped dreamily in the passenger seat of his car as we sped towards my flat. I don't know this man from Adam. I've barely spoken half a dozen words to him. I've seen his cock, but I've no idea what's inside his head. He could be a psycho or a rapist!

Yet the cautious, conscientious medical staff had seen fit to entrust me to him. Who was I to argue? It was Christmas: season of good cheer. After the hassle I'd been through with Harry, it was about time I had some of that peace on earth, wasn't it? Or a piece of something! I giggled again, and Nick's eyes flicked briefly towards me, checked, then returned to their scrutiny of the road.

I seemed to spend the whole journey in a haze of sexy smells. My own Shalimar was still much in evidence, and so was the classic and pervasive man's cologne that drifted from the folds of Nick's jacket, a thick biker-style leather he'd draped round my shoulders to keep out the cold. It was Christmassy smell, Old Spice or something, and invigoratingly light and clean. But its freshness didn't affect me as much as some of the other odours floating around: darker scents; downer and dirtier; mansweat and musk, and the shocking, tangible aroma of my own female arousal.

I couldn't believe what was happening or how I was feeling. He'd nearly blinded me, and now I was lolling around in his car like an easy pick-up, speeding towards my flat where I'd surely ask him inside. Even so, I knew in my soul there was no real danger in Nick. He'd hurt me once, but he wouldn't hurt me again. I didn't just feel that, I *knew* it.

When we arrived, I discovered my body wasn't functioning as well as my mind. My legs buckled as I tried to unlock the door, and within seconds I was in Nick's arms and being Jane to his Tarzan as he carried me through my flat to the bedroom.

What followed would've been either mortifyingly embarrassing or sensationally erotic if I'd been firing on all cylinders . . .

Beautiful Nick undressed me – beautifully. He cleaned off my make-up – working like a surgeon around my battered eye – then washed me and bundled me into a nightgown. He performed the most intimate of services with gentleness and not the slightest lapse in propriety. He even helped me brush my teeth!

When he finally deposited me in my bed and tucked the duvet up round my ears, I was feeling decidedly peculiar, but in a decidedly wonderful way: pampered cossetted and charged with a light sexual fever. Nick's touch had been perfectly neutral, but my body wasn't! I was turned on, but not so intensely it made me uncomfortable. I was floating, my sex felt warm and moist, ready for love but deliciously relaxed. I put my arms up to pull Nick down beside me, then drooped and sighed and let myself be covered again. I felt as if I were outside myself and watching. Watching Nick brush my hair carefully back from my face, adjust the patch over my dodgy eye, then kiss me just once on the cheek.

'I'll stay here tonight just in case. My stuff's in the car. Is it okay if I use your shower? I'm still all yucked up with oil.'

'Mmmm ... yeah ... Shall I scrub your back?' Snuggled beneath the covers, I wondered vaguely if I'd actually got the energy.

'Look, you ... sleep!' He laughed – a soft and incredibly sensual sound – and I must have obeyed because I never heard the water running.

My sleeping dreams weren't as straightforward as the ones I had awake. In the illogical dreamland world, I was sitting on the table in the nightclub with my skirt round my waist and my hand working furiously between my legs. I was the show, and the men on the stage were watching me! The sensation of exhibiting myself was supremely arousing and I was right on the point of coming when my ex-boyfriend Harry elbowed his way through the adoring throng, shouted 'Slut!' and punched me right in the eye! The pain felt like breaking glass and I crumpled into a ball like an injured child. Then suddenly Santa Claus was hugging me better and say, 'Hey, it's all rightl Take it easy!'

'Hey! It's all right! Take it easy!'

One minute I was thrashing around in my nightmare, the next I was cooing and sighing in a pleasant half-awake doze. A strong hand was stroking my shoulder.

Some fragments of the dream remained however. My own hand actually was between my legs, and I removed it as surreptitiously as I could. My eye was prickling slightly, but the sensation was less intrusive than the one running the length of my back – especially in the lower regions where my nightdress had rucked up to my waist. A solid column of heat was pressed close as close and I was being nestled gently against it; while a rather smaller but even more solid column was intent in burrowing itself into the crease between my thigh and the curve of my bottom!

'You were shouting in your sleep,' whispered Nick, still caressing my shoulder and showing no inclination to remove his cock from between my legs.

'I was having a funny dream.' Somehow, I just couldn't seem to help myself pushing back against his erection.

'Yes, I'd gathered that.' As his hand settled over mine, there was a smile in his voice and I blushed in the darkness, knowing that *he* knew precisely what *I'd* been so unconsciously doing.

We seemed locked in a kind of magic stasis – his hand on my hand on my belly, and his cock throbbing quietly away against my leg. It was like hovering on the brink of a huge and very tempting gulf – and wondering if you'd really got the guts to fly!

I suppose some things are inevitable, though. His hips bumped, I went 'Mmmm. . .' again and his hand left mine and started travelling.

One finger slipped slowly and silkily into my cleft, parted the hair, parted the soft puffy lips, then settled like light itself on my clit. The softest of pressures made me groan, and as Nick seemed to be in no hurry, we drifted into a long luxurious limbo time devoted purely to *my* pleasure.

Our bodies lay like spoons, I had his cock pressed snugly against my bottom and his hands at my breast and my crotch – stroking and palpating, delicately caressing and fingering. I suppose in the cold light of day, it could've seemed calculating and manipulative – push my buttons, turn me on – but in the special secret darkness it was a beautiful gift from a stranger. Whimpering and grabbing backwards at his thighs, I twined my feet around his and arched into my first sweet orgasm, my clitoris pulsing in long deep waves that raced on inwards from his steady, rubbing fingers.

He held me, gentled me, and made it happen and happen and happen again . . .

My 'Yes! Yes! Yes!' anticipated his simple uncomplicated questions.

'Are you ready? Do you want me?'

But when I moaned 'Yes!' again, he started to pull away.

'Look, Carrie, I'd better use something. I've some in my wallet . . .'

I couldn't bear not having him against me. 'No it's all right. Try the drawer behind you – in the bedside table.'

'You angel,' he whispered, kissing my neck, then turning away in the darkness. My back felt cool for a moment and there was a rustling, some small deft movements, and then his prick coming at me again, pressing strongly and encased in a condom. He teased it around my thighs, my labia and my moist slit, then took my hips in his big strong hands, tilted my pelvis and positioned himself carefully against my vagina.

'Guide me, love,' he purred in my ear.

It was a moment of perfectly balanced trust. I felt close to tears, loving his male vulnerability as I fed his warm length inside me.

Cradling me, cocooning me, curving his big dancer's body to warm my smaller, softer one, he slid one hand back between my thighs and pleasured my clit as he fucked me. His touch was so sure, so right, so even more beautiful than before that I spasmed immediately around him.

Our movement was limited, but in paradise all motion is relative – I could fly and I *did*! On eddies of hot hard bliss, I rose and rose, buoyed up by my sweet strong Nick, my accidental man from nowhere, with his animal grace, his giving hands and his sturdy hard-driving prick.

It wasn't all one way, of course. Somewhere in my own ecstasies I heard him shout, and felt him convulse and grab and push, push, push as he came. He stretched me beautifully and shafted me deeply, and even in orgasm, he still rubbed and pressed and fondled so I could soar again with him.

Eventually I did get the sleep he'd intended for me, the deep, dreamless healing sleep that only good sex can give you.

I got the waking that goes with it too: a kiss, a gentle shake, and a steaming cup of perfectly perked coffee!

'You're still here,' I observed blearily, scrunching up my good eye as I put aside the cup and focused on Nick.

I woke up faster then. He was still naked, still gorgeous, and I – I realised now – just what I'd always wanted.

'Look, I know this is utterly crazy and you've probably got plans already . . .' I swallowed, wished I didn't look so stupid with my eye patch; wished I could just wake up in bed looking like Madonna or somebody. 'What're you doing for Christmas? Do you want to spend it here? We could make it nice and cosy. Get crackers and stuff . . . If you haven't got anything on, that is?'

For a moment his morning-stubbly face was perfectly expressionless . . . then he grinned, and seemed to sparkle all over with pure sexy merriment. His hand dropped seductively to his lovely, beefy cock.

'Thanks, I accept.' He looked down at the large shaft thickening in his fingers. 'I don't seem to have anything at all on!' Very gently, he took my hand, then folded it around his erection in place of his own. 'But we can soon do something about that!'

Reaching into the drawer, he drew out another condom and smiled as he tore at the foil. 'Merry Christmas, Carrie. Let's start celebrating . . .'

Pretty Young Thing

I'D ALWAYS WANTED to sleep with him. Since the first moment I saw him: when he was just fifteen and I was living with someone else. I'd taken one look at that face and body – and in my mind we'd been naked and fucking.

It'd been impossible then, unthinkable: he was underage and the son of a schoolfriend I'd just re-discovered, and I was working hard at 'me and Peter', a relationship already on the skids without my looking elsewhere.

There'd been everything against Ross and me. All I could do was ogle and dream and blame stress and some kind of early mid-life crisis. But now – three years on – that 'everything' had changed.

I'd invited Joan to the villa for a spell, and though I could see she was dying to accept, she frowned suddenly, then started to dither.

'Can I bring Ross along too? He's really down in the dumps just now. Some little twit's jilted him and of course it's the end of the world. They take things so seriously at that age, don't they?'

I nodded, appalled at my own inner excitement on hearing his name.

It'd been a while since I'd last had sex – what with the bitterness over Peter – yet just that one word, that one short name, and my sex seemed warm, aching and empty.

I was annoyed too: cross with Joan. I was twice Ross Frazetti's age, yet *I* still took things seriously. It was easy for Joan to be dismissive; she'd dumped her unwanted Italian husband with an ease that made me shudder, and with precious little thanks for the beautiful son he'd given her.

It was late afternoon when they arrived. While Joan was happy to settle on the patio with a drink, Ross had disappeared off up to his room, lingering only long enough to make an even bigger impression on me than he had at fifteen. He was still the same pretty young thing he'd been then: a fine-boned, dark-haired poetic-looking boy. But now he was tall and had muscles too. Not to mention a raw, masculine grace, and a thought-provoking bulge in that most crucial of places!

It was more than simple, anatomical assets. This year's Ross had a hint of the big cat about him, a pure, yet discreet alpha-maleness as unstudied as it was exciting. But it was his eyes which really got to me: brown, almond-shaped and enormous, they held a pain that was heavy and dark and sexual. To me, those shadows were explicit; they said that for all his quietness and youth, Ross had loved – and fucked – and lost.

Despite that he wasn't a sulker; quite the reverse. Overturning his mother's pessimistic predictions, he came down promptly for dinner, and though it was obvious that *he* knew *we* knew he'd got problems, he smiled and chatted – and was gently and understatedly charming. I began to wonder what he was like when he was actually *happy*:

devastating, probably; unstoppable; fatal. I imagined myself having an orgasm right there at the table. But he ate next to nothing, and his handsome face was pale under its Mediterranean caramel glow, almost ghostly against the matte black cotton of his sombre shirt and jeans.

I couldn't eat either. Other hungers consumed me, and I drank to make them bearable. I felt a nice, sensual buzz building as I studied his long, slender-fingered hands; his soft, slightly pouting lower lip and those huge, hurting, sex-dark eyes. I wanted to take him in my arms and hug all his troubles away – then take his cock deep into my hungering body and finish the job completely!

And that, I suppose, was what woke me later. It was a shock to actually want someone again. The trauma of my break-up had numbed me. Even before that, out of sight and mind, Joan's black-haired son had been simply an exquisite, but occasional fantasy: something pretty to look at while I made myself come.

It was a hot night, but I pulled a thin shirt over my nakedness as I stepped out on to the veranda. Looking along, I saw that my guests, like me, had both left their French windows open for coolness.

The room next to mine contained Joan, snoring softly and sleeping the sleep of the pleasantly plastered. She'd matched my every glass of wine with a large hand-mixed Martini of her own, but never having had a hangover in her life, she'd probably just get a fantastic night's sleep and be ready to start again in the morning!

Barefoot, I judged my steps carefully as I approached the next window along. Then I stopped altogether. Vaguely familiar noises drifted from between the fluttering curtains.

Muffled sobs, small stifled groans; the sound of someone very young, male, and desperately, desperately unhappy. I hardly dared look into the room, but no power on earth could've stopped me.

He lay like a dark wraith in the middle of the wide white bed. His eyes were closed, his face contorted, and his right hand was wrapped tightly around his cock. Lost in grief, and wracked by unsatisfied desire, my sweet, sad Ross was wanking.

It was the most beautiful sight I'd ever seen, and the most arousing: moonlight, tears and an erection. The combination was intoxicating; my head felt light as thistledown and my sex grew wet and heavy.

I wanted that wide, rosy-tipped club inside me; that penis, that tool; the big, man's cock that sprang up from the loins of a gentle, troubled boy. I must've gasped or sighed or something, because Ross's eyes flew open, then went wide and blank with horror.

'No!' he cried indistinctly, 'Oh, no! Oh, no! Oh, no!' Before I could speak or move towards him, he'd abandoned his stiffened flesh and was dragging the sheets right up and over his blushing face and body.

'Ross! It's all right! Don't hide!' I called out softly.

'Please! Go away!' came a faint voice from beneath the white linen layers. 'Please go away, Mrs Lovingood! Please go. I'm sorry.'

'What's to be sorry for, Ross?' Trembling, I crossed the room and sat down on the side of the bed, 'The tears? Or the fact that you were touching yourself?' I'd seen it now. Seen what I most wanted. I had to stay and make him forget the girl who'd hurt him; or at least try to.

Slowly, feeling as if I were flushing out a scared forest creature, I teased the sheet down to his waist. His eyes glowed up at me from a face burning hot with embarrassment.

'I shouldn't have been—' He paused, snagging that soft lower lip between his teeth. 'I've no right to be doing *that* here in your house, Mrs Lovingood.' He turned away, his perfect profile cameoed by the whiteness of the pillow.

'My name's Amy.' I tugged the sheet clear of him, and his cock bounced up and slapped against his flat, gilded belly. 'And why shouldn't you masturbate here? I do.'

Ross seemed at a loss how to respond. His eyes flicked from his rampant body to my face, and his mouth dropped open in astonishment.

'Sex can heal as much as hurt, Ross,' I said quietly, edging closer. 'I've been lonely ... Why shouldn't I give myself pleasure? Why shouldn't you give *yourself* pleasure? It can only make you feel better.'

His fingers curved slightly on the sheet, and his erection swayed. Something in him was reaching out to me – and I knew now that I could take what I wanted.

Ross. His body. His strong young cock.

'Let's help each other, sweetheart,' I whispered leaning over him and flipping open the buttons on my shirt. With a faint swish, it slid off my shoulders.

Ross's eyes widened even more, but I loved him for the knowing smile that formed on his lush young lips. He was shy; but not *that* shy. I'd surprised him, yes, but he wasn't a helpless virgin, or slow on the sexual uptake. Looking at the rigid bar of his prick, I felt my mouth water and my sex moisten. Foolish girl who'd rejected such a treat! His eyelashes fluttered like twin black fans and he arched his fabulous body towards me in an attitude of complete abandon.

You hussy! I accused him silently. You dirty little

flirt! In need and amusement I pressed my lips to his. How quick he was to adapt, to allure me. I ran my fingers down his flanks as he opened his mouth to my tongue and moaned around it, long and wantfully. His hips lifted as I kissed him, his hot flesh seeking a place to bury itself. In answer I lay full length upon him and massaged his tool with my belly. Two long flexible hands slid around my bottom and began – slowly – to knead.

I'd come with the half-formed idea of 'teaching' this boy something, but as he caressed the cheeks of my arse, and flicked his fingers delicately into my crack, I began to question my own assessment. He could well need some help with his relationships, but as the moments passed – and his hands grew bolder and his touch hotter – it was obvious he knew all he'd ever need to know about the erotic anatomy of women. Maybe that was it? He'd been too much for the chit who'd jilted him! Perhaps he needed someone more ... more experienced? Suddenly, caressing him with my quivering belly wasn't nearly enough!

I pulled a little way out of the clinch and took his cock in my questing fingers. He was like warm, moist suede stretched taut over a tempered steel core. I sighed. There was no hardness like a young man's hardness and I had the crazy urge to wank him to orgasm. I wanted to see his thick white juice come spurting out and fly across both our bodies. I wanted to drink his essence and massage it into my skin like some intimate elixir of youth.

My poise was in tatters now, and ideas of choreographing this lovemaking myself had flown clean out of the open window. One strong young hand closed tight around my bottom, and the other pushed boldly but gently between my legs. A finger entered my vagina, then swirled and probed and explored. I felt my clitoris twitch madly, then almost sigh in my slit as a smooth flat thumb settled firmly upon it and began slowly and demonically to rotate.

How could he know this was my favourite way of being touched? How could he know I liked tiny nibbling kisses at the same time? How could he know I was mellowed-out putty in his oh-so-sweet young hands! When his fingers left my sex, I chuntered like a kid losing its favourite toy.

But I cried out again, with awe this time, and pleasure, as he slid both his hands between my thighs and opened me wide, then took a rock-solid hold on my hips. Following his lead, I brought one leg up and across his pelvis, then let him lower me carefully on to his tool.

'Oh, Ross, Ross, Ross!' I babbled as he nudged into my wettened groove. How could he seem bigger than ever? Thicker and larger than life? As he pulled me downwards, he pushed his own body up – rising into my vagina like a great, smooth missile. I felt impaled, speared, stretched; mercilessly and wonderfully filled. His fingers dug deep in the flesh of my buttocks as he jammed me down harder than ever.

I was in the superior position and should've been in control. But it was this slender young god, prone beneath me, who had the true upper hand. He swung up into me with an imperious strength and force, using my own weight to get deeper inside me. Each plunge dragged deliciously on my clit, and tugged on some secret interior muscle that joined it directly to my womb and breasts. Crouched above him, I reached down to rub myself, just above his sliding cock, then opened my eyes to watch him watching me. He smiled, half smugly, half in wonder, then drove himself on and up right into my palpitating core.

I thought I might burst – then it seemed as if I did. My whole body was one collapsing, imploding mass, locked in a pleasure so intense the very moon and stars seemed to blaze like a fire in my loins.

Dazzled, I found myself slumped across Ross's chest, weeping and drooling, kissing his man-scented neck. His scream of ecstasy rippled beneath my lips, vibrating in his fine young throat as he surged and spurted inside me.

Minutes passed, and we settled down side by side, still half-entangled. Our bodies were all sticky and sweaty, but lying against him – still throbbing within – I felt irresistibly beautiful and young. In my heart of hearts I knew I wasn't technically either, but tomorrow would be the time to face facts.

I closed my eyes; closed out the facts and let love in.

'Amy?' His voice was faint, drowsy, still rough with sex. 'I feel better now. Much better.'

Snuggling closer, feeling better myself, I breathed in his sweetness and slept.

Studies in Red

OH, NO! Why now?

Lacey Hanlon sighed in the bathroom and studied the small splinter-shape of red that'd ruined all her plans.

Why now?

'Why not, dimbo?' she mocked in a whisper, 'It's your own fault for not keeping tabs on yourself in the first place!'

It was her own fault, true, but it didn't make things better. Why now? Just when the sexiest, most beautiful man she'd ever met had started putting out those unmistakable vibes. Why, when she'd been within gasping distance of making love with a man so talented and ideal he was almost a fantasy, had an old and not-very-trusted friend finally decided to arrive?

Goddammit! Why now?

'I've invited the artist to my party,' Jemma had said, 'He only lives upstairs.'

Lacey and her friend had been admiring the focal point of Jemma's new flat – a huge, bold and very passionate-looking abstract oil painting. It seemed to depict nothing in particular, yet to Lacey's eyes, it was surprisingly accessible. Painted by a man, it screamed out the concept of 'woman': robust yet strangely delicate, it was thickly daubed but scattered with small, intriguing areas of intricate unfathomable detail.

It's gorgeous! she'd thought, and still did.

So is he! she'd decided later on seeing the artist himself across the proverbial crowded room. Gorgeous, but not at all in the way she'd expected.

To Lacey the word 'artist' had always been synonymous with 'wimp'. It suggested a pale, long-haired, wild-eyed, limp-wristed aesthete.

Nathan Levay, however, was a muscular, jeans-clad hunk with steady, bright blue eyes, a rich, obviously natural tan, and an almost brutal squaddie-style haircut. He looked more like Rambo than Leonardo.

'You're kidding!' had been Lacey's comment when Jemma had pointed him out.

'Nope, that's the notorious Nathan: artistic genius and all round sex-god. If I wasn't engaged, Lace, I wouldn't let *you* anywhere near him! But as I am spoken for, I'll introduce you . . . Come on!'

Sadly, that first time, it'd been no big deal. Despite her own flaring response to the man, Lacey had detected no answering spark in him. He'd been quietly charming; but nothing more. They'd chatted a few minutes, then Lacey had drifted away, facing the fact that the notorious Nathan Levay was a good-natured, courteous and surprisingly modest man who didn't particularly fancy her. Which was somewhat unfortunate because over the next few weeks she'd spent nearly all her free time fantasizing about him.

At the damnedest moments, she'd see those bright blue eyes, then see them darken as her dream-self made him want her. She'd imagine herself clinging to those broad, muscular shoulders, her nails piercing his smooth, bronzed skin as he bore down strongly and entered her. Nights had been both the worst and the best of times. When she was only half awake, her interior videos were almost pornographic. She saw him naked, erect and about to love her; his brown body imposing, his penis long, hard, and thick. She smelt his male smell, tasted his skin and his sweat and his juices; then had him drink deeply of hers.

That won't happen now, she thought glumly. Not tonight, and probably not ever.

Although, when Jemma had announced this second party, Lacey had hoped ... Boy, how she'd hoped! And she'd prepared herself for it with great care.

She'd fluffed out her brown-blonde curls into a full, soft cascade. She'd chosen clothes that flattered her trim body without being obvious: a white sail-cloth mini-skirt and bomber jacket, a pretty white lace camisole. Her look was inviting but cool, flirtatious yet pristine. Now she felt none of those, because when she'd slipped away to the bathroom, she'd found out her period had started.

Being both confusingly irregular, and so busy she never kept track of herself anyway, Lacey could only thank her lucky stars there was a tampon amongst the junk in the depths of her handbag. It was a blessing, too, that she'd started feeling dizzy when she had. A few minutes more would've seen blood on her chic white skirt as well as her thin silk knickers. It was a bitter thing to happen just when Nathan had taken an interest.

He'd been deep in conversation with another girl when Lacey had first arrived, and observing him

560

discreetly, she'd felt both furiously angry – and acutely turned on. The bastard was looking even more luscious tonight than last time.

Denim seemed to be his uniform, and a faded 501 shirt was a perfect foil for his rugged good looks, its hazy washed-out colour only accentuating the electric blue brilliance of his eyes. Not that those eyes had seemed to notice Lacey. Not until a quarter of an hour ago, that was.

Already feeling wonky, she'd looked up suddenly from her depression and found the man of her dreams standing right in front of her: offering wine and a smile, and with seemingly lots to talk about. Within seconds, she'd felt herself bloom beneath his hot blue scrutiny, and found wit and sparkle from out of nowhere to match his subtle but sexy conversation.

He hadn't touched her, or said anything overtly suggestive, but tonight's Nathan seemed dangerously different. His eyes, his body language, and even the scent of him had changed. It was as if once noticing her, he'd marked her as his, then cut her out from the herd as his prey.

The idea of Nathan as a predator was deeply exciting to Lacey. Not to mention ironic. *She'd* wanted *him* from the very first moment. *She'd* already marked *him* as hers. Then this'd happened!

Feeling ungainly, unhappy and vaguely grubby, she started to insert the familiar white cotton tube – then groaned aloud in intense, unwanted pleasure. Her body spasmed as her feverish imagination made the small white cylinder into something much bigger and smoother and hotter – the stiff, heated bar of Nathan Levay's long prick!

'I thought you had run away,' he said softly when Lacey returned to the party five minutes later, her

561

face white and her hands shaking.

I should've done! she thought wildly, smiling and murmuring a vague excuse. It'd be much less painful to leave now – to weep, drink alone and masturbate – than to stay and be forced into embarrassing explanations.

'Thanks.' She took the fresh glass of wine he gave her, then drank it far faster than she'd intended.

Her body was actually hurting now, but she suspected the discomfort had more to do with frustration than periods. It was a primal but infuriating fact that when she bled, she always felt ten times as randy. Her body would crave sex like mad at precisely the moment a man was likely to turn tail and run in revulsion!

She'd read all the advice in the sex manuals: 'A truly sensual man won't be put off, etc . . .' but her own experiences didn't match the textbook. She'd always met with shudders of distaste, and even with the protecting barrier of a condom, no man had ever wanted her enough to enter a body that was bleeding. Worse still, it was usually the macho men – like Nathan Levay – who'd ended up being the most squeamish.

'Are you all right?' His soft voice cut clean through her pessimism

'Yes, I'm fine.'

In reality she felt terrible. Those fabulous eyes were so kind, so concerned. They only made things worse. For Lacey, gentleness was the most alluring quality a man could possess, a far stronger turn-on than looks, charm, achievements and suchlike. With a few words of tenderness alone, Nathan could've bedded her easily, but as he'd got everything else going for him as well, the sense of loss was so keen it was almost exquisite.

'You aren't fine at all, are you?' He took the empty glass from her hand, sending a shudder through the whole of her body.

Please don't! she shouted inside, wanting him more than ever.

'You look pale. Why don't we get out of here for a spell? It's too crowded . . . you might feel better if you can breathe.'

This was the moment. The moment when two people at a party had the potential to be two naked bodies entwined in a bed.

He only lived upstairs.

Don't do this! Lacey told herself, adoring the weight of his hand on her waist as he guided her from the room.

Please, Lacey, no! she pleaded inside as he pulled her against him on the stairs, the action slow and achingly gentle. Stop him now, you fool! she implored within as he cupped her head in one big, caressing hand and lowered his lips on to hers. She murmured incoherently, then voices physical and mental were silenced by the beauty of his warm, mobile mouth, and the moist pressure of his tongue as it slid between her conquered lips.

Lacey felt her stomach quicker and her vagina flutter around its small, inanimate obstruction. Some part of her was still worrying about blood, but a greater part was crying out for Nathan's strong male body. Her sex was calling out to be propetly filled and her clitoris for the pressure of his flexible artist's fingers. Her breasts felt bursting and tender against his hard, denim-clad chest.

'I want you, Lacey,' he said as they drew apart, so he could open his front door. Desperate to explain, yet nervous beyond speech, she was powerless to do anything but be led like a lamb into his flat.

563

'I—' Her final protest was stifled when he placed one big hand lightly over her lips and used the other to press her smaller hand against his crotch. He was hot and massive beneath the denim.

I'll suck him! she decided in relief. Squeezing cautiously at his fine, hard bulge, she kissed the hand that lay across her lips. Fellatio wouldn't do much for her own frustration, but at least she could make love to *him*.

Nipping playfully at his fingers, she broke away, then sank to her knees before.him, scrabbling at his heavy belt buckle. Taken by surprise, Nathan gasped aloud; but Lacey refused to be fazed and prised open his denims, pushing aside his shirt, and tugged down his white cotton briefs.

His prick was big, stiff and splendidly, throbbingly ready, it was as beautiful as Lacey had imagined and more – already slickly moist at the tip.

'You lovely, lovely girl!' he groaned, sweeping her hair away from her face himself as she dipped forward to take his glans in her mouth. Folding her lips around her teeth and sucking very slowly and carefully, she pulled at his jeans and underpants at the same time, wiggling them down his legs to his ankles. Cupping her fingers around his sleek, hard bottom, she could feel the muscles there tensing as his cock plunged repeatedly between her wet and working lips.

She knew this wasn't what he'd planned, but the thought of how tender Nathan *would've* been had an amazing effect on Lacey. Happy and relaxed, she felt her throat open and go loose, allowing him in far deeper than she'd ever taken a man before.

He was grunting steadily, his pleasure loud and uninhibited, when suddenly he froze to absolute stillness.

Isn't he going to come? thought Lacey, feeling thwarted. She kneaded his taut bottom encouragingly, then to her surprise and bewilderment, felt herself being prised gently off his cock.

'You're too good to me, you wonderful woman.' Nathan's voice was ragged, but his smile was determined. 'It's your turn now.'

'But—' Once again he stopped her complaints; this time with his lips, bending down to her with an astonishing grace considering he was still hobbled by his clothes.

And with that same grace, he quickly and efficiently stripped naked before her.

Even locked in her panic, Lacey had to gasp in awe at the fabulous condition of his body. Strongly but not grotesquely muscled, he was a perfect blend of power, strength and long-limbed elegance. His skin was a glossy toasted gold, and though his chest was smooth and hair-free, his pubic area was densely flossed with black.

Completely nude, he knelt down beside her and pressed the full length of his bare body against her clothed one.

'I know what's bothering you,' he murmured into the tangle of her hair.

'You don't,' she said through gritted teeth, torn between ecstasy and horror as he cupped her breast through its thin silken covering.

'I do!' He pushed down the flimsy garment, took her nipple between his long, nimble fingers. 'You've got your period and you think it'll put me off.'

'I . . . Yes. That's it,' she babbled, falling against him, seeking the comfort of his warmth and solidity.

And yet, she still felt terror. She could feel the ripple of blood inside her, see its redness in her mind's-eye, while everything around them looked so white and unmarked.

The rug they crouched on was white. Her clothes were white. Even golden-skinned Nathan, though darker, was immaculate in his naked peerless beauty. 'But it doesn't matter, my sweet.' His voice was soft as his hand slid up her thigh and cradled her silk-covered crotch. 'I'm a painter. I'm always daubed with colour . . . My hands get covered with it. So does most of the rest of me, given the way I work.' She couldn't see him grinning but she could hear it. She thought of Jemma's painting, then imagined its creation. Nathan moulding the pigment in place with his hands – his fingers, arms, face and chest all smeared not only with red, but with a whole pallette of other colours too.

'It'll get everywhere,' she whispered, then groaned with pleasure as Nathan's pressing palm rotated. Slowly. 'And I haven't got any more—' His lips covered hers, his exploring tongue pushing away all doubts and all inconvenient lacks.

'Don't worry,' he said when he'd subdued both her mouth and her body. Limp as a doll, Lacey felt herself whisked up in his arms, and then being carried into his bedroom and placed in the centre of a large bed. A bed with a milk white chenille bedspread. 'Relax,' he went on, kissing her cheek, his superb body looming over her briefly before he strode away towards the door, 'My sister stays here sometimes. She'll have left everything you need.'

In his absence, Lacey dreamed because she didn't want to think; or worry. Rolling luxuriantly on the soft white bedcover, she kicked off her shoes and shuffled out of her jacket. Would Nathan want to take the rest off himself? Still in her short skirt, with her thin lace top still pushed down off one breast, she followed his instructions and relaxed. Pressing her hand to her belly, she felt one kind of ache recede and another, better one, grow strong. As it did, Nathan appeared in the doorway, then walked, magnificent, towards her.

He dropped a selection of objects on to the bed at her side: fluffy white towels, tissues, packets of condoms and tampons, a drum full of scented wipes.

'There! Everything we need,' he said with a smile, dropping himself amongst the paraphernalia and lying down beside her.

Lacey stroked the long gleaming flank of the most beautiful male body she'd ever seen, then started helping Nathan undress her.

It began with a lot of giggling and squirming and shuffling on her part as they manoeuvred with clothes and towels. Then Nathan explored and stroked and soothed her. Gentle and encouraging, his mouth moved and murmured against her throat as he coaxed her into the final, crucial preparation. A careful tug on the small blue cord that dangled between her wantonly parted thighs. Lacey had one single clear jolt of fear, then forgot it completely as deft fingers plunged her into her crimson-wetness and started to make magic and art.

Within seconds she was coming. Whimpering like a child as her body experienced shocks of pleasure from the touch of her clitoris under Nathan's large, flat and delicately circling thumb.

'I love you!'

Crying out spontaneously, Lacey arched against him, pressing her red-smeared flesh against his hand, 'Oh God, yes, I love you!' Clinging on for dear life, bucking and heaving with bliss, she was dimly aware that it wasn't Nathan alone she so suddenly loved. Yes, she did love *him*, but she also loved herself and her own bleeding body – regardless of the mess it was making!

Blood was everywhere in seconds. In between massaging her to climax after climax, Nathan took up the bright fluid on his fingers and literally painted on her with it. Just a few slight strokes of his genius, and she had birds on her belly, flowers on her face, and butterflies streaming across her breasts.

He decorated himself too. Bold red slashes made him into a crew-cut Indian brave, then all their adornments were smudged to abstraction as he shimmied himself against her, laughing with erotic glee.

It should've been gory, but instead it was only glorious.

Like painted savages, they frolicked and fondled and fooled with each other. As each delight blended into the next, Lacey could no longer keep a count of all the sensual acts they'd shared and the number of times that Nathan had made her come. It seemed that the whole of her body and mind had denatured and reformed into one immense, sublime, and flaming scarlet orgasm.

Everything was beautiful, everything was sacred and right, even her blood. Her blood on his cock; her blood on his mouth as he looked up from kissing her trembling belly and smiled.

'Why the sudden change? Why tonight?' Lacey asked later, in the shower, as Nathan sluiced his studies in red from her body.

'Because you looked vulnerable tonight. Pale and pure ... Like a canvas I could paint on.' He ski~nmed the streaming flow from her hips and thighs, its colour faintly pink but clearing rapidly.

568

'And now you've painted. . .' Lacey held her breath. 'What next?'

'This!' he whispered, sweeping his arms around her squeaky clean body and clasping it to the strong, hard length of his, 'The painting was fine. But it's the canvas underneath I want to keep.' His voice was low and almost shaky, but clearly audible through the steady hiss of the shower.

'Keep? What do you mean "keep"?' Earlier, in orgasm, she'd told him she loved him; but now she knew it was true.

'Just what I said . . .'

'For how long?' He was making patterns on her back with the water now, but to Lacey he was painting with fire on her soul and drawing out their future on her own wet skin.

'As long as you want to stay, my love,' Nathan said softly, tilting up her face for a kiss, 'How about forever?'

Quiet Storm

AT LAST, A real, nice, honest, beautiful man to have sex with.

I'd had that thought, a month ago, when Bryn Stevens had first joined our unit – and I was still having it now, even after four weeks of his total indifference.

Well, that's not exactly true. Bryn had been civil and almost friendly towards me in all our workaday dealings; it was only when the wind blew even vaguely in the direction of sex that he seemed to cool right off. Which was a bit of a problem because I was in a heatwave for him!

I hadn't felt like this in ages. Since my last relationship, I'd been stuck in the sexual doldrums. I hated casual flings and there didn't seem to be anyone around to get in deeper with. I just didn't fancy anybody enough.

Until Bryn walked – or should I say limped – his way into my life. Our new training officer was a modern classic: a tall, dark and sensitive hunk with above-average intelligence and eyes as grey as thunderclouds. It was the idiosyncrasies, though, the deviations from the norm, which made him so irresistibly wantable. He had a rangy, understated strength and a fit man's poise and composure, but it was his barely detectable limp that set him apart as special, vulnerable and different.

It was the same with his moods. His confidence and charm made him a very desirable companion and an accomplished and effective trainer. He was especially good at teaching women, and his off-the-cuff jokes and perfectly judged light-hearted flirting made them far more relaxed and liable to learn than a strictly conventional training style would've done.

He seemed to get along well with his colleagues too. He was nothing short of dynamic in team situations and his ideas were always exciting. But sometimes, just sometimes, when on the surface he was at his most smiling and agreeable, I'd spot this 'otherness' in there too: a kind of storm in the back of his eyes; a discreet but palpable rage that was as puzzling as it was elusive. The strangest thing of all was that it often seemed directed at me. What had I done? I wondered. Except fancy the man something rotten.

But I hadn't been obvious about it; that's not my way. I'd been helpful but not pushy; friendly and approachable but not forwrad. All in all, I couldn't figure out why I was getting these occasional but turbulent black looks. I'm no great beauty, I know, but some men would've been quite pleased to get my attentions . . .

Patsy Colvin doesn't give up easily, however, so without making a major deal of it I set out to get the low-down on the mercurial Mr Stevens. The divisional grapevine yielded swift and intriguing fruit . . .

Eighteen months ago, Bryn had been all set to

establish his own training company – a fact which didn't surprise me given his skills – but just before the final negotiations, he'd had a serious motorbike accident. He'd been in hospital for several months and in consequence his business had folded without ever seeing the light of day – which explained why he was stuck in the backwoods of local government training rather than having a high-profile enterprise of his own. The accident also explained his limp, and the intense physiotherapy and rehabilitation he must've needed afterwards accounted for his superb state of fitness now.

It didn't explain everything, though . . . A certain amount of professional frustration was natural and understandable, but where did the personal resentment come from, the distinct but furious animosity I sensed when Bryn looked at me?

Armed with this scant background knowledge I decided to re-double my efforts. I had my blonde hair cut and restyled, I went on a diet, and I invested in several smart but understated new 'work' suits. I went about my campaign calmly and quietly and although it might've been my imagination, I did seem to start making some headway.

I began masturbating again too. Those erotic doldrums had become a high pressure area now, and one night, after spending the whole day wondering why Bryn wouldn't make a pass at me, I started stroking my clitoris while I thought of him.

No stranger to the joys of self-pleasure, I even dug out my vibrator; a sleek, quiet toy that I'd played with quite a bit in the past and suddenly felt a great need for now.

This time, though, I didn't use pictures from my favourite magazines to get myself going. It was Bryn in my mind as I rubbed myself lightly with my fingers; Bryn as I switched on my vibrant electric friend and skimmed it over my sex. It was Bryn flicking at me and teasing me as the thick pleasure-giving cylinder slid rudely into my body. I didn't usually bother with insertion, but now it seemed a good way to simulate a cock. With the help of a smooth, slightly warm vibrator I could imagine Bryn's hot, pulsing erection inside me and I cried out his name as I climaxed.

Matters came to a head of sorts when, as a team, we all went swimming in our lunch-hour. I was pleased with my slimming attempts because my blue and white stripey swimsuit looked even more flattering than I'd hoped. I got plenty of admiring looks, but unfortunately not from the quarter I wanted.

The man himself looked fabulous, as I'd expected. His body was long, lean and olivey-brown, with muscles that spoke of many gruelling hours in the gym. And he filled out his sleek black Speedo trunks to perfection!

Even his scars seemed sexy: a cries-crossing of thin, pink puckered lines that girdled his lower back and dipped mysteriously beneath the dark shiny surface of his swimtrunks. Whatever had happened to him must've hurt like hell, and I felt a sudden urge to nurture. It was weird, but I couldn't stop wishing I'd known him much sooner and been able to nurse him back to health; been the one who'd restored him to his sex life . . . That black Speedo left nothing to the imagination. As I back-stroked through the water, I fantasized about other kinds of strokings: the long searching glide of Bryn's fingers on my body; the slow, steady pump of his cock as it stroked its way deep into my sex.

He was a superb swimmer, and seemed to be

having fun; until – inevitably! – he caught me ogling his thinly covered crotch. That changed everything. A look of black rage crossed his water-jewelled face and he whirled away and threw himself into the deep end for a series of fast and punishing laps that effectively cut him off from the rest of us.

Strangely enough, he was okay with me afterwards, and at work, but I couldn't help noticing that frown again when we found out that he and I had to work together on a new training pack. It was a rush job that'd been outstanding for far too long, and there was no way we could meet our deadline without taking it home to finish it. Together.

I tried to stay cool and remember it was just routine and that he didn't particularly like me, but as I let him into my flat and we spread out the materials on the coffee-table, I couldn't keep my soaring spirits down. It was deadly boring stuff – a Health and Safety Training Course the unit was hoping to market – but even so Bryn attacked it with his usual competence and enthusiasm, and in spite of the peculiar 'edge' between us, he soon made the whole thing seem fascinating – even worth getting worked up about.

Not that I wasn't worked up already. I'd seen Bryn in a suit, and in his swimming trunks, but not in anything more 'in between'. In jeans and a soft, lambswool sweater, he was even more mouthwatering than ever, and I was soon paying far less attention to safety regulations than I was to his strong, serious face and his lean, die-hard body. Especially the portion concealed behind the faded blue denim at his groin. I kept thinking about how distracting it'd looked in black lycra . . . and when I got up to demonstrate a trip hazard for one of the pack's illustrations, it was hardly surprising I actually went headlong. It was unintentional, I swear it was, but I ended up in Bryn's arms in a classic *Gone with the Wind* clinch.

I've always believed in the power of wishful thinking, and as I looked up into his fine grey eyes, I decided to test out my theories. I hoped. I willed. I silently begged him to kiss me.

And he did.

It was a long kiss, and thorough. A kiss that engaged the whole of his firm, assertive mouth and his mobile, flexible tongue. I responded gallantly and in kind, thrilled to bits that he was just as powerful, sexy and masterful as I'd hoped for.

Happy as a sand-girl, I breezed straight into the next stage. Though his lips were sensual, Bryn's hands seemed strangely reticent. Taking the initiative, I passed searching fingers tentatively across his crotch . . . and suddenly I was on the floor again!

He'd dumped me; all but dropped me. Plunging down from the dreamy heights of the kiss, I found myself sitting on the rug and furiously angry.

'What the hell is it, Bryn?' I demanded, my body as thwarted as my mind. We'd been so close. So ready. 'What's the matter? I thought you liked me . . . I thought you might even be getting round to *wanting* me?'

He was on his feet now, turning away, his straight body hunched as if in pain.

'I do like you, Patsy. And I'd *like* to want you.' Where was the authority in his voice now, the confidence? He was whispering almost, and not making sense at all.

'What do you mean "like to want"? You either do or you don't.'

'It's not that simple,' he said, turning back

575

towards me, and for one second, looking down-wards. Towards his undisturbed groin ... 'I'm impotent, Patsy. A damp squib. I can't get it up.'

In some ways it was the scariest moment of my life, but I didn't feel either revulsion, panic or pity. What I still felt was desire. I was turned on for him and filled with a strange, new, almost missionary zeal. Okay, so we couldn't fuck ... But what else could we do?

'I had an accident. I suppose you know.' Slowly, wearily, he sank down on the settee, then pulled me up from the floor to sit with him. 'Some nerves in my back and pelvis were damaged. Everything else got back to normal, but sadly ...' raising his slender right hand, he waggled a finger forlornly, 'not that.' He sighed and let his hand fall to his long, denim-covered thigh. 'I know it's not an excuse, but that's why I've been so "off" with you, Patsy. Every time I look at you, I realise just exactly what I've lost.'

He smiled then: a soft, wry, very beautiful little-boy smile. At that, my stubborn, determined streak flowed out into a mile-wide river. I reached out and took his hand, folding my own fingers around the one he'd used to demonstrate his deficiency.

'Look, do you know for certain it ... it doesn't work any more? Have you tried?'

'Yes, I had a whole series of embarrassing tests and there wasn't even a flicker.' The smile turned sad, and there was a bitter twist to his sexy kissable mouth. 'I'm sorry, Patsy. There's nothing I'd like more than to be able to make love to you.' His fingers moved in my grasp, swivelling neatly until he was able to stroke my hand and caress it smoothly, delicately and gently. He hardly seemed aware of what he was doing.

'But what about feeling?' I was getting ideas now. Bold, outrageous, exciting ideas. 'Even if you can't get hard, do you still have . . . um . . . sensations?'

'I don't know. I've never thought about it.' When he looked up, I could see he was following my meaning. His eyes were bright, almost wild. 'I've been too pissed off with my body to investigate the situation . . . Too angry.'

'Let's investigate now then.' Bold as brass, I reached for the belt of his jeans.

'Are you sure?' He put his hand over mine and stilled it, but I sensed that he didn't really want to stop me.

'Yes! What have we got to lose?' I wasn't quite the hotshot trainer that Bryn was, but in my own way I was no mean motivator. Personal development had always been my special forte. 'If nothing happens for you at least you'll've tried. And as for me, well, there's nothing wrong with your hands, is there? Or your mouth?' Even as I said it, it dawned on me what I'd *really* always liked best in bed anyway!

Bryn didn't answer. Instead, he prised my fingers gently from his jeans . . . and started undressing me.

He was deft and efficient, as he was in all things; as each garment came off, he caressed the area it'd covered. There was no panic, no fumbling, just grace and pure, sensual enjoyment. His fingertips were beneficent yet probing, skipping lightly over ticklish areas and pressing harder at the parts that cried out for it. When my breasts were naked, he cupped them, one in each hand, and pressed his face between them, his hot breath a pleasure in itself. His faint evening stubble was deliciously abrasive; as if sensing this, he smoothed his cheeks across my nipples, one after the other, again and again and again.

'Oh, yes!' I sobbed, loving the sensation both for itself and for its effect between my legs. I tried to pull off my panties, but again, he stopped my efforts and supplanted them with his. Sliding away the inhibiting white cotton, he tossed it aside, then opened my slit with his fingers.

'Hey, you!' I gasped as his thumb flicked at my clitoris. 'You've still got your clothes on. This's as much for you as for – Oh, oh God! Aaagh!'

I'd wanted him for four weeks and it didn't take much to make me come. A couple of tiny experimental strokes with his thumb-tip and the whole of my wet, needy sex was in motion. For a blank, timeless moment, I completely forgot what I'd been going to say, or even think. All I could do was babble and moan and sob while Bryn coaxed orgasm after orgasm after orgasm out of me with his sweet and rhythmical petting.

When I stopped shouting, he laid me tenderly back against the cushions and pushed my sweat-soaked hair off my brow. I grinned up at him, still panting, my thighs lolling apart and my happy sex gaping and pouting.

'Now you, mister,' I said, feeling wonderful.

'We don't need to,' he faltered. 'It'll be one helluva non-event. There'll be nothing for *you*, Patsy ...' He reached down and cupped his groin, flashing me that beautiful juvenile smile again.

'I still want to try.' I was already tugging at his jumper.

He stopped fighting and succumbed to me, his actions more hopeful than his words had been; especially when I brushed against his nipple with the jumper and got an appreciative 'ooh' in response. I touched him there again when his chest was bare and he shuddered with an unfeigned delight.

'Good?' I queried, feeling hopeful myself now.

'Very,' he purred, holding my fingertips in place with his own.

'How about elsewhere? Any action?'

' 'Fraid not.' He shrugged, and his chest and shoulders glistened like satin.

'Not to worry. We'll keep trying, shall we?'

I was enjoying myself in a different way now to when he'd touched me, but curiously the feelings were equally as exalted. His body was sculpted and magnificent, strangely whole in spite of the wounds it'd suffered. I loved the texture of his skin, the hardness and the cut of his physique; and it was this, and the courage it'd taken to get fit again, that defined him absolutely as a man . . . and not the organ that hung down between his legs.

When he was stripped to his underpants, he hesitated. 'I might as well keep them on. Nothing's happening.' He reached out towards me, ready to take me in his arms and start caressing me again.

But I'd made my mind up. 'No, let me see you. You're not scarred there are you?'

'No. Not at all!' He grinned ruefully. 'It looks fine. It just doesn't work anymore . . .'

His cock was as good to look at as the rest of him. A thick, pleasing length of flesh, circumcised, dark plummy red and nestling in a wiry forest of near-black pubic hair. I allowed myself one single wistful imagining of what might have been, then it was *my* turn to push *him* back against the cushions. I half hoped he might spring to life when I touched him, but willing as I was, no miracles occured. His penis felt alive and hot, and the skin of it was like fluid velvet, but as I handled him he remained quite inert.

At least his cock did. Bryn himself stirred on the couch, moving his limbs luxuriantly and making low sounds of pleasure in his throat. There was still no sign of an erection, but as I stroked him, it was obvious something was happening. I hardly dare ask what he was feeling . . . but suddenly he spoke up, letting his thighs fall open as he did so.

'That's good. So good. I didn't realise . . .'

Empowered by his praise, I set two hands to my task – one tracing the contours of his soft spongy shaft while the other went exploring and voyaging.

I caressed his nipples, his belly and his thighs. Then, as my confidence increased, I went in between the rounds of his buttocks, tickling him naughtily and urging him to tilt his hips. As he sighed and obediently lifted himself, I reached past his balls and touched his perineum and the rose of his anus. He was moaning quietly but continuously now, swirling his pelvis, still flaccid but in all other ways clearly excited.

As I stroked at his tight male hole, and tickled him there, there was the faintest of responses in his cock. The soft chunky organ seemed to ripple in my grasp, and when I pushed more daringly and my finger went right inside him, I felt him throb, then throb again, while moisture oozed thickly from the tip of his cock.

'Oh, please . . . Please. . .' he burbled and I pressed in deeper, feeling for the gland I knew was there but had never sought out before. When I found it he cried out softly, edging his body forward, inviting me to caress him from within.

It was new territory, an unknown land, but so obviously and wonderfully a pleasure zone. I wiggled my fingertip inside him; I massaged and rubbed and blindly circled . . . and within seconds he was jerking like a puppet, shouting and whining, his whole body trembling in my hold. His soft cock fluttered in my fingers like a captive bird and as I looked down, fascinated, it annointed my palm with a veil of silvery fluid.

It was such a small, inconspicuous event, but I sensed that its significance was awesome. As I slid my finger out of him, Bryn rolled sideways and away from me, curling into a ball, a huddle, a foetus. After a couple of seconds, I realised to my horror he was crying – really sobbing his heart out, his strong frame shaking in a great, quiet storm of weeping that terrified me right to the core.

He'd been injured. I'd gone too far. I'd hurt him . . .

But when he unfurled his long limbs again and sat up awkwardly in front of me, his face was as bright as an angel's.

'That was beautiful, Patsy. I never thought I'd feel all that again.' He scrubbed at his eyes with those narrow, graceful fingers of his, then grinned shame-faced. 'I don't know what to say.'

'You don't need to say anything.' I was thunder-struck myself. Overwhelmed. I wanted to kiss Bryn and hug him, do everything all over again for the sheer joy of seeing and feeling his climax. But first I had needs of my own. 'There're some things *you* could do. When you've got your breath back . . .'

I touched my fingers to his, and when our eyes met, his twinkled knowingly. He'd got my drift, and my pussy was already tingling. I looked at his clever, expressive hands and the generous promise of his mouth. I looked at his slumbering cock and thought how fine-textured and silky its skin was and how much I enjoyed just touching it. I thought about all the lovely, languorous things that Bryn and I could do together, and I smiled.

I'd been right after all. I *had* found a real, nice, honest, beautiful man to have sex with!

Perfecto

'TEARS AGAIN?' ASKED a soft, velvet-gentle voice.

I emerged blearily from my misery and craving and saw a crisply folded handkerchief being held out towards me.

'Yes ... Oh, dear ... I'm sorry...' I took the perfect white square and dabbed at my eyes with it. It was embarrassing me always blubbing like this; she'd only been here a week and this was the fourth time she'd caught me crying ...

'Care to talk about it?' that soothing voice enquired again, and I looked up mournfully from the already mangled hankie to the pale, concerned face of its owner.

Maria Samuels was *supposed* to be my new personal assistant, but with me like this, she was already shouldering almost all the office workload. I was luckier than I deserved that those slender shoulders were more than up to it ...

'Look, Sylvie,' she said quietly, 'I've been watching you. You're upset. Why don't you tell me what's wrong? I know we don't know each other too well, but I'd like to help.'

Yeah, she'd been watching me all right. I'd felt

those steady, penetrating eyes on me a lot during the past week. When I wasn't pining for Peter, that was.

They were beautiful eyes too, I realised as she sat down beside me and placed an immaculately manicured hand on my arm.

She was right. I needed to tell someone. But I'd been so wound up in Peter for so long, there was no-one . . . Except her.

So out it came. The story of Peter and me. The story of a capable successful woman acting like a sex-enslaved bimbo over a man who was divine in bed but a selfish, ten-timing monster everywhere else . . . Once I'd started, I couldn't stop. Amongst the sobs and hiccups, I blurted out things I'd never told anybody. How if Peter smiled that filmstar smile of his I was putty. How he'd make me beg for more of his perfect *Joy of Sex* fucking. How he'd make me climax in a way so expert I half expected a judge to pop up and give marks for technical merit. And how afterwards – while my body still sizzled – I'd wish I hadn't been so 'easy' . . .

Maria sat through it: her eyes knowing but not disapproving, her fine oval face composed, almost nun-like. Until I started on the let-downs, the broken dates, the sightings with other women; the fact that even now, I still jumped when he whistled. Then, through a fresh batch of tears, I saw her change. Her deep, dark, golden-hazel eyes flashed with righteous female rage; yet her gently husky voice revealed nothing of it.

'Don't you think you've taken enough?' she said evenly, patting at her smooth, shimmering hair. It was that gesture that gave her away. I'd seen it several times when she was nervous or stressed. While thinking hard, her fingers would flick gracefully to her lovely streaked-chestnut bob – adjust a strand or two – yet never upset its flawless geometric styling.

'Yes. No. Oh, I don't know . . . I'm always like this in relationships! I'm great at business: I love pulling the strings at work. But when it comes to love and sex and stuff, I'm hopeless! It's my nature, Maria. I can't help it. I feel so ashamed, so out of control. I wouldn't mind being this way if Peter wasn't such a total shit! If someone nice took charge I'd be in seventh heaven . . .'

'So the gist of it is' – she took the hankie and folded it into a neat white square again – 'tonight's your anniversary of sorts, and he's leaving you alone and completely miserable?'

I nodded glumly. She was right: I was pathetic.

'Well you won't be!' Something foreign and powerful glinted in her eyes then, and suddenly I felt . . . felt scared. And excited too.

'You're going out with me tonight, Sylvie – to a club I know, called "Perfecto". And you're going to have an absolutely wonderful time!'

'But—'

'No buts! Trust me!' Her eyes flashed again, and her mouth – small, rosy and perfectly sculpted – curved into a smile so determined that my heart lurched heavily inside me, 'You like being taken charge of, don't you?'

I nodded again, feeling peculiarly light-headed.

'Well then! *I'm* taking charge!'

Later, as I got ready, then made my way to the pre-arranged meeting place, the second thoughts began to arrive.

For a start, I'd never been one for 'girlie' nights out: Chippendales and suchlike. And that club –

Perfecto – the name rang a vague beli. It was notorious for something, but for what, I couldn't for the life of me remember.

And another thing: I hardly knew anything about Maria!

Oh, her CV was peerless and her references irreproachable. She was superb at her job, but as a woman – an unknown quantity. All I did know, I realised with a sudden flush of confusion, was that she was quite exquisitely lovely to look at!

Not in an obvious way: that milky complexion and those even, sculpted features were only ever oh-so-lightly made up, and her conservative clothes were aptly matched by her immaculately kept hair, her discreetly polished nails and her generally impeccable grooming.

Yet, even as I catalogued these virtuous and commendable features, I recognised certain others: subversive ones that made me blush – furiously.

Beneath all that bandbox perfection was an equally perfect figure. She had full, voluptuous breasts, a sylph-slim waist and a long, inviting throat which seemed to demand that someone kiss it.

I didn't know why I was thinking things like that, but if Ms Samuels was so gorgeous, it seemed a waste that she go out with me!

Turning a corner, I checked my bearings. Half way down the street ahead was a lighted frontage and discreet neon signs, 'Perfecto'.

Then it hit me.

Several things hit me.

First, Maria was nowhere to be seen, although she'd promised she'd be here waiting. Second, I remembered why Perfecto was notorious.

There were people out on the pavement; people

laughing and drinking and boogie-ing to the dancebeats wafting from the open door; women boogie-ing – *only* women.

Perfecto was a gay club and it was 'ladies night'! I turned away, gathering myself to run . . .

'Hello, Sylvie,' a voice murmured and I turned back towards the club and the women. A slim figure detached itself from the shadows and I realised Maria really *had* arrived first.

But not the Maria I'd expected.

She was still faultlessly turned out. Her dinner jacket – a man's – was cut like a dream. Her leather jeans were soft, gleaming and fitted like a second skin. Her shirt was as pristine as the ones she wore for work, but made of silk crepe, open almost to the waist, and revealing just as white and dazzling in its long inviting vee.

She smiled – half archly, half shyly – and patted her sleekly gelled hair. The gesture was familiar, but this was not the Maria Samuels who functioned so efficiently in the office, and who listened so quietly and calmly. This was another Maria: one who made my pulse run riot and the hair on the back of my neck stand up. To say she unnerved me was an understatement!

'Come on, Sylvie . . . Don't look like that! I won't bite!' She laughed richly but kindly, then took my arm and led me towards Perfecto.

Earlier in the day her fingers had been cool and consoling on my arm, but now they were like strands of flame. Suddenly I was sweaty and breathless, and my head swam with her perfume. She smelt spicy-sweet and musky, the fragrance so strong and heady I could almost see it. At the club door she produced banknotes from her back pocket with a bravura flourish, and we passed like VIPs through a phalanx of smiling, sociable women. Someone called out, 'Hi, Sam! Looking good tonight! Who's your sexy friend?' and Maria turned like a visiting goddess and blew her admirer a kiss.

'S . . . Sam?' I stammered, letting her steer me to a table and sit me down like a child on a teashop outing.

'People call me that.' Her eyes were sultry and oblique, glittering in the subdued light. 'People who like me.' She turned away, signalled for a drink and I caught myself panting.

There was nothing subtle about her now; nothing understated at all. She stunned me with her fabulous cleavage, her berry-stained mouth and her Nefertiti eyes. I felt helpless and wasted, but this time I liked it. She was weird; she was outrageous; but I still felt safe. I had an overpowering urge to call her 'Sam'.

'Okay, I know what you're thinking – about this . . .' She gestured to the women around us, all so at home in their own milieu. 'About me. And you're not wrong.' Her fingers fluttered expressively, then settled on my wrist like a bird. 'But no-one here expects anything of you. Least of all me. All I want is you to relax and be happy. No strings. No pressure. Understand?'

I nodded, then with my heart thrashing in my chest, I turned my hand so hers could settle in it. 'Yes, Sam, I understand.'

Her smile washed across me like a voodoo ray. 'Great! Now let's have some fun!'

And we did. I should've felt uncomfortable in a place so far out of my own experience, but I didn't. Sam – for that was how I had to think of her – was a star in this sky, and even though I was a stranger, I too was bathed in her radiance. With her I felt free and relaxed, controlled yet happy and at ease. The women we talked and drank and danced with were friendly, but there was no pressure.

Except the pressure within. The pressure I wanted. I knew what was happening when she led me to the dance-floor . . .

She moved like a fury, all fire and lissom grace; as I watched, possessed, and tried to move with her, I felt sex jolt heavily in my belly. The same sweet tug I'd felt for Peter, a thousand years ago. It kicked harder than ever now, here in Perfecto, and I was felled like a tree – slain by my divine, different Sam. I was snared by her long, long thighs, so sensual in that thin, dark leather; by her full breasts, swinging proud and bra-less in her cloud of a shirt. As the dance became wilder, she discarded her jacket and showed me more: nipples flirting free as she stretched and swayed, twin red points, stiff and fruity – as dear and kissable as her soft, tinted lips.

We said little to each other – the music was too loud – but we made jokes with our eyes and our faces. We made contact, found meaning, and I felt myself alter. Irrevocably.

'I told you. I don't expect anything,' she said, later, as we crept into her flat.

She didn't look quite so immaculate now, not nearly so perfect. Her shirt clung darkly to her swollen nipples; her fringe was wet and ruffled; her body smelt strongly of leather and sweat and sex. Yet still, with no conscious effort at all, she controlled me.

'Neither do I.' My voice was tiny, my wanting huge. 'But I'd like . . . I . . .'

I didn't know what words to use but Sam heard me all the same. 'Oh God, yes, yes . . .' she breathed as her lips pressed down on mine and her hands enclosed my yearning breasts.

She had a big squashy sofa in the middle of her living room, and as she lowered us on to it, she kept hold of my flesh; kneaded and stroked through my thin silk top . . . Then the silk was gone and she was rubbing my uncovered skin, pulling my nipples, twisting and fondling them with a joy that passed right through my squirming body and gathered in my hungering clit.

'Yes, I know! I know!' she murmured, sliding to her knees and wedging the heel of one hand in my crotch and the other hand under my bottom. 'It hurts, my baby. It hurts, doesn't it,' she cooed, rocking me on her palms; working my cleft from back and front. 'It needs rubbing, my angel, doesn't it? Rubbing and loving and kissing?'

I started to say 'yes, it does', but grunted obscenely when she invaded my panties, then stripped them away and fingered my naked sex.

'Hold your breasts, Sylvie!' she whispered, 'Caress your nipples and it'll feel even better.'

It did. I pinched my own teats, mauled my own body, and felt my legs fall open and my clit rise to her maurauding touch. She wasn't gentle, as I'd expected; she was rough and frenzied and it was exactly what I wanted and needed. She pounded my clitoris, jerked it to and fro between her fingertips, then left it high and dry for three long, cruel seconds . . . I whined like an animal on heat, and in that instant, her beautiful face was between my thighs. Her nuzzling lips caught my bead of lust, and then she was sucking, sucking, sucking and I was screaming, screaming, screaming as a great bowl of light uptipped in my crotch and poured on and out through the whole of my flailing body.

*

The next day, Peter phoned. Puzzled. His plans had changed last night. He'd called me. I read effortlessly between the lines. He'd needed sex; his new floozy had let him down; but there was always ever faithful, ever available Sylvie, wasn't there?

I listened to the spiel, the same old song, and smiled down from a new and blissful height. He started to complain, but other, more appealing sounds attract me: the office door closing softly; the catch falling; light, even steps crossing the room towards me . . .

My heart sings. My loins churn deliciously. A soft hand falls like grace on my shoulder. My perfect one moves to stand before me and my lips form a silent, rapturous greeting. We've only been apart since the small hours, but it seems like an aeon since we last caressed.

Sartorial as ever, she's everything that's wonderful to my eyes. It's 'financier' pin-stripe this morning, not sweat-soaked silk and leather. But still she looks otherly, remarkable, potent. Without words, she's already taken charge. I make as if to end my call, to end Peter-in-my-life by the simple act of putting down the phone, but she shakes her head and grins.

There's a fire in her this morning! Her lips shine; her gel-smoothed hair shines; and her sweet soul blazes in her eyes like a burning torch to lead me from the darkness. She moves closer and closer as Peter starts to wheedle; she lifts my skirt as he asks, aggrieved, why I wasn't available last night.

'Who are you seeing?'

'No one you know.'

I gasp as 'no one' slides her fingers into my panties . . .

'Where did you go?'

'None of your business,' I say, my knuckles white on the receiver handle. Between my legs, the heat and pleasure are 'none of his business' either . . .

'Who is it?' he demands.

'Sam!' I cry, looking straight into her awesome, beloved face.

'And where did you go with this "Sam"?' persists Peter, angry and desperate. 'Where the hell did you go?'

'To Perfecto!' I sob.

'To Perfecto, Perfecto, Perfecto!' I scream, freed forever as I come at the hand of my magical saviour.

The Old Uno Due

I WAS STARKERS when the doorbell rang, and it was a condition I wasn't too pleased about. Surely Ollie wasn't here already? It was only mid-afternoon and my wine and pizza welcome night wasn't due to start until seven at the earliest. I shouldn't have felt cross, I know, but there's nothing worse than being caught on the hop when you want all your preparations to be perfect. Poor old Ollie had been having such a rough time lately, I really wanted this evening to be a treat.

'You're far too early!' I cried, flinging the flat door wide open . . .

A split second later, I slammed it shut again, feeling a complete and utter fool. It hadn't *been* Ollie on the doorstep, getting an eyeful from the gaping neckline of my robe. It'd been the two tall, dark and handsome not-quite-strangers who lived in the flat upstairs; the Italian brothers, Pietro and Paulo di Something or Other, whom I'd been fancying – as unobtrusively as I could – since they'd moved in a couple of months ago.

'I'm sorry about that,' I muttered when I opened the door again, my bathrobe securely sashed across my naked and still damp breasts. 'I don't usually slam the door in my neighbours' faces. But I was expecting someone else and you gave me a shock.'

'I am very sorry if we frightened you, Signorina Foxton,' said the taller one, Pietro, who spoke such exceedingly good English that his diction was better than mine was, 'but we have a serious problem and we would be very grateful if you could help us.'

How could I resist? Not only was he so polite and roguishly woebegone that my feminine heart melted instantly, he was also one of the most handsome bits of stuff I'd ever had the pleasure of setting eyes on. Ditto, his brother.

There they stood on my doorstep, two raven-haired, chocolate-eyed charmers. One was taller and wiry, the other slightly shorter and muscular; but both were gorgeous in snow-white T-shirts which showed off their olive complexions, and tight blue jeans which clung to their slim hips, their long thighs, and their deliciously well-formed crotches. What red-blooded woman wouldn't have wanted to help them?

'Come in, boys,' I said, stepping back into the room and letting them in. 'What's the problem? What can I do for you?'

'Our television is broken,' said Pietro solemnly, exchanging a quick glance with his brother, who I suspected spoke only minimal English. 'It cannot be repaired until tomorrow and our favourite pro-gramme is being shown this afternoon. We are very sorry to inconvenience you, but may we watch it on your television?'

The decision didn't take much making.

'Yeah, sure. Be my guests,' I said, gesturing towards the TV and the settee I usually viewed from. 'I've got a visitor coming this evening but you're welcome to stay till then.'

'*Grazie! Grazie tanto!* Thank you so much!' This was Pietro again, the one who talked. I thought he was going to grab hold of me and hug me, and I was really looking forward to it ... But he didn't. The brothers just settled themselves on the settee and switched on the TV, both wreathed in smiles. Pietro took the handset and began knowledgeably flicking buttons, and Paulo hunched forward, his elbows on his knees, his cute dimpled chin resting lightly on his fists, and his eyes already riveted on the screen.

'I'll just get some clothes on and then I'll come and watch with you,' I said, fully aware that I was simpering. They really were quite spectacular close up and the prospect of having them to myself for a couple of hours was intoxicating. 'What's on by the way?'

' "Football Italia"!' they announced in unison. I just smiled and scooted for the bedroom before my face dropped again. An afternoon of football must be most women's nightmare, and this particular woman was no exception!

I'd been vaguely aware of the Italian soccer coverage on Channel Four, but of course I'd never watched it. That was going to change now, though, and grumbling to myself, I pulled on a scruffy old T-shirt, a pair of panties, and my dilapidated denim cut-offs. As I fluffed out my still-damp hair, I wondered whether I ought to put something better on, but it hardly seemed worth the effort. I looked quite fetching in my skimpy shorts and T-shirt, with my blonde locks all wild and shaggy. But Italian football fans were notoriously the most single-minded in Europe. You could barely get a word out of an English fan when there was a match on the telly, so these lads probably wouldn't even notice I was in the room, no matter how sexily dressed I was.

Sure enough, they barely looked round when I sidled through the lounge towards the kitchen. Charming! I thought, preparing to start crashing things around to express my displeasure. But just then the younger one, Paulo, the non-English speaker, turned from what seemed to be a pretty crucial sweep down the right wing by the team in red and black, and gave me a smile of such dark-eyed warmth and sweetness that the pit of my belly turned to melted honey and suddenly the *calcio* didn't seem quite such a tedious sport after all.

'I'll just get us a drink, shall I?' I stammered, standing there like a lemon.

'*Grazie*,' he whispered, his brown eyes simmering briefly across my not-too-well-covered body before he returned his attention to the screen.

With Ollie in the doldrums, I'd laid in a good stock of wine, so I could easily spare a bottle for my Italians. But to only offer wine suddenly seemed a bit niggardly, so in the interest of Anglo-European relations, I had a rummage amongst all the extra food I'd stocked up with, and flung together a by-my-standards fairly impressive selection of *antipasti*.

Their praise was profuse as I put the tray down on the coffee-table, although I did notice them edging around me slightly so they could still see the screen while they thanked me.

'Thank you so much, Signorina Foxton,' said Pietro warmly. 'You should not have gone to all this trouble. We are already in your debt for permitting us to watch our programme.'

'My name's Georgina,' I answered, knocked sideways by the genuine beauty of his smile, 'but you can call me "Georgia", if you like.'

'*Grazie tanto*, Georgie,' he murmured, turning up the voltage on that grin.

Paulo backed up his brother with a stream of melodic, husky and quite spine-tingling Italian that made not one iota of sense to me, but turned my knees to jelly and made my sex quiver like one. God, these two were so gorgeous they were edible! It was a pity that I'd have to either score a goal or lie down naked in the penalty box to get them to notice me.

Having said that, a curious thing happened when I came to sit down. In what looked suspiciously like a set piece manoeuvre, Paulo scooted to one end of the sofa, and Pietro slid to the other. I sank down in the middle with an Italian striker on each wing. It was the old *uno due*, no less. I wondered if they'd take their eyes off the action long enough to notice how hard and erect my nipples were looking through the thin white cotton of my T-shirt . . .

It didn't seem so. When the wine was poured, and the olives and such handed round, all attention returned to the football. Even mine. Almost before I realised, I was actually following the game and rooting for the team in red and black shirts – Milan, Pietro informed me with pride. I vaguely remembered a neighbour saying that was where the boys were from, and that they'd come over to England to help their uncle set up a new restaurant. Now I'd got a team to support, I decided that AC Milan played very 'attractively', and the sight of those darkly powerful athletes, storming across the pitch, only served to remind me of the two equally dark and powerful males I had on either side of me. Slightly closer on either side of me, perhaps, than they had been originally.

Things came to a head when 'our' centre forward

scored a brilliant goal; rocketing one just past the fingertips of the keeper and putting Milan unassailably in the lead. As the ball crossed the line, both the brothers shrieked *'Forza Milano!'* then turned as one to kiss me. Two sets of Italian lips pressed hot and hard against my cheeks, two sets of Italian arms went around me to hug both me and the other brother – and the glass of wine I'd been sipping at the time was up-ended all over my front. I'd only just topped it up.

I was soaked. Thin white cotton clung like a second skin to my breasts, and if the brothers hadn't noticed my nipples before, there was no way they could avoid them now.

'Mi scusi!'

'Mi scusi!' they chorused, but as I turned from one golden-olive face to the other, I slowly, then rather quickly realised that they already had another national passion on their minds. A passion that flowed as hot in their veins as the football did . . .

In another effortless one-two they moved in on me. Pietro took the glass from my nerveless fingers, then eased the hem of my sodden T-shirt out of my shorts' waistband and pulled it up and over my head. Like an obedient puppet, I raised my arms to help him, and even as I did so, I felt Paulo working on first the button, then the zip of my shorts.

Half-heartedly I tried to protest, but Pietro slid an arm around my naked back and pulled me in close for a kiss. As his wine-scented tongue expertly prised open my mouth, I felt his free hand cup my right breast. His thumb skated delicately across my nipple, and as it did, his brother slid my shorts down over my hips and took my tiny lace panties off with them.

They'd stripped me. Just like that. And all I'd

done was let them ... As his tongue went darting around my mouth, Pietro's fingers played havoc with my breasts. First one, then the other; squeezing, gently rolling the flesh, taking a nipple in his finger and thumb and devilishly rolling that too. The lovely sensations made my pelvis start pumping in sympathy. But those lower zones were now Paulo's special province ...

'Bellissima,' he murmured, sliding a hand beneath my bottom and insolently stroking my cheeks. I felt his fingers splay, and one – the middle one – settle right in the crease and tickle the tiny hole there. His other hand surged into the attack from the front, his fingers combing my wiry curls to get at the treasures within.

With my breasts being tenderly mauled and my anus wickedly fingered, my clitoris woke up and said 'touch me' ... In seconds I was slippery, aching and ready.

But my Italians were devils: diovoli; masters of choreographed teasing. With accuracy and artistry, my labia were slowly eased apart and the bud of my sex exposed. But not touched ...

'Please,' I gasped as Pietro released my mouth and attached his lips to my neck.

'Patience, mi cara,' he whispered against my skin, nibbling his way to my collar bone as his fingers worked ceaselessly on my teats. My own hands rose from where they'd been limply lying beside me and I touched each man on his thigh. Then, without thought or hesitation, slid my fingers lower and covered their denim-covered crotches ...

They were both solidly erect, the heat of their flesh quite distinct through the fabric of their jeans. I shuddered as I lay there between them; my hands on their sexes, their hands not on mine. Both these beautiful creatures would need satisfying soon, but how would I accomplish it? Take them one after the other? Together? I shuddered again – violently – and as Paulo's fingers moved naughtily in my bottom groove, his free hand circled slowly on my belly.

'*Che bella ragazza,*' he whispered, leaning in towards me, his body brushing his brother's as he took the mouth that Pietro had abandoned.

Paulo's tongue was less assertive than his sibling's but just as beguiling; it stroked lightly but surely against my own tongue as his fingers rode the furrow of my bottom.

I was wriggling now, shifting uneasily. They were stimulating my mouth, my breasts and my arse, but the core of my sex was still screaming.

It didn't have to scream for too long . . .

Somehow, I don't really know how, the brothers seemed to swarm all over me. As Paulo's tongue flicked insistently at mine, his brother's mouth cruised down to my nipple. Chuntering with satisfaction, he drew on it heavily, his fingers playing with the other peak and tweaking it to the rhythm of his sucks.

The pleasure in my breasts was fast turning to agony in my crotch, but gentle young Paulo had mercy. He wiggled a finger through my pubes and settled it with perfect precision on my clit. As he pressed lightly there and his other hand palpated my anus, I felt as if a circuit had completed inside me: nipples, clitoris, mouth, bottom. Every sensitive area was covered and attacked, and I came, grunting obscenely around Paulo's probing tongue. I seemed to climax for a long long time; more completely and beautifully than I had for ages. I was still throbbing when the brothers disengaged both their fingers and their mouths and after a whispered consultation in their own language, lifted me bodily from the couch and lowered me on to the rug.

Eyes closed, I just lay there. I knew I had a silly cat-with-the-cream grin on my face, but it didn't seem to matter one bit. My sex felt too hot, too wet and too glowing for me to worry about anything. I heard the brothers moving about nearby, and furniture being moved to make space. As the football commentator still enthused in the background, I heard the rustle of clothing and soft words muttered in Italian. Somebody had just scored when the sound from the television went quieter.

My clitoris and nipples tingled. The brothers were closing in on me again, and this time there would be no Italian football to distract their attention. I opened my eyes and looked towards them . . .

They were magnificent, classical, and superbly male; so different yet so similar. They both had silky Mediterranean tans and soot-black body hair that matched the hair on their heads, but in other ways there were delightful distinctions. Paulo was compact, heavily muscular without being gross, and had a cock that reflected his physique. Jutting out proudly, it was thick and stubby with a tip that was swollen and tempting. Pietro was longer and leaner – everywhere. His body looked slim and flexible and so did his cock. Its shape was narrow and elegant, but its length was breathtaking. He would reach inside me, go deeper than deep, find and touch my soul. And I wanted that so much.

As one, they sank down on to the rug and arranged themselves: Paulo at my side, Pietro between my outflung thighs. Both then carefully lifted me. Pietro raised my buttocks and presented the tip of his cock to my entrance, while Paulo slid an arm beneath my shoulders and twisted my upper body towards his temptingly out-thrust organ. As he rose up slightly on his knees and cradled the back of my head, he pulled cushions from the settee and piled them up beneath me for my comfort.

'*Per favore,*' he whispered, resting his glans against my lips like a sacrament.

'*Per favore,*' I heard from somewhere beyond him, just as Pietro pushed tentatively forward . . .

'Oh, yes! Please! *Si!*' I cried, craning upwards to take Paulo in my mouth while my hips bucked hard against Pietro. Co-ordinating without words, both men surged into me and began to thrust.

Paulo was as careful and gentle as he'd been in everything so far, but it was definitely him fucking my mouth rather than me sucking his cock . . . And Pietro went in just as deep as I'd known and hoped he would. I was locked between them, my body jerking to their immaculate synchronised rhythm as my hands roved blindly over all the hot sleek Italian flesh I could reach.

Not that *their* hands weren't busy . . . A finger, I don't know whose, slid into my slit and rubbed me gently, while other fingers tightened on my nipples. I was pinched and pulled and jiggled and fondled . . . and all in time to the long hard strokes of Pietro's gliding cock.

I wanted to scream with joy but I was gagged by Paulo's thick rod. The sound, caged inside me, seemed to turn back on itself and explode in my sex as pleasure. My vagina clamped hard around Pietro, and my mouth went slack and loose and let in his brother still deeper.

It was too intense to last. The boys were too excited; their cocks too quivering, too bursting, too ready. And I was too full of heat and orgasm and pure, simple love to be able to bear it much longer.

They both cried out as they climaxed. Through a haze and from an enormous distance, I heard 'Gesúmaria!P' and 'Ah! Dio mio!' I couldn't tell which religious exhortation was whose and I didn't care. I felt like praising heaven myself, but I couldn't. I just gulped and gobbled and wept, swallowing warm salty semen and coming like a storm around the cock that was pulsing inside me.

The next coherent thought I had was to notice that the football was over. There was a documentary of some kind on now, probably a very good one, but I was too blissed out and bleary-eyed to make sense of it. Unwinding myself from a tangle of sweaty limbs, I got up, switched off the set and padded away to the bathroom.

When I returned, by way of the kitchen and the fridge, the brothers were still dozing. Two sets of brown eyes fluttered open and two soft mouths smiled when I set down a fresh bottle of wine on the coffee table. Pietro sat up and reached out for me, but as he did, the doorbell rang and both he and his brother pulled faces of eloquent, little-boyish disappointment.

As I shrugged apologetically and turned towards the door, I thought about who I was expecting . . . Then I thought about my two handsome *tifosi* – and everything slotted neatly into place. I didn't even have to bother putting my clothes on this time . . .

Stepping back, I ushered Ollie through, and every mouth in the room – except mine – dropped open. Pietro and Paulo's because they must've thought they were seeing double; and Olivia's because her twin sister – me! – wasn't wearing a single stitch of clothing . . . and neither were the two Botticelli angels sitting on her rug!

'Ollie, meet Pietro and Paulo,' I said, hoping against hope I hadn't misjudged things. 'They came down to watch the football.'

The boys got gracefully to their feet, and I had to stifle my giggles. It was obvious that they were *extremely* pleased to meet my sister.

'Boys, this's my sister Olivia. She's come to stay with me for a few days.'

The brothers both smiled charmingly at Ollie, their open, ingenuous faces every so slightly at odds with the stiff erections that were pointing out boldly from their loins.

Would Ollie approve though? To my mind these two beautiful kindly Italians were just what she needed to help her forget her failed love affair. But there was every chance she might never want to see a man again.

I needn't have worried . . .

'Football fans, eh?' she said with a chuckle. 'Well, it certainly looks like somebody's scored here today!'

Dropping her case, she walked beside me to the rug and the boys, then glanced at the evidence of our 'match'.

'I do have to hand it to you, Georgie . . . Food, wine, *and* naked men! You really know how to cheer a girl up.'

And I had to hand it to the brothers. Ollie was as much a shock to them as they were to her, but even so their teamwork was as faultless as ever. One after the other they courteously kissed her hand, then with a swift nod to Paulo in my direction, Pietro kissed her full on the lips. He was just sliding the shirt from her shoulders as Paulo bore *me* down on to the rug. I smiled and curled my fist around his cock.

Moments later, as Paulo nudged open my labia and entered me, I heard a soft moan of pleasure and looked across to where Pietro was just easing into Ollie. Her pale legs wrapped around him in welcome and when his tight brown bottom began rising and falling, she cried out once again, and louder.

I turned away then, respecting my sister's privacy, and as Paulo starting moving too, I added my own happy cries to the mêlée.

Now, I've always babbled nonsense during lovemaking and this time was no exception. I was noisy; I was incoherent; and I was mindless. But I've got not one, not two, but three other people who'll swear I shouted 'FORZA ITALIA!' as I climaxed!

Stranger than . . .

OOOOOOOH!

Elliot Witter nearly choked on his drink when a slim hand settled lightly on his penis. It was a woman's hand, gloved in leather, and its touch was both devilish and skilful. He felt the grain of the hide kiss the grain of his fine-textured genital skin and a fingertip trace his frenum. He sighed, sadly, and placed his glass back on the bar. It was such a shame that the hand existed only in his mind . . .

Elliot had always had a vivid imagiation, but for the last four weeks, three days and two and a half hours it'd been going bananas. Four weeks, three days and two and a half hours was the exact amount of time since he'd walked into the La Terrazza bar and fallen deep into his very first full-blown erotic obsession.

He'd only gone into the place out of curiosity. He'd been working late and felt stressed out, pissed off and bored with his relatively mundane existence. La Terrazza was a notorious sexual stomping ground, and as a young man whose turn to stomp was long overdue, he'd arrived with high hopes, a genuine thirst, and the beginnings of a very nice hard-on. He'd expected glitzy people, pricey drinks and plush, slightly pervy surroundings; what he hadn't expected was 'The Weirdo' . . .

He called her 'The Weirdo' because by most conventional standards of femininity, she was one. She was also the purest piece of sex he'd ever set eyes on, and when he'd first spotted her, perched languidly on a stool at the other end of the bar, he'd felt an instant turbulence in his trousers.

It shouldn't have happened. Before that moment, he'd liked soft and pretty girls – gentle, pliant little creatures with masses of candyfloss curls and sweet cuddly bodies to match.

But 'The Weirdo' didn't have any of these attributes. In fact there was nothing soft about her at all; she was a hard bitch, and her beauty was brittle and peculiar. Sleek, bright, gel-coated hair matched a sleek, bright decadent image; and though her body was just about as womanly as it was possible to be, she dressed it as if it were a man's.

Elliot knew who she was, of course. On the first night she'd already looked vaguely familir, and on the second, he'd asked the barman about her. It hadn't surprised him at all that she was the famous erotic novelist Diamanda; in fact he couldn't understand why he hadn't recognised her immediately. He had her photograph at home on the back of several book-jackets.

His goddess was as famous for her hedonistic, rule-breaking lifestyle as she was for her passionately purple prose: it was well-known in this city and in others that she liked lovers of either sex and often in multiple quantities.

Elliot would've died for just an instant of her attention, and for four weeks now, he'd seen those silky, painted lips in every one of his dreams, and those glinting, slanted eyes on every woman's face he encountered. Two days ago, she'd turned up wearing a pair of the finest of black leather gloves ... and now, every time his guard went down, he kept feeling their touch on his cock.

The most frustrating thing about all this was that not once had she appeared to notice him. Whether alone or with a flutter of flamboyant friends, his Weirdo seemed to have all the company she required. Elliot had run a million inner scenarios of how their first meeting would go, but when it came to making them real, he was terrified she'd regard him with disdain; or worse still, pity.

Elliot's big problem was shyness. When women got to know him they usually rather liked him; he was no fool, he had a good job for someone of his relative lack of years, and though somewhat fragile-looking for a man, he was moderately handsome in a quiet way. But it was the 'getting to know' stage that was so fraught with difficulty. When faced with a pretty woman, his subtle intelligence deserted him and his pleasant looks turned a furious beetroot red. He'd blush and stammer and he'd know that even though a girl was trying to be kind, inside she was already planning her getaway.

In his dreams, though, he was a tiger. And in the dreams of these last four weeks, with the weird and wonderful Diamanda, he'd stood up on his hindlegs and roared!

He'd walk up to her at the bar, bold as brass and without a microsecond's hesitation. She'd smile that oblique red-lipped smile of hers and indicate immediately that he join her. They'd share a cocktail, or perhaps some suitably 'hard' drink like Scotch, no ice no water, then after about five minutes of his brilliant conversation, she'd tell him she just couldn't wait any more and that she had a suite reserved for them in a nearby hotel.

In a luxurious cream and gold rococo decorated bedroom, she'd divest herself of her severe, man-tailored clothing and reveal herself to be all breasts and voluptuous womanhood beneath. This part he knew to be true, because one night last week she'd shucked off her snazzy designer jacket in the warm, crowded bar, and the shirt underneath had been truly sensational. Classically styled but made from the sheerest and most gauzelike voile, it'd almost made Elliot faint. He – and everyone else in the room – had had a clear sight of her unfettered bra-less breasts. Twin, rounded orbs, high but plump, and with nipples that stood out like thick brown buttons . . .

Back in his dreams, he'd caressed these luscious mammaries with no further ado. She'd sobbed as he mounded and squeezed them, all her hardness turned to miraculous malleable softness, and wetness, and wantonness; for him . . .

'Yes! Oh, Elliot, yes!' was her scream as he first touched her, then entered her. No foreplay was required in this ecstatic world of perfection, and penetration was effected in a single snag-free glide.

Tumbling back to reality, and almost falling off his stool in the process, Elliot sighed with regret. He really loved the 'hotel room' fantasy, although he had to admit it wasn't entirely all his own work. The protagonists – Diamanda and himself – were his choice of course, but the scenario, the setting and the nitty-gritty of the bedroom action came straight from one of the lady's own stories, *The Spider's Web*, which was all about a beautiful, sexually voracious woman who picked up young men in bars and lured them to hotel rooms to fuck them.

Would that it would happen for real, thought Elliot desperately as he considered ordering another drink. It didn't look as if she was coming in tonight.

Two small beers later, he felt the urge to visit the men's room and as he trudged wearily in its direction, he decided that once he'd dealt with his natural function, he'd cut his losses and leave. When Diamanda wasn't in La Terrazza, its crowds of laughing glitterati served only to remind him how lonely he was.

When he returned, he took one last hopeful look around ... and suddenly every nerve-end in his body went 'yow!' – especially the ones in his cock.

Right in the far corner of the room, discreetly tucked away, with a large video jukebox. And standing in front of it – headphones atop her gel-polished hair, and her whole body weaving to the unheard beat – was Diamanda. Alone for the moment, and wearing what seemed to be a leather teddy-boy suit – draped jacket and tight-cut trousers – she was studying the screen before her with an expression of unalloyed enjoyment.

Elliot's heart started to pound like a steamhammer in his chest. She looked so bizarre in her pervy leather suit, but lost in the music she seemed – paradoxically – ten times more approachable.

As he reached her, Diamanda glanced away from the screen, smiled, and before he'd time to open his mouth, looked him disconcertingly straight in the eye.

'I –' Elliot began, but she silenced him with a finger to her glazed lips and mimed that he should wait until the track was over. It was arrogant, and quite typical of what he'd imagined of her, but like a helpless slave, he obeyed.

Up close, her straight-nosed profile was so fine and pure it almost hurt his eyes; and her bodyscents – both natural and artificial – were so potent they made him giddy. It was like standing next to a myth, an illusion, a chimera; and when the number finished Elliot gasped with relief. It felt like ten minutes since he'd taken a breath!

As she drew the lightweight headphones off and hooked them on the side of the machine, Elliot was gripped by panic. He had to speak first. If he just stood here gawking like a loon, she'd think him pathetic and the idea of that was almost physically painful.

'I've been watching you,' he said, nervous but surprised by the strength and apparent calm of his own young voice . . . then even more surprised by the effect it had on Diamanda.

She was shocked; astounded; flabbergasted. It was as simple as that. Elliot couldn't figure out what was so radical about the four ordinary words he'd uttered, so he repeated them.

'I've been watching you,' he said again, 'I hope you don't mind.'

Surprise seemed to soften that pale, sharp face somehow, mute it into something far less intimidating. She looked almost mellow when she answered. 'Now how the jiggery did I know you were going to say that, I wonder? It's uncanny.'

He didn't know what on earth she was on about, but her voice locked him under her spell. It was light, melodic and faintly affected. In a man it would've sounded camp, and even in a woman the timbre was decidedly weird; but to Elliot it seemed. as if every syllable was a gobbet of warmed honey that trickled down his spine and flowed into a pool around his balls. His prick stiffened immediately and formed an aching insistent bar that pushed at the fabric of his trousers. Without thinking, he looked down at the obvious bulge; and to his horror, Diamanda's eyes followed his.

'Oh, wow,' she breathed, 'This gets weirder and weirder.'

'I'm sorry. You don't know me. This's so embarrassing,' he burbled, feeling the blush come racing up his throat and his erection get horrifically harder.

'Don't worry about it,' Diamanda answered airily, her initial surprised reaction melting into something more teasing and confident; a kind of amused resignation that was still ever-so-slightly laced with wonder. 'And I *do* know you – in a way. You're not the only person who watches people . . . I do it all the time. How do you think I get ideas for my books and stories?' She paused, touched a long lacquer-tipped finger to her chin, and seemed, still, to be slightly taken aback, 'Although it doesn't usually work out like this. I must be turning into a seer in my old age.'

A what? thought Elliot, feeling out of his depth and enthralled. 'I've got all your books,' he gasped in a vain attempt to bring some normality to their discourse. 'I think they're great! So well written . . . So real.' Oh Lord, he was only getting in deeper. She'd think him a toadying fool now, as well as a sexfreak with no control af his willy!

But all she did was shake her heacl and smile. 'You sweet, sweet thing,' she murmured, looking down at his betrayingly tented trousers. 'Look, would you like me to do something about that? I don't usually plunge in quite so precipitiously, but after what you said and all . . . I simply don't think I can resist!'

But being propositioned like this, in a public place, quite literally struck him dumb. All the more so because she still seemed to be talking in riddles.

'We could go somewhere right now—' She paused and glanced at her heavy man's watch as if making an appointment to discuss the trade figures, 'Oh shit! I've to meet somebody else and I don't think I've time . . . Just let me check.'

As Elliot looked on, astounded and yet deeply titillated by the sheer outrageousness of it all, Diamanda fished into one of her jacket pockets and rummaged around. The first item she drew out was a book, which she passed to Elliot, muttering 'Hold this!' as she dove in for another search.

Taking the book, he realised it was a thinnish volume, in mint condition, and had Diamanda's own picture on the back.

Good God, it was her latest novel! One he hadn't read but was dying to. It wasn't even due out till next month. He studied the title – *Watching Me, Watching You* – then carefully flipped it open.

Words leapt up from the page at him. Words that in his current hyper-sensitised state, carried arousing and magical weight: 'naked', 'moist', 'distended'. Every letter, every sound in his head, every nuance of meaning seemed to scream to his cock about the body of the writer herself.

'You can borrow that if you like,' Diamanda said, looking up briefly from the wafer-thin portable computer notepad she'd pulled out of her other pocket.

'Er . . . Thanks.' He closed the book, not daring to read further. The prose was inflammatory to say the least, at a moment when his senses were burning already.

One of the strangest, most compelling women

he'd ever met was consulting an electronic diary to see if she could fit him in for a sexual quickie! It seemed about as likely as one of his masturbatory fantasies, and yet it was happening.

'Oh dear, what an absolute drag,' she muttered, flipping off the tiny microcomputer, 'I've to be out of here in half an hour. And tomorrow I'm off to the South of France to research my next novel.' She slid the gadget back in her pocket, and reached out to touch his face. 'We could be hot together, you and I. I just know it!' Her hand dropped to his, took the book, then slid it into his pocket, 'You can read that later, my sweet. When I've gone. . .' She took his empty hand, drew it to her mouth and kissed it moistly, running his tongue over his empty palm. Elliot knew now he could die a happy man. 'Come on! We haven't much time but we can still have some fun!'

With a determined tug on the hand she'd just kissed, she urged him into motion, and led him quickly across the room, her eyes bright and glittering and her fine mouth curved in the most wicked grin he'd ever seen in his life!

Fun? Oh Lord, yes! Thirty-five minutes later his knees were still shaking! It'd been like being back at school; being far too young again; doing naughty things in cramped and uncomfortable places – and loving every second of it! Somehow they'd found themselves in a tiny cubicle in the men's room with their trousers around their ankles and their hands at work on each other's crotches.

He'd tried to protest, but there was no saying no saying 'no' to Diamanda. After only the most cursory of 'reccies', she'd dragged him in, pushed him into the first open stall and bolted the door. Just as she was unzipping her sleazy leather trousers, there was the sound of voices just outside. Lots of them!

'Stay cool,' she'd mimed, pulling her thin and strangely plain white panties down to her knees and leaving them there, stretched, as she took his hand where he could feel her moist readiness. 'Do me!' she breathed, positioning his finger on her clitoris.

He started to rub instinctively, his finger sliding on the big hard bud, then missed as beat as her hands attacked his belt. She bobbed her pelvis at him impatiently, and he managed to re-establish his rhythm, in spite of the fact she was pushing down *his* clothing by now. When his trousers were pooled around his ankles, she moved temporarily off his hand and pushed his briefs out of the way too. When they were scrunched somewhere around calf level, she took his right hand again and crammed his shaking fingers into her slit, then left him to it and took a firm but measured hold on his erection.

In spite of the nearness of other lavatory users, he couldn't suppress his broken gasp.

'Shut up,' mouthed Diamanda, her eyes wild and her own breathing breaking up as she pumped her loins on his hand.

Her fingers were merciless. Working his prick on long smooth strokes, she slid the skin deftly over the inner blood-stiffened pole with – every so often – subtle lateral swivel that was so amazing it almost blew his ears off. Jerking and squirming, he cracked his tossing head on the cubicle wall, and Diamanda laughed soundlessly and re-doubled her digital onslaught. Elliot fought for breath, and wriggled helplessly against the thin barrier that divided them from the unknown men outside.

'What you doin' in there, you faggots?' called out

a gleeful voice.

As Diamanda opened her mouth to answer, with a reaction speed he wouldn't have thought possible under the circumstances, Elliot wrenched his hand from her pulsing sex and clapped it across her lips. Her sculpted eyebrows waggled at him as he felt her licking her own juices off his hand.

'Behave!' he mimed frantically as she nipped at the soft flesh of his palm and began a slow remorseless squeeze of his cock.

'Keep your tongues out, boys!' called the voice again, surprisingly amiably. Elliot bit hard on his lip as the squeezes below turned to a furious milking action. His whole body seemed on the point of explosion as he listened to pissing and washing and general sprucing up sounds ... then at last, footsteps, a slamming door and silence.

'You crazy bitch!' he hissed, releasing Diamanda's mouth. Her lipstick was slightly smudged at one corner; it was the first time he'd ever seen her less than immaculate. 'What the hell are you trying to do? Get us arrested?' he gasped, as she grinned and licked her smeary lips.

'I'm trying to get us off!' she drawled, then before he could do anything about it, she was on her knees, sucking his distended tool into her mouth.

As her tongue worked him, Elliot was aware, principally, of two sensations. One was the cold cubicle wall, so slick and smooth against his working bottom. The other was a great ball of swirling heat and wetness that enclosed his quivering prick.

Diamanda's mouthwork was superb. She seemed to have the ability to create a hard pulling vacuum around him, whilst beating furiously with her tongue on the most susceptible areas of his penis. In moments the semen that'd been suppressed with so much difficulty came spurting out with the most perfect of ease. Elliot grunted freely as each pulse of spunk brought a heavy throb of pleasure with it, a vibration down the entire rigid length of his enclosed and well-sucked prick. If a dozen city policemen had bashed down the door at that very moment, he couldn't have cared less.

Afterwards, he knelt before Diamanda and licked her to a climax she expressed only by the vicious pulling of his hair and the involuntary spasming of her flesh beneath her tongue. More patrons milled about outside as she came, and it was several minutes before the coast was clear and the two of them were able to zip up and sneak out of the cubicle. Even then, and in spite of Elliot's protests, Diamanda insisted on spending several long minutes in front of the mirror repairing her ravaged lipstick. She laughed merrily when he urged her to hurry up because it was, after all, the *men's* room she was preening in!

With her lipstick restored to a gleaming bow, she wouldn't kiss him *au revoir* either, though she did give him an affectionate squeeze of the crotch as she bade him farewell – much to the amusement of several men entering the cloakroom that they'd just left.

'We'll finish this when I get back from France, shall we?' she said as they walked back towards the bar. 'I'll phone you. We'll do Chapter Two then!' She gave him that strange, faintly befuddled look again then, and shook her head. 'Good grief, boy, I don't even know your name!'

'It's Elliot Witter,' he whispered, then tagged on his telephoned number for luck.

'I thank you for that, young Elliot,' she said

archly, whipping out her notepad and recording his 'particulars'. 'And for everything else too. I'll be in touch!'

With that, she'd swept away, leaving Elliot with a wrung-out mind, a wrung-out cock and a pre-publication copy of a racy new novel still stuffed in his jacket pocket.

A few minutes later, he was sitting at the bar with a fresh beer before him which her lingering flavour on his lips made him reluctant to lift up and drink. With the vague feeling that he'd spent the last half hour in a 'trip' at least twice as exotic as its contents, he took out the pristine, unhandled book and thumbed it open at page one. As he began to read, his hands shook, his flushed face drained to dead white, and his penis – unbelievably – swelled up to a new and even harder and more aching erection . . . Was truth stranger than fiction? Or were the two about as weird as each other?

The woman was as unusual as she was beautiful, the first line read, *and as the young man drew close, he felt his flesh grow stiff in his pants. He had to speak – it was now or never . . .*

'I've been watching you,' he told her, his voice nervous but strong . . .

The Man in Black

FUNNY THINGS CAN happen when you're bored, they say ... And one afternoon last summer, in a large Birmingham hotel, boy was I bored!

The lecture was 'Maximising your Selling Potential through Eye Contact' and the only thing my eyes wanted contact with was the inside of my eyelids. The speaker was short and tubby and dressed in Top Man meets Miami Vice. For my part, he'd no potential whatsoever ... The seminar delegates weren't much better: the men were a bunch of yuppie pseuds and the women – with the single exception of a northern lass I'd teamed up with – were hard-faced chainstore power-dressers who'd do a damn sight more than make eyes to get a sale.

Yeah, the selling game was just a great big con, and as soon as this lot was over, I was out of it! This particular lecture was the pits interest-wise, and I'd already tried the usual distractions. I'd counted the pin-stripes on the wimpish back in front of me. I'd drawn seven different doodles on my blank notepad. I'd priced the outfit of the girl sitting next to the wimp. Judy, my Yorkshire mate, was as fed up as I was, but when we'd exchanged commiserations, we'd been furiously shushed by the dedicated types around us. Good God, were they really believing this shit?

After twenty minutes, I'd completely had it. Unbuttoning my jacket, I mussed up my hair and crossed and recrossed my nylon-clad thighs. If I couldn't find a diversion, I'd create one! The plan was to upset all the males on my row, and make it as difficult for them to concentrate as it was for me. I'm not a raving beauty, I admit, but with long, shapely legs, tousled red hair and a very decent pair of breasts, I always get second looks. But today, I wasn't even getting first ones. And especially not from—

Then I saw him. I saw him and I couldn't figure out why I hadn't seen him before . . . Leaning against the wall at the end of my row, was a man dressed all in black: the most gorgeous hunk I'd ever seen. Why he was leaning against the wall, and why he was wearing black denim in a room full of mock Armani? I never stopped to ask.

He appeared to be listening to the lecture, though why I really don't know. He looked less like a sales rep than I did.

He was just my type, though: medium height, slim, dark – very dark. There was black in him somewhere, or maybe Latin. Whatever it was, he'd a deep toffee-coloured tan, jet black hair, and big brown bedroom eyes. He was so perfect for me I could've designed him. He'd got that sexy, dodgy, almost girlish look that gets me every time . . . but with a crotch, in sprayed on jeans, that belonged to no girl I've ever known!

I just couldn't stop ogling it – I mean him! – and any second he was going to turn round and catch me . . .

But he didn't. He just stood and stared at the stage,

a solemn, almost sad expression on his smooth angelic face.

God, he was a turn on! I'd never fallen in lust this fast before. Or fallen this hard. The man in black reached everything instantaneously. My breasts ached, my heart pounded, and my sex became warm and moist. I was a pot that badly needed stirring.

As if he knew I was watching, he suddenly shifted in his sentinel pose. Flexing restlessly, he drew up one leg, flatted his foot to the wall and tapped it in time to some unheard beat. The denim stretched to destruction over his thighs and I thought I'd melt in my chair. His body was long, lean and whippy-looking. His face fine-featured but strong. He'd be fabulous in bed, I told myself. Graceful dynamite. Those narrow hips would pump like a jackhammer . . .

As I thought it I felt it! I swear I did! I was filled, stuffed, stretched. A bar of hard flesh moved inside me . . . I think I moaned – but I can't be sure – and in that moment, he turned towards me, and his face lit up with a beautiful, knowing, narrow-eyed smile – as if he really were on top of me and giving me his all!

'Are you all right, Jackie?' whispered a voice beside me, and I turned away from the man in black and his phantom prick and dragged myself back to reality.

Judy was studying me worriedly.

'You've gone all white, love,' she observed.

'It's okay, I'm fine!' I hissed back, ignoring the frowning faces around us. 'It's just a bit hot in here.'

I wasn't fine actually; but it would've been rather difficult to describe the problem discreetly. Nevertheless, Judy was a good soul and deserved a treat.

I wouldn't be selfish.

'What do you think of *him* then?' I said, nodding towards the end of the row. 'Dishy or what?'

'Who?' she replied, looking puzzled.

'*Him*, you dummy! The guy leaning against the wall!'

But when I turned back in his direction . . . the man in black had gone.

I soon had time to ponder this disappearance. The seminar was a lost cause as far as I was concerned, so I skipped the next lecture and went for a walk around the city. Judy, poor soul, had to make notes for her boss, or she'd have joined me.

I was supposed to be thinking about a new job, but ten seconds out of the hotel, I was dreaming about the man in black. How on earth had he got out of that hall so fast? I'd only looked away for seconds, and the exit was right at the back of the room. Why hadn't I seen him leave? I'd been so tuned into him . . .

The fact he'd been there at all was puzzling. He wasn't at the seminar because I'd have spotted him like a shot. Ditto if he'd been staff.

As I walked, I brooded over what might've been. I would've liked a chance to talk to him . . . Who was I kidding? I wanted to screw him! But a little conversation – between sessions – wouldn't have gone amiss.

I half hoped I'd get that peculiar sensation again while I walked. The ghost of his prick inside me. It didn't happen, but my inventive mind made up for it. By the time I got back to the hotel, we'd done everything I could think of, and a few I'd never thought of before!

Once in the foyer, I scanned around hopefully,

but there was no joy. No man in black to fulfil my lurid fantasies, or deal with their physical consequences. My panties were wet and my sex so inflamed I could hardly walk. If he'd appeared right then and there, I'd have fucked him on the spot!

No, that's exaggerating . . . but I'd have found a way to chat him up.

It dawned on me in the lift just how long I'd been out wandering. The lift was crammed. People were returning to their rooms to change for dinner, and it was hot in the crush of bodies. Leaning tiredly against the wall, I thought of my man in black leaning against his wall. My eyelids drooped and closed . . .

The hotel had nearly a dozen floors, and as I drowsed unnoticed I heard the lift doors swishing to and fro, and people getting out at their stops. The motion and the heat acted like a drug, and I was almost comatose when the lift jolted to a sudden, neck-wrenching halt. My eyes flew open. There – alone in the lift with me – stood the man in black.

'You!' I said stupidly, dazed by having him so, so close at last. He was too close now though. Suddenly I was scared – scared shitless – but just like before, I couldn't stop staring. Staring at a dark, silent figure who stared unblinkingly back at me.

At close range he was sensational: the face seraphic, solemn, and achingly sad, the body a black poem of sex. And I saw something else now . . .

His smooth brown throat was ringed with a scar: livid and fresh-looking, it was a necklace of pain that I longed to kiss and soothe. Irresistibly drawn, I trod the width of the lift and stood before him.

'I—'

It was all I managed. My voice died as the lights did, and we were plunged into utter blackness. All I could see were two flashing indicators: floors one and three blinking alternately. But before I could drawn breath to cry out, arms like iron bands whipped around me, and a strangely cool mouth crushed mine.

It was what I'd wanted, but in the terrifying darkness I struggled. For the first time, I heard his voice. 'No!' he cried, 'No! Don't leave me. Please don't leave me!'

The voice was a match for the face: beautiful – though obviously distressed – light-toned, yet disturbingly rich.

'It's all right,' I answered, gentling him as I'd always known I would. 'I won't leave you.'

It was a ludicrous thing to say, because neither of us was going anywhere. But I see now that there are other ways of leaving.

'Don't leave me!' he murmured, ignoring the fact I'd answered, 'She left me. She said I was too young, too naive; that I didn't know anything.'

He was so upset, so agonised, that it seemed the most natural thing in the world to pull him down to the floor and kiss and hold him as he'd kissed and held me.

'I shouldn't be here,' he muttered raggedly as I tugged open his shirt and licked blindly at the abrasive line of his scar. 'I should've moved on. But I can't go. I need you! I need you so much! Don't hurt me like she did.'

I'd no idea what he was talking about, but I didn't care. My fingers were already working on his belt, his zip, his briefs. Kisses weren't enough for my man in black. He needed the comfort only my body could give.

Delicately, I eased out his prick, and almost wept because I couldn't see it. He was more, far more

623

than I'd dreamed of: big, hard, and already slick with juice. Yet as I ran my fingers along his velvet shaft – then heard him moan as I lightly squeezed the tip – his flesh was quite cold to the touch. But it was a welcome coldness; a salve for the aching heat in my sex. He moaned again, then his hands were in my blouse and kneading my breasts as I struggled out of my lust-soaked pants.

Kicking them away, I lay back and let my thighs fall wide open. With a wordless mysterious grace, the man in black moved over me and pressed his cool prick to my gaping, liquid crevice. There was an uncouth grunt as he pushed it in, and to this day, I can't say whether it was him or me. I only know that having him in me was the most sublime experience of my life. That spectral fuck in the conference hall was nothing compared to this. He felt huge inside me, thrusting and plunging with a remorseless, measured power. Pounding me against the carpeted floor, he wept and whispered against my neck. The words were meaningless, but his tears, trickling on my skin, were what finally pushed me over . . .

All of a sudden I was dying. Falling, coming and flying through space . . . My body grabbed his in a spasm so immense and glorious it seemed to wrench my womb from its roots and send the whole length and breadth of my cunt up in flames. A scream tore from my throat, and twinned with his as we spun through the void in a long, hot, pumping convulsion that went on and on and on and into oblivion . . .

'How do you feel, love?' asked Judy from a great distance, and suddenly I was looking up into her face, then seeing my hotel room behind her.

'What . . . What happened?' I mumbled. My

mouth dry and cotton-woolly, and when Judy held a glass to my lips, I slurped water thirstily. When she took it away, I tried to frame questions.

She beat me to it with an answer. 'Don!t worry, love,' she said gently, 'you've had a fright but you're fine now.'

'But, Judy, I—'

'You were in the lift on your own and there was a power failure. It jammed between floors and you must've panicked and fainted.' She patted my hand reassuringly, 'you were only stuck for a few minutes, but being alone in the darkness must've freaked you out—'

'Alone! What do you mean . . . alone?'

'There was only you in the lift, love.' She eyed me worriedly. 'They brought you here when they got you out, and the hotel nurse checked you.over. She said you were okay and I should let you sleep. That was last night.' She pointed in the direction of the partly drawn curtains. The morning sun was streaming through them.

'Alone?' I repeated numbly.

Judy looked puzzled, but she wasn't half as confused as me. I couldn't remember being carried to my room, or being examined by a nurse. But being flat on my back with the man in black between my legs was as clear as if it'd happened two seconds ago. I still felt sore! Nobody could tell me I'd been alone in that lift.

'You weren't the only drama here yesterday, you know.'

Judy was trying to distract me now. 'There was a suicide in the hotel.' She picked up a newspaper – a local morning edition that she must've been reading while I'd slept. Turning a few pages, she opened it.

'It seems there's been a famous actress staying

here, and she'd got a toyboy with her.' With a horrified fascination I watched her finger track along the print. 'Anyway, they had a massive row and she stormed off and left him; leaving the poor sod so upset he hung himself! In the shower! It's a crying shame. There's a picture of him: he was bloody gorgeous!'

She held out the paper to me, but suddenly I didn't want to see that 'broody gorgeous' dead man.

'When did it happen?' My voice quavered. I didn't want to know.

'Yesterday afternoon, it says,' she said, dropping the paper into my lap, 'It doesn't bear thinking about, does it? While we were listening to all that crap about eye contact, this lovely bloke was choking to death.'

I shouldn't have looked.

But I did.

There, looking back at me, was the perfect, fine-boned face of my beautiful man in black . . .

A Pet for Christmas

THEY WEREN'T THE biggest he'd ever seen, but boy did they look firm!

Niall Christopher spread out his copy of *Penthouse* and gazed at the most gorgeous pair of breasts he'd ever seen. High and delicately rounded they went perfectly with the tiny waist, the long, sleek thighs and the petal-pink, sweetly crinkled sex that peeped demurely yet raunchily through a bush of flossy gold-brown curls.

'Misty – our Mystery Yuletide Pet' the write-up announced, and as his hand slid to his prick – in homage to her beautiful, bountiful flesh – Niall couldn't think of anything he'd like for Christmas better. He'd only bought this mag today, but he was already head-over-heels in lust with pages fifty-two through fifty-nine!

And why not? He needed something to console him and marvellous Misty was keeping more than just his spirits up. Looking at her scrumptious body, he could forget what a crappy Christmas he was having. He could forget this godawful shitty cold he'd caught and – most of all – he could even forget that imminent debacle of all debacles, he company's annual 'do'.

Agh! The 'do'. An event that was both a let-down and a cock-up in one fell swoop.

Things would've been so different if he'd been going with Selina. Or – and his prick leapt like a salmon at the thought – if mouthwatering Misty were his date for the night. As it was, instead of going to the party with the branch sexpot, he was going with the branch 'mouse'. Mary Marwood, a brown-haired, blue-stockinged systems analyst, was the firm's newcomer, and a right plain jane if ever there was one. Niall couldn't believe he'd gone and invited her.

Oh bugger! Oh bugger, bugger, bugger! The biggest bash of the year: a free booze-up at the firm's expense and an 'all-round ' night in a posh hotel. Squiring a stunning blond to the 'do' and then – down boy! – then giving her a seven-inch Christmas present in the room next door to his. Oh God, it should've been perfectamundo!

But now Selina had dumped him, and swapped rooms with mousy Miss Mary . . .

'She's not *that* bad, I suppose,' he philosophised mournfully to the beautiful but two dimensional nude in the his magazine, then poured himself a whisky from the bottle he'd bought – along with the *Penthouse* – to make his life more bearable, 'but I wish to God she was you, Misty, my angel!'

Funny though, he mused blearily, flicking through Misty's spread. The Mouse and the Pet were fundamentally the same animal: woman. So why couldn't Mary achieve the same effect? If she fluffed her hair out, like Misty's, instead of wearing that prim plait; if she wore hot, red lipstick, and clothes that showed her shape . . . Well, she might be halfway decent!

Misty's outfit was totally indecent, and in the big centrefold picture, it showed every last bit of her shape! Her heavy satin wrap rippled across the bed beneath her, its rich plum-purple folds a perfect foil for her creamy, opulent and otherwise stark naked body. Phooaargh! Niall's fingers stroked his hardened shaft as he catalogued her other accessories. A maroon diamanté-trimmed domino surrounded but didn't hide her brilliant electric blue eyes and a pair of sheer lace gloves in the same shade covered her dainty hands. Her right gloved forefinger was pressed saucily into her full red mouth, and her left one pointed artistically yet oh-so-rudely to yet *another* pair of glistening lips.

Mousy Mary had mud-brown eyes that she hid behind heavy unflattering spectacles, and Niall seriously wondered if she had a fanny at all! Yet those lack-lustre eyes had sparkled once today.

They'd been in the corridor, sorting their out bags, when this very magazine had slipped from his hold-all and fallen at Mary's feet. He'd blushed at a prime case of sod's law, and expected Mary to blush even redder at the sight of Misty in all her open-legged glory.

But Miss Mouse had just smiled: a strangely appealing smile in one so dull. 'What a beautiful girl,' she'd commented in her soft-spoken voice. 'Is this your type, Niall?'

For one horrid moment, he'd thought the Mouse was flirting, but then she'd picked up the magazine, folded it neatly, and handed it to him. Afterwards, Niall couldn't figure out for the life of him what'd made him invite her to the party.

But did he really have to go?

I'm far too ill to party, he decided, drinking long and deep of his whisky and rubbing absently at the staple in Misty's naughty navel. I'll stay here with you, my goddess, he told her, beginning to feel distinctly woozy. He'd not had all that much whisky, but obviously even the wee-est of drams was a bad idea on top of medication.

Yes, he felt extremely odd now, although not in a wholly unpleasant way. Perhaps it was the masked temptress beneath his fingers making him delirious with her lush naked body and the promise of sex so mind-blowing he'd probably never ever achieve it with a real woman?

He imagined plunging into that juicy pink furrow, caressing those high, fruity breasts, and gazing into those brilliant, almost unnaturally-blue eyes as he shafted her. In his mind he kissed her sticky red-painted mouth and fucked it with his tongue as he fucked her luscious clinging sex. Oh God, the works bash could go screw itself! The party was right here with Misty, and the stroke of his strong right hand.

He flipped open the brand new robe he'd bought to impress Selina and took hold of the tool he'd hoped would also impress her. This's for you, Misty my darling, he pledged, beginning a slow luxuriant masturbation and wishing he felt just a little more 'with it' to enjoy the process.

To hell with blondes and Christmas parties! It's just you and me, my pussy pet! We'll have a ball together. But reaching out for his drink – with the hand that wasn't clutching his plonker – he suddenly had a slightly deflating thought. As if on cue, there was a soft rap on his door.

Mousy Mary! Knocking back the drink – then regretting it as his head span wildly – Niall quickly fastened his robe and stumbled to let her in.

'Are you okay?' the dark, worried-eyed girl

630

enquired, and Niall could've wept at the difference between the fantasy of a second ago and the drab reality of now.

Yet, spaced-out as he was, he was forced to admit Mary *had* made an effort. Her brown hair was wound in a slightly softer sort of coil, and her fine complexion and regular features were graced with a subtle trace of make-up. Unfortunately, she still wore her gruesome glasses, and the rich fabric of her dress – a kind of burgundy satin that looked strangely familiar – was made up into a disappointingly pouchy shape.

'Thassa pretty dress . . .' Niall was shocked by the slur in his own voice, and even more upset when having stood up far too quickly he fell right down again!

'I'm not pissed, honestly!' he protested as Mary helped him into the armchair and laid a cool hand on his red-hot brow. 'I've got this stinking cold. I'm ill! I'm really, really ill!'

'Yes, of course you are.' Mary picked up the fallen *Penthouse*, and smiled – yet again – at the sight of Misty's beautiful wide-open fanny. What is it with her? Niall wondered through his haze. Is she a lezzie? Does *she* fancy Misty too?

'Is this your cure?' she enquired, shaking her head slowly and looking down at him with such a knowing and suddenly quite sexy look that he almost – in his befuddled state – started to fancy *her*!

'I . . . er . . . dunno,' he muttered, his eyelids drooping. Any minute now he'd probably pass out. 'Thassa a real pretty dress,' he repeated, guilty again at letting her down.

'It's my favourite colour,' she said evenly as she smoothed the hair back from his feverish brow, 'Look Niall, I think you should stay here and get some rest. You'll feel better after a sleep. You might even have a nice dream.'

Niall wasn't quite sure what she was on about: his brain seemed full of cotton wool, his body heavy and powerless. 'A nice dream,' he muttered, seeing the spectre of Misty's fantastic body as the blackness drifted down.

The next thing he heard was the slick of his room door closing. Disorientated, he scrubbed at his eyes, but when he opened them he realised the sound *wasn't* someone leaving but someone coming in. Thoughtful Miss Mouse had dimmed the lights, and in the gloom Niall could just make out a dark shape hovering by the door. A slim figure wearing something long and vaguely wine-coloured. Thank God! It was only Mary come back to check on him.

' 'S okay, Mary, I'm all right,' he called out, 'Don't waste your time on me. Get down to the party and have some fun.'

The figure seemed to sway slightly, although Niall couldn't be sure whether it was his visitor who moved so sinuously or a distortion created by his virus-fuddled brain . . .

'Mary?'

What the fuck was she doing? Suddenly Niall felt slightly rattled. 'Mary! Is that you?' he demanded fractiously – as the hidden one broke slowly from cover.

'Oh God! Oh God, oh God, oh God!' Niall licked his dry lips, and frozen in the act of getting up, he fell back in his chair like a nerveless doll.

Still swaying, but in the most erotic way he'd ever seen because her heels were five inches high, the yuletide *Penthouse* pet sashayed elegantly forward.

I'm hallucinating! thought Niall, deprived of what

little strength he had as his dream woman advanced upon him. He was paralysed; pinned. And as Misty reached his chair and stood before him in all her sensual magnificence, he recognised the exact same mask, gloves and wrap that she wore in the Christmas spread. All in that same rich vinous shade he'd ... he'd seen somewhere else this evening. Somewhere. He didn't know where.

'Misty,' he whispered, still locked in his seat.

The apparition didn't answer but just smiled archly, her gleaming red mouth parting in delicious temptation. What she did next made Niall's prick rise like an iron bar and his heart nearly burst in his chest.

In a smooth dream-like movement she parted her dark satin wrap and revealed the pale, utterly perfect body beneath. She was *Penthouse*-naked under the watery silk and her full, yet delicate shape was as a thousand times more stunning in the flesh than it was on the flat paper pages.

He could see every curve and hollow. The puckered peachy areolae of her peerlessly rounded breasts, every silky cream-white inch of her flawless skin. The achingly sweet curve of her belly. The endearing yet salacious cluster of curls that shielded her fragrant vulva.

Boy, she was fragrant! Niall knew he wasn't imagining things now, because he could smell the pungent, unmistakeable smell of a highly aroused woman! The scent washed over him like a wave filling his head with magic, his crotch with lust and his mouth with a great flood of saliva.

As if reading his addled mind, Misty shimmied like a dancer, then raised one long sleek-toned leg and placed her foot on the chair-arm just inches from his trembling prick. It was a lewd move yet divinely graceful, and Niall surrendered to unbear-able temptation. Opening his robe, he exposed his sex as she'd exposed hers. He could see her fanny quite clearly now, and as her hips wafted slowly towards him, the woman-smell floated potently in his direction. The spittle pooled around his trembling tongue and he was forced to swallow.

He swallowed again as Misty tugged off one lace glove and tossed it away. Again, as she parted her labia with her still-belaced hand an started touching her clitoris with her long, slender and very naked right forefinger.

Niall grasped his cock and jerked it furiously in time to his dream-girl's masturbation. Misty's finger moved faster and faster, rubbing her clit with manic intensity.

She paused only once in her wild race towards climax . . .

Though she still spoke not a word, the flood of juice between her legs was soon so profuse it was audible. Scooping up a shining fingerful, she took it to her panting lipsticked mouth and slurped it with a crude, almost caricatured relish. Then, before Niall could even breath, much less speak, she repeated the vulgar gesture and pushed the results into his mouth.

Her taste was salt, musk and a sea-like richness. Niall moaned out loud at its pure deliciousness and leaned forward hungrily for more. Only to have it denied, and almost weep with frustration as Misty resumed her frantic rubbing.

Within seconds her hips were bucking in an obscene, pumping frenzy, and her beautiful face was distorted – what Niall could see of it – in an animal snarl of orgasm. He could hear the squelch of her spasming vagina and actually see the lovejuice bubbling out of her . . .

Working himself viciously, Niall sobbed as the spunk came shooting up from his vitals, then gave a raw broken wail of purest love as Misty fell forward out of her self-induced ecstasy and took the tip of his prick between her jammy reddened lips.

Niall's last conscious thought was that not a single drop of his semen had been spilt.

A small innocuous sound woke him up, and when he opened his eyes, Mary was placing a steaming cup on the table beside his chair.

'Lemon tea,' she said briskly. 'I thought you'd like some. It always bucks me up when I've got a cold.'

Niall shuffled nervously in his seat, looked down, then sighed with relief. His robe was snugly tied and there was no visible sign of what'd most surely been the finest wet dream of his life. It must've been one, he decided, because his body had that absolutely great, all-round warm contented glow it always got from a truly great come.

He was feeling fine, and thinking about trying Mary's cure-all tea, when he saw her bend down – with a smooth and surprising grace – and pick up something from the floor.

Niall's sense of well-being dissolved like Scotch mist, because what Mary was holding and gazing down at with a small sly grin, was a maroon lace glove. She fingered it slowly, and eased it carefully into shape as if she were about to put it on . . .

Still reeling from the glove, Niall took a further blow when she turned slightly, and for the first time since he'd come to, he got a good clear look at her face.

She was still the same not-quite-pretty Mary with the same ugly glasses, yet at the corner of her soft,

full and untouched-looking mouth was a smudge
. . . a smudge of bright, brazen flame-red that could
only be lipstick. She caught his look and her eyes
twinkled behind her deceiving spectacles. She
smiled, a new smile that wasn't 'Mary' at all but was
bold, moistly pouting and terrifyingly reminiscent
of . . .

A long supple finger rose and wiped away the
incriminating smudge. She smiled again. The smile
that melted Niall's loins every time he saw it – in
whatever form it took.

'Merry Christmas, Niall,' she purred and slid her
finger wickedly, evocatively and oh-so-familiarly
between her lips.

Not Just a Pretty Face

'*I'M NOT JUST* a pretty face, you know!'

To be honest, I'm not even one. I'm more what you'd call 'bonny', but Ellis was either too kind or too clever to contradict me.

'Neither am I,' she murmured, not strictly responding to my tipsy rantings. Who cared anyway? She was smiling that smile again, the one that'd driven me mad for three weeks and posed far more questions than it answered.

Three weeks ago Ellis Delaheigh had arrived from the States to take charge of Jackson-Wordsworth Associates, but for me she'd stirred up far more than the management structure! One look at the divine Ellis and my suspicions about myself grew . . .

Was I a lesbian or what?

Ellis was everything I'm not. Tall, lean and vaguely angular, she had the lightfooted grace of a racehorse. All fine bones, fire and arrogance, she'd stride through the office like the Goddess Diana and confound everybody – particularly me! – with her sexy yet touch-me-not air.

Sexuality . . . One of those famous 'grey' areas for me, I'd say.

Although totally un-Ellislike – that's middle-sized, a redhead, and to put it bluntly, busty – I'd always had my fair share of boyfriends – and sex. But for a while – even before Ellis's arrival – I'd been right off men. Well, not completely off them. I'd fancied one or two, but always the same type. Slim, effeminate guys who reminded me of women. And when I'd put my libido on auto and fantasised I'd always dreamed of pulling women. Until the very last minute, that was, when a rather wacky thing seemed to happen. If I was beginning to like the idea of being Sapphic, why did my dreams stop short of the actual sex?

I'd no-one to confide this in, but I knew the moment I set eyes on her that Ellis Delaheigh would understand. She was Razor-woman, cutting right to the heart of things and splitting the true from the false. Yes, before we'd exchanged a single word, Ellis had looked into my eyes and seen my troubled soul.

Speculation about her was rampant. Fuelled by her imperious air it swirled around her like a purple cloak. The men she'd advanced all fancied their chances; and the ones she'd sacked all called her a dyke!

Me, I couldn't work out what she was, except that she was magnificent! And that she'd singled out me – Rosie Warren, visual futurist – for encouragement and promotion. Not before time either! In a boringly traditional ad agency I'd been having trouble with my far-out ideas. But after some split-second decisionmaking, Ellis had pointed her long coral-tipped finger in my buxom direction and said 'This is the Head of Design'!

And here we were celebrating.

I'd nearly died when she'd oh-so-casually

suggested it. Working on a new layout, she'd popped the bland little question. I'd looked up and felt the full force of something I'd never experienced before: sexual interest from another woman. There'd been more in those big, brown, delicately outlined eyes than a night of pasta, vino and shoptalk. Then I'd blushed and blustered . . . and it'd gone again. We'd been back to a simple meal to celebrate my new job.

Entering the restaurant I'd felt like a lummox. Ellis had led the way to our table, her trimly-turned ankles flashing as she walked; her long, flared skirt swirling out around her. Heads had turned and stayed turned. The watchers thinking, no doubt, 'That's class!' Then they'd look at me and think, 'Who's the fat bimbo?'

We'd come straight from the office, and yet Ellis still looked as immaculate as new paint: cool and composed, with not one of her sleek black curls out of place. While I was looking decidedly blowsy . . .

Once, long ago, I'd tried wearing the kind of drapes and ruffles that Ellis always wore, but on me they'd looked wrong. Like someone else's clothes. These days I'd given in and reverted to type. My short, tight suit and clingy cotton top were tarty, but – unfortunately – very me. What was worse my tawny mop was all over the place, and in spite of a good can of body spray liberally distributed, I was smelling embarrassingly musky. That was the 'Ellis Delaheigh' factor; scary as it was, she was arousing me as I'd never been aroused before. I'd nearly fainted in the Ladies when I'd slipped down my pants and discovered the state they were in!

That's why I'd got squiffy on Italian wine and run off at the mouth, singing my own praises as an advertising designer. I know I'd had my suspicions, but juicing up over a member of my own sex was still one helluva shock!

'I'm not just a pretty face, you know.'

'Neither am I.'

'Oh, Ellis, you're beautiful! You're the most beuatiful woman I've ever seen!'

I scowled at my glass, condemning the wine but knowing in my heart I'd've said it all anyway. Even if I'd been on Tizer all night.

'Am I?' asked Ellis softly, her voice like Dietrich. It made my spine melt and my sex throb like a second heartbeat.

'Yes,' I mumbled, feeling like a soppy, lust-addled fool.

'Thank you kindly, Rosie,' she murmured, then fell silently thoughtful for several long, unnerving minutes.

Oh God, no! I'd blown it: gushed and been completely uncool. Watching her toying with her cutlery and looking vaguely troubled, I cringed and waited for one of her effortless, killer-queen put-downs.

Suddenly, she set her fork down with a decisive 'clomp' and looked up and straight into my eyes.

'Okay then, let's go back to my flat and have sex.'

Things went pretty blurry after that, even though I was instantly stone cold sober. I'd got chills and fever now, fears and longings; I wanted Ellis like hell, but what exactly did 'wanting' mean?

What did lesbians do? Should I start or would she? Dodgiest of all: was I actually a lesbian? Would I end up wishing Ellis had a cock? I'd a sneaky feeling I might, but one look at her beautiful face, her soft, smooth skin and her long, graceful body made it seem less important. Well, a bit less . . .

When we got to her flat – a place as subtle and

elegantly expensive-looking as its mistress – all trace of that briefly pensive Ellis had gone.

'Sit down, Rosie.' Her voice was velvet but unyielding and she gestured to a low squashy chair of coffee-coloured leather.

I flopped down like a brainless dolt and just stared at her.

Ellis towered over me in full control. But somewhere in the hauteur, far back in the mix, was a twinge of something far less self-possessed. I couldn't believe it was nerves, but I was in no state for in-depth analysis – especially when she reached down and took the handbag I was clutching so defensively.

'You won't need that,' she said, flinging it into one of the other chairs. Then, closing the space between us, she leaned over me, dug her hand into my hair and pressed her lips hard on to mine.

I nearly fainted again. There was a world of difference between thought and deed, between words and actually making love. I say 'making love' because for me Ellis was too glorious to simply 'have sex' with. Even though she'd called it that herself.

The kiss was long, sweet and thorough, and in spite of everything, felt right. Ellis's tongue was bold; she tasted of wine and fruit, her lips so mobile and delicious it was impossible not to kiss them in return. When our mouths finally parted, she slid gracefully to her knees, then eased her fine kid pumps off her long, slender feet.

But even barefoot and kneeling, Ellis Delaheigh was no supplicant. Not by a long shot!

'Sit back,' she commanded, 'Relax, but don't move.'

I did as I was told: drugged by her perfume, and disorientated by the sight of such a beautiful woman

641

crouched at my feet. Her silky skirt had fanned around her, but it didn't rest there long. Almost before I knew it she was kneeling up over me, peeling my tight jacket off my shoulders and pushing it down. When it wedged at my elbows, my arms were imprisoned. There was a wild look in Ellis's eyes now, and sweat on her upper lip. But she still smelt clean and fresh. She was all flowers, lemon and spices – while I was far less delicate. Sweat and a pungent woman-smell seemed to roll off me in waves.

With my arms pinned I was at her mercy. My cotton top went next; shoved down like my jacket, trapping me even tighter. My breasts jiggled in my lace bra as Ellis arranged me to her liking. I was her raggedy-doll and she was posing me. I was so turned on by this peculiar foreplay it was mortifying. My pants were saturated now, and I imagined a dark, damp patch on the soft leather beneath me . . .

'Let's see what we've got.' She flicked the straps off my shoulders and dragged my bra clear of my breasts. My nipples were standing out like studs, ruby-red against solid blue-veined creaminess. I felt gross and vulgar. Why couldn't I be slim and lean like Ellis?

But I'd never seen Ellis's breasts, had I? Her lushly draped shirts hid even the vaguest hint of their shape.

She liked mine though!

'Lovely!' Her long, cool hands slid under the mounded weight, cupping, lifting and kneading.

I wanted to scream. Ellis's fingers were soft but her grip was firm. She handled my breasts in the rough way I'd always loved. How could she know what I hardly understood myself?

Bowing her darkly curled head, she took a nipple in her mouth and started sucking with all her might. It was like having my tit in a furnace, yet the still, silent observer in my squirming body saw her coral lipstick smear the peak of my breast.

'Ellis,' I groaned as she shifted her mouth to the other nipple and dragged at it like a starving baby. 'Ellis . . . Oh God!' It was as if she'd wound a fine cord around my clitoris and threaded it out through my tortured breasts. Every suck went directly to my swimming crotch.

'Easy, baby, easy!' she soothed, her mouth full of nipple, then drew back, dropping a kiss on my wet breast.

'Okay, let's see your snatch!' The words were coarse, and her American twang more pronounced now, but to me it was the Song of Solomon. Deftly, with an expression of intense concentration, she pushed up my skirt then gripped my tights and panties in one bunch and hauled them down to my ankles. 'Spread your legs, baby,' she whispered.

For almost a minute, she studied my naked sex, and behind my eyes, I saw what she saw: a page from a porno mag; an arrangement of skin and cheap clothes that was far more obscene than simple nudity . . .

Its very crudeness was uplifting. I was a sacrifice to the divine Ellis, and my breasts and sex had a life of their own, a voice to sing the praises of the woman who bent before me.

She lapped sweat from the crease of my groin. She kissed my belly, my thighs, my fuzzy mound; even my tight-less knees. The clever witch kissed everywhere but the tiny piece of flesh that needed it most . . .

Desperation snuffed out my torpor.

'My clit, for God's sake,' I croaked. 'Suck my clit, you bitch!'

I'd called my boss a 'bitch' and told, no, ordered her to suck me off. But I was beyond caring now . . .

Only my clit mattered. It felt huge and swollen, protruding, caught in a beam of hard light.

In a slow motion movement, Ellis leant forward and obeyed me. Her soft hair fell across my thighs as she clamped her lips around me. Then I was screaming, writhing, coming . . . pumping my hips against her as my hole pulsed like a sea creature sucking in life. It was gorgeous, tormenting, celestial, and I didn't give a damn if Ellis was a woman, I adored her!

I lay half-stupefied for God knows how long, with Ellis's warm face resting on my thigh. When at last she looked up and roused me, her voice had a faintly tentative note. 'Why don't you take a shower, honey? Then we'll go to bed – maybe?'

Confused, and tugging at my clothes, I escaped to the bathroom, and presently, slid naked into Ellis's wide cream-sheeted bed, as she in turn took a shower.

What Ellis had done had been special and beautiful, but now I was hating myself for my doubts. In spite of her unorthodox methods, she'd been tender and supremely giving. She'd made me come; transformed me. But could I do the same for her? Could I touch and kiss another woman's body? A body I still hadn't seen . . . She'd gone into the bathroom fully clothed, with a heavy silk kimono over her arm.

'You're not sure, are you?'

I must've nodded off, tired out by it all, because I'd never even heard her return.

Ellis slid into bed beside me, still swathed in her

exquisite kimono, and in the subdued light, I gazed at her.

Bare of her make-up, she looked younger somehow, and prettier. Yet though still my beautiful Ellis – with her clear dewy skin, and her hair damp from the shower – she seemed discreetly difference, in a way I couldn't put my finger on . . .

I shuddered.

'What's wrong, honey?' she said, her voice alive with a strange edginess.

'I . . . You . . . You're right, Ellis, I'm not sure. I'm not sure of anything,' I muttered, feeling mean and small, 'This'll sound stupid, but . . . but . . . Oh God, Ellis,' I wailed, 'I don't know if I'm a lesbian or not!'

Then suddenly she was laughing: an odd deep sort of laugh that sounded nervous yet relieved, 'Come here, sweetheart, let's see if we can make up our minds.'

'*Our* minds? What do you mean, make up *our* minds?'

'The thing is, Rosie, I'm not sure what *I* am either.' She kissed me then, just once, on the lips, then gently but insistently pushed my hand inside her kimono. Holding my fingers in hers, she slid them down over a hard, flat belly and crisp, springy hair, then closed them around what lay below.

It was a full thirty seconds before it dawned on me what I was holding.

A cock! A warm, stiff, velvety cock!

'Oh God, you're a man!' I cried, instinctively stroking the evidence.

'Yeah, I suppose I am . . . sort of,' he murmured, more vulnerable in that moment than *I'd* ever been, 'Does it bother you?'

I thought about it for a tenth of a second, then shazam! A fatal blow to heart, brain and sex. The grey areas weren't grey any more, and the divine Ellis was still divine.

'No, not in the slightest,' I whispered, smiling. 'So let's get on with it, shall we?'

And with that, I moved over his slim brown body and did all the dirty, daring, delicious things to it that suddenly came so naturally.

And why not? He *is* the woman I love!